REAPER
OF SOULS

To Leslie
Live Abundantly

REAPER
OF SOULS

A NOVEL OF
THE 1957 KENDAL TRAIN CRASH

Beverley East

This book is dedicated to my grandparents
Veronica and Peter Constantine East,
who were snatched away from me along with
other family members I never met:
Phillip East, Constance East, John East, Joseph East, Adelia
East, Olga East, Mary and Carvalho Cork, Madeline Cork,
Philbert Cole, Vera Cole and Iolene Small
at Kendal, Manchester, Jamaica on 1 September 1957.
May they and the precious souls of
the 240 others never be forgotten.

Acknowledgements

'Thank you' usually comes easily for me, but I was dead scared that I might leave someone out, especially since so many people supported the journey of this book. So where do I begin? I'll start with the most obvious: Great House and Michael Grant for the sensitivity and insight they brought in handling me and this important story. I'm told that Charmaine Limonius did some inspired editing on the manuscript.

The International Calabash Literary Festival Workshop gave me two wonderful tutors, Kaylie Jones and Elizabeth Nunez, who helped me find the courage to keep writing when I was so unsure of what I was doing. Long before I knew I had this story to tell, my long-lost friend Uta told me so.

The staff at the Institute of Jamaica, the National Library, The Jamaica Railway Corporation and especially the *Gleaner* Archives were powerfully instrumental in helping me find photographs and crucial research information—in the case of the latter, also providing endorsement for this project. Special thanks to the many survivors of the Kendal Crash who graciously allowed me to interview them, even though they would rather forget than remember. Without their accounts, there would have been no authenticity. My Radio Jamaica Family, Henry Stennett, Hol Plummer, Derrick Wilks and others all allowed me a voice in a place where I could feel safe.

To my family of Easts, who have supported me in so many ways, there will never be enough space to thank you properly. My Aunt Tess (Mrs. Theresa East Headley) who is our family historian, my second mother and my friend, is deserving of a large debt of gratitude for all the daily prayers she sent me. When my back is up against the wall, I can rely on my mum to have my back; Miss Winnie is a source of continued encouragement and inspiration.

Life doesn't stop just because you decide you want to write a book, and my personal life took a severe beating for two years. In the course of completing Reaper of Souls, I was sent some powerful angels who caught me whenever I fell. They rallied around me and I am truly thankful for their love, support and friendship: Rosemary Edwards, Marcia Mayne, Pamela Bell-Peyton, Marcia Bailey, Audrey Hutchinson, Doreen Chambers, Michelle Lowe-Smith, Sydney Stakely, Theresa Lewis, Pam Taylor, Joan Habib, Natalie Middleton, Jennifer Loud, Donna Coley-Trice, Charmalyne Shaw Ruth Dutiot, Jay Bryd, Christine Henry, Avis Charles, Carolyn Cooper, Colin Channer, David Davenport, Don McGregor, Dennis Watson and Clifton Culpepper.

I am blessed to have friends upon whom I can call anywhere and any time. Their answer to me, somehow, is always yes: Rosita Stevens Holsey, Carol Huie, Allison Watson, Cherry Lee, Jennifer Allen, Angie Le Mar, Franciane Selgic, Jean and Frank Russell, Tony Fairweather, Sandy Chung, Diane Watson, Marjorie Scott Anderson and Angela Wynter. The comments of several manuscript readers aided and inspired me to write a better story: Samantha Jones, Sonja Harris, Konrad Kirlew, Dr. Ralph Dimmick, Colleen Douglas, Donna Hemans, Patrice Gaines and Barbara Ellington. There are still a host of people that I have not mentioned but you all know who you are. I am so blessed to have each and every one of you in my life. Thank you for this amazing journey you have shared with me.

Last but not least, I thank my son Diag who so bravely stayed for an additional year in a school he hated because he knew that if we had been apart, no writing could have been done. Jamaica helped turn him into a young man of whom I am extremely proud ...

"Death is nothing at all,
I have only slipped away into the next room,
I am I and you are you;
Whatever we were to each other, that we still are.
Call me by my old familiar name,
Speak to me in the easy way which you always used,
Put no difference in your tone,
Wear no forced air of solemnity or sorrow.
Laugh as we always laughed at the little jokes we shared together.
Let my name ever be the household word that it always was.
Let it be spoken without effect, without the trace of a shadow on it.
Life means all that it ever meant,
It is the same as it ever was, there is unbroken continuity.
Why should I be out of mind because I am out of sight?
I am waiting for you, for an interval,
somewhere very near, just around the corner. All is well."
—H.S. Holland

INTRODUCTION

As a child, I had a subconscious fear of trains. My sweaty palms were always a dead giveaway. The night before a trip, I couldn't swallow any food; I couldn't sleep. Whenever it was time to leave the house, my skinny legs would tremble and make little uncertain steps as my family headed toward the train station, and I would squeeze my father's hand, not realizing that he, in turn, was squeezing mine.

For the longest while, I thought we didn't have enough money to travel together as a family. My dad appeared to be in a panic whenever any of us traveled anywhere by rail. It was worse when all four of us traveled together. And so our trips were carefully orchestrated, like neat little loops on a crochet hook: my mum and I rode in one car, my sister and my dad followed in another, a strictly enforced rule. Years later, I found out that my father had feared losing any more of us.

While growing up in South London, I had learned from a British history book that on September 1, 1957, a devastating train crash had claimed over 250 lives near a town called Kendal, in Jamaica. At the time, this crash was recorded as the worst train disaster in history. Back then, I was four years old and didn't know that I had lost a large part of my family in the Kendal Crash. About six percent of the fatalities were members of my family. No other family suffered as much loss that day.

I often asked my father what had happened to his parents, my grandparents Aunt Vera and Uncle Peter. "They're no longer with us," he would say simply. When I was 18, a recently widowed cousin came to live with us. As I helped her unpack, I saw a silver frame among her things and pulled it out. It was a black-and-white photograph of her, taken in Jamaica. There she was, surrounded by caramel-skinned people. They bore an uncanny resemblance to the both of us. They *were* us.

"Who are these people with you in this picture?" I asked, frantic.

"This was our family in Jamaica," she told me.

"Why do you say, 'was'?" came my query. By now, my thoughts were racing, dreading what this could mean.

"Because they're all gone now."

My cousin ran her fingers across the images frozen in glass. I remember that her nails were well manicured.

"I'll never forget the day this photo was taken," she said calmly. "It was the week before I left Jamaica to join my mother here in England. The same month they all died in the train crash."

"What train crash?"

"You mean no one ever told you about Kendal, Bev? About what happened to us?"

"No," I said.

"Not even your dad, Brother Bertie?"

My cousin's incredulous flashlight eyes now beamed right at me. She stopped unpacking, and then pushed all the clutter to one side. She patted the spot next to her, and I jumped onto the bed.

Slowly, the truth of my family was unraveled. The story had been buried deep in the pit of their souls. For them, it was easier to forget that 14 members of our family left Kingston one bright and sunny Sunday morning for a church excursion to Montego Bay. On the return trip, the train derailed near Kendal and plunged into a ravine—and into the void of my family's memory.

The crash claimed over 250 lives, fourteen of them members of my family. Cousins, aunts, uncles and both my grandparents perished. Only one family member, my cousin Earl, survived. He was 11 at the time, oblivious to danger as he jumped between carriages with another boy as the train flew along the track. He was thrown into the air when the train crashed, and thereby escaped death.

For the next three decades I was absorbed—no, obsessed—with my family's story. I tried to gather additional facts from reluctant relatives; I peppered everyone with questions, searched my father's things, scoured the old books and documents my parents had in the attic; I haunted the library. I coaxed Uncle Howard (my father's youngest brother) to tell me what he knew. He was evasive. My Aunt Tess in Florida was the one most willing to help me. At last, I learned about the devastating impact of the crash on my family, which, in turn, shed light on so many unanswered questions. Finally, my father's fussy rules and strange behavior made perfect sense.

In 1990, on one of my summer visits to Jamaica, I asked my cousin to take me to the Institute of Jamaica in Kingston. If no one would talk to me about it, I would do my own research. Surely the crash must have received newspaper coverage. I walked confidently into the library and asked my question.

"Do you have any information on the 1957 Kendal Crash?"

The stone-faced librarian's eyes widened as if she had seen a duppy (a ghost) and I noticed that others nearby who overheard my request slowly turned their heads in dismay, as if I had asked to see the Pope with no clothes on. *Kendal Crash*. I heard myself say the two Jamaican words that have so much power that hardly anyone talks about what they mean.

The woman walked away and returned dragging her feet, with a yellow, dog-eared file in hand. It was about five inches thick, and covered with dust. I thanked her and took the file, which held decades of answers, to a nearby desk. People in the library stared at me. At best, I was some kind of freak to them; at worst, a ghoul.

Ravenously, I read every line in the piles of documents, and every news item from the *Gleaner*, the island's oldest newspaper. When my stomach rumbled with hunger, I remained transfixed. Waves of emotion swept through me as I sat rigid in the chair, staring at the photos that featured rows and rows of dead bodies. My insides churned a thousand times over and I felt dizzy, my body consumed by grief. I ached all over. Then, I felt a gentle tap on my shoulder. From behind, a voice:

"Miss East, the library closes in ten minutes."

"Huh?" I blurted groggily. "Okay."

I looked at my watch. Where had those five hours gone? I left the library in a teary daze, my mind spinning. As I waited outside, I literally gasped for breath, suddenly asthmatic. When my cousin came back to get me, I couldn't speak. The truth was numbing.

During the past 20 years, I have attempted several times to write this story, but it has been emotionally difficult and, with other pressing projects, almost impossible. On New Year's Eve, 2001, I made the solemn promise to myself and to those who perished that I would spend more time writing it.

On January 3, 2001, my commitment to this project was intensified by what may well have been help from beyond. My beloved Aunt Tess, (my father's youngest sister), mailed me two black and white photographs of my grandparents, Peter and Veronica East. I had never known what they looked like. I could see my father's thin, narrow face in my grandfather, those serious eyes and the large, elfin ears. My mother had told me so many stories of what an endearing father-in-law he had been. *What a wonderful grandfather he would have been to me...* Uncle Peter, as everyone called him, might have shared stories of his time as a soldier in the Second World War, traveling back and forth to build the Panama Canal, or of his life at sea cruising the Caribbean ports.

I stared at the face of my grandmother, Aunt Vera. In her features, I could see my Aunt Ermine (my dad's baby sister) and the faces of some of my cousins in hers. Her slender figure was also a telling characteristic. I had been cheated of her love; she would have wrapped me up in the melody of tomorrows, smothered me in sugar-coated kisses and coaxed me to eat her coconut drops. I was told she would deliver her own sermon on Sunday at the dinner table, giving her version of what Father Eberle's sermon had meant. I was the second of her four granddaughters. Conflicted by sadness and elation, I turned to my son and said in dismay, "Look, Aunt Tess has sent them to help me tell the story."

Like so many of us after the tragic events of 9/11, I realized how fragile life is, how no day is guaranteed. I did not want to leave this life without telling this story, so I suspended my life in America and with my son in tow, I returned to Jamaica in 2003 to research the facts of the crash and give this story the detailed attention it deserved. My journey home was the best decision I ever made. I was embraced and showered with nothing but love. I was living my heart's desire. While on my personal journey of researching and writing this book, I met other members of the East family for the first time. After months of research and interviews, the words unraveled into *Reaper of Souls*.

I think I felt the spirits of my family guiding me. At times, I was overwhelmed by the magnitude of the project, daunted sometimes by the spirits peering over my shoulder. I spent many days not writing, but crying over the images from the archives, hearing echoes of the painful stories retold to me by many of the survivors. I was unearthing the parts of their past that they would rather forget than relive. Reading the Kendal death list and poring over the 1958 inquiry and report often left me too crippled to write. Someone even told me that I was overly ambitious, choosing, as I had done, to write a story that could not be told. The truth was even simpler: I was a handwriting expert, columnist and best-selling author, unable to put one word in front of the other.

In those two years I spent in Jamaica, I felt privileged to hear the victims' voices, visit where they worshiped and imagine their laughter and joy. Their lives have far greater meaning to me knowing how they lived, rather than dwelling too much on the tragic circumstances of their death. Their story is one of profound strength in their faith and love for family. Through people who knew them, I learned that before they left us, there was much joy, love and a whole lot of laughter in the East household.

In every family, there are good and difficult times. There are times when each breath or laughter of a child is a marvel. Right then, life is full. But when your family is suddenly snatched away without warning or reason, how does one amortize such a loss? Is there still faith? As a result, do you dare turn your back on God?

This is the story I want to tell. In some ways, it is my best chance to recreate the family stolen from me. I promise that the main facts of the Kendal Crash are accurate. My characters and many of their experiences, however, are fictional. They allowed me to tell the story of the East family without using the actual gory details, such as how my flesh and blood was so torn and eviscerated that they are still considered missing and presumed dead. I invite you to step with me into the lives of Austin Scott and his two sisters, Esther and Evelyn, three souls determined to overcome the tragedy of Kendal.

Can Esther's denial heal her? Can Eve's faith hold the family together? Can Austin change his heart? This is my gift to those who actually lived and died on that day. And to you.

KENDAL

Since the 18th century, when Jamaica flourished as a British outpost and a haven for pirates, the island has become world renowned for many things: its seductive stretches of white sand, cascading waterfalls, aluminum ore, Blue Mountain coffee, rum, reggae, exceptional track athletes, Rastafarians, ganja, and as a sanctuary for celebrities. Outside of that renown, however, Jamaica is small, and Jamaicans were not prepared for so many to die in a little place on a single day. So Kendal, in many ways, became our Holocaust, and put the island firmly on the world map, setting macabre world records and traumatizing an entire nation. Needless, avoidable and unspeakable.

If you mention the words "Kendal Crash" to any Jamaican over fifty, they somehow all know what those two words mean. Many younger Jamaicans also know, since the event was such a milestone in Jamaica's history. They know it means something big, something horrific. It cut into the Jamaican twentieth century roughly in the middle, somewhere between our innocence and our Independence.

Where is Kendal, exactly? It lies smack in the center of Jamaica, a tiny town nestled just outside Mandeville in the parish of Manchester. A town that requires great effort to find on a map, Kendal is 60 kilometers from my birthplace, Kingston. Drive too fast and you'll hurtle right through it and into Williamsfield, the station that stood mute and forlorn as it waited for the special excursion train to come back through. Kendal is certainly not a tourist resort, like Montego Bay, Negril or Ocho Rios. It is not a town known for seafood, as is Port Royal, nor is it a place like Fort Charles, known for its historic buildings and its battle-marked period of British-French rivalry for possession of our riches. But it is not an ugly place, and at any previous time in history it would have been described as a quaint hamlet. Kendal, in effect, is No-Man's Land, incapable of standing for anything else, a place where blood stained the earth and unidentified victims of the tragedy are buried.

There have been other tragic days of death and devastation in Jamaica. A massive earthquake ruined much of Kingston in 1907; the fabled '51 Storm, Hurricane Charlie, caused widespread loss of life nearly 50 years later; Hurricane Gilbert, the apocalyptic storm that literally changed Jamaican culture in 1988, is still regarded as Jamaica's worst-ever natural disaster. All those events are remembered in folk tales, stage plays and hit songs, but Kendal is not. In fact, the episode has taken on mythic status, a hard-news event that rides alongside the ghost tales it spawned, the scary relative nobody will claim as their own. Many who rode that train survive in obscurity; there is no grave marker at the mass burial site, and except for the old platform steps, the Kendal Station has been erased from the face of the earth. In short, the accident numbed and matured Jamaicans, presenting a fun-loving people with what seemed an impossible level of carnage.

God in His wisdom chose this undistinguished spot to reap His own children. Why did He choose Kendal to reclaim so many of His shining stars? Nothing, not the official Commission of Inquiry, nor the innumerable ghost stories it has spawned, was able to fully explain why. We may never understand, but we may now be able, after half a century, to close the circle.

ONE

I, ESTHER

When I was a little girl, I prayed that my brand-new baby sister, sick and hanging on the frail hinges of life, would die. That's a horrible thing to wish for your own flesh and blood, I know, but at the time I could see no other escape. The responsibility of being Eve's older sister was too much for me to bear.

My older brother, Austin, was the prince among us three. I, the middle child, was the invisible one. I felt sure I'd have no life until that horrible first day of September in 1957, when Eve took sick again and the empty gaze returned to her eyes. It also turned out to be the day my sister actually saved me. I just couldn't appreciate it yet.

"I'm sorry Esther, I hate to go against my word again," my father was saying in his shallow voice, "but you can't come with us to Montego Bay. Your sister can't make the trip breathing like an asthmatic."

"No, don't say it—please don't say it."

I cupped my hands over my ears and shook my head violently.

"Yes, I know what I promised you, my darling, but you just can't come on this trip. You'll have to stay behind and look after your sister."

"But Sarge, I've worked so hard selling tickets for our church trip. And you promised me that if I sold ten tickets I could go. I sold fifteen." Resentment rose from deep within me. My voice screeched with frustration.

"Look after my sister, look after my sister...! I'm sick and tired of being Eve's wet nurse. Just once, Sarge, can't someone else look after her? Please, Sarge, don't break your promise again..."

"You know Miss Ruby can't manage Eve by herself," my father replied, keeping his grip on being patient.

Old Miss Ruby, bless her well-meaning heart, was not always up to the task. Her energy was much less than her love.

"I hate you. I hate you! I wish you were dead!"

"You don't mean that, so behave yourself. You have every right to be upset with me, but I promise I'll make it up to you," Sarge, as everyone called my father, whispered to me as he stroked my hair.

He had this irrepressible presence, eyes as piercing as an owl's. He was firm-jawed, clean shaven, determined and sure of himself. You'd expect a booming voice to come from his large frame, but he only spoke in whispers.

A war wound had split his windpipe, but not his strong spirit. His presence bore down on our house when he came home, creating a heavy cloud of concern waiting to burst. Everyone—except for me and my mother—jumped to his attention.

"Okay," I murmured through clenched teeth. What else could I say? But the words that raced through my head as I glared at him were the opposite: *I wish you were dead.*

My head had been in the clouds for weeks waiting for this day. But now my brown eyes welled up with tears, my head hung low and my heart was as leaden as iron. I stomped through the hallway and past the kitchen, where more than a dozen overstuffed baskets sat, tied up with blue ribbons. Freshly picked fruit, fried fish and bammy, grater cake, coconut drops, Johnny cakes, napkins, plates, and cups for our church outing (the one that I was not going to be a part of) mocked me. I wanted to dash the week's preparations out the window, to destroy them just as my hopeful joy had been.

This was not the first time disappointment had punched me in the stomach. Ten years before, Eve had gotten really sick for the first time, three days shy of my eighth birthday. A big birthday party had been planned for me; my cousins and all my friends from school were to be there. But Eve had developed a high fever and I had to stay with her. Frustration had snapped me up in its grasp. It would hold onto me for a long time.

I'll never forget: sweat seeped from her soft nutmeg-brown skin and through her nightdress. Her collarbone seemed to stand at attention, and the once-crisp cotton sheets were soaked through. Eve was weak, and she would have been a complete rag doll had it not been for all her groaning and tugging at her bushy hair. Even on a good day, she would not let us comb it; if anyone tried to touch her hair, the girl's usually agreeable smile would vanish. I had seen that banshee side of her. We all worked hard not to encounter it.

This was my birthday, but instead of eating birthday cake, I was mopping up Eve's vomit—a smell so vile that I still remember it every time I see cake (I don't eat it anymore. No sir, no more cake). Instead of playing musical chairs and opening gifts, I was on my hands and knees wiping her blood off the floor, changing her urine-soaked sheets, or carrying cups of bush tea from the kitchen to the bedroom. I was the good little red wagon, going back and forth.

I expected to have all eyes on me and my blue taffeta dress—the one Mummy had stayed up night after night to create in the dim light. Instead, all hearts were focused on Eve. Instead of dancing in the new black patent shoes Aunt Pearl had sent from England, or running excitedly through our house with my little sister, I had to listen to her screams.

"Stop it from hurting!" Her voice shot through me. She exhausted herself and us, and then she just lay there, placidly. Her eyes would be closed, her body damp, her breathing uneven and shallow. Gradually, Eve's skin became the color of old prunes and her gaunt face began to take on the look of death.

A cake with pink and white royal icing had been baked for me. I'd hovered patiently by the mixing bowl, waiting to lick it clean. My eyes followed the wooden spoon as it stirred the thick, golden-brown paste. Oh, how I loved the taste of the raw brown sugar and butter, the rum-soaked currants and raisins, all blended together. The mixture on my tongue was worth the long afternoon's wait. My birthday party was canceled, however, and the icing on my cake slowly melted under the glass cake stand, abandoned.

"For God's sake, Eve, get well…" I chanted in my heart. I sat by her bedside for hours, mopping her forehead. I was afraid to eat, afraid to turn away in case she woke up or died. Death would free her. It would be my escape, too. I was sure of it.

On the eighth night, she opened her eyes, looked at me and smiled. She beckoned me to her with a spindly finger. I drew closer, my heart pounding like stampeding horses. I moved my ear close to her dry mouth.

"Don't cry, big sister. God isn't ready for me yet," she croaked. "He takes only his brightest stars so they can shine over us." She squeezed my hand, drew a long sigh and slipped into a deep sleep. Much later that night, Eve's fever broke. She pulled through. I wished she would die, then prayed for forgiveness.

"Thank you, Jesus! Thank you!" everyone cried, jumping up and down.

"What about me, God? What about my birthday?" I asked, audible only to myself. Then I prayed, "Please forgive me for my evil thoughts. Let my sister get well so I can play with her again, so our lives can be normal again. Please God. Please."

God didn't listen to me, and my life was never normal again. The cake, untouched, would become hard and dry. My birthday was going to pass without a mention.

***

"Rheumatic fever," Dr. Young said finally, after looking both my parents in the eye for a long, quiet moment.

"For the rest of her life, she'll be an invalid—or very close to it," he warned. "Her heart is very weak now; prepare yourself for her life to be short. Make her comfortable, because the poor soul will not be here long."

My mother gasped, her knees buckled beneath her long skirt, and she wept in my daddy's arms.

"How long is long?" I thought, but dared not ask.

"Come on, me dear, be brave. Thank God she's still alive," Dr. Young said nonchalantly.

"Have you thought about sending her to England, to your sister, where the health service can offer her advanced medical care? She might stand a better chance to hold on just a little longer," the doctor advised.

"But in the meantime, the slightest upset or distress can send her weak heart into shock."

"Send my sick daughter overseas? She's barely five!" my mother cried.

"But Ruth, think about it," my father said. "You know your sister is more than capable of looking after her."

"Keep her calm. Keep her comfortable. Shhh, don't make so much noise." This was all I heard all day long. Eve did not attend school, did not have to do chores. She just had to stay alive. After Dr. Young's diagnosis, no one assumed Eve would live very long, but in spite of her discomfort and her inability to do the simplest things, she took each day in stride, clinging to life while I begrudged her every breath.

I had loved my sister once, but now I just couldn't.

"Please, save me," I prayed.

"Let Eve get well or let her die, but don't have my life hanging because of her. Amen." What wickedness! But that's how I felt.

Eve had become an inconvenience, and I was secretly jealous of all the attention she received.

"Why did He not just let me die?" she whispered to me one day.

"Let you die? It's my life, not yours, that's difficult!" I yelled at her.

★★★

Eve and I used to sit at the base of the mango tree, shading ourselves from the burning sun as I pulled a brush through her thick hair. I loved styling her hair in cornrows or Chiney bumps, decorating her hair with calla lilies, begonias or allemandes from our garden. She looked as pretty as a picture.

I pampered her as if she were my own personal doll baby. Using the broad leaves from our breadfruit tree, I fanned her as though she were a Greek goddess. I was the first to attend to her if she cried. How I adored her then! I dressed her up in all the dainty cotton dresses Mother bought for her, bathed and doused her in Johnson's Baby Powder until she smelled as sweet as candy.

But today wasn't a day for remembering happier times. Sarge and Austin lifted her tiny frame from the bedroom to the verandah, so she could wave goodbye to everyone. She seemed to be bidding farewell to my happiness along with my chance for a day at the picnic. My glorious September first.

★★★

Our house in Kencot, Kingston, was Family Central. Whenever the whole family of aunts, uncles and cousins came together, there was always wonderful noise as the women preened, the youngsters chased about and the house groaned with excitement. It was that ritual again, this time preparation for a magical train ride to Montego Bay for picnics, games and the beach. I had heard so much about the trip at church and from my friends that the date was carved into my consciousness. Planned for a thousand people, the trip had so many tickets sold that the number ballooned to fifteen hundred. Extra passenger cars and another engine had to be added.

As my relatives struggled with their over-laden baskets, they seemed comical, donkeys walking on two feet. My cousins Donovan and Charles hugged their cricket bats and cradled the game's stumps under their arms. The twins, Colleen and Cassandra, carried nothing but each other's love, swinging their tightly clasped hands and skipping along carefree. Sarge commanded the whole family, as always playing shepherd to his unruly flock. All my aunts, Daphne, Lynette and Martha wore white gloves and their Sunday-best straw hats pulled tightly over their heads, strutting and wobbling in high-heeled shoes, too stiffly dressed to carry anything but their faith and their pride. In their voices there was an accustomed tone of authority that sprawled over everyone else.

"I'm sorry you have to stay here and look after me, Esther," Eve said. "All that work you did preparing food and selling tickets, just gone."

"Don't be sorry. I didn't want to go anyway."

"God will punish you for lying, Esther Scott," she smiled.

"Well, we can have a quiet time in the house together, just the two of us," I said, squeezing her hand. I didn't look at her; my eyes were busy watching everyone rush around to leave me behind.

"You will both be sleeping when we get back, so you be good until we return, my angels." Mother came back into the house to coo over Eve, kissing her forehead. "Esther, I'm sorry you can't go. Here. Keep my rosary beads until I get back."

My cousin Grace hugged me.

"See you, cuz!" yelled cousin Donovan.

"Esther, I promise you a big treat when we get back…" my father said. His weak voice trailed off.

"Yes, Sarge," I sighed, rolling my eyes in disbelief.

"I have a surprise for you," he said.

I tried to imagine what could possibly salve my feeling of abandonment. He couldn't have changed his mind and toy with me like that.

"Austin is going to stay with you too."

Sarge patted me on the back and winked. He knew the gesture would be louder than his voice. I stood on the verandah feeling the warmth of the floorboards seep up through my body.

"Be careful with those baskets!" Aunt Daphne snapped. "We want to be able to eat the food when we get there!"

"Come on nuh man—hurry!" Sarge yelled, "or we'll miss the train!"

The entire expedition packed itself into an little van Sarge had arranged for them. Everything calmed down. I waved goodbye to them, allowing the thump-thump of activity about the house to gradually settle into a sad, vacant lull.

TWO

It was my baby sister Eve, beautiful but petal-frail, who saved my brother Austin's life that day in September. He had jumped at the chance to use her as an alibi, to excuse himself from our church outing. Chuh, why would I want to go halfway across Jamaica with my parents and all my cousins when I could see them any time right in my back yard? He wasn't fooling me. He wanted to see her again. Sweet, spicy Novelette…

"I'll stay with the girls," he volunteered.

"Son, that's so thoughtful of you, to miss cricket on the beach with us, so you can stay with your sisters. I'm proud of you, son."

Sarge slapped Austin on the back, like he was one of the lads.

"Yes Sir," he lied. "It's okay."

"Okay Austin, you're in charge till I get back," Sarge said, overlooking me.

"Take good care of Eve," he said, kissing me on her forehead.

"Come follow us down to the station, Austin, and help with all these baskets. Your mother must think she's feeding the whole of St Anne's church."

"Yes, Sir," he said, grinning from ear to ear.

★★★

Sister Ruth, as everyone called my mother, roasted breadfruit, fried fish, chopped up coconut into tiny pieces to make coconut drops, baked bread and fried fish fritters.

"It's only a day's outing, Ruth, not a trip around the world."

"Sshh, Sarge." She pressed her finger to his lips. "You do what you know best and leave the rest to me."

She spun on her heel and returned to the kitchen. Aunt Martha, Aunt

Lynette and Aunt Daphne flitted from their house to ours, borrowing spices and herbs to season the meats they were cooking. They created smells so sweet, they hung in the air like kites of savory splendor. Austin followed the smell in a trance, all the way to their kitchens. Aunt Lynette and cousins Grace and Donovan were going, but they had no choice. Aunt Daphne was a no-nonsense person, and what my Aunt Daphne said was law.

"Stay behind where? No. You're all coming with us," she yelled at Donovan for the best part of the week.

Baskets crammed with mangoes, naseberries and bananas from our own yard lined the hallway. Aunt Betty had made her sour sop and carrot juice the night before. The excitement and anticipation made everyone seem drunk.

Our families were members of the Holy Name Society of St. Anne's Roman Catholic Church which sat on the corner of Percy Street in Kingston. Every Sunday morning without fail our family occupied the first five pews at church. I and the younger ones nudged and fidgeted through-out the entire service, stifling our giggles, our eyes glazed over after the first part of the sermon. Our heads kept swiveling on our necks in a constant search for anything interesting. Mother was the choir director, and long before Mass started, we were there, watching her organizing, practicing, and getting her charges ready for the day's service.

Part of the success of the excursion tickets was due to Austin's efforts. Like a beggar on a quest for bread, Austin had touted the trip all over the city—even as far west as Trench Town. "Tickets for the St. Anne's outing to Montego Bay! Thirteen shillings for adults! Half price for children!" he'd yell, imagining he was on the BBC World Service, but much, much louder.

"You're a good salesman, Austin," Father Charles Eberle had said. "You and your sister have done a great job. I'm impressed. This is a good start for our building fund."

"Thank you, Father. I'm looking forward to it," the boy lied.

THREE

I remember so clearly the last time we saw my mother. She was impeccably dressed, as usual. Underneath her white pill box hat, her thinning hair was tightly plaited in a French braid and fell just below her slight shoulders. In spite of the birth of the three of us, her waistline was still trim and was tightly cinched by a wide buckle and belt. She wore a turquoise knee-length pleated skirt and a crisp, cotton capped-sleeve blouse which was dazzling white against her velvety brown skin. She looked like a British movie star. She rarely wore high heels, but she decided that day to take the turquoise shoes out of the box that my Aunt Pearl sent her from England. She slipped them onto her narrow feet.

"What do you think?" she said, twirling around in them like a ballerina.

"They look great. You should wear them today," I told her.

"But they are a little high, for me, don't you think?"

"Yeeeeesss… but Mummy, you'll be sitting on the train most of the day," I replied.

"You can manage those heels—but pack a pair of flats just in case," Aunt Daphne advised. "If you don't wear them, Ruth, I'm going to steal them from you and write to Pearl and tell her you not wearing them. Pearl would be so disappointed to know her Christmas gift was sitting in a box collecting dust for nine months. So wear them. Shame on you, Ruth Scott!"

★★★

A hundred "don'ts" sprouted from my father's broad mouth as Austin followed the little van and the family down to the station. His bicycle wobbled from side to side, as he perched the heaviest basket between the handlebars. The basket could have been lashed to the roof but Austin insisted on carrying it. He made the short trip soon after the van did.

"Don't forget—mek sure Eve tek her medicine. Look after your sisters, you hear me?"

"Yes, Sarge."

"Don't bring home no trouble while I'm gone either, you hear me, boy?"

"Yes, Sarge."

"Send for Dr. Young if Eve gets worse. I'll pay him when I get back. I don't want none of those boys from Miss Iris' yard fooling around my daughters, you hear me? Keep them out o' me yard."

"Yes Sir," Austin replied, standing at mock attention.

"Here's the money to pay Marse Jackson when he brings the ice. I don't like the look of none of Jackson's boys either—although the most troublesome one they call 'Blue' gone to England, thank God. Don't mek any of them pass my gate."

He handed his son some silver shillings.

"That boy Clement will be the death of Marse Jackson. Maybe the army can teach him some discipline, because Lawd knows, that's what Clement Jackson needs."

He patted Austin on the shoulder.

"No Sarge, I wouldn't do that."

Sarge raised the corner of his eyebrow in disbelief.

"Don't let me down, son. You're in charge until we get back."

"Yes, sir…" he muttered, still firmly at attention, almost passing out from stifling a derisive laugh. Sarge looked away, and Austin started breathing normally again.

★★★

A surge of people greeted the family at the station, pushing, shoving and nudging their way past them, nearly toppling Austin's bicycle. Droves of eager passengers emerged from buses, cars and trams toward the station, pushing past him without hesitation. Austin elbowed his way through the streams of people as they crammed their bodies and baggage onto the narrow platform.

Higglers, robust women wearing head scarves and aprons of all colors, lined the sidewalks, turning the station surroundings into a bustling market-place, displaying everything from sodas, oranges, jackfruit and pineapple to peanuts and candy.

"Buy some candy fi de outin'! Peanut, oranges, jackfruit—every t'ing you need." Their voices floated and mingled in the chaos like swirls of cotton candy. The Scotts wormed their way through the crowd toward the narrow platform.

"I didn't realize so many people were going on the trip," Austin said.

"Neither did I," Sarge replied.

Anxiety rushed through his body as Austin saw the wooden coaches swelling with excited humanity. It was still fairly dark outside. Everyone going to Montego Bay had to be up early for the special 5 a.m. departure.

"We better board the train quickly and find ourselves somewhere to sit," Sarge yelled at his troops over the noise. He knew there would be difficulty for many who wanted seats, but he was sure he'd be able to cut a path to a place where they could all sit together. He got most things to work for him that way.

Austin took one last glance at them, watching a pair of reckless grins shine from Charles and Donovan's faces. Charles had his tongue out. They knew not to mock their cousin because he would deal with them when they got back.

"Enjoy your day, ma," Austin said, and kissed her on her cheek.

"Have fun, Donovan—and behave yourself, okay? Bring back a nice girl for me from Montego Bay," he whispered in his cousin's ear and slapped him on the back.

"I'm so glad not to be at the hospital today. Today I get to go to the beach. Praise the Lord."

Aunt Daphne threw her head back and laughed. Grace, Colleen and Cassandra giggled arm-in-arm behind Aunt Daphne's back as she and her husband, Cork, bickered.

"Remember all I told you, son." Sarge flashed his stern look at Austin.

"Yes, sir." He took a final look at him and smiled as he raised his arm like a Dickensian footman as he assisted my mother onto the train. Could he command the trains, too?

Sarge wore a short-sleeved Hawaiian shirt and his Panama hat. My parents were a handsome pair. They'd met in Cuba when father and Uncle

Cork, his younger brother, worked on the ships around the Caribbean islands. Uncle Cork had been mesmerized by Aunt Daphne, Mummy's best friend, from the very first day they met. Both couples had had short courtships. A double wedding had taken place shortly after their return to Jamaica. I'd been told a thousand times that the wedding festivities had lasted all week. Goats, shrimp, and chickens had been curried and cooked, mannish water devoured. They'd sang and danced and every person in the community had celebrated the double union. I heard that even ex-lovers had at first felt slighted, but had partied all night.

"Bye, Donovan and Charles! Bye, Aunt D and Uncle Cork," Austin shouted, waving both arms in the air.

"Bye, pretty girls," he said to the twins. "Have enough fun for me, too." He blew a kiss through the air toward Grace and the twins.

With a picture of the family firmly etched in his mind, Austin mounted his bicycle and headed west, not toward the picket gate and the mango tree in the Scott front yard, but to the wide sidewalks and streets of Trench Town.

★★★

How could he resist Novelette? He had kept her a secret from his parents because she was not Catholic. She had a basic education and was being raised by a string of aunts and cousins not much older than she was. Austin sometimes lost track of her ever-changing family details. *Chuh, she was not worth all the tongue-lashing I woulda get from Sarge if he knew about her.* But the secret sweetness of their meetings drove Austin to see her all the more.

He'd met her one breezy day when he'd gone with Sarge to arrest someone. Novelette's tenement yard was a maze of one-room units with rusting zinc roofs. Goats and swell-bellied barefooted children seemed to run everywhere. Itinerant hens scratched and searched for grain. There was one standpipe for the whole shebang. She had stood there amongst all the confusion, a bird of paradise in a bright orange dress, the kind that was tight enough to emphasize her heavy curves and short enough to show off luxurious legs that seemed to go on and on.

Novelette had divine punctuation all over her face, the freckles that dotted her nose and cheeks. She had straight, shoulder-length black hair, and slanted eyes that emphasized her mixed, forgotten ethnic heritage. She could have been half-Chiney with Indian, or one-third Indian, one-third Chiney or one-third black. Who knows? Austin just knew she was stunning. Whatever her mixture, she was an outcast, because she did not look like any of the people around her. A single swan, after all, is hideous in a world of ugly ducklings.

Two days after meeting her, Austin found his way back there. They didn't talk much. There was a lot of kissing and giggling, pure spontaneous combustion. He remembered hitching her up against the zinc fence and pummeling his skinny body into her voluptuousness. The rhythm of their bodies rattled the old zinc fence so much that the whole yard must have known what they were doing. To confirm that, the neighboring children rattled their enamel cups against the other side of the fence in unison with the raspy tune.

In time, their lovemaking became such a public event that they moved from the rusty fence to the sturdy side of the house. Austin muffled his moans and sighs deep in her heavy cleavage as the rhythm of his body pulled in and out of her, the cool breeze brushing against his bare behind. Their bodies learned the tempo of each other and soon they found a way to bury the special climax that came from deep inside themselves. Novelette's aunt liked Austin and so did her best to ignore his rotten manners.

"Austin, you gwine marry mi niece one day?"

"I'm barely twenty, for God sake," he thought, but smiled in reply.

"Yes, Ma'am," he said, the worst lie he ever told.

"Austin come from good family," she would boast to her neighbors. But as much as she favored him, she could not bring herself to buy a ticket for the church excursion to Montego Bay so that he and Novelette could have some privacy for once.

"I'll buy you a ticket," Austin said to her one day with a half-sincerity born out of desperation.

"Is not the money me son, but t'anks—I'm not gwine on no train 'til the full moon come out... I dream say red snake bite me. Is t'ree time now I get dat same dream."

She shook her head at him.

"To dream snake is not a good dream, and den fe go dream it t'ree time. No, sah." She paused. "Somebody gwine dead soon and me not going nowhere 'til de full moon come out."

She said it every time she saw Austin.

***

It was Sarge's idea that Austin go to England and study accounting.

"Travel the world a bit and get some education," he would say.

Austin had a good head for figures, but all he really wanted to do was play cricket and follow in the footsteps of some of the great kings of the game. He wanted to be as noted as Sir Learie Constantine, George Headley or any of the three 'W's: Clyde Walcott, Everton Weeks or Frank Worrell.

Austin's ear was stuck to his transistor radio any time he could listen to the West Indies play. Introduce him to any open space and he could quickly get a bat and ball ready. Three stumps were a permanent fixture in the Scott back yard, where many impromptu games began. Sarge would force Austin to field aggressively, drive the ball to the boundary, or work hard on his spin bowling, one of the true fine arts of cricket.

"Come on, son!" he'd yell. "Get it to the crease, nuh?!"

His passion for cricket was as strong as his son's.

"Get some education behind you just in case you never get to play professionally," he advised.

But Austin's heart was in cricket, not books and figures. Sarge had already received an inquiry about his availability for a junior West Indies XI. He didn't tell Austin at first, but broke down when his pride nearly burst him open. He told the selectors he was thinking it over, because of schooling plans, but Austin knew he'd play and get noticed no matter where Sarge sent him.

The plan was for Austin to accompany Eve and cousin Grace to England. Grace would join her parents, Aunt Pearl and Uncle Dudley, and Eve would experiment with various medicines within the new British health system. Austin would complete his accounting exams and return to pursue a cricket career. His coach said he had great potential. Aunt Pearl had persuaded mother to send Eve to England for a year. She said they were using new medicines on patients who had heart conditions similar to Eve's. Passports were put in order and passages reserved on the *Jamaica Producer* for a departure at the end of October, 1957. Like a trail of ants, many people they had known in Kingston had already made their way to England, one by one, sending for other relatives as soon as they got settled. Eve, Grace and Austin would be the next three to leave.

FOUR

After being curled up like a cat beside Eve, I was ripped from my sleep by an urgent prod. The old grandfather clock in the hallway struck its familiar tone. One time.

"Miss Esther! Wake up! Wake up and turn on your radio! Turn it on quick," Miss Ruby screamed.

Eve and I craned our necks and pressed our ears against the speakers:

A train, on its return leg from Montego Bay, St. James, derailed just outside Mandeville, in the small town of Kendal.' The British voice, calm and assured, came clearly through the speakers. 'The preliminary casualties reported are 50 dead and more than 300 injured. We need every able body, any equipment, any Red Cross volunteers to go to the site as quickly as possible,' the announcer continued. 'This is Radio Jamaica and Rediffusion. I am Merrick Needham. Stay tuned for further details.

"Do you think everyone is okay?" Eve asked.

"Of course they are, my darling. Don't worry," I said.

"Let's pray for them," she said, pressing Mother's rosary beads between our hands. We kneeled, and she led us in The Lord's Prayer:

Our Father who art in heaven,
Hallowed be Thy name
Thy kingdom come
Thy will be done on earth as it is in heaven…

As I rose from my knees, they tingled. I fully expected to find I'd been resting on grains of corn. I watched Eve's every move and murmur. Her breathing was slow and shallow. She barely moved.

"Come on, darling," I said. "Get back into bed."

"Okay. I hope everyone is alright." What a brave girl, I thought.

"They will be. Come darling, open wide and swallow," I coaxed her.

She took her medicine willingly. I bathed her with Bay Rum. Then I fanned and spoonfed her with ceracee tea, everything I had seen my mother doing over the years. Nothing worked. She seemed to slip in and out of consciousness.

"Go call for Dr. Young, Miss Ruby," I said nonchalantly. I had cultivated a that kind of air about everything concerning Eve.

"He and the other doctors are on their way to Kendal, Mrs. Lee told me."

"Miss Ruby, where is Austin?"

"Marse Joe know how fi find him, Miss Esther. Him gone fi find Austin already."

FIVE

"Hey Austin!—Austin!! Whe' you deh, bwoy?"

Marse Joe's anxious voice seeped through the onion-thin walls while Austin lay wrapped in a warm lavender haze called Novelette.

He shot upright in bed when he heard Marse Joe.

"Is what?" he asked, equal parts concern and guilt. "Is Eve…?"

Austin's heart battered the inside of his chest. He hadn't given his sisters a second thought until that moment.

"Dem alright, but you must come wid me. Now. De train crash at Kendal! Come bwoy—fix up yuself! We have fi go look fi your family." Marse Joe hurried along. Austin ran toward Marse Joe's car, but he had to look back.

"Soon come…!" he yelled in Novelette's direction.

★★★

They drove out of Trench Town, onto Spanish Town Road and out of the city, then along winding dirt roads for what felt like hours. Finally, the car joined the mile-long bumper-to-bumper traffic. Marse Joe gripped the steering wheel with his hands close together. He hunched his small body forward as he stared at the chaos ahead. A caravan of bicycles, bulging buses, ambulances and overcrowded cars were crawling along with steady conviction westward, only westward, toward Kendal. Dragon's eyes in red tail lights glared at them as they inched through the night.

"Where the hell is Kendal anyway, Marse Joe?"

"Just past Mandeville, sonny. We been there plenty-plenty times with Sarge when you was smaller."

The sugar-cane sweetness of the thick night air soothed the anxiety in Austin's soul. His body jerked and bounced to an unsteady rhythm as the car negotiated the potholes and bumps along the dirt roads of deep country. This part of the journey seemed endless, filled with engine noise and shouts.

"Hurry! Hurry nuh man—move up, nuh man! Step on the gas nuh! Chuh!" But nothing and no one could get them there any faster.

Then, there was a sudden jolt. Joe had brought the car to an abrupt halt. Austin pitched toward the dashboard; Joe's chest was up to the steering wheel, his eyes on the uniform dead ahead.

"Stop Right Here. Stop Here. Road Block Off." It was a policeman, who sounded the way road signs would if they spoke. "You have to walk from here," he growled, waving frantically at Marse Joe to pull over. The man sweated profusely, more than one human being should.

As they moved ahead, faint screams and the calculated drone of bull-dozers and what turned out to be mechanical saws replaced the unlit silence of the country roads. Austin heard a tiny voice sobbing for Jesus and for help.

Marse Joe yelled at him.

"Come Austin, stop gawkin' nuh man and start look for your people dem." His voice had cracked, but Austin couldn't see if he was crying. He seemed paralyzed by the sight in front of him. Austin's eyes adjusted to the orange flickering flames as planks from the wreckage burned on a bonfire up ahead. The sweetish air had the taint of burning wood and charred flesh. It was still raining, but not enough to stanch the fire or the strange smell. He rubbed his eyes against the smoke and grit, although rubbing them only further blurred his vision. Everything was making Austin's eyes and nose run. He felt the faint sensation of warm urine trickling down the inside of his leg. In front of him, on the sodden soil, was a sea of bodies laid out side by side and covered in old flour bags; others were naked and not yet given their dignity. The darkness made it hard to fully take in the whole scene. The two wondered what other horrors the darkness hid.

Trancelike, Austin ignored his revulsion and carefully stepped over or around the limp bodies. Slowly, he bent down and peeled back the stained covers one by one. Bloodied rags were piled high, bodiless limbs were still scattered everywhere like broken toys. Frantic minutes became two hours. He could find no one he knew.

Crazed now, and oblivious to the carnage, Austin raked through the warm debris with his bare hand, searching only for familiar faces. Between the layers of metal and hot rubble he found bodies sandwiched together.

Still, he began to recognize people from church, but nobody who belonged to him.

Gradually, with the introduction of more volunteers, fires and lanterns, Austin's eyes widened in horror as he beheld severed limbs, torn windpipes, dislocated body parts, arms and legs hanging from the wreckage like so many portions of meat in a butcher's shop. Somebody should have stopped him, but he must have borrowed his father's way of moving through space like he owned it. Tall, lean and strong, with a rakish moustache, a policeman's son had no trouble passing for a cop or trainee out of uniform. Without thinking, or asking anyone in authority, he had gone headlong into the gore and ash, rummaging through what used to be people. Austin had given little thought to who they had been.

"Mother! Sarge! Grace! Aunt Martha!" he cried. He shouted out names in no particular order, into the chaotic night.

"Help, Help!!" Austin heard as he stepped toward where some men tugged at a piece of metal on the train. Muffled voices seeped through an opening. He saw a thin arm stretching through another.

"I beg you, help me," the voice of the arm said. "I beg you—help...!" It was more guttural and insistent now.

"Come, you're going to be alright," Austin said. He stretched out his hand to reach hers, putting some weight on his right side and slowly pulling out a young girl and her baby. The child came out of the wreck dirty but without any wounds he could see. The mother looked about the same age as Grace. Austin saw his own eyes in the light, red as raspberries, reflected in a dirty piece of a lady's mirror. They were burning again from the smoke. His eyes scanned everywhere. Still no Scotts.

Up ahead, a crew of bauxite workers maneuvered a large crane and pulled massive sheets of iron to free some of the injured people. Passengers crawled groggily from beneath the rubble.

"Take your time, take your time—everything is going to be alright," the Red Cross volunteers kept saying as the big industrial flashlights aided their vision.

Where was the track? Austin wondered. He could see at least one engine and several coaches mangled and ripped, but nothing they could have run on.

"Where is the track?" Austin asked the railway worker closest to him.

The man pointed into the air, toward the top of a slope.

"See the light? A few cars from the back still on the track. One coach fly way over so in the yam field. Four more coach dung here in the gully."

He pointed south of Austin. The big Aluminum Jamaica crane had its large fingers swooping down, grasping the damp red clay and debris.

"Easy, easy," another soothed, "there might still be people in this one."

The crane operator stopped his engine, and the flashlights bore down on the ground. Rescue volunteers tapped on the metal, listening for a sound, a return tap, a tiny cry, anything.

In front of Austin, a growing sea of bodies lay side by side on the blood-soaked grass. He gasped at the way rescue workers, photographers and engineers trampled over some bodies with little regard. Austin moved around and occasionally stooped down to turn over a bloodied flour bags and checking possibilities one by one. *A man about Sarge's size. A hat like my mother's. A boy who had his hair cut like Donovan's... All imposters.*

Policemen were ushering injured passengers toward Red Cross volunteers and St. John's Ambulance workers.

"Dis way, dis way," one said mechanically. "There's is more of them down here. Follow me." He kept a rhythm going with his dirty hands.

"Excuse me, Officer," Austin called out, running up beside the man, gasping for breath.

"What you want, young boy?" the cop snapped back. He thought he was addressing a green fellow constable.

"I'm looking for my family."

"You not the only one, son. Look 'round you," he said, waving his hand. "See all this—everybody here for the same reason."

"I'm Sergeant Archibald Scott's son."

"Son, all I can tell you is, look everywhere. Try that fresh pile over there, or the ones under the big tree. Some soon ready for burial—the ones that are odd parts they can't match—and I think people not so badly injured are going on a relief train back to Kingston. Here, take this flashlight." He thrust the heavy lantern into Austin's hand and walked away.

"Come Marse Joe!" Austin shouted.

His feet squelched in the crimson mud. They zigzagged their way through the chaos in hot pursuit of everyone else, toward where two middle coaches had shredded each other as they derailed and plunged down the slope. The cries became louder.

"Help me! save me...!"

Every step he took, he stepped deeper into more mud, more debris. The shattered window glass shone like diamonds. Austin lost his balance for a moment and had to steady himself on a firm piece of wreckage. The wailing rang in his ear.

"Let's try over there...!" Marse Joe and Austin moved randomly through the commotion of pleas for help and shouts of orders that came from behind the station. Bodies were being piled higher.

"Be careful. Take time now; give them some respect."

Men worked furiously in the night digging ditches for the mass burial. The gentle drops of rain hid Austin's tears, softened the red earth and made the digging easier, but it hindered the progress of the rescue mission.

Under the dim light inside the make-shift hospital, his eyes searched up and down, quickly scanning each bed. One of the St. John's Ambulance rescue workers was trying to find a good vein in the arm of a woman, bleeding from the neck. Further down the row of grey blankets, a man was sucking on some ice, tears and blood rolling down the side of his cheek.

"Where is my wife?! he cried in standard English, then "wey me wife dey? I caan' find her!" when he got more anxious.

Heading back outside, Austin spun around, dizzy and dazed. The sound of the bulldozers and the cutting of metal made his insides queasy. He clenched his teeth, sensing that his legs were unsteady in the whirl of confusion around him.

SIX

Hell had made its way up to Earth. On September 2, 1957, the morning sun stretched out its rays of life over the island, as it had done so many days of ages before. But on this day, although the sun shone brightly, the warmth of its rays did not bring any joy to my island. As the morning progressed, the crisp British voice had slowed to a more somber pace:

The scene here at Kendal is unbelievable. The train derailed shortly after midnight last night. The first four coaches are nothing but a pile of iron. Two coaches were ripped to shreds like matchsticks. The fifth coach rammed on top of the fourth one. The rest were split open like the belly of a fish. It is chaos here. Unbelievable chaos. An avalanche of rescue workers, St. John's Ambulance and Red Cross volunteer nurses and doctors have been working steadily throughout the night but the rain here has hindered the fragility of their efforts, making it difficult to rescue all the passengers trapped inside."

The radio announcer's voice faded with exhaustion. Slower, slower the words slipped through his mouth:

"A flurry of photographers are here taking images of the wreckage, the dying, the injured and the dead. The death toll has reached over 100 now and hundreds more injured passengers are drifting in a daze. The stench of dead bodies is inconceivable.

He continued, barely taking a breath.

"Amongst all this horror and enormous tragedy, can you believe it? There are men robbing from these poor souls. Robbers and thieves let me tell you, stealing from these dying souls. Grabbing jewelry, watches, rings, anything they can get their thieving hands on." A long sigh passed through the microphone. "I'm Merrick Needham.

I'm signing off and handing you over to our Chief Minister, Mr. Norman Manley, who will now address the nation - This is RJR reporting from the Kendal site."

The sounds of the rescue continued for a moment, and then silence sucked me in like a cyclone. The familiar tone of Norman Manley's voice flooded the airwaves:

I am speaking, standing on the scene of this unparalleled and appalling railway disaster which happened last night. The damage is indescribable and unless one was here and saw it with one's own eyes, it would be impossible to believe the extent to which the coaches have been destroyed, crumpled, smashed up and the disaster is of a scale unknown in the history of railway operations in Jamaica.

Unhappily, a great number of people are dead. In the final analysis, it will probably be in the order of 250. Hundreds of people who were on this crowded excursion train have been injured. I wish on behalf of the Government of Jamaica to extend to the hundreds, if not thousands of relatives and friends, who are suffering sorrow and bereavement this morning, our profound sympathy and regret. I cannot say how deeply I feel for all who have lost relatives and friends in this tragedy." He paused. "And I pray that God will console them in their suffering. I would particularly wish to mention the members of the voluntary organizations, the St. John's Ambulance Society, the Red Cross, who have been giving extremely helpful service from last night. I would also like to thank the public for the help, cooperation and assistance they have given in clearing up things, finding dead bodies, and assisting to remedy as far as possible the conditions as they exist.

Once again, I would also like to thank, pardon me for adding this, Alumina Jamaica for their human service in cutting a road into the scene of the disaster and providing equipment to help to disentangle the wreckage. Once again, I repeat my profound sorrow and regret and offer my heartfelt sympathy to all those suffering from bereavement and loss at this time...

"I can't listen to this any more." I stormed across the room, heading straight for the power knob on the radio. With a quick flick of my wrist, I turned it off, just as Mr. Manley spoke his last words. I had an immediate emergency right here in my house. I needed help with Eve and Dr. Young was nowhere in sight.

The Chief Minister's words stayed with me for days.

Unhappily a great number of people are dead. In the final analysis it will prob-

ably be in the order of 250.

"I'm taking the radio from Eve's bedroom, Miss Ruby; maybe it will reduce her stress."

"It won't make a drop of difference. Look how many people coming in and out of the house—you t'ink you can keep all this from her?" She pointed out at the window at our neighbors. They had poured into our yard and perched themselves anywhere and everywhere they could find a spot, their faces awash with tears. Miss Lee sat on our kitchen steps holding her knees tightly up to her stomach. She rocked back and forth and bawled louder than anyone else.

"Lawd me Jesus… Lawd, bring home Miss Ruth and her family to us. Do…" she prayed.

"Hush Miss Lee, everyt'ing will be alright," Miss Ruby said.

By two o'clock, the whole community had come to a standstill, their faces filled with despair and their eyes pools of tears. Wherever our neighbors could find a place to sit, squat, or prop themselves up to learn what was going on, they found it.

"Our family will come home to us" I prayed. "God won't take them from us. Didn't you say he only takes his shining stars? Well, Mummy is not one of them." I forced a smile and squeezed Eve's hand.

I felt the blood rush to my face. Once again, Eve's body lay limp on the crisp cotton sheets. The news could not come through the speakers quickly enough.

"So many people unaccounted for," the news announcer was saying. As the midday sun beat mercilessly down on us, the news of the Kendal train crash was on everyone's lips:

"Lawd what a calamity, - what a dreadful t'ing God bring down 'pon us." From Milk River in Clarendon to Black River in St. Elizabeth, from Bull Bay in St. Thomas to Oracabessa in St. Mary, the torrent of oral news about Kendal spread with one theme.

"Everybody dead off inna Kendal."

Radios blared through neighborhoods, in every parish across the island. Every living person had an ear pressed to a speaker for the entire day and September days that followed. I did not want to listen any more. In fact, I tried to keep all the details from Eve, whose heart was already in a state of shock. She was still barely breathing and there was no one to attend to her but me.

The thieves plundered and robbed from the dead and the dying. Rumors ran wild, filtering through the thick green vegetation of Fern Gully in St. Ann, up into the Blue Mountains where our rebellious ancestors had fled from their slave masters, below the belly of the valleys and the soft sandy beaches, along the whispering corridors of haunted Rose Hall in St. James. Not one inch of one corner of Jamaica escaped the horror that was Kendal. I had never even heard of the place until that day. The anonymity of Kendal ended forever, its name springing to life with an irrigation of blood and the loss of too many lives, taken by the Grim Reaper of souls...

★★★

When Austin returned from Kendal, he did not have to break any news to us. We were already broken by it. His bloodshot eyes and haggard face said *I did not find them.* His fingernails were filled with dirt and dried blood. His shoes were encrusted with red mud, his clothes crumpled and filthy. Looking much older, Austin walked in slowly, stopped and sank into the big sofa. he didn't say a word, though Eve lay beside right beside him, motionless. He just slipped his hand into hers.

"Everything is going to be alright," he told me unconvincingly.

How was everything going to be alright without Sarge to make it so? Without my mother to soothe our sorrows, to heal our wounds and to keep us in the light of the Lord?

"I can't believe what I saw there, Esther."

"Tell us Austin, what did you see—and where is everybody?!"

"Rows and rows of them, mutilated bodies everywhere. How could I find them when some of the bodies didn't even have any heads on them? Arms, legs, feet and fingers scattered everywhere. One time, I tripped on something that looked like a football. But when I bent down and looked closer, it was a woman's head, completely bald. Shit! She musta had a wig on." Austin covered his face with his bloodied hands.

"Bodies...just lying there baking under the heat like fresh farm hens."

"What you think they will do with the bodies? Bring them all back to Kingston?" Miss Ruby asked.

"Some are not bodies, Miss Ruby, jus' people piece'n up and can't find no match. They had to bury them there. Rescue workers were more concerned about bringing back the living."

"All that blood and the stench of burning guts and shit…" Austin lowered his head and raised his hand. "Sorry—I can't get the smell out of my head. It still makes me want to heave. I couldn't find them, Esther. I couldn't find them in all that confusion. "

"Don't worry Austin, you couldn't find them because they're probably on a relief train back to Kingston right now." It was Austin that had gone out there, but I was already sure of the worst. The radio made it so clear.

"I hope so, because I don't want to think about them buried in all that stuff. I wasn't alone wandering aimlessly; there were so many people walking around in a daze just like me, looking for their family. I tried, Esther. I tried. Look at my hands."

He pushed them out in front of him.

"I rummaged through the ashes, through all the confusion. I stepped over burnt bodies, so sure that I would find them. Not even a glove, Esther, not even a fruit basket to say they were there. No trace of any of them anywhere," he gasped.

"I found Sister Mary Grace from St. Anne's and put her on the relief train myself. 'I cannot find anyone,' she said to me. She looked completely dazed, Esther."

"I said, 'don't worry, Sister Grace, you just get home safely—the rest of the sisters will find you.'"

"'Tell them you saw me, alright?' she said to me. Her voice was shaking hard."

"'Yes, Sister,' I told her."

"Marse Joe and I searched in every school and church that they turned into a makeshift hospital. I searched every single one of them. I did. They were filled with people lying on beds, on the floor, resting anywhere they could get care. Why such a terrible thing would happen to us, Esther?" Austin fell to his knees.

"Why would this happen—why? What kind of God…?"

"I've been wondering the same thing, Austin," I agreed.

"A good God, a gracious God," Miss Ruby piped up from behind us. She was armed with two steaming cups that made the room smell full of ginger.

"Drink this. It will settle your stomach," Miss Ruby said, pushing the cups of tea toward us. "No worry, everyt'ing gwine be all right."

"My stomach can't settle for now, Miss Ruby."

"I can still smell the blood, I want to…"

Austin ran out the front door and into the yard, touching only one step on the way. His body bent over and he heaved a flood of yellow liquid. I followed, just in time to see him spitting and mouthing curses.

"Hush, me darling—tek time… Everyt'ing in time," Miss Ruby said as she came out behind me. She rubbed his back and handed him a towel.

"Hush, son. Go get some rest. Everything gwine be alright. Just wait and see."

I searched for a quiet corner in which to hide, to cry, to sleep, wake up and believe that this was a dream. My body felt like I'd been beaten with Austin's cricket bat. My insides were hollow, as if Miss Ruby had yanked them out like she did to chickens on Sunday.

★★★

Four relief trains were sent to Kendal from Kingston to bring back the survivors, but not one of those relief trains brought back my family. None of the Scotts was brought in on the white hospital train, either. Not my mother nor my father, not my beloved cousin Grace, not Donovan, not Aunt Daphne nor Uncle Cork, nor the twins, not Charles. Nobody. Not one single soul.

SEVEN

The night my parents went missing at Kendal I settled into their room, much to Miss Ruby's disgust.

"You can't sleep in dere," she said with more than a little annoyance. In Jamaica, a long-time housekeeper is a lot more than an employee.

"Dat's Miss Ruth's room." All things in their place.

"This is my house, Miss Ruby, and you can't tell me what to do anymore!"

I had snapped back at her for the first time, to her surprise and mine. She stood at the door with arms akimbo, watching me curl up into a ball on Mummy and Sarge's four-poster bed. The mosquito netting surrounded me on three sides and appeared to dance in the light from the ceiling fan. I prayed harder for their return.

I lay frozen in bed for a long time, yearning, praying to wake up and find everything in library-book order. I was still in the wrong bed and Mummy and Sarge weren't where they were supposed to be.

My parents' room was spacious and airy. The lace curtains above the open shutters swayed to the relief of a light breeze. This was the room where I'd entered the world. This was the room where I'd stayed when I was sick with chicken-pox. Blinded by tears, I tried to scan the room. The wardrobe bulged with my mother's dresses. Hat boxes were stacked ceiling high. My father's two cricket bats leaned against the wall. My mother's perfume bottles, curated according to size and shape, were lined up on delicately starched doilies on her dark oak dresser. A light trace of essence lingered in the air. I knew which one; it had sweetened the hug she gave me that morning. The tall armoire, adorned with silver-framed photos of all our family, remained stoic, giving all the faces the best view in the house.

Positioning a candle for each one in my family, I set up an altar that second night. I embraced the silence, feeling them, then hearing them. *I belong here with them. They're coming home, and they are not dead. Seriously, how could they be?* My hope was restored, if only for a moment.

"This was just a bad dream." I told myself. *"Everything is going to be alright. I am going to hear the honey-sweet melodic voice of my mother again. I am going to sit by her side and play the piano with her, watch the droves of students tramp our house, dropping cracker crumbs from their hands and the yellow dust from their feet onto Miss Ruby's polished floor. I am going to listen to her and Aunt Daphne giggling like schoolgirls and sharing private jokes about their husbands."* I stared up at the ceiling waiting for God to send me a message, a sign that all was going to be well again.

I fought back tears until I couldn't any longer, then silently cried myself to sleep. I lost track of the total days and nights that my heart ached. My eyes went red as strawberries and my skin taut from the salt of my tears, my body numb and hollow. My mouth felt full of sand.

"Eat some food," Miss Ruby insisted.

"But I can't, Miss Ruby," I told her. "Everything tastes like cardboard." Food was now as difficult to swallow as my recent life. The days began slipping into the void. So did my faith in God.

"Why are you so cruel?" I lashed out at Him. Then, "Please forgive me for all my evil thoughts," I begged.

Then I blasphemed again. And then I heard myself pray.

"Hail, Mary, full of grace. The Lord is with thee..."

I ran my rosary repeatedly through my fingers, pressing hard on them until my hands were sore.

What have we done to deserve this? Dear God, please spare my family, send them home to me. We need them. I need them. Spare at least one of them. But God was silent. There were no answers, just days of uncertainty and inconceivable pain.

★★★

So news on the disaster remained on the *Gleaner's* front pages. Memorial services stretched across Jamaica like a string of misshapen pearls. Some families had very little to bury, some nothing at all. Our government declared Sunday, September 9th as a Day of National Mourning. Hundreds of members of St. Anne's Roman Catholic Church poured into our tiny building for the service. A slow cadence of silent steps entered the small building which might have burst at the seams to receive its mourning members.

It seemed every living soul across the island attended some kind of service in honor of the dead. Makeshift altars were erected in both the established and the impromptu hospitals. By the second morning there was a mass grave at Kendal. Prayers and burning candles kept going. Hardly any music came from any radio or gramophone—especially not *If You Should Leave Me My World Would End*, the song many were singing when the train derailed. Smiles were washed from nearly every face; heads and eyes were lowered in sorrow. Soaking-wet handkerchiefs were everywhere.

Austin, Marse Joe and Miss Ruby attended the requiem mass at St. Anne's. Everyone in the community went, except for me. To do so was to admit defeat. So I just sat in the rocking chair on the verandah, watching everyone as they passed our house on the way to do the right thing. The only thing.

My brother returned from the service for my family and our church family. He did so coolly, swallowing up his pain.

"There was not one dry eye in the church," Austin said.

He was too noble, too manly somehow to show that he too could cry. The sorrow that begat mourning would be shed across the island for days, for months, perhaps years. *My family was coming home, so why should I mourn them?* I asked myself. I believed it every single day, though as the days slipped by, the possibility of their return seemed improbable. I was illogical and dishonest, but I believed. I didn't cry, either.

Every day became a replica of the day before: I dragged myself out of bed without showering, slumped into the rocking chair on the verandah and stared up at the pale-blue marbled sky as if some miraculous answer were coming. I wanted a sign to read:

YOUR FAMILY MEMBERS ARE ALL COMING HOME

or

YOU CAN FIND THEM IN MAY PEN OR LOOK DOWN ORANGE STREET —THERE THEY ARE!

but the blue emptiness stared right back at me, telling me nothing.

"Come put on dis dress today," Miss Ruby would say in the voice she reserved for Eve or Austin.

"Eat this. See, I mek some nice puddin' for you." She made a potato pudding that was so good, it could have been served to royalty after hundreds had fought and died for a taste.

"Come on home, Sarge, Come on home—Mummy, anyone," I mumbled over and over.

The only time I ever moved from the verandah and didn't feel numb was when I checked on Eve. I sat on the edge of her bed one day dangling my feet like a five year old, listening to her uneven breathing. I lay my hand across her forehead to find that her temperature was going down. Her hazel eyes opened and her long lashes blinked at me. Then she smiled, and I was connected again to Mummy and Sarge and all the Scotts there had ever been.

"I'm going to be alright, Sis." She took my hand in hers and kissed it.

"I love you, Sis. Everything is going to be alright. Just trust in God."

"Yes," I said in an uncertain voice, "of course."

I rarely heard a word that was spoken by anyone unless is was repeated or shouted. I wandered through the house dazed and deadened, not eating, not sleeping, and not knowing what time it was. Sometimes I never even knew what day it was. I'd wear the same dress for days on end, until Miss Ruby laid out a fresh one on my bed.

***

I don't remember making a conscious decision that I'd never again set foot in church. It just happened that way, and I know I didn't go back to Mass until much later, the year Austin summoned me to London. For endless hours and days I stared into space, not going anywhere. Just as no one passed through the gate to come in, neither did I step beyond it. I didn't go to college as planned, not to the market, not to the movies with my friends. I just hovered around the house for days, for months. For years, actually. It didn't seem that long. I was waiting for my parents.

"Darling, why you don't take a walk over to Miss Lee's house," Miss

Ruby coaxed. "She made some nice potato pudding—even better than mine."

"I don't want anything outside," I said. "I just have to wait here for them to come home."

How could all of them die like that? Austin had not found one piece of identification, not Aunt Daphne's pretty pink hat, not Mummy's turquoise shoes, not a glove, or a blue-ribboned basket, not one whole body of any one of them, not a limb, not a piece of fabric. So they must be alive.

"Okay, okay."

"A miracle will happen. Just wait and see, Miss Ruby."

★★★

The *Daily Gleaner* headlines read:

THE WORST TRAIN CRASH IN THE HISTORY OF THE WESTERN HEMISPHERE

CALAMITY AT KENDAL

SURVIVORS CAME BACK

"As devastated as in the aftermath of previous hurricanes, the little town of Kendal could never settle back into anonymity again. Some residents moved away while others became spectators, storytellers, investigators, and shop keepers, selling food to visitors or selling handpicked flowers for the mass grave that was dug behind the railway station. The railway company managed to get service restored by the next day but nobody traveled by train across the island for months..."

I stopped reading the newspapers. I could not look at the published photos of the wrecked coaches, the death list, or those assumed missing. Each day the newspaper came, I folded it in half and put it in Austin's suitcase. I couldn't listen to the radio commentaries or to the interviews of the survivors. The accident remained on the front page of the *Gleaner* for 28 days, a whole month, more or less. For all those long and unbearable days, I waited and hoped for my family to come home. If I looked, if I listened for them, I should hear them come tumbling through the gate and up the path. The Iron Horse had not taken them from me. Surely, there was going to be a miracle and I...

But no one came home.

Austin had returned to Kendal twice.

"Go back and look for them," I yelled at him again and again.

"But they're not there, Sis! They're not there."

My faith in God reached rock bottom, and I let Him know it. "You are a wicked God. A wicked, wicked God," I cried in desperation. "How could you take them away from us like this?" Except for the odd morsel from Miss Ruby, I refused to eat. And then, like a slap in the face, I snapped out of my trance when Austin said, "Esther, I think you should come to England with us."

I sprang from the bed.

"No, No!" I said at the top of my lungs. "Are you crazy? I won't go. You can't make me go. The plan was for Eve to go with you and Grace, not me. There was never ever any talk from Mummy and Sarge about me going to England. I am registered to start college in the New Year, you know that. I have a place at Shortwood Teacher's College. I'm not coming to England with you. I'm staying right here."

"Don't talk foolishness. How can you stay here alone?"

"I'm not going, Austin. I'm staying here; I'm going to wait for them to come back."

Resolute and unyielding, I folded my arms and flung myself back on the bed.

"My darling sister, it's been three weeks now. Nobody is coming back. They are all dead. I saw the wreckage of the first four carriages. I saw the unmarked coffins. Their remains were probably in one of them."

I covered my ears with my hands.

"Don't say that. Where is your faith? I will make a way for myself. Somebody has to be here when they come back. I'm staying right here and that's that."

"But you can't stay here alone. You don't even know how to keep house and cook," Austin protested.

"Miss Ruby said she will stay here with me."

"Miss Ruby!! Miss Ruby? When did you two become bosom friends?"

"Miss Ruby loves this house and loves our family. Where will she go if she doesn't stay here with me? She says this is all she knows. She says she'll wait for them with me."

"Miss Ruby is going to wait here with *you*? Me, I could understand, Eve I could understand, but you, Esther Scott?"

"Miracles happen, Austin, and I am staying right here to greet them."

"No one is coming home, Esther. They are all *dead*." It was the first time anyone had said it.

"You don't know that. None of their bodies were found. Not one body from our family. So how do you know they're dead? Tell me that!"

"Because it's been nearly a month now, and not one of them has come back."

"Maybe they got hurt somewhere. Maybe they lost their memory. Maybe the train threw them away from the site. Maybe they're wandering the streets of Mandeville or some little district," I cried desperately.

"Maybe they're *dead*, Esther. Look," he said, resting his hands on my shoulder, "Marse Joe went twice. Miss Ruby's cousin and I went back there two times too. I searched the hospital in Mandeville and Spauldings and right here in Kingston. I searched the morgues and me and Marse Joe looked through every inch of Manchester. How many more people do you want to go looking for them?"

"Someone has to be here when they come home."

"Hush, Esther. It hurts me to hear you talk like this." He placed his arms around me.

"No matter what you say, I'm staying right here."

I stormed off the verandah and into my parents' room, slamming the door behind me. I closed my eyes and embraced the silence. My heart ached to be in disagreement with my beloved brother but I was not going with him. I could feel Mummy and Sarge in the house. I could hear them. I belonged there with them.

With my face toward the ceiling, I climbed into their bed, planning my new life.

"I can do this. I can make a life for myself right here." I muttered to myself. I had been invisible for years and nobody knew or cared much about my existence. I could teach piano like Mummy. I could ask Marse Joe to work the land and help sell the fruits. I could live from the land. *Yes, they would be home soon and someone has to be here,* I reassured myself. *They would be home long before January when college starts.*

★★★

At sixteen, my sister Eve was a wisp of a girl. She wore two plaits, thick as rope, around her oval face. She could have passed for twelve. She would walk barefoot across the bedroom floor, her stride slow and uncertain. Her hazel eyes shone bright, always reminding me of the sharpness of her mind. Her matchstick legs were thinner than her arms and stuck out from under her daisy-print nightdress. Her shapeless clothes hung off her body like a tent. She was still weak but didn't call me for help anymore. She placed her spindly fingers on the leather-bound family Bible. 'Now it's time for Scripture,' she mumbled. Eve picked up her rosary and held the book closely to her flat chest. I stood by the door in awe of her.

"Eve, are you up already, my darling?"

"Yes, Esther," she said, turning around to me slowly. "If I'm to travel soon I'd better start being upright, or else Austin will ship me over to England in a trunk," she smiled.

I held her soft hand and we made our way toward the morning sun piercing the room. We took one certain step at a time, like two doddering seniors. *How could I ever have wished her dead? How could I have been so stupid?* I'd never seen strength like hers.

★★★

Eve and Austin's departure date crept up on us much sooner than any of us anticipated. Eve and I curled up in bed together like newborn puppies, sucking on the silence of our throbbing hearts. Never a word of complaint escaped her lips, never a sigh of despair, always a faint smile on her gentle face. Why had I resented her so, praying for her death? I'd spent all those wasted years, praying for her to die.

Occasionally Austin joined us, perching on the edge of the bed, resisting us but lacking the courage to ignore us. Overnight my brother had become a man; he'd become our father, our protector.

"Here, have some nice cocoa tea," Miss Ruby coaxed, as she lit the candles on Mummy's dresser. I knelt before the dull flame, clasping my hands and threading my fingers through the rosary.

"Please God, let Eve and Austin travel safely to England. Please, God." Miss Ruby packed a basket full of mangoes, naseberries, guineps, June plums and gimbelin. I packed crocheted doilies for Aunt Pearl and for Uncle Dudley, and all the back copies of the *Daily Gleaner* since 3rd September with the details of the crash.

While the world spun around us with news of desegregation in an American school in Little Rock, Arkansas, of interest rates being raised to 7% by the Bank of England and Prince Abdul Rahman Putra becoming the Chief Minister of the Federation of Malaya, my island limped along in sorrow. Condolences poured in from neighboring islands and powerful nations. The Pope said he would send a special emissary. There was even a message from the Queen herself, and the Union Jack was flown at half mast.

Survivors' ordeal emotionally paralyzed each community; families began putting their jigsawed lives together again. Stories of ghosts and strange occurrences surfaced everywhere and every person somehow seemed to know at least one:

Two girls get into a taxi and engage in spirited conversation, excited about going home after a trip. They arrive at their Kingston destination and leave the car without paying. The cabbie pursues them, but alas, their family says they were lost at Kendal and could not have just entered the house.

A photograph is taken in a northcoast house, showing family members and their long-serving maid, who died at Kendal. She is clearly shown in the picture, even though it was taken some time after the tragedy.

At the scene of the crash, a distraught woman makes a beeline for a bloody severed penis lying near the wreckage. 'Lady,' someone says, 'you can't be sure that it's your husband's. He may still be alive.' The woman remains steadfast. "Who feels it," she insists, "knows it."

In the most popular stories, the dead and missing were showing up in bedrooms and on balconies, floating about and banging on doors. Speculations and arguments flowed as to why the train had crashed. Some said, "The driver was going too fast."

Others said, "Too many passengers on dem old rickety trains."

Still others were sure, "De bad bwoy dem was fooling around with the emergency brakes."

The church people said, "Too much badness going on pon de train, dat's why God strike dem down; a so everybody dead."

A Reverend somewhere said, "Retribution and damnation from the high and mighty…"

And so it continued.

I folded all the newspaper articles on the top of Austin's worn leather suitcase and closed the lid tightly. The day I had prayed for, to be away from Eve, was finally here. Now that it was here, I wasn't ready to let her go and she wasn't ready to leave, but time determined otherwise. Miss Ruby and I followed them down to Kingston Harbor. We waited until it was time for them to board the *Jamaica Producer*.

"If you change your mind I will send your passage—any time you're ready," Austin assured me.

"I won't change my mind," I said softly.

"I'll be back in five years, anyway. I promise. When I finish my studies, I'll work two years and save all the money I can. I'm going to build a big memorial for them. You watch and see."

I did not flinch. Neither did I look him dead in the eyes and ask him how the hell some stone was going to bring them back. A big stone with my parents' name on it meant nothing. But this was my brother Austin—always full of grandiose ideas—and this was another one. I just didn't have the heart to tell him.

"Don't be too proud to say you want to join us. Promise me?"

"Yes, I promise," I said, ignoring the fire of Liar's Hell licking at my ankles.

He kissed me. I threw my arms around him and squeezed. I had not been this close to him for a while. Then I hugged Eve, feeling her fragile body through her cotton dress. Maybe this would be the last time I would see her alive, especially if the treatment in England failed.

"Promise me you'll write," I whispered, as I pulled her tighter to me.

"I will. I'll tell you everything. When Mummy comes home, tell her I love her."

"Here, take these." I gave her the red beads. "You keep Mummy's rosary."

Miss Ruby and I stood at Victoria Pier, amid the craft sellers and the errand-men and their handcarts, waiting for the ship to fill up and the gangplank to be moved away. Eve and Austin were among the first to go aboard. We had insisted. Miss Ruby cried. I thought I was in tears too, but my cheeks were dry. We waved them off from the quay as the air filled with the vessel's smoke. Now a fragile remnant of my family was to be taken across the ocean to a country far away. A country with all those stories of chivalrous kings and enchanting queens, of pirates and peasants. The same one that had plundered the wealth of Jamaica.

Austin and Eve's gentle farewell waves disappeared in the distant dark water. Soon, the ship became a tiny toy on the horizon, gone to England. I stuck my chin out and made my way home, beginning my own journey without them.

48

EIGHT

October arrived very quickly and there I was, six weeks without my mother, alone with Miss Ruby in the otherwise empty house. Miss Ruby, of all people. Before all this happened, before Eve got sick, I was a happy child and life was carefree. All I had to do was stay out of the woman's way. Miss Ruby was supposed to be our housekeeper, but she did not iron, wash clothes, clean, or cook. All she did was oversee everybody else. She assigned others to do the chores that she felt were beneath her. What exactly she did was hard to figure out back then.

Miss Ruby arrived at our house in the dead of night—so I'm told—with a small black box that bore home-made remedies. She also had a brown paper bag with her clothes. Some people say she was a descendant of the Maroons and had lived in Accompong but I thought she was an Obeah woman come to haunt me. Exclusively.

Mrs. Lee sent for her when Mummy was having difficulty with Austin's birth. He entered the world feet first weighing a resounding 10 pounds, 2 ounces. Miss Ruby helped my mother through her fifteen-hour ordeal and stayed with her ever since that day. She delivered me and then Eve, although our births were much easier.

Miss Ruby's peppery tongue sweetened when she was near my parents; she was sympathetic to the ailing Eve and doted on Austin, but her long face somehow soured and her upper lip curled whenever I appeared.

"Get off my clean floors wid those dirty shoes!" she would snarl.

"Stop making such a ruckus on dat piano," she hissed. "Your sister is sleeping—and me can't hear meself t'ink, " she'd yell at me.

She dared not speak to me that way when either of my parents were present. Her face lit up whenever Mummy entered the room, walking behind her, praising her, singing, fetching and carrying anything Mummy asked for. But as soon as my mother's back was turned, Miss Ruby's heavy brows knitted and her tone tightened. I quickly learned to stay out of her way.

She was as tall and as wide as a regular man, and always wore a pair of black men's oxfords. They were easily a size twelve. Her skin was dark and smooth like molasses, and she had a scar across the bridge of her nose. A black head-tie usually covered her hair, except on Sundays when she wore a wide brimmed hat to church to hear my mother play and sing. I never saw her hair, and wasn't very sure if she even had any.

Miss Ruby rarely smiled, and she walked with her head erect and her back straight like she was royalty. Her face radiated that sense of urgency as if she had a train to catch. But she mostly moved slowly, so it must have been a slow moving train in her mind. Her wide hips swayed to some secret ancestral rhythm she held deep inside her soul where only she was aware of her legacy of greatness. She wore two colors: purple and navy. I later found out that she only had three dresses. The purple one had a white lace collar which she wore on Sundays to church or special occasions. The blue ones were for everything else.

Anyone who came to work for us, in her opinion, was 'unsuitable, lazy and could not be trusted.' That was all I ever heard her say. Helpers were fired at will and there was always some reason or incident that she used to justify their dismissal. I learned not to get too close to anyone because their service with us, somehow, would always came to an abrupt end.

Cynthia, a sweet girl not much older than I was, came to our house to work once. Her grandmother had sent her from Chapelton in the parish of Clarendon. She worked hard and my parents, especially Sarge, liked her a lot. She rose at the crack of dawn to start the day's washing. She starched and pressed all our uniforms, Austin and Sarge's khakis, and my tunics. She even bleached and beat out the grass stains from their cricket whites. Whenever I stood close to her I noticed a strong smell of bleach, and I saw that deep red dye stains were permanent in her palms and on her fingers.

She fell into bed late after the sun had gone down, when the late light had dissolved into black. No task was too much for her. She walked with her head down and her hands behind her back and quickly stood to attention when Sarge entered a room, although it was not necessary. I drew close to her because she, like me, was invisible.

I would show Cynthia all the gifts that Aunt Pearl had sent me from

England and I sometimes read my books to her. On the rare weekends she had free, Sarge drove her back to Chapelton and I stayed with her family. Her brothers gave up their bed for me and slept on the floor. From what I saw on their table, each of Sarge's meals could feed Cynthia's whole family.

Cynthia would take me down to the river where we would play and soak our feet in the cool water. Further down in the bend of the river an entire community of women knelt over wet clothes, beating the dirt out of them with stones.

"You home dis weekend, Cynthia?" they seemed to call in unison.

"Is Miss Esther that you have wid you? What a way she growing."

"Can I help?" I chirped behind her.

"No baby, you don't have to help, de way your father raise you, and you will never have to be on your knees, like us."

Miss Ruby of course, did not approve of my weekends away from home.

"Suppose somebaddy run wey wid har, Miss Ruth?" she fussed at Mummy.

"She'll be fine," Mummy reassured her.

"Don't be so familiar with the help," she barked behind Mummy's back.

"Why not?" I asked.

"Because you can't trust none of dem girls. As soon as dem get comfortable dem slack off and start get shoddy with the cleaning, cut corners and all that. Before you know it, dem run off wid your mother's jewelry and your farder money or some can be facety enough to t'ink say dem can take your farder too," she said with no irony whatsoever.

"But Miss Cynthia is so nice—and I like her."

"It's not her place to be your friend, Miss Esther."

Miss Ruby glared at me, her upper lip trembling. "She is here to work and work only, so don't get in her way."

She grabbed my arm, pulling me along with her.

Sarge left home before I awoke and usually returned well into the night. He was a man of few words, not shy but talked only when he had something specific to say. He chose his time to talk with precision. I saw him on Sundays only at the breakfast table, then later on at mass. But one thing I knew for sure was that my father did not like his porridge stirred. He enjoyed the 'crust' that formed on the top of his cornmeal or banana porridge. Every new helper was given strict instructions about this.

One morning I woke up earlier than usual and saw with my own eyes Miss Ruby tiptoeing into the kitchen and quickly departing. When Sarge went into the kitchen, all hell broke loose, which was so unlike him.

"Who in God's name stirred the porridge?" he bellowed as best he could with his weak voice. The sound came out squeaky, but you knew it was angry sound.

"Is Cynthia stir you porridge, Sarge," said Miss Ruby quickly, pointing her finger at young Cynthia.

"I never stirred nothin', Sir. I never stirred nothing," she cried, clutching her few belongings in a carrier bag.

"You is a lyin' wretch!" yelled Miss Ruby. "Is you stir Sarge porridge. Is *you…*"

Before I could finish getting dressed for school, Cynthia was already shuffling down the path, sobbing. Her tears were to no avail; she was banished for good. From that day onward, I acquired a distaste for porridge— and a greater one for Miss Ruby. She was ruthless and had no qualms about securing her place in our family's nest.

***

Our home became the center of village commerce for the Kencot area. Every transaction, legal or not, passed through Sarge's hands. If anyone wanted documents signed or notarized, Sarge did it. For documents to travel to England, Mummy completed the forms and then Sarge signed them. If anyone needed extra money, Sarge loaned it. If anyone needed a reference for a job, Sarge wrote one even if the man hadn't worked with him. Sarge sometimes even put up the bus fare to get to the interview.

His biggest believer was Mr. Jackson, and although Sarge didn't like Jackson's sons, he tried on several occasions to help them find work. Sarge was not only our protector but he belonged to the whole community as well. How I adored him then.

It wasn't until after the train crash, when I saw his name in the newspaper on the Kendal death list, that I knew his full name. It's funny how common it is that West Indians don't know their parents' full names or age or birthplace. There it was —Neville Archibald Augustus Scott, next to my mother's name, Ruth Miriam Cassandra Scott and my other family members.

Sarge had an indomitable spirit. Everyone knew when he was home.

"How is my Eve?" was the first thing he said when he entered the house, the screen door slamming behind him.

He'd bend down, pick her up, place her on his knee, and sit in the rocking chair while she read to him.

"Esther, get me a nice cold drink please, honey."

"Yes, Sarge," I said, grateful for the slight recognition.

He and Austin would play cricket late into the night. When he thought we were sleeping, the front verandah transformed into a domino club while Miss Ruby watched over everyone with a cautious eye.

I loved the land around our house, and for hours at a time I daydreamed while idling through the corn stalks scorched by the sun. As far as the eyes could see, all the land around us belonged to Sarge. He acquired 10 acres of land in St. Elizabeth in recognition of his services in the Second World War. He fought two hard years in the trenches of Picardy along with British soldiers. He returned home with several medals and the title papers for his plot of land. Although the soil was rich and red he didn't want to be a laborer, so he sold his title to the bauxite company and bought our house in Kencot community near the center of Kingston.

Sarge loved the power and authority that a uniform gave him and as soon as he returned, like so many other Jamaican men, he quickly registered with the Constabulary Force.

Sarge planted everything he thought possible, with the aid of Marse Joe's magical hands. Coconut, mango, banana, ackee and breadfruit trees dotted the yard. All year round, we had food galore. Marse Joe was a miserable man who lost no opportunity to lament the loss of his crops in the howling winds and rain of Hurricane Charlie in 1951. Every time I saw Sarge and him together, they were quarreling about something. Sometimes the content of their interaction wasn't a fight at all; it just always sounded like one.

Behind the house, Sarge grew everything he could put his hands on from callaloo, yam, dasheen and cassava to tomatoes and pepper. He even tried his hand at avocados, and until the stubborn seed finally sprouted, we had no peace. The land around us prospered and became a second income to supplement Sarge's meager salary as a cop. He quickly gained a reputation within the community for being able to provide food for the entire neighborhood. He loved putting his hands in the dirt. "The soil sustains my soul when I leave home to do my job every day," he often said. The land became my first love too, and I spent more hours out there with him than inside with my books.

***

Like an oversized heart, our house thumped with life. The smell of fried plantains, fish and baked bread wafted through the air all day long, while the uncertain melodies of students pounding the keys of our piano were a constant reminder that my home belonged to every child in Kencot and parts of wider Kingston. Children tumbled into our parlor before school, during school and late into the evenings—and all day long on Saturday.

I sat in the rocking chair whenever my mother's students came, especially when Mr. Jackson brought his sons Junior, Clement and Clifton. Clement, tall for his age, was easily the most handsome of the three boys. He knew it, and that made him full of himself. His friends called him 'Blue,' but I didn't know why.

My mother sat on the edge of the stool, her body seeming so tiny next to his. I watched them from the corner of my eyes, turning the pages of my book while Mummy placed his fingers on the keys.

'Too limp,' she said when his wrist rested on the piano, her voice as soft as a lullaby. She lifted Clement's hand and pressed his fingers firmly on the keys. Clement followed her lead, his large frame hunched over the black instrument. *Ding.* His big fingers timidly touched the keys while barely making a sound.

The only time I felt I got my mother's undivided attention was when I sat beside her and played the piano on Sundays after church.

"One day I will play as good as you, Mummy."

"I'm sure you will play better than me one day, my darling." She said.

"You've got my voice. One day you could sing in front of thousands."

"No, I'm too shy."

"You're shy now, but you will grow out of it. When you go to college and get real training, your teachers will show you all you need to know about commanding a stage and using your gift."

I loved to listen to my mother sing in church or at home, but mostly in church, where she took on the aura of American jazz singers like Lena

Horne, Billie Holiday and Ella Fitzgerald. She had an incredible ear, and learned most of the songs from the radio. She had studied music in Cuba before she met Sarge. Once was all she needed to hear a tune and she could replay it or sing it again and again.

Austin, Donovan and Charles bounced around the house like princes and only three things concerned them: food, cricket, and girls. When new teenage students arrived for lessons, the boys just sat slack-jawed, gawking at them as if they had never seen girls before.

"You boys better move from here and find something to do," Mummy would say firmly from behind the piano without looking over at them.

NINE

When starting a new life, one typically considers the best timing for transition. We make preparations for the changes and we have some idea of when that new life may begin. But when death comes knocking there are no announcements, no warning signals, no decisions can be made to stop it, no specific month or day is assigned. It just comes. Just jumps out, snaps you up and eats you alive. Austin felt that the London weather had hit him as brutally and as unexpectedly as death. His teeth chattered as if they were speaking their own language.

"Shit—it's freezing!" he muttered, hunching his shoulders up toward his cold, numb ears.

He wrapped his arms around himself and tried to tighten the embrace as the icy wind whipped all around. There were hundreds of brown-skin people being met at Victoria Station. The interior was like a huge factory with a cast-iron skeleton of girders and a ceiling that hovered what seemed like fifty feet above them. The massive Train Departures board dominated the platform about twenty feet up, and would have been a very welcome landmark for Austin and Eve if it had been blowing hot air. Like most of the West Indians arriving that day, they were inappropriately dressed for the cold weather. Eve wore a cotton floral dress with a matching jacket and Austin, a short-sleeved shirt and thin tailored suit. He felt the chill running up and down his spine.

"I'm so tired," Eve piped in from behind him.

"Let me put the suitcases together to make a seat for you," Austin offered. He shed outer his jacket and placed it around Eve's shoulders. "Is that better, sis?" That was the gentlemanly thing to do. Sarge would have been proud to see the way his son took care of his sickly sister. Austin felt the chill as his and Eve's eyes searched through the dense crowd for a familiar face. The swell of voices enveloped them and mixed in with the wheezing and humming of the train and the thud of the doors. Austin cupped his hands over his ears.

He pulled himself up to his full height as he caught sight of her face. There was something distinctly different about Aunt Pearl. Austin could not quite put his finger on it, but from the moment he saw her on that crowded London platform, he knew she was not the same person that left Jamaica. The glow which once radiated from her oval face had been replaced by an ashy grey. She was as beautiful as he had remembered, although it seemed she had aged almost ten years. The day she left Jamaica for England five years before, he was at the cricket club on South Camp Road, close to scoring half a century and would not tear himself away to say goodbye to her. *Shame on me. Chuh, cricket was closer to my heart than Christ.*

Her sunken eyes harbored an undisguised sadness. Huddled under layers of winter clothing, she could not hide that she had lost a lot of weight. Her protruding collar bone gave her away immediately. She wore a navy blue coat with a fake fur collar. The strong resemblance to his mother was obvious, with her ballerina posture, her full lips, and her cat-like eyes. Looking at her made Austin's stomach ache.

"Aunt Pearl!" Austin yelled, slicing up the air with his arms.

"There you are! My dears!" she cried, her arms flailing out from under her heavy winter coat.

She welcomed Eve and Austin with an ear-to-ear smile, as they stood shivering on the platform among the bulging baskets, overfilled trunks, and suitcases.

"But stop!" Aunt Pearl said, taking a half-step back. "You too big to give your Aunt a kiss?"

She wrapped her arms around Austin, just as he noticed two things: he was now two heads taller than she was and she had a peculiar smell—the dry musty odor of stale tobacco, both on her breath and on her clothing. He said nothing about it, but pulled her close to him.

"It's so good to see you again."

Austin squeezed her tightly, trying to ignore the smell. In the warmth of her arms he realized how much he missed his own mother's embrace and tenderness. She hugged Eve and they both began crying, shaking and screaming like they had got the Holy Spirit.

"How you have grown," she said with her newly acquired British accent, her sunken eyes scanning us up and down.

Although Austin was tired from the fourteen-day voyage at sea, followed by a three-hour train journey from Southampton to London, the odor surrounding Aunt Pearl bothered him.

Is this how you smell when you come to live in England? he wondered. *Furthest from my mind before I arrived was the fact that my aunt, a staunch Catholic, a Jamaican woman from Rocky Point, Clarendon, was now a chain smoker to rahtid!*

"Come, let me get you both home into the warm."

She pulled them without hesitation in the direction of one of the 'Way Out' arrows, then toward the exit doors of the overcrowded terminal.

Austin flinched as the crisp November air greeted his face. Outside, the hubbub of arriving and departing passengers seemed greater than what was left behind. Aunt Pearl summoned a taxi with great efficiency.

"Mitcham Street in Kennington, please." Austin and Eve threw their few pieces of worn leather suitcases into the luggage compartment and jumped into the cab. As they stepped into the black taxi, the yellow digits in the small black box on the side of the car started ticking over. The three of them huddled together on the black vinyl seat talking and sharing their excitement. Two of the faces still glowed from the sunshine of home, but their hearts were heavy.

The taxi pulled away from the overcrowded pavement and zigzagged in and out of the rush-hour traffic, overtaking sardine-packed red double decker buses and other vehicles. It proceeded south toward Westminster Bridge where the River Thames lay tranquil beneath the evening chaos.

The rain beat heavily like pebbles against the window pane, as if trying to force itself inside. From the taxi window, Austin could see commuters dressed in layers of clothing, raincoats, water-repellent hats and boots huddled together, clinging to their upright umbrellas in the anticipation of more London rain.

Although she had waited three hours for them, Aunt Pearl was as dry as sand. She sat on the vinyl seat, her body limp, clinging to Eve's hand. With her other hand, she held on tightly to her experienced leather handbag until she needed to retrieve something from it.

"My God!!" Austin yelped. The 'something" was a packet of Senior Service cigarettes. She pulled one out and placed it between welcoming lips. She lit it and closed her eyes as if in prayer, tilting her head backwards as she inhaled its vapor. Both Austin and Eve's mouths hung open.

"Aunt Pearl, you smoke now?" they asked in unison. She held her body erect with the dripping umbrella at her side. Her dark eyes stared back at them as she took a long defiant drag of warm smoke.

"Don't look at me so. You don't understand," she snapped back at her nephew, her body and head rocking from side to side.

Her words were now pronounced with an intonation a lot more like Miss Ruby's.

"It's bad enough that Dudley makes a fuss every time I have one."

Her eyes followed the circles of smoke fading into the thick air.

"I don't need any aggravation from you two as well."

The only people Austin had seen smoking in Jamaica were men. Uncle Cork rolled tobacco, Uncle Winston smoked a pipe, and on occasion his father smoked a Cuban cigar when he played bridge. But no woman in the family—or any woman he knew—was a smoker. Wasn't that something only female movie stars did?

"When did you start smoking Aunt Pearl—and why?"

Eve nudged Austin the moment he asked.

"What?" he turned to Eve. "You want to know, just as much as I do."

Austin shrugged his shoulders, looking his aunt squarely in the face. Aunt Pearl crouched forward and took another drag from the object of discussion.

"How is my darling Esther?" she said, ignoring her nephew's question.

"I wish she had not been so stubborn and had come with you both, but your sister was always so different."

"I wouldn't call Esther different, Aunt Pearl. She is just a stubborn mule." Austin retorted.

"Listen to the pot calling the kettle black."

Pearl shook her head.

"Stubbornness seems to run in our family, Aunt Pearl."

Austin tried to disguise his irritation, as she continued to avoid his question. He had already forgiven Esther for wanting to stay behind in Jamaica without blood-relative supervision, but the overwhelming emotions that rushed through his body quickly dispelled any irritation.

Finally, she leaned forward, stubbing out the cigarette in the taxi's concealed ashtray. Her habit was genuine; only a true smoker would have known its location. Although he was getting soaked, Austin was thankful when she wound the window down. Being in the presence of Aunt Pearl warmed the heart. It felt like having his mother back.

The taxi, with its ever-ticking meter displaying the fare of 5 pounds and 35 pence, approached the famous Oval cricket ground.

"Look, Austin, this is where you're going to play cricket for the West Indies one day." Aunt Pearl pointed at the closed whitewashed gates of the cricket grounds. The taxi took a sharp right and turned onto Kennington Road and then made an abrupt left onto a short narrow street. The small row of brick houses were identical, with red tiled roofs and smoking chimneys. The only distinction between them was the color of their front doors.

The cab driver decelerated.

"What number, love?" he yelled from behind the glass partition. But no number was necessary. The cabbie took his cue from an animated man hopping about on the doorstep and waving his hands frantically, showing himself to be Austin's favorite uncle. Dudley was a stout man with a sanguine face. He had a horseshoe of receding hair and specks of grey in his beard. Uncle Dudley was still doing a jig when Austin reached into the pocket of his brown corduroy pants and pulled out his wallet.

"What you doing?" Aunt Pearl said as she pushed his hand away.

"I can pay for the cab."

"Your Jamaican shillings no good here bwoy."

They tumbled out of the taxi and entered the door to a new life. Yes, there was something distinctly different about Aunt Pearl. She was no longer an aunt but Mummy Scott's replacement. *She'll give us the love she had stored for her own daughter, Grace.* The difference in Aunt Pearl was that she was now an anchor for hope and future happiness—or so Austin thought.

"What a nice big house you have, Aunt Pearl," Eve squeaked from behind Austin.

Aunt Pearl vanished into the darkness and up the winding staircase. The Scott siblings trundled in behind her, through the narrow passageway, the naked bulb assisting them with vague light. Eyes strained as unsure feet stepped carefully onto the frayed stair carpet. Eve and Austin stumbled up four flights of stairs, heaving and banging the suitcases all the way up, chipping the banister's red paint on the way.

"Take time with those suitcases," Aunt Pearl said softly.

"We are almost there," she reassured as she panted for breath on the penultimate step.

Behind one door leaked sounds of African music, drums and a rough kind of flute. A mixed aroma of curry chicken and tobacco wafted up just before she opened the door of her flat.

"Here we are," she said as she flung the door wide open.

Aunt Pearl and Uncle Dudley's living room had high ceilings, with two large bay windows adorned with net curtains and pink-and-white frills around the ends, layered behind red velvet drapes which did not match either the wallpaper or the carpet. It was the same red floral carpet and wallpaper that had greeted them in the hallway. It seemed that nearly every inch of floor space was occupied by a piece of furniture.

A large mahogany cabinet with glass doors dominated the room. It was stacked to the top shelf with bone china serving dishes, featuring an entire dinner set with the Queen's profile from her Coronation. Long-stemmed crystal wine glasses stood with pride among her sherry decanter, Pyrex dishes, two crystal candlesticks and a silver cruet set. This was Aunt Pearl's pride and joy. The contents of the cabinet never saw the light of day unless some outstanding event warranted their use.

On the wall, facing the door was a picture of Our Savior. No matter where you stood in the room, his piercing blue eyes seemed to follow. Uncle Dudley's indispensable radiogram extended itself along the entire side of the wall. It would become a source of comfort to Uncle Dudley and Austin on the really cold nights when they huddled by the instrument, listening to the World Services or 45s and LPs of Fats Domino, Nat King Cole, Harry Belafonte and the beloved West Indian calypsonians, Sparrow and Lord Kitchener.

On top of the radiogram was an array of starched multi-colored doilies that stood like ballerina dresses under porcelain ornaments, and an entire photo gallery of Austin's family. He moved closer; his heart sank as he picked up the silver-framed photograph, the one with himself and Sarge in their cricket whites when he was a little boy. Austin barely recognized himself. He had filled out since then and now sported a goatee, which he imagined would have been to the distaste of his mother, God rest her soul. Just as his sisters had taken all their delicate features from their mother, Austin resembled his father. He had the same red-brown cinnamon-like skin, the same aquiline features and long straight nose, which clearly emphasized that the blood of slave masters ran through the Scott veins.

Austin looked deeply into his father's eyes, forcing back the tears from his own. *Why did you have to die? I need you so much… How the hell am I going to make it through life without you, Sarge?* he wondered.

The sepia photo of Grace, the largest photo of all, stood in the centre of all the other photographs. She had inherited the same Queen Nefertiti eyes as her mother and Aunt Pearl, but it was her manner that had really accentuated her beauty. Austin had guarded her from his friends and their evil thoughts as he did with his own sisters. Of all his cousins, Grace had been his favorite. She was too kind, too delicate, and too graceful to have survived this cruel world. God had chosen her to be with Him to watch over the family. Had she not been his cousin, Austin would have fallen in love with her as all his friends had done when they met her, and glued their eyes to her striking features.

"Stop eyeing up my cousin, chuh," he would keep telling all the boys, killing their gaze. Now he and Eve had taken her place in a new home. They would never fill Grace's shoes, but they'd somehow have to fill their Aunt and Uncle's hearts. It was not possible to fill her shoes. and both of them knew it.

Above the vacant fireplace was an unframed picture of Queen Elizabeth II, held to the wall by a drawing pin. Substituting for a coal fire stood a paraffin heater, ejecting blue and orange flames while providing insufficient heat for a room so large. Austin and Eve huddled around the nauseating glow of the paraffin heater, which would become their greatest friend during those long winter nights. They could not feel any heat unless they were sitting right up close to it. The settee and armchairs surrounding the heater had certainly seen better days, but that is where they placed themselves every evening, regardless.

The family tragedy had an opposite effect on their new guardians. Aunt Pearl had lost a substantial amount of weight, while Uncle Dudley had become heavier, with a barrel belly that protruded like a woman's in the last term of pregnancy. He stuffed himself with food at any given opportunity. Without a doubt, the nightly Guinness and sweet-milk that Aunt Pearl prepared had added the unwarranted pounds. He wore grief well though, and most of the time, he was jovial, even when he feigned those brave smiles of his. The only time he got upset and fussed at Aunt Pearl, to no avail, was when she smoked. It comforted Austin to know that he was not the only person affected by Aunt Pearl's smoking. But she was yet to give him an answer about it.

Aunt Pearl was in and out of the kitchen, constantly cooking. But if you blinked you missed when or what she ate. At dinner she moved the food around on her plate but rarely did any go into her mouth. Leaving a full plate of food, she always found a reason to go back to the kitchen to get something for someone.

"Anyone want more rice, or potatoes?" she would ask.

"Come sit down nuh Pearl? Every minute you leave de table," Uncle Dudley complained.

"We all have two feet and can get anything we want from the kitchen. Come sit down, woman."

She hissed through her teeth, ignored him and shuffled off into the kitchen once again.

***

Things weren't turning out as the youngsters imagined. First, Eve had to find out that Aunt Pearl's place wasn't the whole house she had seen from the outside. Now, Austin was stunned to discover that his entire bedroom would be a folding 'Z' bed in the kitchenette. Of course, he said nothing. *What a something—and my spacious bedroom is still back home.* In Jamaica, when he drew back the curtains, he was bathed in the daily sunlight. Here, he might be bathed if someone splashed in the sink.

Chuh, what could I say? He asked himself.

He was now in the care of Aunt Pearl. Sleeping in the kitchenette had its advantages, though. It was the warmest room in the flat. Austin fed the gas meter with extra shillings and slept with the oven on most nights. "It's dangerous to do that," Aunt Pearl fussed.

"But I need the oven to keep me warm," Austin said. The bitter evening cold seeped through his bones, and he tossed and turned throughout the night. The recurring dreams of Kendal haunted him.

The toilet for the entire household was four floors down, and there was no bath. A path with cracked paving and overgrown weeds led from the house to the outhouse. Considering how shabby the rest of the house was, the toilet was spotless, with rolls of tissue paper, lavender-smelling toilet freshener, and a bottle of Dettol, the West Indian's quintessential disinfenctant. Taking a bath was an ordeal. It meant taking a bus to the public baths (but that's a whole 'nother story for another day).

An abandoned concrete coal shed filled with old junk occupied the entire garden; there was no space to swing a cat, much less have a game of cricket. Aunt Pearl would lean against the shed, her shoulders hunched, as she dragged on what Austin called her 'comfort stick.' On the rare days when the sun forced its way out, Austin sat on the flat roof of the coal shed and enjoyed its cheerless rays.

★★★

"Although this is the so-called 'Mother Country' and your father and other men fought in both World Wars on the invitation of the Crown, we certainly are not welcome here," Aunt Pearl would say without prompting.

"The banks won't loan us any money and rooms to rent are almost impossible to find. Landlords are afraid to rent to us because of the backlash of their neighbors," she said, appearing from the kitchen.

"So the rumors I heard back home are true then, Aunt Pearl?"

"Yes my darling, every word. The signs 'No Dogs, No Irish, No Colored' and 'WOGS go home' are real facts, my son. 'Keep Britain White' are the facts about our Motherland."

She paused, then looked all around her before speaking again.

"They are too ignorant to realize that when they call us WOGS, it really means someone of high status. Workers of Overseas Government Services, that's what it really means, and not just any and everybody can get that position."

"This is just temporary," she said, patting Austin's shoulder. "Better days are ahead, I promise you."

★★★

Once they had settled in, Eve and Austin spent most of the first three days sleeping away the lingering effects of their journey. Uncle Dudley patiently waited until his nephew was fully rested to probe him about every single detail of the horror at Kendal. Alternating between heavy sighs and shakes of the head, Uncle Dudley shifted his weight from one side of the armchair to the other as he read every inch of the Jamaican papers over and over again. Aunt Pearl, on the other hand, never asked any questions about the train crash or Jamaica. Her main interest and concern seemed to be Esther.

"Esther should have come—Esther should have come with you," she said over and over, shaking her head.

"Yes, Esther should have come with us, but I just could not get her to understand that waiting in Jamaica was a bad idea. She really believes they're coming back."

"Everybody deals with their grief differently. She'll soon come round. I just hope we find a place before she asks us to send for her…"

"I'm going to have a smoke," Aunt Pearl said abruptly.

She stepped aside, opening the window to have another cigarette. She never smoked in the living room or bedrooms, but she would stick her head out the window—bringing in all the cold air—or she would go downstairs to stand by the coal shed as if it were a neighbor she could talk to. Sometimes Mr. Vincent, our neighbor, joined her. In those moments, it was as if the train crash had never happened at all.

★★★

Uncle Dudley proudly gave Austin a tour of the whole house in the grand style of a landlord. He had waited for five years to see his beautiful daughter, and he had already rehearsed his script that would mention when the house was built, how many square feet of living space it offered, and so on. He had imagined walking through the building with Grace and introducing her to everybody. Now all he had was Austin , now that he could no longer brag about "My Grace is this, and my Grace is that," and take her photograph to work in his breast pocket. All the London Transport workers knew everything about Grace: what she ate, her likes and dislikes. In his own way, he'd prepared the world for her; now, all he had was a nephew following his uncle sheepishly around the house, knowing that he could never be anything Grace had meant to him.

"We are all one big happy family here while we are away from home.

We all try to help each other as best we can," he said as we climbed the stairs. "But I will never forgive Vincent for giving Pearl her first cigarette. Chuh."

"Is him spoil up me wife."

"Is that how she started smoking, Uncle Dudley?"

"Yes, son. When your aunt got the telegram about the crash, I wasn't here, so she ran downstairs to Vincent and he tried to calm her down. When he didn't succeed, he offered her a cigarette. What a fool!" Uncle Dudley sucked his teeth.

Aunt Pearl never sat still longer than five minutes. Fidgeting like a five year-old, she was either cooking, cleaning, knitting, mending Uncle Dudley's socks, or studying for a nurses' exam that would take her to a higher position at the hospital. She still ate small morsels of food if any, and disappeared countless times down the stairs to smoke. The only time she stood still was when she smoked; then, everything came to a complete halt. In the middle of cooking dinner, she would suddenly disappear downstairs and out into the cold air. Her shoulders hunched up around her ears as she puffed away beside the abandoned coal shed.

Austin could not ignore his aunt's behavior any longer. One night when she slipped out, thinking he had not noticed her, he followed her out into the narrow garden. He found her perched on the edge of the broken brick wall. Austin took up a similar position beside her and sat still and quiet, watching her blow circles of smoke into the night air.

"So, Aunt Pearl," Austin said, interrupting her thoughts, "I wish you wouldn't smoke."

"Oh, chile, why you bother me so?"

"Because I love you, Aunt Pearl."

"If you love me, you would leave me alone and go back inside and wash up my plates." She blew the smoke from her mouth without looking at him.

"I'll do that for you later. It just hurts me to see you smoking like this."

"Did Dudley send you out here?"

"No, Aunt Pearl, not at all."

"Austin," she paused, "I have to smoke if I want to stay alive. I don't want to but I have to. I smoke to stay sane, my love." She rubbed my shoulder.

"Well, Aunt Pearl, if you won't stop smoking, then I am going to start smoking with you." I reached out to take a cigarette from her.

"You crazy, bwoy?" She pulled her body away from me. "I beat you dead first before I mek you tek up this bad habit. Don't think just because you're taller than me now, you too old fe a good ol'time beatin.'"

"But I can't watch you do this to yourself every day, Aunt Pearl, I love you too much."

"I wish I could stop, chile, but I can't," she sighed. "I started smoking the day Grace died." She slumped forward, her face full of sadness. "The day of the train crash," she said slowly.

"When I got the news, I wanted to set myself on fire and burn the way my baby had burned on that terrible day. Burn the way your mother burned and all our kin folk; your daddy, Uncle Cork and everybody we knew. The pain was too much for me." She pressed her hand to the center of her bosom and pulled once more on her cigarette.

"Dudley wasn't home when I first got the news." Her body rocked to and fro, comforting the cigarette like an open flame.

"I ran downstairs screaming to Vincent. Poor Vincent. He didn't know what to do with me, so he gave me a cigarette and made me a cup of tea, which had more brandy than tea." A half-smile surfaced on her pained face.

"I nearly choked on it at first, but now I can't stop myself. Some days I smoke a whole pack. It soothes my hollow heart, my aching stomach." She stared into his face, her own face tearless but guilt ridden. Austin placed his arm around her arched shoulders.

"If only we had worked harder to get Grace here sooner, she would not have been on that train..." She paused and took a long sigh, "but then...," she said, folding her hands in front of her, her body still rocking. "It would have made no difference. Your mother was still on the train, so I would have been in the same pain I am in now. So I smoke against my husband's will, against my church and my God. I go to mass and confession and pray for forgiveness and hope that God will forgive me and understand me."

Her Jamaican accent was now stronger than white rum.

"I have forgiven Him for taking my only child from me, my darling sister, my brother-in-law, my cousins. Fourteen beautiful lives stolen from us without a warning. Just like that." She snapped her fingers as she said it.

"I have forgiven Him. So He must forgive me for I am not sinning, I'm just in pain. A pain that won't go away," she exhaled.

"No one should say anything to a mother who has lost a child." She paced up and down the concrete path. "She doesn't live any longer, so she exists the best way she can."

She threw the cigarette to the ground, pressing it out as she would a cockroach.

"To live with the guilt every day, the anger, all our dreams shattered." She turned to Austin, her body now taut as a board against the coal shed.

"I wanted Grace to be a doctor," she smiled." She would have been a good doctor too, you know. She was clever." Austin patted her hand, and comforting her the best he could, he rubbed her back with his other hand.

"Yes, Aunt Pearl. Grace would have been good at anything she did."

"No one, not even God, can tell me what to do now. I do what I need to do to stay alive and sane. When you get settled you will see plenty of mad people walking around in London town, let me tell you chile, and you better learn how to hold your corner."

She looked Austin dead on in the face.

"Imagine, one day we are a complete, happy family and in one short journey across the island, all our lives are shattered, all our dreams lost. Our family gone forever."

She wrapped her shawl more tightly around her shoulders.

"But now I have you and Eve," she smiled.

"Don't worry, Aunt Pearl, I am going to make it alright for you. I am going to work hard and build a big memorial in their honor. I am going to be the biggest name in cricket that anyone has ever heard of. Nothing can bring our family back, but I am going to keep their memory alive, you just wait and see." She reached out for Austin's hand.

"Let's go inside. It's freezing out here."

She pulled Austin into the warmth and the mixed aroma of their new home. It was a home that was so much less than he was used to, but a home filled with as much love nonetheless. He never accepted that she smoked but he never made another comment about her actions again, either. As agonizing as it seemed, he just sat with her most nights, watching her puff the grey circles into the air, sucking on her pain.

TEN

My empty days were like an abyss. The heavy November rains pelted the wooden shutters on our house, the drops as heavy as my heart. Our house, once full of noise and life, had fallen silent. The piano keys still lay untouched just like on the first day of September when they all left. Miss Ruby set the table in case anyone came, but no one ever did.

My grief bubbled up inside me, not like a sharp pain but a constant throb which never seemed to ease. I stayed behind because I truly believed in my heart that I'd hear my mother's voice again, feel the softness of her blue-black skin, be scolded by my father, walk in Grace's shadow and lie to Uncle Cork about Donovan or Austin's whereabouts.

I told myself, one day I'll wake up and not feel so weak. One day my heart will not ache for them. I'd slip in and out of this conscious thought and just sit right there on the verandah with my crochet. I know I sat there on the edge of insanity, immersed in longing and sorrow. My eyes were fixed on the gate, waiting for it to open and for them all to come bounding back into the yard.

I'll mark time with each loop. One stitch at a time. I'll weave my new life crocheting these doilies. For every week I'm here waiting for them, I'll crochet something. Slow and precise like a waltz.

Long before this quilt is finished, I told myself, *"they will all be home. I know it in my heart."*

★★★

Every day dissolved into another. I unwillingly pulled myself out of bed. I walked to the verandah staring at the pale blue sky, waiting for an answer to appear. I wanted it to read, "Your family are all coming home tomorrow," or "You can find them in May Pen" or "Look for them in Savanna-la-Mar."

But there were no messages in the sky.

"Eat something before you fade away," Miss Ruby said, pushing my breakfast in front of me.

"I can't, Miss Ruby. I can't."

"Just a likkle sip for Miss Ruby."

She pushed the spoon toward my mouth.

"Just a likkle sip," she smiled. I pushed the food away. Food was as difficult to swallow as my life had become.

"You have to eat something or you will waste away, Chile."

"I can't."

"What can I do to you to make you feel good?" she patted me on my knee.

"I wish you would move into one of the bedrooms closer to me, Miss Ruby."

"But, Miss Esther, I like my little room round the back there. "You will be just fine where you are. I can see and hear everything." She smiled and wheeled away from me.

***

By a certain point—I'm not sure when—I think it was rumored that I was mad. I'd lay awake in the intense heat, tossing and turning, straining all night for the sound of any of them. I waited for the creak of the door as it swung open back and forth all day long with students coming for their lessons, or for the sound of Sarge's hoarse voice saying "Where is my Eve?"

There was no chuckle from Aunt Martha, no cooing hellos from Christine and Cassandra, no pounding of the piano keys or the crack of the ball and the bat. I waited and waited, but I heard nothing. I was certain the two of us would go shopping downtown to Issa's or Nathan's again. We would pick out pretty dresses for Eve. I knew that one day would pass when I would not shed a tear for my family. I stayed on my knees praying, looking up into the sky, hoping that they were out lost somewhere and searching for home, and that when they found their way I would be here to greet them. I dozed off to sleep.

All the years I had lived in Eve's shadow, I had wanted to be my own person. Now I was alone. My days stretched longer, my sadness bounced off the walls like echoed whispers. I could hardly breathe without Eve or Austin flooding my thoughts. *How are they doing? How are they surviving that cold English weather?* I wondered.

As much as I missed them and my heart ached for them, I could not go to England. I had to stay right where I was. Although my faith had slipped, I knew that God would deliver my family to me.

"I know you are watching me, God," I'd say. "I know you're making me suffer for my evil thoughts. I've got the message, God. I've learned my lesson!" I yelled at the stifling air.

If I was not staring at the sky, my eyes were fixed on the trail of ants making their journey across the polished verandah, precise and certain. When I wasn't watching ants, I sat for hours staring at the gate, willing and waiting for someone to walk through it. The only person who came through it was Mr. Buchanan.

"A letter from England for you, Miss Esther," he would yell. Gingerly walking up the path as if I might pounce on him, he bent toward me, placing the letter in my lap.

"How are you today, Miss Esther?"

He mouthed the words at me the way you would talk to somebody who was in a long coma.

"Fine, thank you Mr. Buchanan. Just fine," I lied.

"Say howdy to your sister and Austin when you write back, okay Miss Esther…?"

My sister's letters were better than any book I had read. Her words brought comfort. So many times, I wanted to write and tell her that I would join her and Austin, tell them I wanted them to hurry home. Five years without them seemed like a prison sentence, but I had created my own prison.

What irritated me the most was Marse Joe's attitude. Since Sarge was gone, Marse Joe took it upon himself to be master of the land, doing nothing but sitting under the mango tree, eating or watching Miss Ruby work.

"You nuh have nuh work today, Marse Joe?" Miss Ruby yelled at him.

"Sun too hot, Ruby. Chuh."

"Sun too hot every day for you, Marse Joe, since Sarge gone. You better watch yuself 'cause Duppy know who fi frighten."

"Shet you mout', Ruby. You me boss?!" He barked back at her, spitting orange pulp as he spoke. He continued peeling his orange, the skin snaking around his knife.

***

The days of Christmas spirit floated through the air, but there was no baking, no potato pudding, no poinsettas lining the verandah, no red bedspreads, no sorrel shelled and drawn, no extra cleaning, no trips to the Ward Theater to see Christmas pantomime, no carols sung around the piano.

It was another series of long, hot and humid nights. My eyes were accustomed to the dark from being awake until morning, so many times. Beads of sweat settled on my forehead, in the creases of my neck, and in the crevices of my arms. I drifted in and out of sleep, tossing and turning on the starched sheets, listening to the gentle humming of the ceiling fan as the inadequate breeze failed to cool me.

The shadows of the mango tree danced on the wall. Somebody? One shadow, unfamiliar, suddenly appeared long across the ceiling. My heart stopped beating. Before I could make a sound, the shadow's thick fingers and sweaty palm had covered my mouth. Sweat dripped insistently from his face, down onto my cheek and into the corner of my mouth as I tried to scream. "Shh…" was all he said. A man's sandpapery skin and the stench of his body consumed me. I was rigid with revulsion.

"Me sorry for your loss, Miss Esther, but you can't lie here every night and t'ink say you gwine get away wid it," he hissed in my ear as he pinned my body to the bed.

"Girl, you know how long I've been patient—how long I've been waiting?!"

He pressed his body harder against mine. My body was paralyzed with panic, the sparrow under the lion's paw. I was trapped.

"I been patiently waiting for my money. Don't you scream, young miss. I'm not going to hurt you as long as you do as I tell you. It's not your body I want. Me never fight a woman fi her body yet. I just want what is owing to me."

He must be drunk, I thought, but as badly as he smelled, there was no essence of liquor on his breath or body.

"If I move my hand, you won't scream will you, Miss Esther?"

My eyes widened. I shook my head the best I could to reassure him. The rough hand scraped over my lips and cheek as it freed my mouth.

"Your farder owe me money since the devil was a bwoy, and I want every red cent of it right now. Me sorry 'im dead, but a promise is a promise. Sarge did tell me say if anything 'appen to 'im I must tek part of de land fe me payment."

He pulled a crumpled handwritten note from of his pocket.

"Look 'ere," he said, pushing the note in front of my eyes. It was too dark to read or to tell whether it was really Sarge's handwriting. He must have carried it around a long time.

"If you don't have it, Miss Esther, then you have to give me the land and the house."

"What kind of money could Sarge owe you, that you think I can just give over our house and land to you, just like that?" My trembling voice betrayed my fear.

"Gambling debt, me dear. You t'ink say your farder was some kind of saint or something just because him was Catholic and go to Mass wid your madder on Sunday? God rest her soul."

He made the sign of the cross on his chest. "You farder was a big ginnal."

"Well, if I'm to give you the money, then let me get up."

He wiped his nose on the back of his hand and moved his body to one side. I dislodged myself from underneath him, disguising my relief.

"Don't try any funny business, young miss." I rolled out of bed, my legs as weak as a colt's. He followed close behind me.

"It's okay, man... I'll get it. I'll get the money. "

"Don't mek a sound, you 'ear me," he hissed, close enough for the sound to be in my head.

My mind raced to an escape plan; my body shook. I scanned my mother's dresser for a heavy item I could use as a weapon.

Think quickly, I told myself. *Think girl, think.*

"I think there is some money hidden in the kitchen under the floor boards."

My voice trembled as I pointed toward the kitchen.

"Mek we go get it." He pushed me in the back.

I fumbled my way down the hall toward the kitchen, guided by the light of the moon. My heart was racing so fast I felt dizzy, but my legs gained steady momentum.

As I entered the kitchen door, I saw Sarge's cricket bat. I walked toward it. I bent forward toward the floor where there was a split floor board; grabbing the bat with one quick swoop, I swung my body around and hit him across his head. *Whack!* I heard something break. The blood gushed everywhere at once, spraying me and the walls. He staggered backwards holding his hands over his bloodied face.

"You likkle bitch," he spat.

"Get away from me!"

I hit him again, this time with more force. He fell to the ground. Hard. I looked down at his body, my own stiff with fright. There was a slight movement from his left eye as the blood oozed from his head onto the floor. He moaned. His lashes flickered and his left lid opened. His eyes held only a blind, empty gaze. He sighed and tried to move his lips but only a shallow sigh escaped. He took a deep breath, then stopped breathing. I jumped back in simultaneous horror and relief.

"Oh my God, what have I done?!" I heard myself shriek.

I bent down over his lifeless body, trying not to think of him as someone I had known for so many years, someone who had climbed a coconut tree and picked the biggest one just for me. I wanted to forget that there had been a past between us. *No, he was an intruder, a stranger who had come to hurt me, I tried to convince myself. Yes, it was self-defense, because he had come to hurt me.*

I took one last glance at his motionless body then ran barefoot out of the kitchen, my feet slapping the wooden floor up the hallway to Miss Ruby's room, my whole body trembling as I went.

"Miss Ruby, come quick, come quick. It's Marse Joe, It's Marse Joe." My voice broke from the terror.

"What's wrong with Marse Joe now?"

"Come quickly, I think he's dead."

"Hush you mouth, what you talking 'bout? You must be dreaming, girl."

I pulled at her thick arm.

"Come let me show you, come Miss Ruby."

Her body was heavy and full of sleep as she pushed her feet into her slippers. She got up and dragged herself toward the kitchen. To where I'd hit Joe. I'd hit Joe, but there was nobody. No body.

"Where him gone? The body gone!"

"Chile," Miss Ruby said sleepily, "I told you, you were dreaming."

She rubbed both her eyes with her fists.

I turned on all the kitchen lights. "No, look! See the blood... there!"

I held the lamp high and followed the red line away from the spot where I had left him. Miss Ruby followed, but not as closely as before. Joe hadn't got far. There he was, face down in a pool of blood.

"Oh, mi sweet Jesus."

Miss Ruby placed her hand on her chest.

"What you do, chile?" She bent over his lifeless body, then turned him over onto on his back. Touching his wrists, she placed her ear close to his heart. Miss Ruby shot her chin up to glare at me.

"Me Jesus, him dead fi true...!"

"What we going to do, Miss Ruby?"

"We? How him end up dead so pon me floor?"

"He came into the bed, talking about money Sarge owed him, and I hit him with Sarge's cricket bat, and, and..." I stuttered. "I didn't mean to hit him so hard. We have to get the police!" I sobbed at the top of my voice, wringing my hands.

"Get the police? No, me chile. We can't get no police in dis business."

"Why not?"

"Too much mix-up-mix-up. You don't need all dis trouble in you young life right now—after all you been through already. Wid you family dead off inna Kendal. We just gwine have to get rid of the body."

"Get rid of him, Miss Ruby?"

"Nobody don't do business wid Marse Joe, Marse Joe was careless wid him life, nobody gwine come look fi 'im."

"But I killed a man, Miss Ruby," my trembling voice whispered. "It was self-defense."

"You wan' go jail, gal? Kingston jail a no pretty place for nobaddy, much less s'maddy like you, Miss Esther. You don't know no rough life," she said.

"But it was self-defense."

"You t'ink you can go teacher training college wid murder record a hang over you head? All you family business out a door; you farder owe nuff money a road. Lawd have mercy!"

She placed her hand on her forehead.

"Him was a man who use to gamble hard. We don't know who else coming fi dem share." Miss Ruby placed her hands on my shoulders and stared at me with piercing intensity.

"Let me tek care of it. If word get out you could lose the house and the land, even if dem find you innocent. You farder owe nuff money, you know. Sarge was able to keep ever'baddy at a distance because ever'baddy did 'fraid of Sarge."

"Sarge owed money?"

"Yes, yes—look, me chile, dis is not de time fi family confession. Come, trust old Ruby. Miss Ruby ever let you down yet? Just trust me."

She wrapped Marse Joe's body in the blood-soaked rug. We dragged the weight of him through the kitchen door and out into the yard, pulling him over the flower beds, behind the calalloo patch and around the broad-leafed banana trees and across the gully.

The hem of my nightdress and my feet were both wet from the night dew on the grass. My arms ached as his body became heavier toward the end of the yard where the abandoned pit toilet stood. My trembling hands struggled for a moment with the broken latch. Then with one mad effort I pulled the broken door open. It dangled on its rusty hinges.

We struggled with the weight. Lifting a bit of his body at a time up onto the seat, we hauled him up head first. Once his shoulders were through the large, rotting hole, we let go. His body fell into the blackness below, along with his wallet, his pen knife, his smelly flannel checked jacket and glasses, two bloodied towels, and the rug he soaked with his blood.

"Take off your clothes. Get rid of everything you have on." Miss Ruby said. I quickly undressed down to my underwear, which was soaked bright red with blood.

"Come on nuh; tek off everyt'ing."

I hesitated for a moment, my heart pounding.

"Girl, hurry! There is nuttin' you have that I don't see already. Mek haste." Her peppered tone returned. She threw her dressing gown around my bare shoulders, my body trembling under the crescent moon.

"Mek haste before mornin' come," she hurried me.

"I'll hide his bicycle down inna de bush and you go back to the house and clean up the mess," she marshaled.

"I've got to cut down a whole heap of banana leaves."

"Banana leaves! What for, Miss Ruby?"

"To keep down the smell when him body start rot. Gwaan." She shooed me away like I was a stray fowl. "Just mek haste and don't ask so much question."

I ran into the kitchen, filled the aluminum bucket with water and carbolic soap and tried to scrub the blood stains from the floor. My hands and knees ached from a position to which I was unaccustomed. I scrubbed and scrubbed, but the stain would not budge. The blood, now dried, had seeped like quicksand into the crevices of the floor boards. Now I had a bucket full of red soapy water and a trail of red stains to deal with.

"Why did he have to get up and move?" I cursed the dead.

By the time the sun peeped through the early morning skies, we had hidden all evidence of Marse Joe's existence. I scoured my hands until the skin was sore, trying hard to wash away the shame. I changed the sheets on my mother's bed, then crawled in, drained with exhaustion from the night's untimely events.

"Are you there, Sarge?" I called into the air. "You see what you've done?" I fell into bed and wept like a baby.

"Hush, me chile," Miss Ruby said, rubbing my back. She sang to me:

"There is no secret what God can do, what he does for others he will do for you. With arms wide open, he will pardon you, there is no secret what God can do."

"Hush. You get some rest now, me chile."

"Do you think anyone will miss Marse Joe? Should I tell...?"

"You say not'ing to no one, you hear me? Don't write to Austin or Eve, not to chatty Miss Lee or any of our neighbors. Leave all the questions and answers to me. Tonight never happened, Miss Esther, you hear me? You must never talk about tonight to anyone. Trust nobaddy," Miss Ruby said, shooting me a stern look.

"Okay..." my shaky voice murmured.

"You get some rest. Don't you worry about a t'ing. Miss Ruby gwine tek care of you good." She pointed her finger at her chest.

Her face was lined with years of hidden secrets. I leaned toward her and wrapped my arms around her full waistline. I buried my head in her heavy bosom. Her heart pounded equally as fast as mine. She remained calm and still.

"Hush, it's all over now, me dear. He can't hurt you no more."

This was the woman I hated as a child, the one who I thought hated me, and now without question she shielded me and made me feel safe.

How many times had she protected our family? How many secrets did she have locked inside her heart? Was this the reason she chased away so many helpers in the past? What other secrets did Sarge have? All these questions surged in the back of my mind. A certain nudge of reality surfaced. I really didn't know my father at all. I knew he broke small promises to me but I didn't know that he broke promises to other people as well. He was a gambler. He had lied and had a vice that almost cost me my life. I took a life in defense of my own. I wanted answers from him and where was he? Was he really among the smoldering ashes and steel buried deep in the dark soil at Kendal? "Where are you, Sarge?!" I screamed again into the air.

"How can I thank you, Miss Ruby?"

"Your mother would want me to look after you. Tonight never happened, you hear me. Get some rest, mi chile." She kissed me on the forehead for the first time. I in turn wrapped my arms around her so tightly.

"Esther, I cannot breathe." She pulled my arms from her waist.

"Everything is going to be fine. Just trust Miss Ruby, you 'ear?"

"I am sorry for all the times I was disrespectful to you, Miss Ruby. Sorry for all the displeasure I caused you." Tears rolled down my face.

"Hush chile. No time for confessions now. You and Eve were the girls I never had. I loved your mother like she was me own daughter. I would do anything for Sister Ruth. Your family was the family I dreamed of. I—I owe you. You go to sleep now."

I walked toward the door.

"Where you going?"

"I think I'll sleep in my own room tonight," I said imperiously.

"But Miss Esther," she said, her hands on her hip. "dis is your room. You make it yours since the night of the crash. Don't let Marse Joe run you out of it now. It's yours."

"Will you sleep in here with me too?"

"I'll mek up my bed over there on the chaise."

"No Miss Ruby. I can't let you sleep there. The bed is big enough for the both of us."

"No, Miss Esther, I couldn't sleep in Sister Ruth's bed. No, not at all, that's not right. What would I tell her? I know she's watching us."

"I won't tell a soul."

"No I won't do that, but you got to realize say, dem not coming back Miss Esther, none of dem." She paused.

"They really aren't coming back, are they?" Tears ran down my face as I let her hold me in her arms. For the first time in months, I went directly off to sleep. And dreamed nothing.

★★★

A distant pounding outside my window woke me up. Bang. Thump. Bang. Bang. Thump. Jumping out of bed, I looked at the clock. It was almost 2.30 p.m. Half the day was gone. I rushed to the window, drawn to the sound. Miss Ruby stood with hammer in hand, nailing a sign to the gate. I dragged on my dressing gown and ran barefoot down the path.

NO DOG HERE BUT BEWEAR OF GUN.

The sign was hand painted in red with unequal lettering on a piece of floor board. "Miss Ruby, what are you doing?"

"Protecting us from anyone who t'ink say dem bad enough fi come 'ere at night time again."

"But we don't have any guns in the house."

"Who tell you so?" She barked back at me. "Mek haste. Come inside." She pushed me back up the path.

"Sarge have one or two guns in the house."

From a cupboard in the hallway she pulled out a Remington Model 14 pump-action rifle and two Smith & Wesson .38 pistols. One was a long Police Special, the other was a snub-nosed short version of the same gun.

"Here, keep dis one under your pillow." She pushed the hand gun toward me. I recoiled from it like it was a piece of rotten fish.

"No, Miss Ruby, I can't take a gun into my room."

"Alright then, I am going to stay up all night and mek anyone of dem t'ink say dem bad, fe come inna dis yard any time after dark—fi *any* reason. Me ah go shoot dem dead."

★★★

When there's an old black woman of dubious background sitting guard night after night under a tree with a powerful rifle, word travels fast. It wasn't long before everyone heard that Miss Ruby would shoot you after dark if you set one foot past our gate.

For four full weeks as night follows day, Miss Ruby sat on the verandah in the shadows of the mango tree with Sarge's rifle. Only Miss Ruby knew how many other debt collectors like Marse Joe were out there with 'I owe you' notes. Only she knew who to look for. Like a loyal soldier she would die first rather than let anybody tarnish our family name.

"Good Morning, Miss Esther; Good Night, Miss Ruby," we heard each day from a safe distance outside. Our neighbors called at toward the gate, but not one soul stepped inside our yard again, and I never set one foot past it either.

So no one came, not even in the daytime. A few questions swirled around from our neighbors. "Where is Marse Joe?" they'd ask.

"Mi hear say 'im gone a fareign to 'im sister," Ruby would tell them in her normally abrupt tone.

★★★

Just as the fever passed through Eve for four days and nights, the guilt of my actions seeped through me like a fever. I was delirious and my temperature did not return to normal for almost three weeks. Bathing three times a day became a ritual: early morning, after lunch, and before bedtime. I washed my hands more than I could count during the course of the day. But I thought I could still see Joe's blood between my fingers. At night my mind ran wild, and I paced up and down the floor, back and forth, listening to the creaks of the floorboards beneath my bare feet.

Stricken with guilt, I barely spoke, barely ate or slept. By midday I took to bed and stayed there until the sun went down. Killing Marse Joe meant nothing to Miss Ruby. She went about her business like nothing had happened, humming to herself, piling her plate high with food, while my stomach heaved at the smell of it.

"Here, I make your favorite dish for you," she coaxed me, but everything she did failed.

"I don't want it." I pushed the plate away from me.

"Well I have to go back into my black medicine box." She said. On top
of my guilt now came a layer of curiosity, covered with remorse, piled high
with suspicion and disillusionment. What kind of man was my father? What
else was I going to learn about him? I wondered.

I sank deeper and deeper into despair. I woke up in the middle of the
night hot and drenched with sweat. Marse Joe's image danced around in
front of me every time I closed my eyes. I clutched my stomach howling and
crying like a baby. I climbed out of bed and stormed through the house doubled over in pain.

"Sarge where are you? Where are you? Come home, come home," I
cried through the hollow house.

One night in a fit of rage I ran through the house, pulling every picture
of Jesus and all the crucifixes off the walls. I ran into Austin's room, my room,
and my parents' room, gathering all the Bibles in the house. Carrying them
stacked high against my chest, I stumbled out into the yard and threw them
in a heap on the ground. I ran into the kitchen for kerosene oil and matches.

"What is all this ruckus I hear? What are you doing, me chile?" Miss
Ruby screamed after me.

"You can't burn the Holy Book and the Lord Jesus—is crazy you going
crazy, gal?" she said, pushing me away and pulling the Bibles from my grip.

"How can there be a God, Miss Ruby? How can there be a God?" I
screamed at her.

"I don't know, me chile. I don't know why God take them from us but
burning the Bibles won't help you one bit." She pulled me inside the house,
wiping the tears from my eyes with the hem of her big blue skirt.

Miss Ruby now sang to me often, the way she had done when Eve was
sick while placing cloves of garlic at the top of each door. Burning candles,
mixed cubes of blue and a yellow liquid the color of urine with candle wax,
humming and praying as she concocted her secret potions. She dug deep
into her secret black box, now tattered with age, and pulled out a chicken
feather and a bottle of black ink.

Drawing the sign of the cross over my bed, she said, "There. Keep Marse
Joe from haunting you," she said, staring me squarely in the face.

"Nobaddy gwine worry you no more, Miss Esther, dead or alive I
promise you dat."

But I was already haunted by guilt, by the spirits of my father.

"I must go to the police, Miss Ruby. You can't protect me forever. I will tell them what I did. I am the daughter of a respectable Sergeant. The law would be on my side." I cried.

"Is what wrong wid you Miss Esther? Ah fool you fool or what? No reason to do that now," Miss Ruby argued with me. "Just let time pass nuh?" She pushed a pile of blue airmail letters under my nose.

"Four letters come for you from England, Miss Esther. When you goin' to open dem? Long time me no hear you read de letters. I longing to know how my Austin and Eve are doing. Read dem!" she demanded.

The tissue-thin air letters bearing the Queen's profile were now a welcome escape. They came beautifully scripted in Eve's copperplate handwriting. Eve's letters were my biggest source of comfort in my first year without she and Austin. Every inch of the paper was used and at the end she closed with a quote from the scriptures.

"Thou wilt show me the path of life:
in thy presence is fullness of joy;
at thy right hand there are pleasures for evermore."
—Psalm 16: 11

I now lived my life vicariously through Eve's letters. Her words sustained me like air. I read them and reread them as often as three or four times a day and at night I pushed them under my pillow. I read them aloud to Miss Ruby, who awaited their arrival as anxiously as I did. When the next one arrived, I carefully stored them in Mummy's shoe box after reading it. I replied to her the next day. My letter sat on top of the piano until Mr. Buchanan came on Thursday.

★★★

Eve and Austin survived their first winter. They came to accept that they had to start new lives, but that didn't prevent them from asking why they had to start over in the middle of the London cold... When the snow came to Austin's new world, it didn't look anything like the Christmas cards Aunt Pearl used to send to Jamaica. They were so clean and peaceful. The snow meant more clothes to wear, more paraffin to buy and more precaution from the children who pelted him mercilessly with snowballs and then ran and hid if he retaliated. The grey slush which often turned into chunks of ice created havoc for drivers and pedestrians and caused many accidents. In his mind, the Christmas cards were a lie, like so many other facts about 'Jolly Old England.' England was not even close to 'Jolly.' *To rahtid.*

By now Eve and Austin knew all the other tenants in their new home at Mitcham Street. Uncle Dudley did not waste any time giving them a tour around the rest of the building. The first introduction was to the infamous Mr. Vincent Agabi.

"I don't know if I want to meet this man, Uncle Dudley."

"Why, son?"

"Well he's the one who started Aunt Pearl smoking." Austin said.

"Yes, yes, but he's really not a bad chap at all." Uncle Dudley tapped on the door.

"You in there, Vincent?"

Mr. Agabi appeared from behind the chipped door like a Masai warrior, his skin as black as charcoal. He slouched forward as if to apologize for his height. As Austin entered his flat, the stain of old pipe tobacco hit his nostrils. He fanned his nose and tried to adjust to the smell.

"Come in," he said in a deep baritone. Vincent Agabi stepped aside, bowing his upper body and sweeping his right arm royally in front of me.

"So this is your nephew Austin? Welcome to the Motherland. Is it cold enough for you?"

He rolled back his head and roared with laughter.

"Vincent is studying to be a doctor. He loves to read so you will both have a lot in common— but he doesn't know how to play cricket. We're still working on that."

Vincent Agabi's room was half the size of Aunt Pearl's living room. He had a twin bed, a table with no table cloth, one chair near the paraffin heater and a transistor radio. There was no television and no carpet. Part of the linoleum floor was ripped, showing the bare floor boards underneath. His clothes hung around the room on wire hangers and where furniture should have been, all Austin could see from ceiling to floor were stacks of books, mountains of papers, files folders, magazines and more books.

In the centre of his table rested a glass ashtray filled with cigarette butts, and a ceramic pipe. By his bedside table, there was a dog-eared Bible and a photo of a woman with three small children competed for space. The windows had no curtains. Sheets of newspaper kept out the natural light and the naked bulb provided little light to the room. In one corner stood a single-burner hotplate crying out to be cleaned.

"Would you like a cup of tea?" He asked and pointed to the kettle sitting on the hot plate.

"No man, we are not stopping. I'm just doing my rounds to get this young man settled."

"Any time you get fed up with your Uncle Dudley and his dominoes and his music and you want some peace and quiet son, my door is always open to you. Nice to meet you, Austin. Welcome to England." He shook Austin's hand with a firm grip.

They left Agabi's and climbed the stairs to meet Miss Duncan.

"Lawd Mr. Dudley, what a way you nephew handsome. Come in, come in," she said, tugging at Austin. A little girl with two big brown puppy eyes appeared behind Miss Duncan's knees. Her four plaits were as thick as naval rope and had a red ribbon hanging from the end of each one.

"This is Margaret," Miss Duncan said, pushing the little girl forward. "She just come up last month herself, so she not too used to everybody yet."

Miss Duncan's room was furnished in a very similar way to Aunt Pearl's and Uncle Dudley's, but there were toys scattered everywhere on the floor: a doll house, bright plastic tea cups and plates, dolls of every description and a photo gallery of loved ones left behind covered the cabinet top.

"I hope Pearl has plenty of long johns for you because you going to need every single last one of them."

She squeezed Austin's arm.

"Sorry to hear about the loss of your family, son. They are all in God's hands now."

One more flight, where Mrs. Morgan was eagerly awaiting them.

"Come here and let me see if I can still feel the sun on you." She pulled Austin close to her body.

"I miss home so bad. You have the nicest family anyone could have asked for as neighbors. Me sorry to hear about your loss. Lawd me bawl, me bawl so till for your Aunt Pearl when she tell me the terrible news. Your Aunt Pearl... she is a Trojan, though. I don't see her cry yet since she get the news about her one-daughter." Mrs. Morgan talked ten to the dozen, as if she had

had no outside communication with the world until the Scott youngsters arrived.

"When I first came, I cried every night. I was so homesick and bwoy the cold just bite me to de bone. Is your Auntie and Uncle dat comfort me, you nuh. Is dem mek me believe say I could stay in England and mek a life. Now me still homesick but at least me not crying everyday like before. Me send for me daughter. She soon come join me," Mrs. Morgan said, looking Austin over, "she is about your age."

Her tiny space seemed to generate its own plastic. There was plastic fruit, flowers, tablecloth, table settings and furniture covering. A large shipping barrel sat in the middle of the room with a Trelawny address written on the side. Austin stared at it.

"Oh, this is for home. I'm sending down a barrel for me family for Christmas."

"Muriel, you don't need Christmas to send a barrel," Uncle Dudley joked with her.

"Every little bit of money she earn she send it home."

"How you ever going to move from here, Muriel, if you don't keep some for yourself?"

★★★

A little paradise soon arrived from Jamaica. Mrs. Morgan's older daughter was a welcome distraction and brightened up Austin's miserable days in those early months in London. He would kiss dear Eve goodbye and then sneak into Mrs. Morgan's flat to get some morning juice from Harriet Morgan.

Harriet was a big-boned girl with wide hips and pouting lips. She blocked Austin on the stairs one day, opening her dressing gown and showing him her fullness. Without saying one word to him she dragged him down the staircase and pushed him up against the coal shed. Their bodies were jammed together against the cold concrete, but their first encounter was not the least bit enjoyable for Austin.

"Let's go inside into the warm," he encouraged her.

"Okay, come on then."

She pulled and tugged at his clothing, their bodies pressing against the cold enamel sink. Like rabbits and other such animals, they were not peculiar about where they united—as long as it wasn't outside. Sometimes, he propped her up on a kitchen table that could hardly carry their weight. Harriet was loud and he often had to cover her mouth to stop her mighty groans and moans.

"Shh—the whole house will hear us. Tek time, nuh...?!" Austin whispered. But as much as he begged her, and the more she enjoyed him, the louder she groaned. They graduated from the kitchen to the back of the flat in the bedroom. Austin even pushed her head inside the wardrobe to muffle her sounds, but with little success.

His time with Harriet cheered up the days, but they were short-lived. One day he was in the throes of passion when Kiss me neck! He felt a sharp crack across his back. Mrs. Morgan returned unannounced and found them half naked, Harriet's head jammed in amongst her Sunday clothes in the closet and Austin bare-arsed and humped over behind her daughter.

"Get off me daughter, you dutty dawg," she yelled at him, whacking him across the back with her umbrella. Austin scrambled and fell upstairs with his trousers halfway down his ankles.

Mrs. Morgan never mentioned what she saw to Aunt Pearl, and Harriet was shipped off to Bristol to be with another family member. Austin never saw or heard anything from her again.

Austin went and knocked on her door. "Mrs. Morgan," he said in a sheepish voice that leaked through the chipped paint, "I am sorry for my behavior."

He pressed his ear against the door, waiting to hear some movement behind it. She opened the door and stuck half her face out from behind it. She looked Austin up and down with a snarl and without giving him a chance to open his mouth further, she slammed the door in his face. Bang!

When they passed each other on the stairs, her brown eyes were cold and filled with scorn. Like a menacing mosquito she whispered in his ear, "Is you spoil me girl-child."

"I am sorry, Mrs. Morgan... I take full blame," Austin kept saying in a small voice. But it made no difference. Although he took the blame for his actions, he knew for sure that the way Harriet maneuvered her thighs around him, those were not, by any means, her first encounters with man-sex.

***

It was Austin's job to supervise the amount of paraffin needed in the house. It was also his responsibility to light the heaters in each room every morning and to extinguish them at night.

"Mek sure them shut off everything good. Check the gas stove; we don't want no fire in here," cautioned Aunt Pearl. "Always mek sure you buy enough, because if we run out like Muriel did one time, we will have to wait for a whole week in the cold 'til the paraffin man come again."

Uncle Dudley warned him: "We nearly dead from the cold that time."

The jarring clang of a bell, audible from halfway down the street on Thursday nights, announced the arrival of Andy the Paraffin Man. This was one sure way to know how many other black families had joined the neighborhood, especially anyone Austin's age. It wasn't long before he met the others. They called themselves the "Heater Men." The warmth of an entire household rested on their young shoulders. As the winter months faded and 1958 promised to dull some of the edge of the Kendal tragedy, they became the first young men under twenty-five to start a cricket club in South London.

After a full day of walking the London streets looking for work, instead of a cup of tea, there was work to do at home. He made his way home the best he could, slipping and sliding all the way.

ELEVEN

"It's five months now since you don't leave the house Miss Esther. Come downtown wid me nuh?"

"I just can't go."

"All you have to do is put one foot in front of the other and open de gate and go through it Miss Esther."

"I can't..."

"There is no such thing as can't. You mother ever teach you that word? I'm going to market Friday because Saturday too busy," she said, "Too much batter-batter with ever'baddy. You don't want to come wid me and buy something nice?"

"No, no, Miss Ruby. Whatever you buy is fine with me. It doesn't matter. My heart is too empty to worry about anything."

"We can pour some love back into your heart by shopping. You used to love to shop with your mother."

"Not this time, Miss Ruby. Maybe next time."

"I decided to postpone teacher training for one year Miss Ruby."

"What!!! What you saying to me? Now you really gone crazy fi true."

"I'm not ready, Miss Ruby."

"You never going to be ready, Esther chile, if you don't at least try to be ready."

"I wrote to the Principal already. Look, she wrote back." I produced the letter and read it aloud. 'Take all the time you need. A place will be here for you when you are ready.'

"See?" I nodded my head waiting for some kind of approval from Miss Ruby.

Instead she rolled her eyes, shook her head and shuffled out of the room. But as the months filtered into another year the possibility of attending

Shortwood seemed as far as away as the journey to England. My progress was slower than a turtle's race. There were days when I did not stay in bed the entire day, but those were few and far between. I gradually moved off the verandah and into the yard.

"Now Marse Joe is gone, the work is piling up around the yard. I'm going to do some of the gardening, Miss Ruby."

"But you will spoil up your hands and your reputation," she barked at me. "Who will want to marry you if you work in the ground like some field laborer all day in the hot sun?"

"But I like working in the soil. Just the way Sarge did. It makes me feel closer to him."

"Girl, you worry me to death. You don't seem to have a bit of sense some days."

But as much as she scolded me, staying on my hands and knees tilling the soil soothed me. The softness of the damp earth, the smell of the dirt quenched me. Sarge was flawed, but he was my father. I could feel him right there and it comforted me. I learned to ignore Miss Ruby's comments, but was forever grateful for her presence.

★★★

Darkness fell quicker than the sun rose and every now and again the clouds parted and let the moonlight filter through our house, where the silver streaks shone in bright shards across the wooden floors.

Listening to the music of the crickets and watching the dancing lights of the peenie-wallies, I lit the lamp on the verandah. I settled in Sarge's rocking chair, the chair that Eve once sat in while she waited for me to come home from school. I looked at the crochet hooks and threads, ignoring the vivid colors and patterns that were once my joy. Anything red now looked like Marse Joe's blood, anything dark now looked like dead flesh. My serenity was disturbed by a faint voice beyond the gate.

"Good night, Miss Esther, Good night," came the plaintive call.

"Miss Ruby, there's someone at the gate," I whispered.

"Me ready fi dem," she whispered back at me as she positioned herself behind the window, clutching Sarge's loaded rifle. She shouldered the weapon and cocked it, pointing it directly ahead of her.

REAPER OF SOULS   89

"Who is it?" I said.

I stood up with the oil lamp above my head, straining my eyes into the darkness. So sure the police had come to arrest me for Marse Joe's murder, I jumped back and almost dropped the lamp. My embroidery fell from my lap off the edge of the verandah and down the steps as if to greet my visitors. A familiar feeling returned. It was my heart pounding in my chest.

"Who dat?" Miss Ruby echoed.

"Is me, Miss Esther... Buchanan. Don't shoot."

"Oh, come in—come in." I sighed with relief.

"I have someone for you. Miss Esther," he said, standing to one side. *Wait. He said 'I have* **someone***' for you.*

Behind Mr. Buchanan stood a tall man, his soiled clothes bursting over his large frame, his bushy hair unkempt. I recognized him immediately. I ran down from the porch two steps at a time and down the path toward the figure.

"It's Donovan, Miss Ruby."

"Donovan!!" I let out a scream as I ran to him. I flung my arms around his neck, my body trembling and tears running down my cheeks.

"I found him wandering around the place. He don't remember who he is though, or where him come from, Miss Esther."

"Oh my God, it's you!" I shrieked, "It's you!" I pulled and tugged at his wiry hair and planted kisses all down one side of his cheek. My lips met a salty gritted face that wore a harsh beard. He just stood there, not moving at all.

"Come. Come, take a seat."

I pulled him toward me, squeezing him tightly.

"I can't stop, Miss Esther. I have to get back to the shop. Me wife not too hearty tonight. I just wanted to bring him home for you."

"Thank you, Mr. Buchanan. Thank you so much."

I led Donovan up the steps and placed him in my chair like he was a blind man. He gave me a blank stare.

"Donovan, it's me, your cousin Esther. You don't remember me?"

"I don't remember anything, but your face looks familiar."

He forced a smile behind his unkempt beard.

"I'm Esther," I said again. He sat in my chair deaf and mute. I sat on the edge of my chair, rubbing the palms of my hands on my knees.

"Donovan, I am your cousin, niece to your mother. I have an older brother called Austin and a younger sister called Evelyn."

"Where are they?" he said, looking for them to appear through the walls.

"No, they weren't on the train. They're gone. To England."

I bolted into the house, grabbed a photo from the piano and pushed it under his face. His eyes ran over the photo with a blank gaze.

"Oh, don't worry. Something will jog your memory soon. Don't fret. I'm so glad to have you home."

I ran back into the living room and brought out a photograph of Donovan, Austin and Sarge in their cricket garb.

"Look, Donovan, there you are. There is your father, there's my father and my brother Austin—and you."

He fixed a hollow stare onto the frozen images and pushed the photo back into my hand. His dark brown eyes roamed the room, his head moving slowly like a baby searching for its mother's breast, searching for some familiarity, but nothing jogged his memory. I flung my arms around his neck and kissed him again. In turn, he slowly put his long arms around me. I'd seen indigent men walking around the city before, but never hugged one. Donovan smelled faintly like rotting cabbage.

"My prayers have been answered," I whispered. "Thank you Jesus."

"Here, Mr. Donovan, drink some of this," Miss Ruby said, placing the teacup in his hands.

"Thank you ma'am." He looked up at Miss Ruby as he sipped his steaming tea.

"Can I stay here for a while?"

"Of course you can, my dear. You can stay here as long as you want. After all we have been through, we certainly need a man around the house."

"Shh." Miss Ruby nudged me. "Don't tell him anything," she whispered. "Especially like how him head not so good already."

★★★

Donovan rolled out of bed around noon, and ate everything in sight. Starting with his dessert, his favorite rum and raisin ice cream or a plate of guava, sliced papaya, pineapple, melon or mango, he then ate his leftover dinner. Around midnight, he ate a breakfast of banana porridge or fried plantains. It was easy to know what he ate. He left a trail of broken eggshells on the counter, crusted bowls of porridge and half-opened jars of honey, with the spoon stuck tight in the jar. Sometimes the sugar jar was left open with ants crawling everywhere, or the milk left out to curdle in the midday heat. This annoyed Miss Ruby to no end.

Every time he passed the piano, he would hit one key—*ping* with his index finger or run his hand across the entire keyboard. Sometimes, he'd press the 'C' key and pause for a moment, staring at the photos on top of the piano. He would cock his head to one side, sigh deeply and then rub his shoulder against the walls like he was searching for an answer to come out of them.

Donovan had no external scars. He didn't walk with a limp and had no limbs missing like so many other survivors, but he was as hollow as a seashell. I'd jump out of my sleep awakened by his loud screams and run down the hall to his room.

"It's okay, it's okay," I'd say, rocking him in my arms. "Sshh, I'm right here."

Our eyes followed him from one day to the next, from room to room. With bated breath, we waited for him to speak.

When he sat down to eat, Miss Ruby and I screeched our chairs forward toward him, joining him at the table, folding our arms, peering into his deep dark eyes waiting for him to speak. Our plates were never piled as high as his. We thought good food might bring him back to himself, so we let him eat all the more. Finally, we asked the question.

"Will you tell us what happened on the train, Donovan?"

"I better go back to my black box," Miss Ruby said. "Here we are. This should work on him good," she said, pulling out two hairpins and a clove of garlic.

She boiled three eggs and placed them beside four burning candles on the dining table. She put the garlic in a spoon and held it over the candle flame.

"I like that smell," were the first words he said.

"I like that smell," he said again. "It smells like Christmas."

"What do you remember about what happened on the train,

Donovan?"

"What do you want me to tell you?"

"Everything."

"I need to sleep now. I don't remember much, but I do remember that Chris was with me."

He stretched his long arms above his head, took one look at me and left the room.

★★★

"Who lived here with you before the accident?" Donovan asked out of the blue one morning.

"Our family. Everyone."

"Tell me about them. Tell me, Esther."

"Well there was Sarge, my father, and my mother Miss Ruth. Sarge was the eldest of five. There were rumors that more were scattered throughout the island, especially in May Pen. Their features were so distinct that he told us that he had discovered his sixth sibling, Aunt Martha, by chance when her donkey cart lost a wheel on the way to town. He told her to come live with us in town."

"At first, Aunt Martha didn't want to come. She liked being by the Bay, but eventually Sarge got his way and Aunt Martha uprooted her family from St. Ann's Bay and moved to town to be closer to us. Aunt Martha had twins, Colleen and Cassandra. They were nine years older, and an older boy Charles, who was the eldest of all of us. Charles was twenty-two."

Aunt Daphne, your mother, worked in the emergency section of the hospital. Why, no one knows," I smiled. "She could not stand the sight of blood nor all the groaning and crying, and watching people suffering upset her so much. Every evening she came to us with all the trials and tribulations of her patients and the daily drama that unfolded in the hospital. We got a blow-by-blow account. The only difference was a news announcer would tell us something different every day."

'Lawd, Ruth,' she would say to Mummy, 'I have to leave that place before those people kill me off or drive me to drink.' You came here every evening with them, ate dinner with us and left just in time before it got dark. On Saturdays, a pot big enough to bathe four babies sat on the stove boiling up some kind of soup for all of us. Seventeen mouths to feed. Red peas soup or pepperpot soup with thyme and spinners was your mother's favorite."

I sighed for a moment and took a deep breath.

"Donovan, I'm so glad you are here. I stayed behind because I truly believed that they would come back. Austin was angry with me at first but I didn't care."

"I'm glad you are here to tell me everything."

"Then there was Grace. Cousin Grace was so special, she was everyone's favorite. She was bright and she zipped through her homework and always helped me with mine. She wanted to be a doctor to cure Eve, she told me. Grace lived with us, because her parents had already moved to London. She was going to join them that October with Eve and Austin."

"Well—Austin, my dear brother, just seemed to skid through life with not a care in the world. He played cricket all day long and went missing for hours with Sarge."

"Did I play cricket with them?"

"No, you seemed quite content just reading and playing the piano with Mummy. You're a natural on the piano, Donovan, a real natural. You should play it sometime."

"Why don't you play it?" I led him toward the piano. "Here sit down, just play it."

Donovan placed his fingers gingerly on the keyboard and slowly moving his fingers among the black and ivory keys. He smiled. "Oh yes," he whispered. "This feels good. This feels so good." Three torturous days went by. Donovan got up every day and went straight to the piano, where a smile surfaced on his face and a sweet melody came from the keyboard.

★★★

"Well," I said, as I looked into Donovan's face one day.

I followed him around the house like a lost child and just when I had given up hope that he would tell us anything, he started talking.

"Esther," he said, "so many bad things happen but I don't remember how it all happened. I just know a lot of bad things happened on the train."

He paused. "Chris was with me. I remembered this morning that Chris was with me. He could tell you everything better."

"Chris? Bow-legged Chris? But I thought his grandmother had said he couldn't go."

"Yes, Chris was there. He just turned up at the station," he said, jumping out of his chair.

"Are you sure?"

"Yes, I'm sure he was with me when the train crashed. Do you know what happened to him? Did he come back?"

"I'll have to ask Mr. Buchanan if he has seen him," I said. But I can't leave the house.

"Why not?"

"I just can't go past the gate."

"I don't remember where he lives."

"When he comes on Thursday, I'll ask Mr. Buchanan to send for him."

★★★

Friday dragged its way through and Chris hobbled into the room on crutches. I walked swiftly toward him, kissing him on the cheek.

"I'm so glad you came, Chris. Thank you for coming. I can't leave the house, you know.

I'm sorry, but you do understand why I can't leave the house?"

"No, but Donovan told me to come. Glad to know you're alright, man." He slapped Donovan on the back. "I've been so depressed that I've just stayed in bed most days. I don't know if I will ever get through this."

"Yes, everyone is having a hard time with it."

"Well, where do you want me to begin?" He smiled at us, showing his crooked teeth.

"At the beginning from the time you got on the train. Tell us everything." Miss Ruby and I said in unison.

Chris took a deep breath.

"Well, Sarge and Uncle Cork tried to find a decent place for all of us to sit together." Miss Ruby and I quickly pulled up a chair toward him.

"Yes," I said, bobbing my head.

"It was impossible at first to find somewhere to sit. The train was so full.

We all nudged and pushed our way through the packed railcar, Sarge leading the way, constantly looking behind him to see that we were all together. He had used his connections at the gate, you know, the way he usually does, to get reserved seats." Chris nodded his head as he spoke.

"When we got to our coach, it was already half full and the reserved sign was crumpled on the ground. We settled ourselves the best we could. Two to a seat squeezing up beside each other. We had the heavy baskets on our laps."

"Where all these riff-raffs come from?" I whispered to Donovan.

"Maybe they decided a church outing is what they needed," Grace said. "Your cousin always had a kind word for everyone."

"It looks like every known criminal is on this train," Sarge said, leaning over to us.

"We must stay close together," he warned us.

"This coach is full. You can't come in here."

Sarge jumped to his feet, as more unwanted ragamuffins pushed their way through the door.

"Well, you can imagine the cussing that followed – 'Go wey! Yuh t'ink you nice? Later fe yuh brethren,' they yelled back at him, forcing their way through the doorway. 'You b-c.' Excuse me language, yu hear, Esther?"

Donovan raised his hands in the air, sighed deeply and began walking away.

"Where are you going?" I asked Donovan.

"I can't listen," he said.

"Don't stop, Chris. I need to know everything, no matter how hard it is to listen. I need to know."

My stomach churned as I adjusted myself in my chair.

"All kinds of roughnecks planted themselves in most of the coaches, like flies on cowshit. They set up their little rum stations, gambling with cards, slamming down dominoes so hard the girls jumped every time one hit the table, and cursing at the top of their lungs." Chris stared straight ahead of him.

"I recognize some of those faces," Sarge told us. "We have some hardened and wanted criminals amongst us; they must have skipped bail…"

"Let me see your ticket, young man," Sarge said to one of them.

"Don't worry 'bout my ticket—you a conducta?!" the young bwoy growled back at Sarge.

"You are off duty," Ruth gently reminded Sarge.

"Don't get involved Sarge. Everything will be all right," she said.

"We're all in God's hands."

Donovan returned, leaning against the wall, one foot inside the door. We ignored him, hoping he would come all the way in.

"Well, the whistle blew and the old train creaked and rocked on the iron wheels and left the station."

Chris swayed his body from side to side.

"I think there were about twelve coaches."

"You know what I remember? I remember colors."

Donovan piped up from the doorway, moving back and forward like a rocking horse.

"I remember colors. When I looked outside the windows, I could see colors. Bits of red in all the shades of green. The scenery outside was just beautiful, but inside our carriage was vile and spoilt by all the cursing and vulgarity of those ruffians."

He dropped his chin to his chest and let out a big sigh.

"Yes," said Chris. "Those rogues weren't on the train for any good reason; to them it was just a free joy ride."

"Grace started crying."

Donovan eased into the conversation again this time, not looking up.

"I hate to see Grace cry."

Donovan rocked and swayed from one foot to the other, while I sat as stiff a pole at the edge of my seat, hanging on to their every word.

"We tried to ignore them by singing hymns over their raucous laughter, but the louder we sang, the louder they got. I was so embarrassed I could barely hold my head up because their language was so foul."

Donovan raised his head and moved toward me, pulling up a chair beside me. He took my trembling hand in his and I rested my head against his shoulder.

"The train rattled into Spanish Town then on to Hartland. We counted every stop. Do you remember doing that, Donovan?"

Chris looked over into Donovan's blank face. Donovan shook his head.

"It was the farthest point we had ever traveled, wasn't it Donovan?" Chris looked at Donovan again for confirmation.

"Yeah," Donovan replied, nodding.

"At Old Harbour, the train eased into the station and fisherwomen pushed their goods through the window at us. "Peppa shrim's...! peanut and cashew!" he mimicked at a high pitch. "We traveled across May Pen Bridge, above the Rio Minho, and then the train crawled up through the hills of Porus and Williamsfield along to Greenvale and downwards to Oxford and then on to Balaclava."

Chris flattened out his hands and made a roller coaster in the air.

"I must have dozed off and missed Maggoty and Ipswich."

"See your tea 'ere, Mr. Donovan and Mr. Chris."

Miss Ruby appeared with a tray of hot cocoa tea and a plate with large slices of bun and cheese.

"Thank you," Chris said, enveloping the cup with his large hands before continuing.

"I think it was about midday when we arrived in MoBay. We all jumped off the train so quick. Bwoy, the fresh sea breeze felt so good on my face."

Chris held his head up toward the light as a slow smile spread across his face.

"I must admit I forgot all about the confusion, the noise and vulgarity from Kingston. It was exciting to take part in all kinds of activities."

For the first time, the enchanting smile I used to see on my cousin's face returned.

"The little kids scrambled to the beach, screaming and running. They skipped rope, they ran the three-legged race; they even did the egg and spoon race. Later, Father Eberle preached and I felt so good to your mother sing 'Ave Maria'.

"'Sing it, Sister Ruth, sing.' They were urging her, like your soft flowers against the breeze." Chris paused and sipped on his tea.

"Sister Ruth found a shady spot on the beach for us. She and your aunts spread out the tablecloths and we gobbled down every basket of food that had been packed."

Chris closed his eyes, threw back his head and licked his lips as he spoke.

"The days of food preparation disappeared just like that."

He snapped his fingers.

"Your mum didn't keep those high-heel shoes of hers on for long. I remember watching her and Sarge holding hands, strolling barefoot on the beach like two teenage lovers, while the girls bickered back and forth at each other."

He rolled his eyes up in his head and grinned.

"Your cousins Grace, Colleen and Christine sunbathed and Charles, Simon, Donovan and I went off to play cricket with our friends until the sizzling midday sun scorched our bare backs and heads until we were parched and exhausted. I cooled myself down in the soothing seawater and dragged my feet through the seaweed until it felt like I had wet rags between my toes. Donovan and I swam a little too before we joined the others."

Chris paused, letting out a big sigh and opening his eyes, looking at me for encouragement or approval. A big smile engulfed his lean face.

"Go on, Chris."

"I can't listen anymore," Donovan said.

I slumped forward in the chair, my stomach in knots, as he walked toward the door. Then he spun around.

"I saw the funniest thing," he said.

"What did you see?" I said, turning toward him.

"An old Austin Morris with no driver in it, spinning round and around. How they managed to do that I don't know, and no one could tell us, but it was really clever. Do you remember that, Chris?"

"Yes, yes…"

Chris looked up at him and smiled.

"Come sit back down, Donovan."

Chris patted the chair beside him.

"A car with no driver in it. Now there's something you don't see every-day. We had so much fun, it was one of the happiest days of my life."

Chris paused and sipped his tea, both hands hugging the mug.

"Miss Ruby, this is delicious," Chris said, looking down into his cup.

"I mek it just how you both like it." she smiled, pushing her chest out.

"Wid just a sprinkle of grated nutmeg on top," she continued, folding her thick arms in front of her.

"Anyway," Chris continued, "all good things had to come to an end." He sighed.

"Our departure time was around six and Sarge rallied the troops, ushering us back onto the train. Esther, the return journey was living hell."

Donovan covered his eyes with his hands.

"The crashers out of control. The strength of the rum was working its toll on them. They staggered from side to side through the passageway and they were talking slow like rumheads." Chris shook his head.

"I'm going to press charges as soon as we get back to town!" Sarge said.

"Sarge said he called for help at the Montego Bay police station, but was told that there was not enough manpower to assist us with such an unruly mob, but there would be enough police waiting for us by the time our train returned to Kingston. Police were going to be ready at the Clarendon Park, May Pen and Old Harbour stations just in case any of them bad boys tried to jump off the train before we arrived in Kingston, he told us."

Chris shook his head and continued staring dead ahead.

"Your mother asked Donovan to get her some water, so Donovan and I pushed our way through the crammed carriages. We jumped from coach to coach, squeezing our way through the dazed passengers. Drunk from their own tiredness, tired from the constant disruptions, a lot of the passengers were slumped over and sleeping. The nuns huddled together in constant prayer, their rosaries clenched tightly in their fists. One bwoy wouldn't stop switching the lights on and off."

"'Somebody said, 'Stop that, nuh?!' The bwoy jus' kiss 'im teeth."

"For some reason, the train picked up speed. Every carriage seemed to be busting out with passengers. The hooligans forced their way all 'bout the train, picking pockets and groping some of the women. Their hands went everywhere, even forcing their rum breath on people. The nuns weren't treated with any respect or dignity from what I hear. Father Eberle walked from coach to coach, saying 'The Lord is with thee. Everything is going to be alright.' He said it over and over again, but it wasn't alright; everything was getting worse. Outside was pitch black and I couldn't tell where the hell we were. I pushed my way past a toilet and I heard an awful scream like a woman was being raped. Three ruffians were blocking the door—they were big with broad shoulders—blocking the toilet door so nobody could get in.

"'Move from here, church bwoy,' one said, just like that. 'Move, ah say!' He pushed me aside. 'Move from ya before I bus' up you mout'.'

Chris' body was shaking, but he kept staring in front of us, never looking at me.

"I felt like a coward, Esther, but what could I do?"

He shrugged his shoulders with a helpless look on his face. "All the odds were against us, Esther."

Donovan's eyes stayed tightly closed. His body was a metronome, rocking back and forth.

"I tried to make my way back to our coach, but the train skidded down the slippery hills like a roller coaster. The grating sound of the iron wheels against the track echoed through the gullies."

Chris placed his hand over his ears. "When I try to sleep I can still hear the loud grinding sound, the wheels screeching against the tracks."

His hand stayed over his ears and his head. His body trembled. I sprang out of my chair, rubbed my hands down the side of my thighs and put my arms around his shoulders.

"Hush. Stop a little, Chris. Stop."

"I'm okay, Esther," he said, his chest heaving.

"The train jolted to one side and then there was a big bang. My body jerked forward. Next thing I knew, I felt something fling me into the air."

Donovan stopped again and moved a hand to the back of his head. Miss Ruby reached out to him, wrapped her arms around him.

"It's alright boy," she said.

"I'm alright Miss Ruby—seriously," he sighed.

"When I came back to myself, everything was black-black. I couldn't hear anything, really. I thought I was dead, but through the haze I could see some light. 'I'm definitely in hell' I was thinking. I don't know how long I was lying in the gully," Chris continued.

"My back felt like it was broken in two. And I couldn't feel my legs. I couldn't move anything below my waist. The longer I lay there, The more I knew that I wasn't dead and I wasn't in hell. God saved me."

"I heard a groan beside me. I said, 'Donovan, are you there?' I kept thinking he couldn't be far from me. So I stretched my arm out beside me and felt a body. 'Donovan, is that you?' I moved my arms up to my face and everything was wet; my fingers were covered in blood! I turned my head to the man next to me, but nothing came from his mouth but blood—his black empty eyes just looking right at me, blood dripping from his neck, his ears and the corners of his eyes. I pulled away my hand quick-quick. I started to pray to myself, but I was all mixed up:

The Lord is my Shepherd, I shall not want, I fear no evil, thy rod and thy staff they comfort me...

I wasn't conscious the whole time; I was going in and out. I heard shouts, heavy groans, and both men and women screaming. They couldn't hear my little crying because of the bulldozers. I could hear 'Over here, over here!' and see flashlights all around out of the darkness. I tried to scream out, but only a whisper would come. 'Over here!' I kept hearing—I think I was shouting that too…"

"I lay there, wet from the rain and cold from the night dew. The air was so thick I couldn't see further than a few inches. I even tried to shout but it made everything hurt. I'm not sure how long I was there, but eventually a stray dog found me. A dog! He started to lick my face, then the cuts, and it was his bark that they heard when they came for me. He barked and barked like a howling wolf until somebody finally came."

Chris gave another deep, heavy sigh. I adjusted myself on the chair, my body rigid.

"*Now all I had to do was find Donovan,* I thought, but I was delirious when a Red Cross volunteer found me. 'Over this side!' a young man was screaming. Then I heard, 'Here—this one is still alive!' The St. John's Ambulance volunteer asked me my name and if I could feel anything, you know? I couldn't answer; I had to just shake my head. My thinking was all mixed up in my head. *Where was everyone? Where was Donovan, Sister Ruth, Grace, Sarge, everybody?*

Then one—two—three! They lifted my body and just swung me up onto a stretcher. Believe me, my body hurt even more. My right foot was bleeding under my knee. On my back, all I could see was metal rubble, tangled limbs, bloodied clothing, droves of people searching through the wreckage. 'Can I look for my friend?' I asked the Red Cross worker."

'You need medical assistance—keep still, someone will find your friend, don't worry; everything will be alright,' he said.

The large cranes from the bauxite company swooped down and lifted the burning pieces of the mash-up train, piece by piece. The Red Cross and St. John's Ambulance volunteers used the really big flashlights to help them find the injured and the living. All I could see personally was confusion, smoke and chaos. Two of the carriages were split wide open and they used the wood for a fire that could light up the darkness.

I could see volunteers pulling away rubble with their bare hands, searching for anyone; anywhere they heard a murmur or a lost voice. There were bodies everywhere. 'Look if you see mi foot…!' I heard somebody saying. The volunteers kept saying 'Another one over here!' I saw two of those men taking off a watch from one of the dead bodies—stealing from the dead."

My body shuddered and goose bumps rose around my neck and up to my cheeks as Chris talked.

"You're sure that is what you saw, Chris?"

"For sure. I couldn't believe it at first, but yes. I did see it. I saw robbers heartlessly fingering pockets and purses. Can you imagine? Injured people, dying and dead. They were rummaging through everything, robbing from the victims, ripping off rings from their broken fingers. While they were lying helpless; no mercy for any of these poor people, no respect for the dead or barely living. 'Stop thief!' I tried to shout, but my voice was too weak.

'My friend is in there somewhere; his family is in there somewhere. Save them, save them.' I kept saying over and over again, 'Find my friend.' 'Please find my friend. He can't be too far from here,' I begged.

'Hush, son. We'll find them for you.'

That's all I remembered before I blacked out."

"Where did they take you, Chris? asked Donovan, "because Austin, Marse Joe and Miss Ruby's cousin all came searching for me with no luck. They looked everywhere, but not one item, not a basket, nothing that looked like any of us was found. It was as if the family had never been on the train."

"I woke up a few days after," Chris continued, his body shaking violently again, "in a make-shift bed on the floor of the hospital."

"They took you to the hospital in Spauldings?"

"Yes."

"But Austin went there. He didn't find you."

"They moved us around as the more seriously injured people came in. Every nearby school or church was turned into a place of refuge or hospital. My injuries were not so severe, so they bandaged my arm and leg and the doctors told me I should be sent back to Kingston. They needed my bed for others who were more badly hurt, like those who needed urgent surgery, amputation or blood transfusion. They gave me a Red Cross blanket and put me on a relief train back to Kingston. I thought I should try to find Donovan, but it was impossible through the masses of people." Chris continued to shake.

"I searched the town for a familiar face too." Donovan edged his way back into the conversation. "I was looking for somebody or something, but nothing looked familiar to me. So many people were searching for anybody they recognized, just like me. I just drifted through the streets and slept on the sidewalk and ate whatever I could. I begged a little food here and there. Then one day I'm drifting through town and this man comes up to me.

'Donovan Scott,' I hear him say, but I don't look up.

'Donovan Scott,' I hear him say again. He came up to me and hugged me. He said, 'Oh me Jesus!! Donovan, you don't know who you are, son?'

"Who I am?" I said to him. "Who are you?"

'I'm Mr. Buchanan from the post office, son, and you are Sergeant Scott's nephew. I hear say dem never find any of you so me glad fi see you fi true. You alive. I saw Austin and Marse Joe looking for you,' he said.

'Sorry to hear about your family, son,' Mr. Buchanan said.

"My family?" I said.

'You are Donovan Scott, nephew to Sergeant Neville Scott, Mr. Scott's wife Sister Ruth teaches my children piano. Son, let me take you home.'

Donovan let out a big sigh. He did not speak again for an entire week.

"Well, I suppose I should be going home now." Chris rose and brushed off his trousers.

"Thank you for coming and telling us everything, Chris. Don't make yourself a stranger. Come back whenever you can. Give my love to your grandma. Come and have dinner with us soon, hear?"

"I would like to do that. I would like it very much, Esther."

He placed both hands around me and kissed my cheek, his body still shaking.

"I find it so hard to do anything. I can't sleep at nights. I can't concentrate on anything for any length of time. What kind of life will I have now, Miss Esther? I can't even walk good—look at my leg." He thrust his leg far out to the side of his body.

"I know its hard for you, Chris, but you've got to be strong."

"I hope Donovan can get his memory back soon. I miss my friend bad."

"Any time you want to come here Chris, just come."

"Thanks Esther. Thanks a lot."

Chris hobbled down the path, dragging his left leg behind him. I dragged my body to bed, exhausted from all Chris had told me. I curled up in bed and cried the entire night.

"I'm so sorry I wished you dead, Sarge, I'm so sorry." I cried myself to sleep.

Two weeks later, they found Chris' body floating in Kingston Harbour.

TWELVE

"Be careful of what you ask for, because you may just get it," Mummy often whispered in my ear. I prayed for someone to return from the train wreck at Kendal, but I didn't prepare myself for when that person came or how he might fit into my cocoon.

As soon as the sky turned from powder blue to purple, Miss Ruby and I had shaped a comfortable routine for ourselves. Early to bed and early to rise. Now Donovan, our lone survivor, was back in the house. He had no routine and didn't look like he wanted to fit into ours.

He wandered around the house staring into the corners of the ceiling, staring at the walls as if it was the first time he was inside. He picked up photos, gazed at the images behind the glass, then placed them back in position. He would walk backwards with his eyes still set steadily on them. Then he'd pace the floor in deep thought with his head hung low, or he'd run through the house from room to room like a child playing hide and seek with an imaginary playmate.

"I can see you," he shouted from behind the furniture.

Donovan was now almost 20 years old. He was not an athlete like Austin, but as a child he'd spent ages under the mango tree sketching objects and reciting Shakespeare. Now that he was back, he showed very little interest in anything; like me, he did not want to return to his schooling. I could not encourage him as I had set no example. But two things sparked his interest: the piano and the rum bars downtown. Every single one of them lured him like a seductive lover, and women swarmed him like bees to honey. He had the same striking looks as Sarge and Austin. It was clear as day that the men in our family were related. Their skin tones were an exact match—a cinnamon red-brown. Donovan's complexion was a shade darker perhaps. He had a square, broad face, bushy eyebrows and deep-set dark brown eyes. Even after resurfacing, he never shaved or combed his hair. His head was just one big bush, but he was still an attractive man who women found irresistible.

His temporary memory loss gave my cousin an added but innocent sex appeal. There were hundreds of survivors from the Kendal crash, but my cousin Donovan became the most popular in our community. He had no scars to show, no stories of ghosts to tell, no money to spend on the women that fluttered around him, but they still hankered after him anyway.

"Tell me about Kendal, Donovan," they whispered in his ear. But the word 'Kendal' never fell from his lips.

Night after night, like a mother hen, I paced up and down in my nightdress, the balls of my bare feet slapping the floor.

"Where is that boy? Why can't he come home at a decent hour?"

"What is the point of scolding him? It makes no difference," Miss Ruby said. "He's going to do what he wants to do anyway."

"But until he comes in, I just can't sleep."

When I finally went to bed, I'd jump out of my sleep at the shrill sound of him singing at the top of his lungs.

"Onward Christian soldiers, marching on to war... with the cross of Jesus..."
Or his fingers pounding away at the piano. Once he was home, he would stumble through the hallway and into the kitchen to cook a full meal for himself. Two or three courses. Donovan never made a snack. Instead, he labored in the kitchen cooking his favorite dishes. Anything from curry mutton, rice and peas, oxtail with butter beans and carrots, to stewed beef and vegetables. He boiled cornmeal dumplings as big as oranges, served large slices of yam and dasheen as big as a rock stone. He sometimes made a pot of gungo peas soup with spinners and thyme, large enough to feed an army.

I combed my mind to think of a time when he would have learned these culinary skills, but for the life of me I could not think of when I'd ever seen him—or any of our men folk, for that matter—in the kitchen.

"You are using up all my provisions," Miss Ruby bellowed at him, but her fussing made no difference.

"I don't want to sound like I'm complaining," I said. "After all, I did ask God for someone to be saved from the train crash."

"God certainly answered your prayers. Esther," Miss Ruby shook her head and wiped her hands on the end of her apron.

"Him send your cousin Donovan. Now you just have to mek do wid him. Don't fret yuself 'bout what him doing, Miss Esther—Mek him stay same way."

★★★

"Esther! Where are you?" Donovan shouted through the house like a child.

"Yes, my darling, I'm right here," I replied.

"Come play the piano with me now."

"I can't."

"Come now," he commanded me like an army officer.

"Esther, come play the piano with me…!" he yelled.

"Pleeease…" he begged in his best five year-old's voice.

"Okay, okay, I'm coming."

The first time I ran my fingers across the keyboard, my stomach churned and tears welled up in my eyes. I had not played the piano since they all left that September morning. My aching for my mother hadn't changed. I sat next to Donovan, staring at the keys as if they were my enemy, my fists tightly clenched and my body rigid. I flattened my fingers onto the keys and Donovan put his broad hands over mine.

"Just touch them, Esther. Start with C."

He took my index finger and placed it on the key.

I touched the key gently. "See, you can do it," he said with a big grin. He caressed the keyboard as if it was a woman's body and the most melodious sounds emerged. Sometimes he'd play American jazz, sometimes mento, some calypso sounds, but mostly classical. Beethoven, Handel and Bach. Beyond my mother's training, he was a natural player and wallowed in the attention that playing the piano stirred in everyone that heard him. With Donovan's gentle persuasion, I eased into a regular routine.

"It's great having Donovan home," I wrote to Eve one morning. *"He breathes life into me every day, Whew!! Sometimes more life than I or Miss Ruby can manage. We never know from one day to the next what to expect of him. That's a good thing, right? I'm happy to have him home here with me."* I wrote every single detail to Austin and Eve in England.

Donovan's nightmares tormented him. He would scream out into the stiff night air, and I would run to him. He consumed too many bottles of white rum, but when his fingers touched the keyboard, all the chaos in his mind disappeared and the resulting melodies soothed my aching heart.

"I think we should continue the school," he said one day out of the blue. "What do you think, Esther?"

"I don't know if I'm ready. That's plenty responsibility."

"None of us will ever be ready if we don't get started," he said.

"I need more time."

"How much time do you think you need?"

"I don't know."

"Can I start?"

"I don't mind if you start but don't ask me to do anything until I'm ready. Promise me that."

"Esther," he said, placing his hand on my shoulders, "our pain may never go away completely but we have to go on. Sarge, your mother and mine would want us to be happy. They had a happy life. A terrible thing happened to all of us, but we are not alone. It was God's will to take them from us, and we can't change that."

★★★

As I adjusted to my new life with Donovan, I began to feel a renewed respect for Eve's life in England. Her letters were full of promise and hope and I was in such awe of her ability to transform her life, while I, the 'healthy' child, stayed stuck in mine:

Dear Eve,

I am so sorry that you have written to me twice. I wrote one morning before the bedlam of the day began. Donovan has started the piano lessons again. During the past three weeks we have had 15 new students. They come from as far as May Pen or Bog Walk. Do you remember Sister Charlene the organist at the church? She passed away, so I have now inherited her students from Spanish Town.

Miss Ruby makes the best drinks for the students and often they stay longer than the lesson. Your favorite mango and pawpaw drink is a popular request. I must admit I am selfish with the sour sop juice when she makes it. It is still my favorite. Mrs. Lee says that Donovan has brought life back into the neighborhood. She missed the sound of the piano and now she is back on her verandah listening to him.

*My heart still aches for Mummy but it is surprising what a healer time is. I think
I am getting stronger each day. Donovan, with all his madness and memory loss, has
been my savior. He has helped pull the pain from my heart. But I like to believe that
my work here with the students is keeping Mummy's memory alive. Be good to yourself and know that you are always in my prayers.*

    Love you always,
your loving Sister
    P.S. Tell Austin it is about time he replied to my letters.

★★★

The silent echoes of our house were gone and were now a distant memory. From sun up to sun down, students of all descriptions tramped through
our house asking for music instructions or attending lessons. I often caught
myself humming or singing the same songs Mummy had.

"We want Donovan to teach us, not you, Miss Esther," the students
chanted.

I didn't care one iota. He was a better teacher than me. The same innate
gift he had for playing the piano matched his natural ability for charming his
students. Life with Donovan was so precarious. I anticipated anything and
everything at any time.

Not a day passed without him luring someone in to playing the piano.
Mummy's students had been mostly children, but Donovan now encouraged
a handful of grown men to play too, but the majority of students were young
single women. So many of them, traipsing through the house, most of them
not the least bit interested in learning to play the piano at all, but just curious to sit beside my handsome cousin.

Women of all ages, shapes and sizes came. They arrived in groups of
threes and fours, hours before their lessons, fanning themselves, women fluttering their eyelids on over-painted faces. I saw skirts hitched up higher
above the knees than appropriate, and tops tighter above their thin waists,
emphasizing watermelon breasts. The cheap perfumes lingered in the air
long after music classes ended for the day.

"Watch dem, nuh...?" Miss Ruby kissed her teeth in disgust. "Dem
favor poppyshow."

Donovan was oblivious to their advances. After weeks of trying to get his attention, they became discouraged, realizing he didn't have the slightest interest in them. Some of the women paid more attention to their lessons; those who were not serious about learning to play the piano in the first place, simply disappeared.

Donovan found his love interests downtown and disappeared for hours. He was known in every rum bar from Dirty Dick's to as far as Port Royal. Sometimes he'd take the bus to Cross Roads to Sloppy Joe's. Mr. Buchanan or some other faithful always staggered back with him, shoulder to shoulder, arm in arm singing at the top of their lungs. He never gave his students a chance to complain about his lateness. He'd slide into the room and shower them with compliments, even charming their mothers until their sourness simmered.

"Sorry I'm late," he said with a broad smile, darting through the house to immediately start the lesson.

"It's alright, Mr. Donovan," they sang in unison, fluttering their eyelashes, swaying from side to side. Mothers accompanied their daughters and after a while with the supervision of Miss Ruby and me they realized that their daughters were safe, despite the handsome face that greeted them.

Donovan never wrote anything down, never collected any money or kept a timetable, but he knew every student by their first name, how many sisters and brothers they each had, what school they attended, when they started, what grades they were in. There was never much discussion about fees but everyone paid on time. Miss Ruby made sure of that.

Miss Ruby eventually took down her sign from the front gate. The original,

PIANO LESSONS HERE

was back. I became the banker and organized the class schedules. There were rarely any cancellations.

"Pay this into our post office savings account," I'd say to Miss Ruby as I sneaked a bundle of money into her hand. "Just in case."

THIRTEEN

It was a chilly, dark morning. Even the sun had overslept. A gentle breeze swept across my face and I squinted to adjust to the morning light. The entire house was quiet. I looked at the clock, and its hands told me that half the day had gone.

"Oh my God!!" I yelped.

I jumped out of bed half dressed, pulling my robe around my shoulders. I ran down the hallway. There was no smell of fried plantains or dumplings coming from the kitchen. No pots and pans clanging, no water running in the sink, and no sound or sign of Miss Ruby either in the kitchen or anywhere in the yard. I peeped around her open bedroom door. There she was, fast asleep and slumped forward in her chair, her chin in her chest and her rifle in hand.

"Miss Ruby...! I shook her shoulders as my heart raced.

Was she dead? I thought. *And why is she still patrolling with a rifle...?"*

She stirred just a little, her large frame shifting in the chair. But she did not wake.

"Thank God," I sighed.

I ran down the hallway to Donovan's room. The door was closed, and without knocking, I pushed the door open. The room was dark and stuffy with a smell of stale carnality.

Donovan never closed either the window shutters nor his door at night, and slept with all the lights on. My cousin lay in deep sleep, wrapped in the arms of a woman, his face covered in a mass of thick black hair. It was the happiest I'd ever seen him. I tiptoed out of his room holding in my surprise until I was back in the safety of my own.

Donovan's new love came to visit him often. Too often. She disrupted his lessons and showed up unannounced. He never seemed to mind at all, but it annoyed me to no end. She said her name was Lucy. She had skin that was soft and ochre like olive oil. She wore a lost look on her face. Her deep-set grey eyes stared at you as if she had seen the world four times over. She never smiled or frowned, but stood looking at me expressionlessly. She was pigeon-chested and had no hips. Her legs seemed to surpass her waist. When she was alone with Donovan, I watched her giggling, singing, and whispering to him.

Her black hair fell loosely below her waist. She wore the same pair of shoes every day, but a different frock style, all in shades of blue. Some were short sleeved, some had collars, some were extremely plain. But no attempt was made to match the striking turquoise shoes on her feet.

From head to toe she was decorated in jewelry. Beads and more than one crucifix hung around her neck; three clip-on earrings hung from her ear lobes, every finger including her thumbs had more than one ring on them. With every move she made, she jingled. She heard me one day mumbling about her strangeness. All she said to me was, "I'm an instrument of my own devices."

When she visited, the strangest feeling came over me. I instantly felt cold no matter how warm the day or evening was, and when she left, her smell, something like camphor and thyme, lingered for hours. It was an odor so odd, I just wanted to throw up.

I did not like Lucy at all. When I looked down at her feet the shoes she wore looked exactly the same as the ones my mother had owned. The same turquoise shoes Aunt Pearl had sent from England. My fixation on the shoes made it difficult for me to be nice to Lucy or to focus on anything she said. I could not take my eyes off her feet. Without any thought or preparation, I blurted it out one day.

"Where did you get those shoes, Lucy?"

"My cousin gave them to me," she said nonchalantly.

"Oh, really?" I asked, unconvinced.

I pursued the line of questioning.

"They are an unusual color, aren't they?" I said.

"Of course they are. I like unusual things."

She brushed the thick hair out of her face. I was positive that her shoes were my mother's. *But how did she get them?* My mind sank to the many horror stories I heard about the Kendal crash. *Many of the dead and injured were robbed at the Kendal site. Was she one of the thieves?* I thought.

How was I going to approach Donovan? This was the first time he was happy since he came home. His face lights up every time she comes here.

"You just got to tell him, Miss Esther," said Miss Ruby.

"Look how he rushes to the kitchen and makes a fresh fruit drink. Cutting up pineapple, orange, melon or sour sop for her. He finishes his lessons early to be with her. His students are in such awe of him they never seem the least bit bothered by Lucy's disruptions."

"It's okay, Mr. Donovan," Esther would say, mimicking them, swaying from side to side. "They sound like a choir when they talk to him."

"I don't want to upset Donovan or have him think that I'm going crazy, but I can't take it any more, her coming here night after night in Mummy's shoes."

"Langalala Lucy is a dam' t'ief," Miss Ruby mumbled under her breath every time Lucy went by.

"Who she t'ink she favor, dress up like a dam Christmas tree, inna har blue frock dem and blue boot. She t'ink me no have no sense?"

Donovan and Lucy were passionate lovers. Their lovemaking could be heard throughout the entire house, sounding like howling wolves. Miss Ruby and I walked through the house with our hands over our ears, shaking our heads. But like everything about Donovan we grew accustomed to it. We were grateful for those sounds of pleasure because when they were finished they fell into a deep sleep and nothing could stir them.

One night, when the howling had stopped, Miss Ruby and I tip-toed behind each other like thieves into his room. We picked up the shoes Lucy had left at the foot of his bed and crept out of the room to examine them in the light.

"Look at de soles—as smooth as a baby's bottom," Miss Ruby said.

"And look, a size 8 and the same brand as your mother's shoes." We examined the box they had first traveled in from England. Everything matched.

"See dere now, everything de exact same." Miss Ruby smiled like she had solved something Agatha Christie wrote.

"...Talk 'bout har cousin give dem to har. She too lie," said Miss Ruby.

"We have to wait."

"Wait for what?"

"We have to find the right time to tell Donovan his girl is a thief. I don't

The Daily Gleaner

LARGEST CIRCULATION   ESTABLISHED 1834   Price: THREEPENCE

KINGSTON, JAMAICA, TUESDAY, SEPTEMBER 3, 1957.   SIXTEEN PAGES

Death ... destruction in the night ... world's worst rail smash ...

171 KILLED IN EXCURSION TRAIN WRECK
DISASTER NEAR KENDAL
700 injured of 1,600 on trip

Death rode the rails

Coaches break from engines, derail, crash

GLEANER CENTRAL BUREAU
MANDEVILLE, Sept. 2.

WHOLESALE death and disaster rode the rails to Kendal last night. By midday today Jamaica's worst railway accident by far—and one of the gravest in world railway history—had reached at least 171—159 bodies removed from the scene to Mandeville mortuary, and three deaths from injuries at Mandeville Public Hospital and nine at Spalding—with an estimated 600 to 700 injured.

[body text continues, largely illegible]

Special meeting of House proposed

Previous big rail wrecks

NEW YORK, Sept. 2 (AP) — THE worst train wreck in United States history—"...that" the "World Almanac", was a Brooklyn accident near Malbone Street in 1918, when 97 were killed and 100 injured.

Heartbreak and relief ...
As survivors came back

Gleaner Staff Reporter

THERE can be involved in the disaster at Kendal brought this Kingston at 3.55 a.m., eighty survivors grouping scenes of passengers brought to the wreck and 690 other survivors with them of the midnight horror.

[body text continues]

National mourning on Sunday ...
Govt. setting up Inquiry Commission

THE Government of Jamaica, in expressing its profound sympathy with the injured and the relatives of the dead has announced, through the Chief Minister the Hon. Norman Manley, that a Commission of Inquiry, with the Chief Justice as Chairman, is being set up forthwith to examine the cause of the tragic railway accident.

[body text continues]

DEATH LIST

[names, largely illegible]

Two engines: one driver?

'They had trouble with a wheel'

Gleaner Central Bureau

MANDEVILLE, Sept. 2.

[body text continues]

Little girl only survivor in coach

Gleaner Central Bureau

MANDEVILLE, Sept. 2.

A MIRACLE in the midst of disaster was witnessed last night when a little girl of barely five years old was rescued alive from, beneath a pile of dead bodies — apparently the sole survivor from the coach in which she was travelling when the Montego Bay — Kingston train wrecked.

[body text continues]

Chief Minister: I send my sincerest condolences

BEFORE leaving Kingston to visit the scene of the accident yesterday morning the Chief Minister, the Hon. Norman Manley, issued the following statement.

[body text continues]

JLP's 'sincerest sympathy'

MR Donald Sangster, M.H.R., Deputy Leader of the Jamaica Labour Party, issued the following statement yesterday:—

[body text continues]

Major Island disasters

[list, largely illegible]

MEMORIAL SERVICE

[body text, illegible]

for maximum stability fit HI-MILER by GOODYEAR

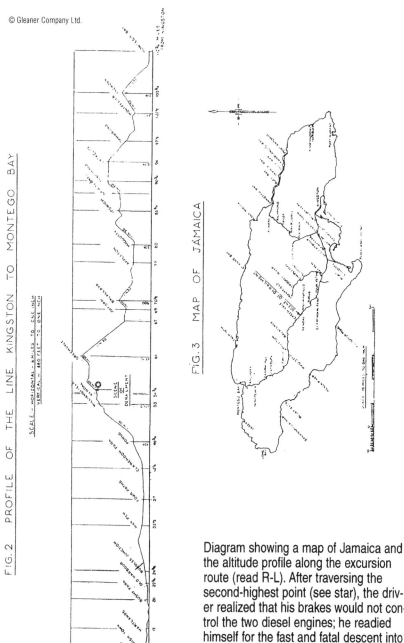

FIG. 2   PROFILE OF THE LINE KINGSTON TO MONTEGO BAY

SCALE — HORIZONTAL — 6 MILES TO ONE INCH
VERTICAL — 880 FEET TO ONE INCH

FIG. 3   MAP OF JÁMAICA

Diagram showing a map of Jamaica and the altitude profile along the excursion route (read R-L). After traversing the second-highest point (see star), the driver realized that his brakes would not control the two diesel engines; he readied himself for the fast and fatal descent into Kendal. He knew something had gone horribly wrong as soon as he made his test application of the brakes. Just before the derailment he exclaimed, "We dead now—we dead now!"

The façade of St. Anne's Church has changed little since it advertised the special Montego Bay excursion (below, left) in the weeks before September 1, 1957.

Right: One of the St. Anne's Church memorials to the Kendal dead.

A Jamaica Railways scene from the first half of the twentieth century, taken at Gregory Park, the second station stop after Kingston.

14053

Left: Rev. Father Charles Eberle, rector of St. Anne's Church at the time of the Kendal Crash. When the train excursion became oversubscribed, he requested a second engine and more passenger cars. Right: The thirteen-shilling adult ticket for the special excursion. Many who turned up for the 5 a.m. departure refused to board the train, concerned by the chaos they witnessed on the Kingston platform.

British engineers and Jamaican laborers bridged rivers, cut mountains and tamed spectacular terrain to establish the Jamaican railway. Established in 1845, it was one of the world's first.

Police, volunteers and onlookers swarm the mangled No. 305 and No. 505 passenger cars as they lay in the cutting. As the train derailed, falling cars that were coupled at the center tore through each other, creating the worst of the casualties.

The author's grandparents, Peter Constantine East and Veronica Teresa East.
Like more than 1500 others, they excitedly made their way to the Kingston Railway
Station to board the 5 a.m. special excursion train to Montego Bay on September 1.
They never returned, and their bodies could not be identified at the crash scene.

Rescuers and volunteers got a clear sense of the carnage at daybreak. Because
so many victims were unidentified, the final death toll, including those who died
from injuries in the ensuing days, would surpass 250.

Left: All that remains of the Kendal Train Station is the platform foundation. Right: The likely location of the Kendal graves, between the station and the crash site, is based on eyewitness accounts, newspaper archives and the author's research.

Left: This picture of Kingston Station shows the waiting room today. Though there is no passenger rail service, it is preserved by the JRC. Right:Kendal remains a small but notable spot on Jamaica's maps, courting obscurity but always remembered for the horror of September 1, 1957.

want to upset him, Miss Ruby, or have him think we're going crazy."

"Miss Esther, me no mind what him think, but him have to know."

For several days we watched them on the verandah holding hands, listening to their lovemaking. Lucy sprawled out on the front terrace like she owned the land. She never made any attempt to acknowledge us, and on every visit she showed up in the same shoes, jingling and clanging with every move she made. Then one night I just blurted it out.

"Donovan, I need to talk to you," I whispered, grabbing him by the arm.

"What's wrong?" he said.

"It's Lucy."

"What's wrong with her? Isn't she beautiful?" his eyes wandered toward her.

"Yes she is, Donovan, but you see the blue shoes she's wearing?" I took a deep breath as my heart raced ahead of me. "They don't belong to her. I am positive they belong to Mummy. I am positive they are the same shoes that Aunt Pearl sent from England."

My words rushed out of my mouth more quickly than I'd planned. My eyes searched his for an answer. I took a step backwards waiting for a response from him.

"Donovan, darling, I wouldn't say this to you if I wasn't sure."

He stood silent, looked at me with no expression on his face and left the room without saying a single word. He stormed out onto the verandah where Lucy was sitting in my rocking chair and in a soft voice said, "Lucy you must leave. And don't come back here."

"Why?" she asked, seeming only mildly concerned.

"You make my cousin uncomfortable with those shoes you're wearing. She thinks they belonged to my aunt. Wherever you got them from they were stolen from Kendal."

The smug smile she wore evaporated from her face. She promptly stood up straight, stepped out of the shoes, peeled off every item of jewelry, the rings, the bangles, the necklaces, brooches, pins, earrings and rings from all parts of her body and placed them beside the shoes. Without saying another word, Lucy left the house in her bare feet.

"Well that's that," said Miss Ruby, clapping her hands together.

"I can't play the piano, now Lucy is gone," Donovan mumbled. He shut the door behind him.

"What we gwine do now?" I had to ask.

"He'll get over her," Miss Ruby assured me. "Just give him some time."

***

Donovan paced the floor, wringing his hands, staring into the corners of the ceiling, running through the house playing hide and seek again. Then suddenly one day, out of the blue, he appeared from behind his bedroom door dressed in a blue suit, blue shirt and navy tie and polished shoes. He was well shaven and clean-cut. Both his beard and his bushy hair were gone.

"Where are you going, Mr. Donovan?" said Miss Ruby, "dress up like puss a look fowl?"

"Just going down to the library."

"You going to the library to do what? You going to read book now?"

"No, I am going to look for Lucy. She said she worked there."

"Mr. Donovan, no badda bring dat t'iefin' gal back inna mi house."

"I just want to see her one more time."

"Why you want to see her again? De girl is no good and she's a damn t'ief," Miss Ruby said.

"I just need to see if she is okay." He rushed passed me and through the gate.

"Wait, Donovan!" I shouted, but he was gone.

I hadn't told Donovan this, but whenever I'd frowned at Lucy, the students would ask me, 'Why you make you face like dat, Miss Esther? Who trouble you?'

"What you mean?" I would ask them. That was when I realized that I, Donovan and Miss Ruby could see her, but they could not.

"Miss Ruby, you see what I see, don't you?"

"Yes me dear. Me see har, me see har good and clear." She said, folding her arms in front of her.

***

"We have no Lucy working here," the curt librarian said.

"Yes, Lucy said she worked here. She is tall with an olive-colored complexion and..."

The librarian interrupted, "Look here, I tell you already young man, we have no Lucy or anyone with that description working here."

She turned on her heel and left Donovan standing aghast. As he moved toward the door, he could see that pinned on the wall were photos under the heading:

PRESUMED DEAD AND MISSING PERSONS FROM THE KENDAL TRAIN CRASH

Donovan walked closer to the wall and looked closer at one photo that seemed to reach out to him. There were those grey eyes, the light complexion, Lucy's long face. He stepped back, his mouth dropped open and he let out a loud scream as he ran out of the library. Sweat poured from his forehead and across his back. He undid his tie and gasped for breath. He headed down to Dirty Dick's.

"Give me a shot of rum, man!" he yelled at the barman.

"Wha'happen to you, Donovan? You look like you seen a ghost."

Donovan knocked back four shots of rum, then four more before he stumbled back home.

"Here he comes, Miss Esther. Here he comes," said Miss Ruby with her arms crossed over her breast.

★★★

It wasn't long before Donovan found another girl, and another girl, and another, until Miss Ruby said, "Lawd Mr. Donovan, you don't have to mek you wey through de whole of Jamaica. Leave de people dem girl pickney alone nuh."

The piano lessons stopped abruptly. No one came to our house for several weeks. Whispers and rumors surfaced through the neighborhood that Donovan "bring grey eye duppy gal" back with all the jewelry from Kendal.

Miss Ruby cleaned and polished the shoes that had caused so much contention. She burned a candle around them for two days and returned them to the shoebox that had traveled from England. Carefully, she removed all the Scott's jewelry and put them away. The rest that Lucy had left behind, Miss Ruby laid out on straw mats and rested a sign next to them.

COME COLLECT YOU TINGS ONLY IF YOU ARE HONNEST.

A string of curious busybodies came from miles inspecting the jewelry, trying on rings, picking at pieces of gold and silver pieces. Heads tilted and bobbed at the array of shiny pieces that came from Kendal, but no one took a single item.

One week faded into two, two into three and the pile of gold and silver bangles, rings, watches, crucifixes and brooches sat out in the sun for two months. Miss Ruby polished every single piece for five days, humming as she cleaned. She wrapped them in an old bandana and put them away in another shoe box next to Mummy's turquoise shoes. None of us ever mentioned them again.

FOURTEEN

Two years passed, with dawn and dusk sometimes drifting into one another. It became difficult to account for time, because time had lost all definition after I lost my parents. Today the afternoon sun drifted behind the clouds, and I listened to a playful breeze tickling the coconut trees. I sipped on my freshly made glass of sour sop juice, enjoying the lull of the day, before the stampede of students muscled their way into it.

I heard a soft voice calling from the gate. I raised my eyes but kept the crochet hook close to my work. Behind the gate stood a young girl not much older than I was. She was of average height, with her hair pulled back off her face, revealing a high forehead and slanting eyes. She wore a faded dress which seemed two sizes smaller than her body, the better to emphasize her large breasts and long legs. She clutched the hand of a child in one hand and in the other, she held a small suitcase. There was no need for her to introduce herself, as the child's face did that. The boy had the same red-brown skin, straight nose and square face as Austin, the same as Sarge, and the same as Donovan.

"Good morning, Miss Esther," she said and smiled timidly as she leaned on the gate.

"Can I come in?"

"Yes, please come in." I stood up, placing my embroidery beside my drink.

"I don't think you remember me," she said walking closer to me. " It's only one time I did meet you. I'm Novelette Norris."

"Yes, Novelette, I remember. Have a seat." I pointed to the chair next to mine.

"Hello, little man," I said, bending down to the boy and patting his head.

"I'm sorry to come to you like this. I know is not right to come without any notice."

"It's okay," I said.

"I never came before because I didn't know how to tell Austin I was pregnant after him reach England. My aunt told me, 'You make your bed, you got to lie on it.'" The words quickly spilled from her mouth.

"Now I get a chance to work in America and I am asking you if you will keep Austin Junior until I return." My mouth dropped wide open.

"Keep him until you return? I don't know one thing about children."

"He's no trouble, Miss Esther, and I would not be gone long."

The skinny, cinnamon-red boy ran toward me, raising his hands for me to pick him up. "Auntie, Auntie," he repeated, waving his hands in the air. I bent down and pulled his little body close to mine. Once I held him in my arms, his baby skin touching mine, all thoughts of letting him go were gone.

"Why didn't you tell us before?"

"I didn't know how to tell Austin or you. He wrote me four letters from England, but with all he was going through, the loss of your family, I just felt I should stay away. Austin loved his father so much, I just couldn't add any more pain or confusion to his life at the time, so I said nothing to him." She spoke ten to the dozen.

Miss Ruby came to the verandah and stopped dead in her tracks, her arms akimbo.

"But stop! Is Austin baby dis?" She picked him up and swung him around as if she had known him all along.

"Hello, beautiful boy, where yuh been all me life?" Miss Ruby gushed, nearly smothering him with her big hug. She kissed him all over the face.

"Well, I must be going then." She got up and pulled down the hem of her dress.

"I'll be back soon. Be a good boy for Mummy and don't give your auntie any trouble."

She wrapped her arms around him and kissed him on both cheeks.

"Thank you, Miss Esther. He will be no trouble, I promise you."

★★★

Novelette left as quickly as she came. She wrote to us once with no return address, just a passport photo of herself signed to Austin Jr.

"From your Mummy. Love you always, my special boy."
N. Norris

I often wondered what I would do if she returned to Jamaica and wanted her son back.

Nothing jolts you into reality more quickly than a small child. It took me all of one day to adjust to Austin Junior. He was a joy. He never slept in his own bed that we made up for him at the bottom of mine. Instead he steadily worked his way through the week alternating between my bed, his Uncle Donovan's bed and Miss Ruby's bed. Sometimes all three beds in one night.

It took me three weeks to write to Austin and tell him that he had a son. The small gift of a child. The pure innocence in his laughter was like a new gentle wind to me. Neither my conscience, Miss Ruby, or Donovan allowed me to hide my nephew. Of course, I wanted to hide Austin Junior from his father because I knew my brother so well. There would surely be a fight between us as to how long I could keep him. *'Put him on the next boat with a family friend and send him to me.'* I could see the words on the airmail letter already.

"Miss Esther, when are you going to write to tell your brother about his son?"

"Tomorrow I will."

"Two days ago you said the same thing, Miss Esther."

Two weeks later, I wrote words of joy to Austin.

★★★

Donovan stopped drinking, just like that. Austin Junior was his new best friend. As soon as day broke they were both in the kitchen having breakfast, and then out into the yard playing cricket.

"Hold the bat like this, little man." Donovan coaxed little Austin. "Back, leg forward, swing. That's right. Forward like that." When the midday sun was too hot to play, he propped Austin Junior in his lap and showed him what he knew best, the piano. With Donovan's large hands smothering his, he got his first piano lessons. "Press this one," *Ping* came the sound from the piano. "Press 'C.'" *Peng* came the other sound.

"This is how your grandma played." A big child himself, Donovan ran through the house playing hide and seek, ran out into the yard behind the banana trees and down to the bottom of the yard where the pit toilet was. Every time they went that far, my heart skipped a beat.

"Play where I can see you both," I yelled to Donovan, but to no avail.

Miss Ruby taught Junior to make shaved ice and coconut drops.

"You'll rot his teeth," I protested, but my complaints fell on deaf ears.

"Lawd, missis, leave me alone nuh, me raise nuff more pickney than you." she replied.

I taught little Austin to read. By the time he was enrolled for school he was so far ahead of the other children that the teacher moved him up from kindergarten to first grade. The demands of a small child pushed my emotions in all directions, and suddenly I found myself wanting to go to the shops, to buy books and clothes for Austin Junior. *I just got to get past the gate. Over two years have passed and I have not stepped past the gate. I've just got to walk up the path and open the gate.* I said to myself. Just one foot in front of the other. I walked down the path and stood there, looking over it to and to the other side.

"Nobody coming, Esther—you can go, you can go," said Miss Ruby.

"Come, me chile, you want us go widout you?"

"No. you can't do that. You can't go without me. Tomorrow I'll go, I promise."

★★★

"Miss Esther and I are going downtown to buy books for Austin. Are you coming, Mr. Donovan?"

"Esther gwine leave the house? You think I can miss that? Of course I'm coming."

"Just don't mek a big t'ing of it, just in case you scare her."

"But it is a big t'ing. Esther don't leave the house since, how long now?"

"No badda remind her how long she stay lock up in here. Me just as guilty fi mek her stay lock up so long."

"Where we going, anyway?"

"Jus' come, Mr. Donovan. Me know you only recognize Kingston streets at night time, so jus' come."

"I can't miss this at all. Esther leaving the house."

★★★

All night I shivered in my bed, and when I could not sleep anymore I got up and got dressed.

I walked down the path and toward the gate. I stood there staring at it.

"I have just have to open it and walk through it. I just have to walk through the gate." I told myself.

I kept saying that until the light of dawn appeared in the skies.

"How long have you been standing here?" Donovan said.

"Oh, I don't know. I couldn't sleep so I thought I would just get dressed and be ready when everyone was ready."

"We don't have to go today, if you aren't ready, Esther."

"Oh, yes we do," said Miss Ruby, stepping up behind us. "Me and Austin Junior ready to go shopping."

"I'll be fine."

I took a deep breath, unlatched the gate and gingerly stepped through it. The planet held up; I didn't fall through.

"Hurray!" Donovan and Miss Ruby cheered, clapping their hands in mock adulation.

"See, it wasn't so bad," Donovan said, stroking my back.

"I did it," I said, turning around to look at the gate behind me.

"Hurray!" mimicked Austin Junior, clapping his hands in the air without actually making contact. "Hurray for Auntie Esther!"

★★★

I must have been a real sight, seeing me with my jaw hanging down to the ground and my eyes popped out of my head as I stood in the middle of Orange Street. I spun around and around, staring at everything. I jumped at the sound of every bus or car that honked their horn as they passed me.

"My God, why is everyone in such a rush? What is all this madness?" I asked, cupping my hands over my ears.

"All of that is the world, me dear. It has to get used to you again. Come on, you'll be fine," Miss Ruby comforted, putting her arm through mine.

"Just think about all the clothes, books, and toys we have to buy for Austin Junior."

"It will be worth it," Donovan edged in, taking Austin's little hand.

"Come on, Auntie…" Austin's little voice rose from below my waist, tugging on my skirt.

"Your Auntie is coming, my darling. I'm coming."

FIFTEEN

The telegram from Esther had come three weeks after Austin's arrival. It stayed sealed on the dining room table for a long time until Austin came home one evening, angry at the world. Everyone in the house all looked at it with scorn and dread that the contents within would bear more bad news. As much as they each tried to put on a brave face, none was strong enough or ready to accept any more devastating news.

"What's wrong, Aunt Pearl?" Austin said as he entered the flat. Pearl looked as if she had awakened in an open grave.

"Another telegram. Here," she said as she pushed it into his hand.

"What does it say?" She turned away from him, wrapping her shawl around her hunched shoulders.

"I couldn't bear to open it until you or Dudley came home."
Austin peeled it open carefully like he was with the London Bomb Squad.

"Let me sit down first." Aunt Pearl sat down, leaned forward, took a deep breath, and held Eve's hand.

"Okay, we're ready," she said.

Austin took a deep breath, and tried to swallow the lump in his throat. It read:

DEAR ALL,
DONOVAN IS HOME WITH ME ALL IN ONE PIECE. HIS MEMORY HAS GONE BUT HE IS FINE. PRAISE THE LORD. LOVE YOU ALL.
ESTHER

"Oh God," Austin sighed with relief, and ran toward Aunt Pearl and Eve. He hugged both of them. Aunt Pearl made the sign of the cross, muttering something about Jesus and Thank You. Then she shuffled down the stairs to the garden. It took Austin over an hour of coaxing her to get her to come back into the house.

Uncle Dudley took the following day off from work to buy some clothes to send home for Donovan. "You think this will fit him?" he said, holding up a pale blue shirt against Austin's chest.

"Sure," Austin said, although he didn't have the heart to tell him that Donovan hated all the other pale blue shirts he had sent home to Jamaica for him.

Austin stayed awake the entire night, trying to figure out which prayer God had heard, why He chose this precious soul to return to the living. *Why Donovan? Why not my mother? Why not Sarge? Why not Grace?* Donovan was alive and all he knew was that there really was a God.

Esther had been adamant about staying in Jamaica, and her waiting had not been in vain. Maybe God sent her a separate message, maybe God had told her to wait. There was some relief for the family after all. Be thankful for small mercies, Mother would have said to them.

Austin pinned the telegram to the wall under the picture of the blue-eyed Jesus, and in the weeks that followed, he looked up at the heavens and chuckled, giving God thanks for bringing his cousin home from Kendal. A man was in the house to help Miss Ruby and Esther until he returned. Esther's letters got to him full of Donovan's struggle to sleep. Austin felt normal when he read those lines. Both boys were struggling with what they had seen at Kendal.

The piano lessons and all the comings and goings in the house were described in great detail. Sometimes it was days before Austin felt comfortable with the news.

He became the official letter reader in the house as if everyone else were illiterate. Before the telegram came, everyone had read their own letters Esther had written to them, but now Aunt Pearl, Uncle Dudley and Eve waited for Austin to return home. As tired as he was from his days in search of work, he could not say no to either his aunt or Eve.

"Another letter has come," they'd say as soon as he stepped into the door.

He knew exactly what his role was. Becoming the official letter-reader kept Austin updated with the family's life back in Jamaica.

Aunt Pearl and Uncle Dudley were accustomed to everyone borrowing everything from them, from sugar to paraffin to umbrellas. So whatever the household needed, Aunt Pearl made sure she had extra.

Enrolling for night school was not a problem, but looking for work in London was frustrating. Austin's daily search for work became a steady rhythm of rejections. The doors would shut in his face before he had a chance to say a word. Everything was fine when he called ahead of time, and the potential employers seemed keen to meet him. But as soon as he arrived and they saw his black face, all he heard was "Sorry, son, the position is already filled."

Austin was finally spared the indignity of searching for work, when Uncle Dudley announced that he had secured a job for him in the accounts department of London Transport. The job was originally to be for Grace, but when the manager heard that Grace had died, and that Austin was having difficulty finding work, he offered it to the youngster.

He settled into his job very quickly, eager to make some quick money and go back to Jamaica. As a rule, he arrived at work one hour early every day and stayed an hour and a half after work until it was time to go to evening classes. Most days, Austin worked through his lunch hour and even went in on Saturdays, grabbing any available overtime. Sleep became a luxury. And since it was hard to sleep anyway, he worked, studied and walked the streets at night, saving every single shilling he earned.

***

Austin was the only black face in the accounts department and often was mistaken for a canteen worker or bus driver.

"Where's your uniform?" he was asked one morning by one of the transport inspectors when he walked through the doors for work.

"I'm not a driver, I'm in administration," he said, disguising irritation. But gradually, his color became of little concern, once he demonstrated how efficient he was at balancing the department's books.

The wet days of January dragged on into smoggy February nights. For three consecutive weeks, the traffic inched along the streets, the fog so thick Austin could barely see his own hand in front of him. Sunshine was a notion in the distant past, and he tried not to think of home because it felt even worse. The life he had left in Jamaica was so far removed from memory, even the beautiful letters from home did not stir him anymore. Other concerns were sounding in his head. *Roll on, spring time, so I can play cricket again.*

***

West Indians in Britain remember the summer of 1958 as a tumultuous time on the streets of London. Anti-black rioters roamed the streets like fox hounds, lynching, looting, and firebombing the homes of black people. Notting Hill made a mark in British history as the home of the first major race riot in London. For four consecutive days and nights the fighting in the streets of Notting Hill was headline news. Everyone in the flats at Mitcham Street watched in horror on the black and white television set, trusting a wire hanger to keep the reception connected to the story.

Esther's letters to Austin came fast and furious, expressing concern. Norman Manley, Jamaica's Chief Minister, came to London to reassure the Jamaican community that all was going to be well. Dinners and meetings were hosted at 10 Downing Street by the tall, distinguished white-haired Prime Minster, Harold Macmillan. But the riots and chaos could not push us out.

Although Austin was only staying for a few years, many of his fellow Jamaicans were here to stay, and no racist, no cold weather, no signs of 'Keep Britain White' would dismiss them so easily. Aunt Pearl feared for his safety because Teddy Boys stalked the streets looking for their next victim.

Austin's trips to late-night haunts were not deterred by any of them. He searched the city by night from the neon lights of Soho to Piccadilly, from Paddington to Brixton. Never sure what exactly he was looking for, he absorbed the new surroundings and noticed the differences from those he had once known at home. As Austin became more accustomed to the London streets, he became fascinated by the size of the buildings and their architecture, and was appalled by the dirty, crowded, confused city in which he found himself late at night, and the number of homeless people begging for bread, a penny, anything. He had seen shacks in shanty towns across Jamaica's landscape when he traveled with Sarge, but didn't expect to see such poverty here. Not in Jolly Old England.

The strangeness of London, the echoes of a lost empire whose language and customs he mimicked and endorsed as his own now irritated him. So entwined were British customs with Jamaica's, that people had almost forgotten that they were African and that they were different from the British, with a completely different past.

In Jamaica they sang the national anthem 'God Save the Queen,' hung portraits of their kings in their homes, and in their courthouses, wore the wiry white wigs against their black skins. They lowered the Union Jack when King George died, and welcomed young Elizabeth when she was barely twenty-one. They lined the streets from Rodney Memorial to Kings House, from Matilda's Corner to The University of the West Indies, waving miniature Union Jacks to welcome her and her sister Princess Margaret when they visited.

Now Austin was in their country. They didn't notice him. His presence was insignificant. They didn't have a clue or care that his father had also fought for their freedom, fought to save their empire. He too had a right to be there. Captain Henry Morgan and many others had plundered and pillaged his island without pretense or apology and now that he was here on their island, they had the nerve to reject him. What bloody cheek.

On his night outings, Austin never looked for trouble at first, but trouble always seemed to look for him. Walking through Soho one night, he heard shouts and screams. He ran toward the commotion.

"Hey, what the bloody 'ell are you doing?" he shouted.

Not waiting for a reply, Austin charged forward like a bull to a red rag to help this poor black boy. Three Teddy Boys were kicking and beating the shit out of him.

"Get the fuck away, you bullies! " he yelled, and pulled out a flick knife.

The blade gave off a glint under the street light. Austin zipped the blade across the face of one of the buggers, not for one moment thinking that he was outnumbered to rahtid. They turned on him like a pack of hounds and he felt a blow to the mid-section. Then another to the groin.

"Oh, shit…" Austin whimpered doubled over in pain and fell to the ground. He had been flailing as he was attacked and was sure he had got in some good licks of his own. One white youngster bawled for his eye.

"Get out, niggers!" Austin heard as he blacked out. "The only good niggers are dead ones…!"

He was out for what seemed like minutes, but the sun was coming up. Austin felt an odd wetness on his face and sensed the smell of urine. One of them had peed on his face.

One other poor bastard, his eyes puffed up like a boxer and blood oozing out of him, lay in the alley until the early hours of the morning when a newspaper boy found them and called the police.

"Are you two alright?" the cop yelled at them. The sound of sirens brought cars screeching up. An ambulance took them swiftly to Hospital.

When Aunt Pearl arrived in the Emergency room, her greeting wasn't as sympathetic as Austin thought it would be.

"Is try you trying to get yourself killed? Why you don't listen to me, Austin? Why you have to walk street so much?" She kissed her teeth.

"I keep telling you to keep off the streets late at night. Me can't tek it if anything happen to you or Eve, me heart not strong enough for any more death."

She waved her finger in his face. Austin's body throbbed for days, and every move he made seemed to stretch the cuts and bruises open, but he got up and went to work anyway. He was soon back on the streets again looking for the Teddys.

When Austin's 'Heater Men' heard about his ordeal, they said "Blood haffi draw." They combed the streets with Austin, carrying their cricket bats, bottles and knives, looking for Teddy Boys.

"It doesn't matter that you can't identify the ones that beat me?" Austin asked, his cricketer's sense of fair play intact.

"Teddy Boys are Teddy Boys, so any one of them will do," yelled his friends. It wasn't until the night he was arrested for a brawl outside a pub that he stopped, took a breath and thought, "What am I doing? This is foolishness."

"What kind of shame and disgrace you want to bring in pon us?" Uncle Dudley asked when he arrived at the police station for the third time.

"Is this the way Sarge and Ruth raise you?"

"But Uncle, I'm sick of these people thinking they can just beat us up like this," Austin shouted. "Sick of them thinking that they can treat us this way."

"This is not the way to make change, son. You become as ignorant as them if you feel that this is all you can do," Uncle Dudley pleaded.

"I did not come to England to get killed or cause you or Aunt Pearl any more pain. I'm sorry."

Austin stayed off the streets for two weeks to appease his guardians. But he was quickly drawn back in. As usual, he couldn't sleep much at all. Sometimes, in the middle of the night, he could hear the rumbling sounds of the bulldozers, the sorrowful cries of passengers pinned between sheets of steel inside his head. The faint cries that surfaced from the debris haunted him night after night after night. His mouth would feel dry and swollen, his stomach churning.

Any time Austin saw a flame, it brought back the smell of that night, the smell of burning wood, bloodied rags, the burning flesh. And the heart-wrenching cries. Although many of the bodies had been dispersed quickly, no facilities were available to control the stench which lingered in Kendal longer than anyone cared to mention.

When Austin closed his eyes, he never had pleasant memories of Jamaica, things like his times with Novelette up against the back of the house. It was sheer torture thinking about the pleasure she gave him. He could no longer smell the lavender behind her ears but he could remember the smell of burnt bodies. Neither could he get a clear picture of being by his mother's side playing the piano, or Sarge giving him cricket lessons. What stayed with him was mass destruction, decaying bodies and death all around.

Austin walked the London streets at night because the memories of Kendal were etched so deep into his mind and heart. He yearned for Sarge to return and make his life normal again. He was so ticked off with God for changing his promising future. He tossed and turned in bed at nights, haunted by his father's voice. "Why didn't you find us, son, and bring us home? Why son, Why?" He could hear Sarge's distinct whisper. "Why did you leave us there amongst those murderers and thieves? Why didn't you find us and bring us home?" Those were the sounds of his Jamaica. That was what he heard replaying in his head. No matter that so much time had passed, that night in September was still as clear as day. *How can I sleep easy when I can't find my family?* he kept thinking.

There was a time when his father made all the decisions in his house, or so he thought. A time when his sisters sat on the verandah longing to go to the places that were forbidden to them. A time when he rode his bicycle as far and as fast as his legs could take him, to run errands for his mother and carry women on his handlebars and whisper sweet nothings in their ears. Those carefree days were gone.

Austin walked the London streets because his bed tormented him. Sleep became his enemy. Every living soul in Jamaica had lost a little part of themselves on September 1. Austin felt as if he had lost all of himself. He didn't have a clue about how to reclaim it.

SIXTEEN

Another winter melted into 1959 and Aunt Pearl's household ticked over like a reliable grandfather clock. She seemed to work constantly in two—sometimes three—shifts at the hospital, cleaning and wiping up the mess of ungrateful patients.

"I don't want no blackies touching me," the patients bitterly complained to the ward sister. But Pearl arrived on the 6 a.m. shift anyway and often stayed way beyond midnight, emptying bedpans, wiping up vomit, blood, and remaking beds. Never did an unkind word pass her lips.

Uncle Dudley escaped behind the wheel of his bus. He didn't have to talk to a soul until he came home. That suited him just fine. Although a skilled cabinet maker by trade, Dudley worked long grueling hours on the London Transport buses. He knew every inch of London from the night echoes of the deserted city streets of St. Paul's to the bustling lights of Piccadilly and the manicured lawns of the Greenwich and Black Heath suburbs. He worked every single bus route from the No. 36 to the No. 171. When the summer weeks arrived and Eve was in better nick, he sometimes took her on his route with him. He turned down promotions, but accepted minor pay increases as if he had won the lottery.

★★★

From Monday to Friday, everyone except Eve left for work. Austin was the last to leave and the last to return. Every Friday at 6:30 on the dot, a stout silver-haired man came to collect the rent. He had a cauliflower nose and walked with a limp. It was said that an injury to his leg had prematurely ended his army career. He never smiled at any of us.

"What's his problem? Is he scared of our dark skins, Uncle Dudley, or is he just rude?"

"No man. Don't tek no offense; is so him stay. The British, like the weather, can be cold and unpredictable," Uncle Dudley chuckled.

"Not like us back home. We spoke to everyone, or at least acknowledged them with a bow or a smile. Tilted our hats at the ladies, but not here, mi dear. Everybody is as cold as ice."

"Do you think Mr. Carr wants more rent now that Eve and I are here?"

"Mek him dare ask us for another penny for this hovel we living in!"

***

On Friday nights, Uncle Dudley brought home fish and chips wrapped in newspaper. That was the one night Aunt Pearl did not cook. She had other business to attend to outside of the kitchen. That business was the partner, or the "box," a form of savings club. Each person in the club put in a certain amount of money each week. At the end of an agreed time, usually six months or longer, he or she received a large sum of money, usually the entire weekly pool.

From Friday to Sunday evening, between fifteen and twenty people with whom Austin quickly got acquainted filed through the house to leave their hard-earned money in the care of Aunt Pearl. She was their trusted banker, and Austin's too. On any given weekend, there could be from 300 to 700 pounds in cash enriching Aunt Pearl's kitchen drawer, and each week without fail, someone would come and collect their bounty. Most of them were saving to purchase a small house—since the banks would not give them loans—or they were saving money for passage so another family member could join them from Jamaica. As for Austin, with every pound he saved, he felt closer to going home.

Aunt Pearl established a reputation as sound as any banking establishment in the city of London. Every member of the savings club was carefully vetted and came highly recommended with two references from respected people in the community. Word got out, and over the years Aunt Pearl's partner club expanded to over a hundred members.

There was only one little hiccup in her system, when Miss Irene's nephew, Everton, ran off with a share of the partner and was never seen again. I had never seen my Aunt Pearl cry since the day I set foot in England. I stood riveted and helpless, watching her small body heaving as she shook with rage. The months of tears she had not cried for Grace came flooding down her face.

"Lawd have mercy, you see me dying trial…?" she sobbed. "Lawd have mercy. That money was to help us move."

My Aunt Pearl bawled the living eye water all night long, and nothing and nobody could console her. She paced the floor and she wrung her hands. I felt just as sorry for Miss Irene, Everton's aunt, as I did for Aunt Pearl.

"Me caan' believe de one Everton, dat likkle dundus bwoy, would do dis to me," Miss Irene sniveled.

"Mek some likkle blond girl from Essex fool 'im up." Aunt Pearl kissed her teeth.

"Pearl, I will mek sure every penny put back in your hand," Miss Irene promised, wringing her hands.

"I shoulda follow me mind, but me mek Satan tek me over."

"Here, Pearl." Uncle Dudley pulled out a wad of money from his pocket.

"This is from my domino club. It's a good hefty sum we collect for you."

"No, no." She pushed the money away from her. "I don't want your money, Dudley."

"But Pearl…" he protested. "We all trying to help you."

She turned away from him, pacing the floor for four days and nights. She held her head low. She did not cook, hardly ate, and did not go to work. She sat looking through the window, as if expecting some message to come to her. The only thing she did with regularity was to go down to the garden, sit on the wall and puff away, burning out a part of her own soul.

"Aren't you going to do something, Uncle Dudley?" Austin said.

"The best thing is to leave her be," Uncle Dudley advised. "Give your aunty time."

So time passed and we waited. There was nothing any of us could say or do. Eight days later, she got up and put on her starched uniform.

"No point crying over split milk," she said, as she threw her cape around her shoulders and plopped a wooly hat on her head. "What's the point of making a big fuss over it? What's done is done. I've got so much to do; got exams coming up." She acted as if the incident with the missing money had

never occurred. During the months that followed, Miss Irene paid back
every penny. Aunt Pearl, in turn, treated her with tenderness.

"When I find that one Everton you see, is me and him. I going give him
a bloody good hiding. You watch and see."

Austin searched the streets night after night looking for Everton to give
him a good working over for hurting my aunt, and stealing everyone's hard
earned cash, including his. But he never found Everton. It was just as well,
since the result might have been a stretch in Brixton Prison—and not for
the thief.

In the hope that he could help her, Austin started taking his chances at
the betting shops. He was never lucky enough to win any substantial
amount of money.

"What do you think you're doing? Gambling is not going to help you.
Here, give me that," Aunt Pearl said. She prized the little money from his
grip. "Until you get some sense, Austin Scott, I'm keeping your money."

"I'm not a child, Aunt Pearl. I can manage my own money," he protested.

"When I can see that you can, you can have your money back." The
subject was closed.

"Well if you're going to take my money, I'm going to take your cigarettes."

"Take my cigarettes!!! You must be losing you mind."

Austin stretched over her to snatch her bag. He took out the packet of cigarettes and crushed it.

She stood without flinching. "You think you're hurting me?!" Aunt Pearl
yelled at him.

"You can't hurt me. I hurt every single day. You can't stop my pain," she
added, pouting like a child. And so the dance with Austin's money and her
cigarettes continued until he was too tired to fight with her anymore.

"You win," he said to her one day. She smiled and snatched the cigarette packet from him and put them back in her bag with a triumphant grin.

***

On Saturday nights, half of the London Transport workers, bus drivers,
conductors and canteen staff ploughed through Aunt Pearl's home and con-

verged in the tiny kitchen. The shuffling and slamming of dominoes could be heard until daybreak as the tiny white tiles hit the kitchen table. Shouts and all kinds of name-calling became familiar occurrences throughout the game. Even Mr. Vincent became addicted and joined in.

Aunt Pearl's entire household attended mass on Sunday, except Austin.

"Why should I go? he huffed at her. "What kind of God would take my whole family from me like that?"

"Hush, son, don't say so. Forgiveness is the key to survival."

Aunt Pearl repeated this to him every Sunday to no avail. "You think by staying at home and serving other gods they can help you?"

She picked up the half empty bottle of wine he had guzzled. "Cheap wine at that," she scoffed, shaking her head.

Austin had secretly gambled all the little money he won at the local betting shop, hoping that he'd have a windfall so he could return to his beloved Jamaica. He would build the memorial that he felt was deserving of his family. Austin's mission to finish his exams and go home grew stronger. God couldn't help him to do that. All he had to do was work hard and save harder and get out of London. His savings, however, amounted to only four pounds and seven shillings.

Austin Scott had received an exceptional education. He had been taught grammar well in school. He had read more than his share of books about history, science, mathematics, and Sarge had taught him the finer arts of cricket: how to beat the batsman as a bowler, how to watch the ball, hold the bat and drive the ball to the boundary, how to field quickly and effectively. From a young age, Sarge told him stories of his service in the War, his travels to Panama to help build the Canal. He never told him Anancy stories, but instead about the great black leaders like Shaka the Great, Nanny of the Maroons and Marcus Garvey. 'Rise up you mighty Race,' he would make Austin repeat, raising his arms and balling up his fist in front of his son. Austin's mother had taught him the scriptures and how to value each day. He knew Jamaica from the maps he had studied, but no one had prepared him for the hurt he would have in his gut for months on end. No one had prepared him for survival.

He declared himself a man who could not cry in order to feel better. He watched Uncle Dudley get up each morning, study the news by reading the newspaper articles over and over again, then put on his dark-blue

London Transport uniform and get back on the bus. Austin was drifting into nothingness. Unlike his uncle, routine began to decay his spirit. Aunt Pearl quarreled with him about his drinking and gambling. He even turned away from Eve, not because he didn't love her, but because she got so sick and needy at times. He feared losing her too. More than that, he hated England, the coldness, the aloofness of the British, the blatant racism for which he was unprepared. The end of his five years could not come quickly enough.

"Why did they place advertisements in the *Gleaner* inviting us here if they didn't want us?" Austin asked Uncle Dudley.

"We are here to build up their country—do the jobs they don't want to do. We are a part of the Commonwealth. Don't you worry about them. We have a right to be here."

***

At weekends, Uncle Dudley and Austin went to every cricket trial possible. They exhausted all the local clubs and then traveled by bus to Lancaster, Leicestershire and even as far as Wales. The thought of living so far from family and being so isolated bothered him, but it did not bother him enough not to go to the club trials. Austin tested both with ball and bat, answered all the questions and passed all the medicals examinations, but still every letter he received from the cricket board began something like this:

Dear Mr. Scott,
After much consideration of your outstanding skills, we regret that we cannot offer you a position with our team at this time. However, we hope you will continue to play and possibly reapply at another time…

The one thing that he woke up for every day in Jamaica had become a sore point in his soul. Austin eventually joined the Surrey County Cricket Club with the help of Uncle Dudley. At first, he was welcomed with curious eyes and indifference, but gradually his team mates welcomed his sharp skills. In his first season, Austin took over 52 wickets at 9 runs a piece. He was an outstanding batsman and a lightening-fast wicket keeper. No matter what position was thrown at him, he could handle it like a pro. He brought all the cricket-playing 'Heater Men' with him and most of the time they thrashed the opposition mercilessly.

Their skills so outclassed their British counterparts, that the sport now became as much their game as it was theirs. The 'Heater Men' did not have the same passion for the game as Austin did, however, and many times a slight shower of rain stopped them from showing up at a match. Austin could play rain or shine and believed that the true test of a good batsman is not how many runs he can score on a good wicket, but how many he can score on a bad one.

As good as Austin was, the likelihood of his playing cricket professionally or otherwise looked slim. The British weather hindered the game most of the time and in his first summer in London, they played only five Sunday afternoons for the entire season, while they watched and waited for the rain to ease. Away games were even more problematic, because Austin hated to take a train. He could not even work up the courage to travel on a train to work. He took the bus everywhere, which took twice as long.

★★★

Austin wasn't sure which came as the bigger shock: the telegram saying Donovan was alive, or the letter announcing that Novelette had showed up out of the blue with his boy. *Me, a father! Not a pot to piss in or a window to throw it out of, but I had managed to become a father.* He smiled with some joy, but at the same time he felt confused, proud with a tinge of sadness. *While my family was being crushed to death, I had planted life inside Novelette.*

His only relief was that I, his sister, wanted to keep his son. Thank God for good sense. What would Austin do with a child in England? He doubted if Aunt Pearl would have minded, although such news guaranteed a tongue lashing from her. It wasn't hard to imagine.

"How you manage to have sex and you not married? What kind of irresponsible behavior is that?" The berating from Aunt Pearl would continue for days and then she'd simmer down and accept what was unchangeable.

I am going home, he kept telling himself, so Sis could keep him until he returned. His son was in good hands with Miss Ruby, Donovan and me. He made Eve swear not to tell Aunt Pearl, and she promised, but Aunt Pearl found out anyway. How, he never knew. Maybe he talked in his sleep, but the verbal harangue that he anticipated came fast and furious as soon as she got wind of the news that she had a grand-nephew.

Disillusionment began to seep between the cracks of his interior. *Suppose I don't pass my exams, and make the grade as an accountant? Suppose I don't ever get to go back home to the land that I love? Home to Esther and Donovan? Home to build my memorial in honor of my family? Suppose I just turn out to be a complete failure?* In the face of what should have been good news, Austin withdrew from everyone. Esther had written to say that St. Anne's church had mounted a marble plaque on the back wall in honor of the lives lost at Kendal, but that was not sufficient and not worthy of what he felt was needed to honor our parents and loved ones.

If I build a memorial for them, their voices would go away, he believed. Sarge would forgive him, and their souls could rest in peace. Austin had chosen the passage of scripture for the tombstone. He had several sketches on paper for the type of headstone, its shape, its color. The Virgin Mary would be placed at the top, and on both sides the names of each family member would be carved with their birth date. The first verse of Ave Maria would be at the top of the headstone. All he needed was to save enough money to pay for such a grand gesture.

None of Austin's family seemed to think it was important and every time he broached the subject, there was silence or indifference.

"If you really want to honor your father's memory," Aunt Pearl said, "finish your studies. Don't worry yourself about some piece of stone."

Her words were painful to his ears, and hit him as hard as any personal insult could have.

★★★

No matter what time Austin arrived home, the light under Mr. Vincent's door suggested he was still up. He tapped gently on the neighbor's door.

"Come in, Austin, my boy."

His presence soothed more than anyone else's did. Mr. Vincent never asked questions unless he thought they would be welcome; he never used criticism; he just listened. He was also good at explaining any mathematical formulas Austin didn't understand. The man was a genius.

"Don't let the cold weather get you down, my son. Get what you came here for." He was always ready with a pat on the back.

"So many people fall by the wayside, disillusioned, some too ashamed to go back home because of pride. Don't be discouraged in this country."

He rubbed his hands together, hunching his shoulders.

"This weather is enough to dampen anyone's dreams and spirits." He turned up the wick of the heater, rubbing his hands together again. "Stay focused son, and move on to the place you want to be. Keep your eyes on your final reward."

Vincent Agabi pulled up his chair in front of me. "Look," he said leaning forward, "you say you want to be an accountant? Then you can be an accountant. You want to play cricket? You can play cricket, semi-professional or professionally. You want to go home and build this memorial for your family? Then all is possible, my boy."

"But none of them upstairs seem to care about the memorial," Austin said, his eyes raised to the ceiling.

"Don't make excuses. When you make excuses, you begin to live a lie. The only person who is limiting you, is you. You want to build this memorial for your family you can build it. If that is what is important to you. Remember you are not building it for Pearl or Dudley, or your sisters. You are building it to get closure. Everything is possible, son. You just have to believe it. Read your Bible more."

He took his enormous dog-eared Bible and opened it, turning it to face Austin.

"Here, read," he said, putting the Bible on Austin's lap. "Read Mark 9:23. Nothing can bring your family back to you, not even prayers. But you owe your parents the honor to be successful, to keep their names alive. Keep their memory alive by living and not by giving up, my son." Mr. Vincent poured some lukewarm tea into his guest's cup.

"How was class this evening?"

Austin shrugged his shoulders while the man rambled on about his own dreams, and in his tired state, he dozed off. Agabi gently nudged him.

"Go on upstairs. Leave your papers with me. I'll look over your homework and give it all back to you tomorrow."

"Good night," Austin said, "thank you," and stumbled up the stairs to his cold wire-spring bed.

What the hell am I doing in this Godforsaken place? he wondered as he undressed. *What is my life about? Why should I complain? I have a decent job com-*

pared to most of my peers and my studies were going well. But he just couldn't shift his feelings from sadness and self-pity.

★★★

The tube was jam-packed. Newspapers hid the many unfriendly faces and umbrellas poked his sides like large needles; screaming school children disturbed his muddled thoughts. Across the crowded train, Austin saw her. More precisely, he saw the smile, a gap-toothed smile and a dimple that lit up her face and his heart. She was chatting away to a woman who stood in total awe of her. Austin missed his stop that day because he could not take his eyes off her.

He took the tube every morning at the same time, his search for her surpassing any apprehension. Each day he looked for that face, searching for that dimpled smile, the gapped teeth, the orange wool overcoat. No luck. He could not travel by bus anymore. Suddenly, his life depended on the trains he despised. And on finding her.

Then one morning, on a day when Austin was more weary of his world than usual, tired of sleeping on the cramped 'Z 'bed, tired of the brainless work he was doing, and tired of haunting the London streets at night, there she was. He wormed his way through the crowded train, unable to resist her, drawn in like a magnet.

"Good morning," he smiled, interrupting her conversation.

She turned around, tilting her head to one side. There was that smile, the smile that welcomed you without words, the smile that captured his heart.

"Where have you been all my life?" he boldly asked.

"But stop…" she snapped. "Do I know you?" she asked, her brown eyes scanning him from head to toe.

"No, not yet."

The woman beside her had an oval face and a her hair pulled back in a tidy bun. Her dark eyes matched her brown wool coat, which was a size bigger than she was. The mousy woman put her hands over her mouth, lowered her head and giggled, as Austin continued to flirt with her cousin, an Amazon beside her.

"I'm Austin Scott." He shot his hand out at her. "But my friends call me Red Bones."

She stared right back at him holding on to the railing above.

"I would shake your hand, but if I let go of the rail I might fall." she said.

"I'll catch you if you fall," he smiled.

His heart pounded inside his body. Then a big smile surfaced on her face. Her gap teeth appeared and he knew that was where he wanted to be. That was the beginning of Inez and Austin; but it was a bittersweet one, because with the rose of her affection came an old thorn: her best friend, Clement 'Blue' Jackson from Kencot.

SEVENTEEN

The first time Eve met Inez Wright, she tried her hardest not to like the woman. It wasn't that Eve had a vicious bone in her body; that's not how her mother—God rest her soul—had raised her. She secretly decided to hate Inez ever since Austin had come home, to wake her up in the middle of the night, more excited than she had ever seen him since they had arrived in London.

"I met this girl," he kept on saying, shaking her out of her sleep.

"You meet girls all the time. You can't expect me to get excited about another one, Austin".

"She's different Eve, I'm telling you, she's different. You'll see." Even Austin's eyes were grinning.

When Esther wrote to them, telling them that Donovan was alive and home with in Jamaica, Austin kept saying, "Praise God." Since that day he had not shown any more excitement or interest in anybody or anything, so Eve knew she had to be someone special. And she was.

Aunt Pearl unlocked her precious china cabinet.

"This is a special occasion," she said as she carefully took out all her best china.

Inez Wright, you're in, Eve mused. That single act told her that Aunt Pearl had accepted Inez, sight unseen.

Inez was officially introduced to the family on Aunt Pearl's birthday. Aunt Pearl had not celebrated her birthday since Kendal.

"To celebrate anything, to be happy, seemed to be disrespecting Grace and our family's memory," she said.

"Just have a small dinner party for the five of us," Austin pleaded.

"Okay, okay," she said.

His aunt was a far better cook than his mother and always cooked more food than was necessary. Austin and Eve soon became accustomed to leftovers that somehow tasted sweeter the following day. In Jamaica, their meals were prepared daily and the thought of having leftovers was unheard of. At home, in Jamaica, we had helpers who cooked, but both Uncle Dudley and Aunt Pearl worked long, ungodly hours, so cooking every day was not an option now that we were in England. Eve knew how to cook, with all the time she had spent hanging around the house with Miss Ruby and the other helpers, but neither Aunt Pearl or Uncle Dudley would hear of it.

"No, no, no! You'll be on your feet too long," was all she heard from them.

Uncle Dudley parked himself at the head of the table. "So who's saying the grace, then?" He looked directly at Eve.

"Okay, I will."

"That's my girl."

Aunt Pearl had outdone herself. She cooked at least eight different dishes: curry chicken, rice and peas, fried fish, roast potatoes, roast beef, carrots, sweet corn, more. She stood in the kitchen for over an hour grating carrots to make carrot juice with condensed milk and nutmeg. Uncle Dudley added a shot of white rum, giving it an extra kick. The Jell-O and the custard cream dishes sat on the window sill, chilling until it was time to serve them.

Inez arrived promptly at 5:00 p.m. She wore a snug purple and black wool dress which stopped just above her knees. Her matching jacket had raglan sleeves delicately trimmed with four covered buttons of the same fabric. She wore a pair of patent stilettos with the highest heels Eve had ever seen. How she stayed balanced without falling over, Eve couldn't tell. But she couldn't deny it—Inez looked outstandingly chic. A little overdressed, she thought. *Where do you find those clothes anyway?* she asked herself.

Inez was probably two inches shy of six feet; a little plump, not fat, just well built, with ample breasts, curvy hips and thighs. Everything about her seemed big in comparison to Eve's frail frame. She had a roundish face, skin the color of caramel with a sprinkle of brown freckles on the bridge of her nose. She had full lips and when she smiled the deepest dimples appeared in her cheeks.

Her hair was comb-pressed flat on her scalp. How did she get short hair to look so good? Eve wondered. A thousand questions raced through Eve's mind as she scrutinized Inez. Every feature on her face was distinctive, which made her stand out spectacularly from other women.

Inez looked directly at you when she spoke, as if she always had a clear thought in her head and never had to think anything through. Not like Eve. She pondered and hesitated about everything and sometimes had to pray really hard before she could make a decision. Inez exuded confidence and oozed sex appeal.

Eve watched Inez through the corner of her eye to see if she was familiar with the intricacies of table etiquette. If she wasn't, she certainly fooled Eve. Although she ate like a horse and had generous helpings of curry chicken, too many slices of roast beef, and Eve lost count of how many roast potatoes she gorged, she ate with decorum. No slapping of her jaws was heard. Eve was amazed. Miss Ruby would have called her 'craven.' Inez never talked with her mouth full, nor did she slurp her drinks or slouch over her plate. But had anyone ever told her it was unladylike to pile her plate so high? She obviously had no class.

Extra cutlery was placed on the table to confuse her, but to Eve's surprise, she knew which utensil to use with each dish. I feel guilty, Eve thought. *Was I a snob or just an insecure fool?*
She could hear my mother's voice faintly whispering. "Don't judge a book by its cover. We are all God's children."

How could Austin be remotely interested in this woman with cropped pressed hair, loud, form-fitting suits, devil-red nail polish and lipstick? Who does she think she is?

"So how long have you been here?" Aunt Pearl broke into the gentle clatter of knives and forks, swallowing a mouthful of food in the moment before she spoke.

"I've been here ten years."

"Are you a Windrush Girl then?" Uncle Dudley asked.

"Yes, I left home on my sixteenth birthday and bought my ticket for 75 pounds," she said, pushing her chest out with a big smile.

"It took a whole lot of begging and pleading for my father to get me papers to travel. I told my father that I was coming to England to be a nurse. I had to get away from my family or I would have turned out to be nothing, stifled and suffocated in the little town of Happy Grove, Portland." She said it the way a tour guide would. "There was absolutely nothing happy about Happy Grove," Inez frowned.

"As hard as life is here, I'm never going back there."

Eve took a big gulp of her drink as she listened, watching Austin's face fill with admiration as Inez spoke.

"I lived with my father and my four brothers. My father believed that I was responsible for all of them, keeping them fed and watered after my mother died. He was a cane cutter and harvested cane for the rum factory."

She stretched over to refill her glass with carrot juice. Inez spoke about her job as a nurse's aide with indifference, but quickly turned the conversation to her dreams. Her posture changed to an upright position and the tone in her voice sang a melody; her eyes sparkled as she spoke.

"I want to be a famous dress designer one day and have my name on the label of elegant dresses and suits." How ridiculous, Eve thought. Nursing is such a good job. After all, you can buy clothes in a shop.

"How nice." Aunt Pearl smiled politely, nodding her head.

"Did you design what you have on now?"

"Yes, I did," she said, chest forward with peacock pride.

"My father," she continued, "would not allow me to come to England alone. So my cousin Madge came with me."

"Where do you both live?" Aunt Pearl asked.

"Madge and I live East of the Thames in Stepney Green. It took me two buses and a train to get here.

We rarely cook when we're home," she said with a big smile on her face, her speech quickening, "so I'm really enjoying your food."

"Thank you dear," Aunt Pearl said. Help yourself to more. There's plenty here... But why don't you cook?"

"We're usually too tired and also we don't have a proper kitchen."

"You have an iron cooker on the landing, too?"

"Yes. How did you know?"

"That is so typical in most of the homes they rent to us. That is why I took this place, although it's on the top floor."

"Cooking is such an ordeal. We have to climb three flights of stairs for water. That's too much work."

"Yes, chile, that is too much work," Uncle Dudley piped in.

"It's so nice to eat some home-cooked food, Aunt Pearl. This is delicious." She pointed to the half-eaten chicken leg on her plate. Eve looked over at Austin, who was tearing into his roast beef, hanging on to her every word.

"So how do you eat?"

"Oh, we have acquainted ourselves with the corner chip shop," she announced proudly. "Madge and I have worked our way through the sparse menu. Fish and chips on Friday, saveloy and chips on Saturday, pie and chips on Monday, even curry and chips sometimes on a Sunday." She covered her mouth and let out a child's giggle.

"The chippy knows us by our first names now," she said and grinned at them. "We have our other meals in the hospital cafeteria."

She turned to Austin. "I'll love you for life, Austin, with an aunt who can cook like this." Eve feigned a smile, while everyone else roared with laughter and approval.

"Inez, let me get you some more carrot juice," Eve piped in.

"Yes, please, I'd love some more," she said, pushing her glass over. Eve stood up with the jug of carrot juice, missed her step and tripped, splashing the juice all over Inez.

"Oh dear," said Aunt Pearl, rushing toward Inez with a napkin and patting her down.

"Watch out, Eve! How come you so clumsy, girl?!" Austin yelled at her.

"It was an accident!" Eve yelled back.

She threw her napkin on the table and huffed off to her room, slamming the door behind her. Austin had raised his voice at her for the first time ever.

Eve's deepest desire, to prevent this woman from having her beloved brother, was unraveling before her eyes. As long as she could remember, Austin had always put her first, and now there was Inez. She felt that not even other family members came between the two of them. In her mind, Austin belonged to her and cared for her. Now he had slipped away into the magic spell of Inez Wright. Eve's thoughts raced around in her head as she cried behind the closed door.

"Eve?" It was a gentle voice from behind the door.

"Yes," she answered, sniffing into a hankie.

"Please come back to the table, my dear. A little carrot juice is not going to spoil my suit. It was a cheap old thing anyway."

"I can't," Eve sobbed. "I feel like an idiot. I'm such a clumsy fool."

"Come on out. You are not clumsy at all. If I hadn't been so greedy, it wouldn't have happened.

"Come Eve, open the door."

Quickly wiping her tears, Eve slowly opened the door and pushed her head around the small gap she had allowed. "Come here." Inez gently pulled her out and hugged her, warm as cocoa. The active mind Eve had cultivated while she was so sick in Jamaica kept working fast:

Austin was as much hers now as he was mine and I just have to adjust to the fact that I have to share Austin with someone else. Surely Austin would not want to marry her and if so, what would happen to me? Where would I go? He couldn't possibly want to marry a woman who didn't want to ever go back to Jamaica and Inez didn't look like the type of woman who you could persuade to change her mind, either.

Eve was trying her hardest to push her away and ignore her, but the irrepressible Inez just bounced right back. Inez had no intention of competing with minor details like a jealous, insecure, weak and ailing sister. She was too busy chasing her dreams to let Eve or anything else, for that matter, interfere. Eve would have to be quickly changed from obstacle to ally, but she was too innocent to understand that yet.

After dinner, Austin and Uncle Dudley withdrew from the table, leaving the women in the kitchen to clear the table and wash the dishes. The red lipstick smudges clearly identified the utensils Inez had used. By the end of the evening, she had won everyone's hearts forever, and in the months that followed, Eve grew to love her sometimes more than she loved herself. Inez became her big sister, her teacher, and her hope that even after losing someone, one could survive and live on and be happy. Inez would become her refuge.

Inez was relentless, and before long there were more conversations between she and Eve than there were between Eve and her precious Austin. On short notice, she invited Eve everywhere. Each time she had to decline, because there was always a hospital appointment that she had to keep. The refusals did not deter Inez at all.

★★★

"Eve, would you like to come with me the next time I go to Petticoat Lane?" she said one Saturday night while she was visiting Austin.

"Yes, yes, I would love to."

"You have to be careful with Eve because of her condition, Inez. She tires so easily."

"Aunt Pearl!!" Eve protested.

"All that up-and-down in the market in the cold may be too much for her."

"We won't stay long," Inez reassured her.

"I can't stay cooped up in the house forever. I have to get out now and again. There's a whole world out there beyond the hospital doors waiting for me."

Eve threw her arms around her aunt's neck and kissed her. "Please, Aunt Pearl, please."

"I have plans for you Eve," Inez promised. "If you like to sew, you could help me with some of the hand work, the hemming, button holes, the beading. For pay, of course."

A big smile rose on Eve's face.

"It would be great to earn my own money."

"You'll be sitting down too. It won't be too strenuous."

"When do you plan to go to Petticoat Lane?"

"Tomorrow, " Inez offered.

"Tomorrow!!!"

"But tomorrow's Sunday. She'll miss mass," Aunt Pearl persisted.

"Sunday is the best day for all the bargains and a wider choice of fabrics," Inez said.

"Aunt Pearl, didn't you say if you carry God in your heart it doesn't matter where you pray?"

"You girls have an answer for everything... Inez, don't keep her out too long. That's all I beg of you. She'll suffer the pangs of hell the next day."

Next day, Eve was up, washed and dressed before anyone stirred, and waiting for Inez. They took a bus and a train and arrived in Petticoat Lane. Soon they were weaving in and out of the dense crowd, stopping at different stalls. There were stalls for everything, from pots and pans to fruit and vegetables, and from shoe laces to alarm clocks. Some vendors perched illegally on orange boxes.

"Some of their stuff's fallen off the back of a lorry," Inez whispered as she nudged Eve.

"Come back in an hour and they'll be gone before the cops come and ask them any questions. But I am not interested in any of that stuff." Inez dismissed the household and fruit vendors with a flick of her wrist.

Eve stood in awe of the amazing sights around her. Even in Jamaica, she had never been as far as Coronation Market, or downtown to the big stores like Issa's or Nathan's, and she had never ridden a tram car. Her mother always felt the journey would be too much for her. Back in Jamaica, she would sit on the verandah anxiously waiting for her and Esther to return to hear all about their trip and what they had brought back for Eve.

There she was, on a Sunday morning, missing Mass, in the centre of London in the hub of Petticoat Lane, looking at fabric, buttons and colored threads. *What would my mother say if she could see me now?* she wondered.

"Our first stop is the button shop," Inez announced, doing her best double-decker bus conductor's impression.

"Then threads, and our last port of call will be fabrics, and if you're hungry we could stop and get a bite to eat at Rachel's Café. They make the best salt beef sandwiches in all of the East End."

"Salt beef sandwiches," Eve echoed.

"Me dear, nothing like what you have ever eaten in Jamaica. Doorstep slices of rye bread, filled with steaming hot slices of salted beef, smothered with mustard, and a large pickle on the side if you so desire." Inez smiled.

"I'm ready to try anything." Eve tried to disguise her excitement. She sounded like a five year-old.

"You don't know what you've been missing, but we'll have to get the sandwiches before we buy the fabric. I don't want to be lugging all the heavy stuff around."

"Whatever you say, Inez." Eve's mouth was already watering from the description and her anticipated delight.

As soon as Eve entered the button shop, she stopped dead in her tracks. It was the Pearly King and Queen, adorned with thousand of buttons sewn on their suits serenading shoppers coming in.

I'm getting married in the morning
Ding dong the bells are going to shine ...
put up the shutters,
don't make a ruckus.
but get me to the church on time...

They sang at a screeching high pitch, knocking silver spoons on their shoes and knees as they kicked their feet in the air like Parisian can-can dancers. There were buttons of all sizes, colors, shapes, and designs all through the shop, in baskets, in showcases and boxes stacked ceiling high.

"Who could have guessed there could be so many buttons in the world?" Eve said in awe.

"The wrong button can change the entire style of a garment. A cheap button can spoil a nice dress. One little button can make a difference to a boring piece of fabric. It brings it alive," Inez said.

"Look at these." She thrust out her hands as if she had gold nuggets in them.

Inez purchased several buttons and danced out of the store with the Pearly Queen, kicking her knees in the air as high as theirs.

"Come back and visit us again soon, me luv," they called out after her.

They moved across the street to the thread shop. Here Eve was more at ease, because she had spent so many hours on the verandah crocheting doilies with her mother, but still the range of colors was amazing. Fifteen shades of red, from poppy red to magenta and fuchsia. There were silk threads, cotton threads, threads for embroidery, coarse army threads.

"Can you believe that such an insignificant item as thread could be so critical in the making of a garment? Thread embroiders nice designs; it is the thread that holds the button to the outfit; it's the thread that weaves the fabric together in the first place."

Inez ran her long fingers over a spool of silk thread. "All praises to thread."

The pair knocked spools of thread together in the air as if they were champagne glasses.

"It's the truth, my sister." Eve giggled, pulling her hands over her head.

Her laughter stopped suddenly when she felt a severe tug on her arm. When she looked up, she saw that a young boy had run off with her handbag.

"Thief! Thief!" Eve yelled, pointing ahead of her, legs shaking beneath her skirt.

Inez sprinted ahead in hot pursuit; the young man behind the counter ran out of the store behind her.

"Stop thief!" they screamed, charging down the street behind the culprit like a pack of hounds. Eve felt dizzy and her feet began to buckle beneath her. She grabbed onto the edge of the counter and took a deep breath.

"Are you alright, my darling? Let's get you somewhere to sit," said the storekeeper.

"I'm alright. Honest, I am."

"Here we are," Eve heard from behind. There was Inez, dangling the broken strap of the handbag like a prize.

"I think if the bugger had known Inez was going to be running behind him, he'd have had second thoughts," said the storekeeper.

Everyone clapped and cheered the two of them.

"Bloody thieving rascal. What the heck would I tell Aunt Pearl if something happened to you?" Inez said. "I swore I'd look after you."

"I'm alright. But I'm hungry," Eve said.

"Then let's go eat and you can take a load off your feet."

Rachel's Café was filled with shoppers and the aroma of fried bacon and chips saturated the air. In the tight atmosphere Eve struggled to breathe, but she didn't care, and certainly wasn't going to mention it to Inez.

The salt beef sandwich lived up to its expectations. It was like nothing she had ever eaten before. Even the mustard was splendid.

"I don't want to appear greedy but could I have another one?"

"Rachel," Inez hollered across the counter, "Eve is hooked. One more sandwich for my sister here."

What impressed Eve the most about Inez was not her knowledge of fabrics and threads, but that everybody in the whole market knew her like she was a famous person, and she knew everybody by their first name. Even when the thief tried to steal the bag, without a second thought the shop boy followed in pursuit right behind her.

Their last stop was the fabric shop. Eve was very tired, but dared not complain.

Each stall owner lured them in to view their wares.

"I've got some beautiful silks from India over here, me luvvy," a man yelled from across the street.

"I've got diaphanous organza, taffeta, velvet, mesh for crinolines, plaids, polka dots, stripes, herringbone, houndstooth. Everything your little heart desires," another beckoned.

"Come over here, deary, and take a look."

"Every kind of material on God's earth." Inez said.

"Sequins are very popular with my clients, although they are hell to work with."

She turned to the assistant.

"Give me eight yards of this, two yards of that one," she said, pointing to a roll of emerald green organza, and fifteen yards of the white Italian lace. "That's for Cherry's wedding dress." Inez pointed to the sales assistant with precision.

All Eve knew about fabric was gingham, khaki and the floral cotton prints that Mummy used to buy for our dresses. Those fabrics were nowhere to be seen amongst the mountains of emerald green, violet, blue, purple and magenta silks.

"How do you know so much about this stuff, Inez? How do you know where to go to find it?"

"I go to night school three nights a week. I learn pattern cutting, design and textiles. I love it."

"Mama taught me to sew by hand, but since I've been here, I bought a second-hand Singer machine and I've mastered it. I work the graveyard shift at the hospital so I can go to school."

"How do you stay awake?"

"I just drink a lot of coffee. Me and cousin Marge share one bed. Marge works the day shift, and while she is at work I sew during the day when most of our nosey neighbors are at work. I can't let my landlady know that I'm bringing extra work home, because it might just cause a problem." She said, giving Eve a devilish grin.

"My policy is what the mind don't know, the heart can't cry over."

She nudged Eve.

"I take a cat nap in the afternoon and then get ready to go to school. I have a strict plan for the future, me dear, and nobody is going to change it."

"And what about Austin?"

"What about him?' she smiled. "He'll change, just wait and see," she said confidently as she nudged Eve again.

"My cousin in Manchester wants me and Marge to join her there. Rooms to rent are much easier to find and cheaper too, so she says. But I don't want to live in Manchester. I want to be here in London in the heart of the city."

"I want you to stay here, too," Eve said, trying to disguise childish notions.

"Every day my Aunt Pearl goes out looking for somewhere for us to move to. She comes home so distressed and disheartened. There are four of us so it's much harder to find somewhere big enough."

"Marge wants to send for her daughter, Madeline," said Inez.

"Marge has a daughter? I didn't know she was married…"

"She's not."

"Oh."

"Just a little mishap she had with some young boy from Jones Town. But what a blessing this little accident turned out to be. Look…"

Inez pulled out a passport photo of a little girl.

"She is the sweetest little dumpling you ever seen, eh?"

"Oh, yes she is a sugar dumpling alright. Who is taking care of her?"

"She is living in Spanish Town with her grandmother until Marge can get her papers and her passage together to send for her."

"That's why sometimes Marge don't seem so friendly. Her heart is aching and until she can get her little Madeline here she won't be happy. Not a day goes by Marge doesn't shed a tear. Sometimes my heart aches just listening to her cry."

They wormed their way through the market. A slight drizzle shortened their expedition. Weighed down like two donkeys, they muscled their way through the crowded streets, up onto the sidewalk, behind the carts, around the stalls, anywhere they could find an opening until they could see the main street of Whitechapel Road.

"Taxi!" Inez screeched. The black bulldog of a car slowed down to a stop. She opened the door, pushed Eve in first, then got in behind her, almost before she could sit. Inez threw her bags into the back of the cab.

"Stepney Green, please. And then on to Kennington. Phew…!"

"Wow! That was fun, wasn't it?" Eve exhaled.

"Buying fabric is the next best thing to sex. I love it." She nudged Eve, threw her head back and laughed. The blood rushed to Eve's face.

"You love sex?" The words flew out of Eve's mouth quicker than she had a chance to stop them.

"Of course. And your brother is a master. But don't ever tell him I told you so. He's already too big-headed," she said.

"Austin, an expert lover?" Eve shuddered at the thought of her brother naked. She had never even heard a woman admit that she liked sex before and she'd never even considered Austin as a sex machine, although she was aware he had had several lovers. He shared everything with her except that aspect of his life.

"So how do you know what to buy for each customer?"

"Too embarrassed to talk about sex, Eve?"

"UhUhmmm, yes. So how do you know what fabric to buy?"

"Don't be ashamed to ask questions about life. That is how you learn. I am your sister now," she said, nudging the younger girl again.

A flush of blood rushed through Eve's body when she heard the word 'sister' and although Inez rambled on about her customers, she was still stuck on that one word. *Inez is here to stay whether I like it or not, but was Austin aware or did he care about this major decision being made around him?* she wondered.

Eve listened to Inez. Her brown eyes sparkled. She had never been so passionate about anything the way Inez talked about clothes, fabric and her customers.

"When I was growing up," she continued, "all my father cared about was his machete, his donkey and his sugar cane. I was a girl with no mother and I think I was an inconvenience to him. I couldn't lift heavy loads like my brothers or chop cane, although sometimes they made me do it. I dreamed that one day I would have a wardrobe full of dresses; not wear hand-me-downs and torn-up baggy trousers and not to have to wash another shirt, boil water, cook food, wear ragged clothes and smell the sweat and grind of three grown men all day. I knew my life could be better than that, if I only had a chance."

"Oh you are so sure about your life, Inez," Eve said, smiling up at her.

"Stepney Green," yelled the voice from the front of the cab.

"Here."

Inez rolled a pound note into to a ball and placed it in the palm of Eve's hand. The money felt clammy and cold, but it was as if Inez had given her the keys to the Kingdom.

"This should be enough to cover your part of the fare as well."

"Thanks Inez. I'd love to come with you again. This was so much fun."

"Anytime, my darling. It was nice having your company. Cousin Marge would rather stay in bed than come shopping with me."

"I'd be happy to come again."

"Just check that it's okay with your brother and Aunt Pearl. I don't want either of them fussing at me."

"They are going to make a fuss anyway, you know that."

She kissed Eve on the cheek and got out of the car. The cab continued its way toward Tower Bridge and south across the river. It took Eve three days to recover from her day on Petticoat Lane, but the next invitation could not come quickly enough.

EIGHTEEN

Nature has a funny way of protecting you from what you can't manage, like the way they say God only gives you what you can bear. Esther, her beloved cousin Donovan, Aunt Pearl and Uncle Dudley were all that remained of Eve's once bigger-than-life-sized family. She thought that nothing could ever come between any of them. They had been each other's heartbeat. Yet, the rest of her family had been snatched away from her without warning, without a single sign. God had spared her the pain of having been on that train, but gave her different challenges instead. During those miserable days that followed the crash, the investigations and inquiry, she was in a state of semi-consciousness, barely alive. Of the siblings, she was the one least affected by the crash because she was already dying.

After the Kendal crash, she prayed for death to sweep her away swiftly the way it had devoured her family. She went along with the rhythm of things, knowing that her days were numbered. In fact, she sometimes prayed that since she had no place on earth without them, no purpose for living, she would join them soon.

How could I live without Mummy, without Sarge? If I died, Austin and Esther could stand over my grave, weep and pray for all of us. They would be rid of me and not be burdened with an ailing sister for the rest of their lives. Donovan's return gives some hope and I was glad that Esther had some company. How I envied her at times… I had no intention to ever cause my family any heartache, any problems.

She had grown accustomed to being the spare wheel every time Austin and Inez stepped out of the house on a date. No one seemed to mind Eve's presence, except Eve. The last time she protested that she didn't want to play gooseberry any more, that she would never go anywhere again with them, was the last time she needed to say it. That was the night she met Clement, Inez's best friend.

Inez had a full social calendar. Every week there was some event to attend: a wedding, an engagement party, a christening, a gift shower for this or that. Her clients invited her to every function they were hosting; she had dressed them for the occasion so they always wanted her to be present to show her off. They were never short of party invitations.

Although Aunt Pearl fussed and complained that she was not getting enough rest, Eve would not refuse any invitation that came her way. Despite her feeble start in life, Eve benefited greatly from the medical treatments she received. It was really no longer a major undertaking for her to go outdoors. She had many days of clear breathing and strong movement. She grew an inch and put on more weight. And she now had Inez. In fact, Austin and Eve were now the once-maimed children behind the gap-toothed magnet. So it became customary to see all three of them out together. At most gatherings, Eve took a seat near the back and accepted her role as spectator. She didn't dance. She only spoke to those who spoke to her. It was enough to entertain herself with the constant buzz of life all around her.

And then, one evening out of nowhere, a penetrating voice said, "How come you're not dancing?"

"I—I can't dance," Eve stuttered, looking up to see to whom the sultry voice belonged.

"What you mean you can't dance?" He threw his head back and gave a raucous roar.

"Everyone born in Jamaica can dance my girl, even me granny."

"I'm sick, and it takes too much energy." she said.

Without invitation, he pulled up a wooden chair beside her, scraping the chair along the floor as he moved in.

"Well, Evelyn Scott, tonight I am going to steal all your energy and then breathe it right back into you again." She could feel his piercing eyes on her as they ran up and down her newly filled-out body.

"How do you know my name?"

"Isn't that your brother Austin over there?" He pointed across the hall. "I know your family from home."

"You do?" She tried to contain her excitement.

"But I don't remember you at all."

"No, you wouldn't remember me. You were too young. I'm Clement Jackson, but my friends call me 'Blue.'" He stretched out his hands, pulled her hand toward his mouth and kissed the back of it. Her heart skipped and raced. She had seen her own body differently lately, noticed the late pul-chritude and brightness in her eyes, the kind of thing a man like this might be drawn to. In her mind, however, she was still little sickly skinny Eve, and not a target for a man like this. The mirror said differently.

"Blue? What kind of friends do you have that they would call you Blue?" she said, desperately trying to catch her breath—and shift the obvi-ous topic, as she had tried to do that first time out in the world with Inez.

"Not Blue as in sad." He smiled, his gold tooth shining back at her. "Blue as in blue the color—you know the little cube of blue your grand-mother used to whiten clothes."

"Oh, that blue. How did you end up being called that?" She was back in control now, and managed to act just a little bored and disdainful.

"I lived with my grandmother for a while in Frankfield. She put my white clothes to soak with the blue cube and forgot about them. When she remembered, the blue had spoilt all my clothes so everything that I owned that was white turned blue. There was no money to buy a whole set of new clothes so until they were torn, too small or had gradually washed their way back to white, I had to wear them blue. You can imagine the heckling I got at school, so I stopped going to school. Then my grandmother found out that I was not going to school and she beat me. So I went to school with my blue clothes and became officially known as 'Blue'."

"Oh, you poor thing."

"Poor is an understatement! Even chicken back was too expensive to buy for Sunday dinner. We ate meat only once a month and the rest of the time mannish water and hard dough bread. Don't feel bad for me though. Those dark days back in Jamaica made me tough, made me ready for the life ahead of me. And when I lay hungry and dirty in the trenches during the war, I could bear the hunger pangs because I'd known hunger so many times before."

He looked out at the dance floor and stood up. He seemed to go up twelve feet.

"Come, let's dance." He pulled Eve to her feet.

"All this good music going to waste."

"But I can't," she whined, pulling away from him.

"Come, I'll make it easy for you."

She craned her neck to look at him. Clement Jackson stood at least six feet four inches tall. He was a solid man with broad shoulders, with conked brownish hair that had wavy kinks and a part on the left side. Yes, that hair was styled like Nat King Cole's. The color of his hair complemented his complexion. His skin was as dark as coffee, with just enough red underneath to reflect the light. He had thick bushy eyebrows and a pencil-thin mustache that sat over his broad upper lip. He wore a brown pin-striped double-breasted jacket that covered the better parts of his body. His trouser legs were wide and baggy. Gold cufflinks glinted at the end of his white starched shirt and a timepiece dangled from his pocket at the bottom hole of his waistcoat. All he needed was a top hat to look the perfect part of a Charles Dickens city gentleman. He was the eldest of four sons, and although she did not remember him, their paths had crossed briefly several times before in Jamaica.

He reminded her so much of Sarge. He was self-assured and charming, but a lot more boisterous than Sarge would ever have been. 'Vulgarity and loudness in men are unnecessary,' Sarge always said to Austin. "A man can prove himself by his manner and not his mouth."

"Just put your feet on my shoes and I'll lead the way," Blue said gently.

"I can't stand on your feet, your shoes are so new and shiny." She looked down at his two-toned brogues. She saw her face in them.

"Just do as I tell you before I carry you across the room," he cajoled.

"I feel so awkward," Eve said, raising her hands onto his broad shoulders.

"Look. No one in here is worried about us."

"Okay, Okay."

"Just put your feet on mine."

She obeyed like a child and tiptoed carefully onto his shoes. Only a few curious eyes stared at them.

"Never mind them. Just hold me tight. You are so light. This makes my job easier."

Eve was overwhelmed by the smell of his cologne. She pulled her head back a bit to avoid it, but it made no difference. By the second dance, she didn't care. She pulled her body closer to his, and he held her tightly around the waist. Eve was grateful the music was so loud; it drowned out the sound of her heart as they glided across the dance floor.

"Why me? There are so many women here. Tell me…" she insisted.

"I'll tell you later," Blue whispered in her ear.

He held her even tighter and they danced to Nat King Cole, Fats Domino, and Jim Reeves, whatever they played. She just didn't want him to let her go.

"Don't overdo it, Eve. Remember your condition." It was Austin, hovering now close beside them, his arms folded across his chest, prison-guard style.

"She's fine, man, she's in good hands with me," Blue said smugly. Austin glowered at him. They stopped turning, and Blue walked her back to her chair. He pulled up his trouser leg at the creases and lowered his large frame into the chair beside Eve's.

"What can I get you to drink?"

"Nothing, I don't drink."

"Not even a Babycham?"

"No, but some lemonade or cola would be nice."

Blue strutted across the hall. Eve's eyes stayed glued to the back of his neck. On the way, he picked up a little girl and swung her in the air, kissing her on her cheek before putting her down. Mid-way back, a petite woman in a floral skirt and a white lace blouse pulled at his arm to get his attention. He whispered something in her ear as he rubbed his hand across her back, around her waist and down her right thigh. She giggled, throwing her head back, and slid away.

Eve's eyes remained fixed on him. As much as she tried to fool herself that his absence didn't matter, it did. It had only been minutes, but her heart sank every minute he was away from her. She was already hooked and intoxicated by him. Eve looked at her watch and counted each minute before he made his way back. Forty-three, to be exact.

"Here we are." He pushed a small bottle of Schweppes tonic water in front of her. "They have no more cola." Eve took the bottle and the glass from him.

"Thank you very much." She knew that Austin was watching their every move, although he kept his distance.

"So what are your plans this week? You fancy going to the pictures?"

"Uh, I, I don't know."

"You don't know what you are doing or you don't know whether you want to spend another evening with me?"

"Umm… I don't know if I can go."

"It's just the pictures, my love, down by the Coronet. They're showing 'Porgy and Bess.' I'm in love with Dorothy Dandridge—and you of course, my dear."

"Is that the film with Sidney Poitier?"

"Yes, the same one with Sammy Davis Jr., Diahann Carroll, and Pearl Bailey. All the top black American actors."

"Okay, okay. Wednesday."

He never left her side for the entire night.

"So you didn't finish telling me how you know my family?" I asked.

"I used to deliver the ice at your house many years ago."

"You were the ice boy, in the red truck. Mr. Jackson's son?"

"Yes, that was my father's truck. I watched you sitting on the verandah playing the piano or reading. You never noticed me. Your sister and your mother would play the piano and sing to you. I would watch them teaching you how to play and how frustrated you would get when you hit the wrong key. Your mother played so beautifully and she was so patient with you and all her students."

"You knew us then?"

"You were so small. I didn't expect to be noticed by you. Your father wasn't raising his daughters to notice the likes of me. He shooed me away like a stray fowl if I came too close to the house. I was so shocked to hear they died at Kendal. I am sorry for your loss Eve." He leaned forward and took her hand. Her stomach fluttered in that familiar kind of dread, but this time only for the moment when he mentioned Kendal.

"Although your father didn't like me, he was the type of man that I looked up to."

Clement knew so much about her, and she hadn't even known of his existence. A tinge of sadness rose inside Eve as memories of her beautiful family flashed through her mind.

"I loved music so much and your house was one of the few places where it was appreciated and heard all day long."

"Those were happy days for me, although I was sick," she sighed, adjusting her body in the chair.

"I craved what you all had. Everything your family had, I wanted. I had nothing. After the hurricanes washed away my father's crops, he worked day and night and got himself out of the cane fields and bought that old red truck and started selling ice. Your father was one of our best customers. Mr. Scott encouraged other people to buy from us. Anything your father said, everyone believed and followed."

"Yes," she nodded. "I remember. He did have that way about him, didn't he? Everyone jumped to attention when he spoke."

"I worked hard because I knew if I did, one day I could be just like your father."

He ran his index finger over the rim of the empty glass. "I'm sorry he died. My father pulled me out of school at the drop of a hat to help him, so my learning was not steady. I wanted more, so when I saw the advertisement inviting us to go to war, I signed up with the RAF. I did not necessarily want to fight a war for a country I did not know much about or had any love for, but my father felt it would be good learning for me. None of my brothers were interested, so I came to England on my own. 'England will mek a man of you' my father said. 'Me can't offer you any good education and nothing better than ice-selling, so go to war. Fight for the Mother Country.'"

Clement looked down at the floor.

"Is there something you need, Eve?" interrupted Austin, moving toward her as if Clement did not exist.

"Austin, this is Clement Jackson. He knows us from home."

"I know who he is, dear," he replied, without turning his head to look at Blue.

"If you would excuse me, I would like to have the company of my sister."

"Don't leave," she said, reaching out to touch Clement's arm.

"It's okay, my love, I'll share you with your brother, at least for the moment." He winked at her and stepped away taking his devilish grin with him.

"What do you think you're doing with the likes of him?" Austin whispered.

"Oh, Austin…! Hush your mouth. I'm not a baby anymore. We're just talking. He invited me to go to the pictures on Wednesday."

"Eve, that man has a million women and he's twice your age. You don't want to get mixed up with a big ginnal like him. He has such a reputation…!"

"Austin, I'm just going to the pictures with him. That's all. How many men do you see knocking on my door, for God's sake?"

"That is not the point. In fact, that is the point. The first could be the worst."

"Can we just get through one day without an argument?"

"I'm not fighting with you, I am just trying to be a good brother to you. I am just protecting you. That's my job now."

"Well, you've just been fired from your job." She smiled and kissed him on the cheek. "Go protect your own love interest." Eve pointed at Inez as she stood in deep conversation with another dashing young man equally as handsome as her brother.

"Are you trying to get rid of me, little sister?"

"Yes," she said, pushing him away from her. "Move. Go away. You're giving me a headache."

★★★

"Inez , I have a date with Clement."

"I noticed him breathing hot and heavy all over you like a dragon. He had asked me about you before, but I knew Austin wouldn't approve, so I told him you were seeing someone."

"What!!? How long ago was that?"

"Oh, I can't say. You would kill me if I'd told you the truth."

"How long have you known him?"

"He was one of the first men I met when I arrived in London."

"Were you lovers?"

"No, luv. I don't think I'm Clement's type, although I'm not sure what his type is. But every woman in London knows him. Ooh la la, Mr. Hot Stuff." Inez waved her wrist in the air. "Careful Eve, he's got a reputation."

"He's really nice. A real gentleman."

"He is a ginnal, not a gentleman. You be careful, little petal. He has a silver tongue—and not everything he tells you may be true."

"Will you straighten my hair, before my date with him?"

"Straighten your hair?! Oh, I don't know about that, Eve. What will Austin say?"

"What can he say? It's my head, it's my hair," Eve insisted. "Please Inez.

Please? It doesn't matter what Austin says. I'm so tired of looking like a schoolgirl, tired of wearing my hair in plaits, tired of pulling the comb through this bush."

She tugged at her hair.

"It would be so manageable if it was straightened. Please, pretty please."

"Okay, my sweet. Please don't whine. It's so unbecoming. I'll come later this afternoon, this is the only night I don't have classes."

***

The iron comb and curling tongs sat on the top of the two-ring burner. Inez sectioned and greased Eve's hair with Dixie Peach pomade, pulling and tugging the hair preparation through it.

"Girl, your hair is as coarse as a horse's mane."

"Ouch! Not so hard!"

"Hush, baby. You're so tender headed…"

Taking one small section at a time, Inez pulled the hot comb through the strands. Eve could feel the heat against her scalp and as the comb touched her virgin hair, it sizzled and smelled. She winced and squirmed in the chair, hunching her shoulders as she felt her scalp burn.

Her hands shot up toward her head, but she did not get to touch the cooking hair.

"Stop that. Get your hands out of your head." Inez hit her with the the handle of the comb on the back of her hand.

"Now Miss Eve, I'm fixing you up pretty to go on a date, but no hanky panky with Clement, you hear me?"

"I can take good care of myself."

"Like hell you can. You don't know a thing about the likes of Clement Jackson. He is all sweet talk and you are greener than grass."

"There, look." Inez held a mirror toward Eve. "Well, what do you think?"

"Oh, my hair looks beautiful!" Eve cried out. She pulled the mirror closer to get a better view. The thick, straight hair now rested on her shoulders. Fat curls cascaded down the side of her face. For an eternity inside a moment, Eve did not recognize the person.

"I don't look like a girl anymore, but a woman."

"What a difference a hairdo can make," Inez said, her hands akimbo.

"What the hell is going on here?" It was Austin flinging open the door. Eve's triumphant moment was short-lived, as she jumped out of her skin. The iron comb slipped out of Inez's hand onto Eve's ear, shoulder, scorching it on the way to burning her shoulder.

"Aarrrgh!" Eve roared, grabbing at her singed parts.

"What do you think you're doing to my sister?" Austin shouted.

"I'm pressing her hair. What does it look like to you?" Inez retrieved the hot comb defiantly.

"She doesn't need to have her hair pressed. Her hair is fine as it is."

He was livid, snarling as he shouted at them. "Look at how you burned her. You're dressing her up like a dinner pig for your friend Blue, right?!"

He stomped toward them, and before they knew it, he had grabbed the burner, comb and tongs off the table and threw the whole bloody lot out of the open window. Inez and Eve were dumbstruck. A succession of clings and clangs synthesized as the iron instruments hit the concrete pavement, making an unholy tune as they fell.

"Oy mate, watch out!" two voices bellowed in unison from below.

"What the hell did you do that for?"

"Why do you insist on corrupting my sister?" Austin charged anew.

"Corrupting your sister? I'm straightening her hair. I'm not teaching her to striptease, for God's sake!"

"Have you lost your bloody mind?" Inez and Eve yelled back at him.

"She doesn't need her hair pressed, straightened, whatever you girls call it."

"It's my head, Austin. When are you going to realize that I'm not a broken doll but a real person?"

"Wash it out immediately, Eve," Austin yelled .

"You have got to be kidding. It just took Inez two hours to get it looking like this."

"When I get back, Miss Evelyn, you better have all that stuff out of your hair."

He disappeared as quickly as he had entered, slamming the door behind him. Eve ran to the cabinet to protect Aunt Pearl's sacred china, which vibrated and trembled within.

"Sometimes I just can't believe I love that man," Inez said.

"Well, I am not washing out my new curls at all."

"Do you think Clement will like it?" Eve pushed up the curls with the palms of her hands.

"Why wouldn't he? You look damn good girl, even if I do say so myself."

Inez took a step backwards with her hand on her hips. A big grin came over her expression.

"If I can make my short hair look good, then I can damn sure work wonders with yours," Inez promised. "Never mind Austin. He'll get over it."

The burns on Eve's ear and shoulder were painful but the burning hate in her heart was worse. Over the weeks that followed, the injuries turned from pink to light brown, until the skin began to repair itself. The rift between Eve and her brother was getting ready to widen.

***

Every item of clothing from her wardrobe was scattered all over the floor and on her bed. What should I wear? What kind of questions will he ask me? Eve stood in front of the mirror rehearsing her possible answers. She restyled her hair a dozen times and checked her face in the mirror for blemishes, pimples, anything that would mar her complexion. She was simply dizzy from excitement until Wednesday rolled around. Her mind flooded with thoughts of Clement. She eventually chose a blue twin set and a tweed skirt that Aunt Pearl had given her for Christmas. Eve wished she had some high-heeled shoes to make her look taller for him.

Aunt Pearl and Eve wore the same size but she didn't dare ask. She could already hear the response:

"What you going to do in those high-heeled shoes? Remember your condition." As if anyone ever gave me a chance to forget 'my condition.' My condition isn't going to stop me tonight, Eve thought as she sprayed her neck and wrists with her favorite Blue Grass perfume.

"Aunt Pearl, can you help me with my makeup?" she yelled into her Aunt's bedroom.

"Yes, dear. Just wear a little powder and some lipstick. It will brighten up your face." Pearl came over and dabbed the powder evenly across Eve's forehead, smiling into her face as she did it.

"There," she said, kissing her niece on the forehead and stepping backwards. "You are as pretty as a picture... the phone's ringing."

"Maybe it's him."

"Hello? Yes, she's right here, Inez... Eve, it's Inez."

"Have fun with Mr. Hot Stuff," Inez yelled at the other end of the phone line. "Whatever you do don't go back to his house, don't get in the back of his car, keep your wits about you, don't drink any alcohol... and if all else fails, call me and I'll come and get you wherever you are. I've already warned him that he will be in big trouble with me if he messes around with you."

"Thanks Inez, but I know I'll be okay."

"Okay, me darling. Clement is a sweet talker but a ginnal. Before you know it, he will be having his wicked way with you. Men like Clement are used to having their own way, no disrespect to you. So say no, or you will be old news before the paper is printed."

"Okay. you're sounding like Sarge. Love you. Bye." Eve hung up the phone before Inez could say another word.

***

It was sixteen minutes past seven when the doorbell finally rang. *Oh my God, it's him*, Eve almost said aloud. She felt dizzy, as though she had done a thousand somersaults.

"He's late," Pearl sneered teasingly.

"Just throw down the key," Eve shot back. "And if you can't say something nice to him, then say nothing or leave the room."

"Come right up," Aunt Pearl shouted as she leaned outside the sash window. Blue stared up at the light that produced the voice. He tracked the gleaming bits of metal coming at him, adjusted his feet and caught them expertly with one hand.

Eve stood behind her Aunt, hoping that her heart would not collapse from all the excitement and cause her to fall flat on her face at his feet.

Blue entered the room and was more handsome than the week before. He wore a navy blue pin stripe suit, a white shirt and a pale blue tie.

"Good evening, everyone," he said, removing his hat.

"These are for you, Aunt Pearl." He handed her a box of Cadbury's Milk Tray chocolate.

"Oh, thank you." She raised her shoulders and cooed with delight.

"Well, are you ready?" Blue asked, looking at her.

"Yes, of course." Eve picked up a small clutch bag she had borrowed from Inez.

"Don't keep her out too late," Aunt Pearl said. "She tires easily. She's not going to tell you this, but she has a 'condition.'"

"Oh Aunt Pearl, stop embarrassing me."

"I'll take good care of her Aunt Pearl, don't worry yourself." Clement said, smiling at Aunt Pearl.

"Blue...!" Austin's sour voice rose from the corner of the flat. He emerged from a darkened room and walked toward the others.
"This is my sister you are leaving here with. Let me tell you, if you hurt her, country boy, you better run. You better hide, you better take the first boat back to Jamaica because I'll hunt you down and kill you. You understand me, boasy bwoy?" Austin was primal now, snarling and narrow-eyed.

"Stop that...!" Eve pushed Clement through the door, just as he was raising his hat to Aunt Pearl. There was just enough time for him to throw a big smirk at Austin.

"Yes, Boss. I hear you loud and clear. I'll take good care of your little sister, don't worry yourself..."

Eve led them both down the narrow staircase. The smell of Mrs. Duncan's curry dish greeted them. Clement followed closely behind her. Outside the house, he quickly took the lead so he could reach the car first. He opened the passenger door and Eve climbed inside his brand-new Aston-Martin.

"We can still make the eight o'clock show if we hurry," he assured her. Blue smiled at Eve as he brought life to the car and made it purr. They sped off through the narrow streets.

★★★

"You smell nice," Blue said, putting one arm over her shoulder and the other inside her coat around her waist.

I wish I could say the same about him, she thought. *My good God, he reeks of that Old Spice again.*

The Aston-Martin made good time. As they pulled up to it, Eve craned her neck to get a better look at the grand dome and articulation of one of Europe's oldest movie houses. An architectural appreciation would have to wait, because Blue took her by the hand as soon as they parked, and led her straight through the doors. Adjusting their eyes to the dark, they clumsily found their seats inside the grand old Coronet cinema in Notting Hill. Blue held her close, whispering that he was sorry they had arrived a few minutes late.

Eve hardly saw any of the film. They kissed unabashedly. Blue fumbled with her blouse. Too insistently, because Eve now became aware of her own opposition.

"Stop," she pleaded. Confusion was creeping in, and she felt dizzy.

"Are you coming back to my flat, afterwards?" he whispered in her ear.

"No, I can't," she answered sheepishly. She could hear Inez's warning floating around in her head.

"What, you don't trust me?"

"No, I don't trust myself," she giggled. Blue continued where he left off, covering her neck with his kisses. Eve admitted to herself that she did not want the night to end.

***

Despite the caustic comments from Austin, Clement visited Eve again and again. Every date began with a plea, an argument, an ugly comment from Austin, but nothing any of her family said kept her away from him. *I have him and nothing to lose,* she thought.

From the time she was a child, Eve's life expectancy had been predicted to be only a few years. *What difference did it make if he broke my heart? My heart had been broken the day all my family died. I'm not going to live very long anyway.*

Clement had breathed life into her, she felt. He taught her to dance at the Lyceum. They ate in ritzy restaurants in Regent Street and Piccadilly. They were regulars at the Palladium. Eve enjoyed the performances of Paul Robeson, Sammy Davis Jr., Satchmo and so many other traveling black artists.

He introduced her to high officials and businessmen in the Jamaican community. Her once limited life was now filled with social engagements. Inez had been the only other person with whom she had explored the outside world. And Clement never ever considered her sick or ailing. 'Her condition' was of minor concern to him. He was considerate, though, when she tired, and he slowed his pace to accommodate hers, instead of treating her like a delicate, dying flower. She loved him for that alone and their courtship lasted, despite the disapproval of her family.

From morning to night, Eve's mind was flooded with thoughts of him. She didn't have time to write letters any more to her sister in Jamaica. She also missed several hospital appointments. Just as the fever had ravaged her body when she was a child, the charm of Clement 'Blue' Jackson swept through her like a new affliction. Her body yearned for him, her nipples became erect at the sound of his voice and the love between her legs moistened whenever he touched her. Eve hugged her pillow at night, pretending that his body was close to hers, praying that one day it would be. She prayed for forgiveness for her wicked mind as it galloped away with sexual fantasies. She even feared that her thoughts of Clement were out of control.

Eve took Inez's advice. She did not sleep with him, but was not sure how long she could hold that promise. Her whole body was made weak yearning for his next touch, his breath on her neck, a wink, a smile, a naughty whisper in her ear, or the way he grabbed her around her waist and undressed her with his dark puppy eyes. Nothing, not one word from anyone could sway her from him.

All her life, people had comforted Eve, fetched and carried for her, been at her every beck and call. Indeed, she had been a true invalid, and although she was grateful for their love, his indifference to her illness was refreshing. What tired her most were the constant quarrels with Austin. Uncle Dudley mostly kept quiet, but his face constantly wore a look of concern. Aunt Pearl, on the other hand, helped her get dressed for every date. She even bought Eve a few new outfits.

"You going out with him again?" she heard Austin's voice behind the door.

"I sure am."

"Why you want to mix up yourself with someone like him, Eve?" Austin protested.

"Oh, you sound just like Sarge. How many boys do you see knocking on my door? None, Austin Scott, absolutely none." She played with the buttons on her dress. "You make sure to keep all your male friends as far away from me as possible."

"That's not true. I just want the best for you."

"The best is right here. Clement is established in the community, he works hard, he is kind to me."

"I'm a man. Clement is a boasy bwoy as transparent as glass; plus he is twice your age."

"You give me no credit."

"You are only seventeen, Eve, and inexperienced with men."

"How will I ever get experience when I'm not given a chance to make my own mistakes?"

"But you are jumping in the deep end."

"Then let me drown in happiness." She raised her hands in the air and shook her hips.

"How you so fool-fool?"

"I know what you're thinking. What does a man like him want with a sick girl like me? He told me everything about his life, Austin. How Sarge ran him from the house, told him never to set foot anywhere near me and Esther, or his land. That the likes of him was not worthy of his girls. Did you know that? Even threatened to have him arrested."

"Eve, he is lying to you, giving you some sob story. And of course you've fallen for it."

"It's because of those harsh words from Sarge that he has made something of his life."

"Well, good for him." Austin crossed his arms.

"He went from nothing but an ice boy to the RAF and then into business for himself. That's some achievement, don't you think? Give credit where credit is due."

"I heard he was dishonorably discharged from the Air Force."

"Wicked rumors and gossip. You know how tongues wag and stories are exaggerated. Now he is in the process of buying a house in Dulwich."

"Whatever Clement has achieved it is because he is a thief, a wheeler and a dealer. Nothing he does comes from hard work, but from other people's misfortune."

The air in the room suddenly went thick and heavy. Eve paused and took a deep breath.

"He asked me to marry him, Austin." She paused again. "And I said yes."

"You said what? Are you crazy, girl?!"

"Austin, I said yes. So there."

"You barely know him. What are you thinking, girl? You think you can manage a man like Blue? Alright." His voice softened. "Go out on a few dates with him if you must, get to know him a little bit more, but please, Eve, don't marry him."

"Austin, please listen."

"No you listen to me. You marry that *ediat bwoy* and you are a dead woman." He paused and took a deep sigh.

"Listen to me, my sweet darling." He lowered his voice and came closer to her. He took her hands in his.

"You and Esther are all I've got now. I'm fighting with you because I am fighting for my family. You're young and you don't have much experience with men," he sighed.

"I just can't give you over to somebody like that. Sarge would expect more of me."

"All I know, Austin, is that I love him and he loves me."

"Who couldn't love you, my precious darling? But men like Blue don't know what love is. Mark my words, my sweet sister. It will be short-lived happiness. Men like him are so predictable."

"Don't judge everyone by your standards. Until you met Inez you weren't exactly a saint yourself."

"Clement has children in every corner of London. Remember, a leopard doesn't change its spots, my love. He will deceive you and break your heart. Eve, I'm begging you. I don't want to see you hurt."

"No, Austin you are wrong about him."

"Evelyn Mary Scott, listen to me. I am your brother and I forbid it." He grabbed her by the shoulders and shook her.

"If Sarge was alive you know he would forbid it too."

"But Sarge isn't here anymore and you are not my father," she snapped back at him.

"I wish Sarge would jump out of his grave and slap you right now…"

Austin quickly softened his tone. "Eve, all Blue can give you is heartache."

"I don't want you or Aunt Pearl and Uncle Dudley to be looking after me all my life. You have your own lives to live."

"So that's your reason for marrying him? You're marrying him to get out of this house?"

"No, Austin," Eve sighed. "I'm marrying him because I love him. Please don't deny me my one chance at happiness. Please."

"Your one chance of happiness. You are not giving yourself a chance." He paused, raising his hands in the air. "Fine! Don't listen to me. You marry him and see what you will get. Old time people say if you can't hear you must feel. You mark my words, hard-ears Eve. Since you came to England the cold must have frozen your senses. You marry Blue and I wash my hands clean of you. Clean-clean."

He slapped the palm of his hands together. Livid, he turned and left, slamming the door behind him. Aunt Pearl's china rattled and creaked inside her prized cabinet.

NINETEEN

"I can't get the time off work," Uncle Dudley had said, excusing himself from going.

Austin stood firm to his word and did not attend. The only person present at the wedding from Clement's family was his first cousin Jocelyn from his father's side.

Much to her family's disgust, Clement and Eve were joined on Valentine's Day at the inconspicuous Registry Office in Camberwell Green, south of the River Thames, one week after her eighteenth birthday. There were no bridesmaids, no bouquets of lush flowers, no choir boys, and most painful of all, no give-away father, not even a brother or an uncle to substitute for Sarge. Nothing that she had dreamt of as a girl. There was just a red-nosed Justice of the Peace who resembled a walrus. He read their vows with an annoying nonchalance between intervals of sniffles. Faithful Aunt Pearl and Inez stood teary-eyed and shivering in the unheated room.

Inez had designed a long white lace dress with a matching jacket that had bell sleeves and a mandarin collar. Eve felt like a queen, although she had chosen a most uncomfortable pair of satin shoes that squeezed her toes. Her feet hurt so much she found it hard to smile. She was filled with mixed emotions, deliriously happy that she was getting married, but deeply hurt that Austin had decided not to come.

"It's unlucky to cry on your wedding day, my darling," Aunt Pearl said as she squeezed her little gloved hand.

"I wish Sarge was here to see me getting married, Aunt Pearl. I wish Grace could have been my maid of honor."

"They are all here with us right now in spirit, every one of them."

"You think so? I just wish Austin had changed his mind."

"Don't fret yourself about your bull-headed brother, Eve. He'll come around. You'll see."

There was no wedding reception with the three-tiered wedding cake, no music or plates of rice and curry coat, no bouquet thrown. Instead, they left on the afternoon ferry to Calais and then caught a smelly old train to Paris. It had always been Eve's dream to travel. She had traveled through the magazines and geography books, her imagination exploring the landscapes of exotic places from the verandah back home.

Sarge had traveled to France, Germany and England and before the war he had lived in Cuba, Panama and Curaçao. Esther and Eve would sit on his lap as he told them tales of every trip he took. Beyond the streets of London, she had no experience. She presumed that she would see the famous landmarks: the Eiffel Tower, Notre Dame and all the wonderful sights Paris had to offer.

But naive as she was, she didn't realize that honeymoons were not for sightseeing and exploring a new city. Clement had other plans. He had patiently waited until they were married. He had made numerous advances to persuade her but she kept her promise to Inez. As weak and as dizzy as she was with excitement in his presence, she managed to contain herself and steady her head.

"Don't let him spoil you," Inez warned Eve.

"Let him wait. I was already spoiled before I met your brother and I regret it now," she told her. "So I know what I'm talking about. These men make promises and then they don't keep them. They say anything to get between your legs. When they are soft they are hard, and when they are hard they are soft." Like a wise owl, she spoke firmly to Eve like that before every date. She blushed every time Inez spoke with such frank honesty about sex, but she learned to listen even if she did not respond or fully understand.

"Clement can get sex anywhere he wants. If he spoils you, he won't marry you. Let him wait," she said.

And wait they did. It was the hardest thing she had done in her entire life, apart from staying alive. Every time she was in his presence, she melted. Every time he touched her, she went weak at the knees. As difficult as it was to say 'no,' even in an uncertain whisper, her response remained the same. The more she said no, the more obsessed Clement became.

Then it happened. He undressed her slowly and gently under the starless Parisian sky, unraveling, unbuttoning, peeling off layers of silk and satin garments until she was naked. He spoke softly and made no hurried movements. Eve lay quite still as he cupped her small breasts, sucking on them in a manner suggesting that he imagined them much larger. He ran his hot tongue over her body, kissing every part of her.

Eve had no knowledge of these intimate matters, apart from what she had seen at the cinema or read in love stories and biology books. Neither Esther or Austin or her parents had ever discussed such intimate details with her.

Clement caressed Eve's body from head to toe, working his lips and tongue softly and slowly into every crevice of her body. He nibbled and kissed each ear lobe and down her neck, across her shoulders and along every inch of her spine. Shying away, she suddenly pulled the covers up, hiding herself, so conscious was she of her lack of experience. The only people who had seen her entirely naked were her doctors and her mother. And now she was truly a woman on her own, in some kind of heaven.

Alone for so many nights, she had fantasized about what this moment might be like, but she could not move, could not respond the way she felt she should.

"Don't cover yourself. I want to see all of you," he whispered as he parted Eve's slim legs with his knees and moved his head down her body, below her waist and then slowly and gently between them.

"I won't hurt you, my darling," he whispered.

It was not until the third night of their honeymoon, after he had explored her entire body, that he penetrated her, and when he did she was relaxed and ready for him. Eve took all of him with ease. She wasn't sure how her small frame would stand the weight of him, but he turned her body sideways to lessen the pressure of him. Eve had no experience to measure the joy she felt and no words to describe the sensations that radiated from his hands, his tongue, his body. Were there any words in the dictionary for these emotions? Their bodies shuddered in unison again and again under their enthusiastic rhythm.

Eve no longer lay stiffly but moved to his manhood and his rhyme. With little experience, she had no idea how much was enough, since each time was better than the last. They lay in bed until the late mornings, in a cocoon of indulgence, their bodies snug and safe, listening to conversations they did not understand coming from below their hotel window.

Clement ordered room service, which never came until midday, but Eve didn't care. They feasted on each other's bodies until there was food. She craved only him, and abandoned all ideas of sightseeing, staying in bed for days. She was deliriously happy. Her expectation of life had been so limited before. All she or anyone else had expected of her was simply to stay alive for as long as she could. Outside her family, Eve had not known love. To be loved and married had just been a mere fantasy. Now there she was, wed and in bed, lying in the arms of her husband. It was every girl's dream, and hers had come true. Her husband was Blue.

"I will always love you with all my heart," he whispered. "I loved you from the first day I saw you. You don't know how long I've waited for you. Sarge never thought I was good enough to even set foot on his land, much less marry one of his daughters. But now you're mine."

It wasn't until the fifth day of the honeymoon that they finally got to visit the Eiffel Tower. They dined on the Seine while curious onlookers, unaccustomed to seeing the maitre d' serving blacks sometimes slowed down to gawk. Eve didn't understand one word of all the commotion they caused every time they entered a restaurant; she just floated on air. Onlookers, some uncomfortable in their presence, shifted in their seats or feigned a smile. Clement translated for her. His words were slow but confident from his wartime experience, as he worked his way around the menus and the streets of Paris.

Eve was not bothered by the legendary rudeness of the French. She was hanging on her husband's arm. Now without her parents, without her cousins and beloved family, she could begin a new life. What more could one ask for? Prayers had been answered. God was giving her another chance. *I exist for Clement Blue Jackson only,* she said in her mind. She had long resigned herself to being a spinster for the rest of her short, unpredictable life, so the thought of love, marriage, a house of her own—and the prospect of having children of her own—had always been just a mere fantasy. Her husband was loud and unrefined, but she didn't care. Of all the women in the world from London to Birmingham, Clarendon to Kingston, he had chosen her, and she was indebted to him for her happiness. She was now Mrs. Evelyn Scott Jackson and she would hold on to that for dear life. Whatever it took.

***

The house at 10 Orchid Crescent became Eve's new home. The house stood on the prettiest road in all of South London. The last terraced house on a tree-lined cul-de-sac. It was a great place to see the apple blossoms push their way through to signal the beginnings of spring. For three and a half weeks, the trees swayed majestically like ballerinas, with their pink petals rustling in the insistent breeze. They fell like velvet confetti, covering the entire pavement.

The new Jacksons were the only black family on Orchid, much to some of the neighbors' distaste. For miles, there was not another black face to be seen. And as beautiful as nature made the street, it lacked the friendliness to which Eve had become accustomed. She and Clement were welcomed with polite grins, but never with the warmth or sincerity she had experienced back home or even on Mitcham Street when she lived at Aunt Pearl's. People just peered from behind their net curtains and front gates, but they never spoke to her.

The house had four unused upstairs bedrooms. The stairs were too much for her to climb frequently, so Clement turned the study on the ground floor into their bedroom. The place had a large living room with bay windows, and a Victorian fireplace with a marble mantelpiece. The kitchen was enormous, with more cupboards than she had pots and pans to put in them.

Clement spared no expense. He furnished the house with "only the best," as he kept saying. A Chesterfield leather settee with matching wing armchairs nearly filled an entire side of the living room. A horseshoe-shaped bar full of every kind of bottle occupied too much space. A twenty-inch screen television, which needed no indoor aerial, stood against the north wall. One day Eve came home from a hospital appointment, and there in the corner was a Steinway grand piano. She cried with a mixture of joy and pain as the piano pulled her back into the past. When she closed her eyes, she could see her mother sitting at the piano, her delicate hands on the ivory keys. Producing the most harmonious sounds, she had soothed Eve or gently persuaded her students to play the way she did. It didn't take long before Eve amused herself on the keyboard, especially on rainy afternoons. It was this one act of love that convinced her that her husband was the kindest, most thoughtful man in the world and that her brother was wrong about him.

★★★

Eve loved to walk through the carpeted house barefoot, with her tiny hands trailing lightly against the silky wallpaper. Radiators in each room and hallway meant that she never experienced the nauseating smell of heating paraffin again. Visits to Mitcham Street were as rare as a sunny day in London. She encouraged her family to come and visit, but everyone stayed away.

She enjoyed the garden the most. It looked nothing like the fruit-laden trees back home, but just the open space reminded her of Jamaica and the land she had left behind. There were no bananas, no coconut or mango trees, no ackee; only one solitary apple tree that stood at the bottom of the garden.

In September, it bore the tiniest Cox apples. Eve picked, stewed and juiced every apple that came from the tree, making apple pies, apple crumble or sometimes just apple juice. But no sour cooking apple could replace the delicious taste of a Millie or a Julie mango. Nevertheless, this was now home.

***

Within months, reality slapped Eve in the face. She knew her husband drank and had an expansive social life, but now she felt that this side of him was beginning to interfere with their time together. She was so weak for so much of the time that she could not accompany him on his many business socials.

"Where have you been? Where are you going?" became her new and constant chant at Clement. Most nights he stumbled through the doors, his shirt hanging outside his trousers, his tie loose around the collar.

"I'm home, my dear wife," he would slur, or say "give me a kissss, wifey," and spray spittle all over her as his hands fumbled at her slight body.

"Where have you been?" Eve would ask.

"I'm back now, honey, so come give your husband some good loving."

"You're drunk again." She pulled herself from under him.

"Just a few with the boys, Eve. I'm not drunk. I drove home all by myself." He flashed his big teeth at her. "Say a prayer for me, Eve. Pray for me."

His words were slow and slurred as his heavy body slipped into sleep.

"Let's get you into bed," Eve said as she coaxed him up off the sofa so he could lay out comfortably.

She peeled off his jacket, his tie, shirt and trousers.

"Come to bed nuh, Eve?" he murmured. "Come to bed. I promise this won't happen again. I promise you Eve."

With that, he was out for the count.

"Mary, Mother of God, help me," Eve prayed.

This was her daily dance, the new married life. Clement, with all his flaws, was now all hers. He had given her more than she had ever dreamed conceivable and he loved her. He told her so. He had breathed life into her, and some days she was filled with such happiness, Eve felt she could just burst. Misgivings slipped in and out of her thoughts and she wondered how long her marriage would last, but didn't entertain the notions for too long. She pushed them aside and hugged dearly to each day, no longer feeling sick and ailing, but gasping for the breath of his love. *Just pray*, she kept telling herself. *But where are my rosary beads? Only the two of us in this big house. They can't be far.*

"What are you looking for?" he said the next morning, from behind her.

"I can't find Mummy's rosary beads anywhere. I've looked through each drawer and under the bed in all the rooms. Have you seen them?"

"No m'love. You can pray without them, can't you?"

"But I need them. I need them. They belonged to her."

"I'll buy you another rosary."

"It won't be the same, I need to find hers. They have to be in here somewhere," She said, crawling on her hands and knees.

For days, she searched for them but found nothing.

***

Eve longed for children of her own, but disappointments and caution from several doctors convinced her that childbearing would be almost impossible.

"Your body is not strong enough to endure childbirth," the doctors warned. "You or your child could die."

As she did when she decided to marry Blue, Eve tossed caution to the wind. *I've come this far,* she thought. *Who knows what I can do? I've survived two healthy parents, moved to another country; I've even forgiven God for taking my family from me. I've survived longer than anyone had expected, so I have nothing to lose.* The new treatment was working. She was breathing much easier. Although the doctors convinced her that she now had a longer life expectancy, they were not hopeful that her body could manage the birth of a baby. She and Clement tried and tried, but after two miscarriages and buckets of tears, Eve surrendered to barrenness. Thereafter, she poured her love into the garden.

For hours on her knees, she tended herbs and flowers as if they were her children. Esther had written from Jamaica telling of how much she enjoyed working the land, so Eve decided to follow her sister. Though Eve had acquired rose bushes from the previous owner of the house, she now planted daffodils and geraniums in the back garden. Clement built a rockery and an herb garden of rosemary, chives and basil. Some herbs she was unfamiliar with, but she gradually learned their value and how delicious a few sprigs of rosemary could taste on a leg of roasted lamb come Sunday.

Eve planted thyme and mint, and there was always a wonderful smell from every corner of the garden. All around the patio grew wild bluebells entwined with clusters of ivy and honeysuckle. From the French doors in her bedroom, she could smell the thyme and lavender. She savored the mingling scents and peace of her newly acquired wealth.

On the rare days when there was no rain, Eve went out to the garden and hung sheets on the wash line, letting the light wind blow the wetness from the laundry. Her neighbors on either side were so uncomfortable when she was working outside that Mrs. Goldberg would hide her whole body behind her washing to avoid talking to Eve.

Refusing to be ignored, she called to her. "Good morning, Mrs. Goldberg. How are you today?"

"Fine. Very fine," she mumbled, peering from behind her washing with an awkward smile and a nod.

"Pay them no mind, love, they don't know any better," were Aunt Pearl's words of comfort. "If they would just open up their little minds, they would know what they were missing. You're a wonderful person and would be such a good neighbor to them if they only gave you a chance."

The front garden gave Eve a better view of the comings and goings on the street, so she saved Saturday mornings for that garden. When more people were at home, she paid Milky and the paper boy promptly—and often in advance —to dispel any rumors that the Scotts lived above their means.

This notion was prompted when they woke up one morning to find a sign pinned a neat white paper sign to their door:

NIGGER GET OUT. WHITES ONLY. GO BACK HOME.

Eve cried at first, uncontrollably. "Don't cry," Clement said. "We are here to stay. This is our home. Don't let their ignorance scare you."

"It's your right, girl." Uncle Dudley reminded her. "Your father and Clement fought in both wars for them, so you have every right to be here. We've paid our dues, so don't worry about those silly words."

★★★

Eve sat in her bay window waiting for the postman, waiting for any news from home. She observed that Esther wrote often at first until Donovan came, but she still waited for her letters. How she envied Esther's life. She had Miss Ruby and Donovan were together. All Eve had was a house of empty potential.

She amused herself by reading some of her letters over and over. She had to read them herself, now that Austin wasn't speaking to her. In turn, she communicated with a pack of lies. *God forgive me, but I can't tell my sister the truth.* Eve replayed in her mind the messages and the stories Esther had written her. Sometimes her mind was so disturbed by the stories that Chris had told her, like the accounts of women being raped on the train. Those hurt her the most. Eve went as far as to wonder whether her dear Mummy, Aunt Daphne, or any of her cousins had been raped. Her eyes welled up with tears. A familiar nausea returned when she imagined the many indignities they might have suffered before they died at Kendal.

The only story Esther did not tell them was about Lucy.

What does it matter that I don't know my neighbors' names, what their husbands did, what schools their children attended? At Mitcham Street, we lived in and out of each of our neighbors' flats, but what should I care? I was now Mrs. Evelyn Mary Scott Jackson, mistress of 10 Orchid Crescent, owner of acres of land in Jamaica, married to one of the most successful and prominent Jamaican men in all of London. What do I care that my neighbors did not speak to me or did not welcome me?

Eve tried to fool herself into believing it didn't matter that she was lonely, that she missed Austin, missed her family. It was all, however, for naught. In the splendor of her new surroundings, she wept every day and night until the coming of Mrs. Harris.

★★★

Through his personal connections, Clement had arranged with the social services for Eve not to have any more hospital visits, but for a district nurse to come to her at home.

"I can't drive you back and forth, sit in the cold hospital waiting room for hours then drive you back home again. That's half my day gone," he complained.

The few times he accompanied Eve, he spent most of the time eyeing the nurses, instead of paying attention to what was being said about her health or progress. Her family, her beloved mother and Sarge, and even Esther, had scheduled their lives around her, and Eve was now certain that Clement could not—or would not—do for her what they had done for so long. And so came the need for a Mrs. Harris.

Mrs. Harris stood on the porch almost as wide and as tall as the door. Her large body was covered with a navy cape, and she looked something like an oversized superhero. Her brown hair, which was thinning at the temples, had more grey streaks than brown. It was pulled back into a tight bun that made Eve's head hurt just to look at her. Her Wedgwood-blue eyes peered over metal-framed glasses, and her blank expression remained after Eve opened the door.

"Good morning. I'm here to attend to Mrs. Jackson."

"I'm Mrs. Jackson," Eve said dryly.

"Mrs. Evelyn Jackson?" She glanced down at her clipboard, then back at Eve, squarely in the face, stuttering over the name. "Mrs. Eve-lyn Jackson?"

"Yes, I am she."

Her face turned several shades of red. "Oh, I am sorry, me dear." She fumbled over her words, clutching her nurse's bag for dear life with both hands. "Oh, I'm sorry. I didn't know c-c-coloreds lived on this street."

"Neither did I," Eve said calmly.

The woman gave an awkward smile. Eve stepped aside and gave the woman leave to enter.

"What a lovely home you have."

Her cold eyes scanned the hallway as she shed her cape and threw it carelessly over the nearby banister. She was light on her feet, considering how much weight she carried around the hips. Her starched uniform rustled like newspaper as she walked toward the master bedroom. Eve sat on the edge of the bed as the nurse efficiently measured medicine and prepared a syringe. She noticed that the woman hummed gently to herself.

Mrs. Harris first broke the awkward silence between them. "Are we ready for your treatment then, luv? Although a nice cuppa tea would do the trick before we got started."

"Oh, yes, that would be nice," Eve replied, "but you better make it."

"Not a problem, luvvy." She set about making tea. She made it strong and black.

"At least you came in." Eve smiled. "The last nurse refused to attend to me and left without taking the position."

"Oh, that was Betty Wilson. Silly woman. I'd heard about the fuss she made about "things not being satisfactory" at your address, but I didn't know what the reason was. Betty's always got something to gripe about. Well, me? I love to take care of people so you could be blue, black, green, or yellow. We're all God's children."

She leaned backwards and looked Eve over.

"You did throw me a bit back there, I must admit, but I'm sorry about what happened. Your color really don't make no difference to me. Not one iota. I'm widowed with three children, so I just want to do a good day's work to keep my kids fed. I was just genuinely surprised that some of these hoity-toities around here allowed you to settle on their street, that's all."

Without waiting for a response, she began massaging Eve's legs and joints. Soon, she had remade the bed, and to show how well she knew her business, she cheerfully fluffed the pillows as if Eve would be her only patient that day.

"So where in Africa are you from, then?"

"Excuse me…?"

"Aren't you African?"

"No, I'm not African; I'm from Jamaica."

"And where is that?"

"Jamaica is in the Caribbean Sea, near Haiti."

"Haiti? Never heard of it."

"Wait a second, I have a map. Let me show you." Eve walked over to a drawer and pulled out an old geography book. She opened the pages to

North America. "See? There we are…!" she gushed, pointing to the small shape of her homeland with pride.

"Ooh, it's not very big, is it?"

"It's big enough for us. Small, tough island, just like England."

They both threw back their heads and laughed.

Mrs. Harris was as amazingly punctual. She arrived at 11.30 a.m. sharp every other day. Not a minute before nor a minute after. Eve could set the clock by her and over the years that she visited and cared for her, Eve grew to depend on her to fill the empty days.

After the first week of visiting, Mrs. Harris announced, "I'm going to change my schedule."

"Oh, are we tired of Mrs. Jackson already?"

"No, Luvvy. I just love being around you. I learn so much and you're such a good patient, I decided I want to end my days with you before I go home to my monsters."

The days were filled with precision. Eve listened to the World Services and the soft tones of Una Marson, who brought news from home. That was when she liked to write home. Using every inch of the paper, Eve wrote detailed letters full of lies to Esther. Some days, her breathing was difficult and walking was more than a struggle, but she took every day in stride. *I'm married and alive. Not a day passes that I don't ache for my parents, for the laughter of Grace, for the teasing of Colleen and Cassandra, the constant bickering between Uncle Cork and Aunt Daphne.* The nurse couldn't replace any of them, but if she could just have a baby to keep her company, then she felt sure it would help to fill the void. Her entire ordeal would be worthwhile.

Although Aunt Pearl, Inez and Uncle Dudley visited regularly, Eve's heart ached for Austin. It had been almost a year since she had last seen him, but it seemed like a lifetime. She hadn't believed him when he threatened not to speak to her if she went ahead and married Clement. She thought he was just letting off steam, the way he usually did. Austin's absence threw a wet blanket on her life.

Eve once went to a wedding reception that her brother and Inez were attending. She thought it would be a chance to break the ice, sitting within striking range of him, hoping he would look over at her even once and smile, nod, give any kind of acknowledgment. But he gave her nothing. The highlight of the evening was Clement showing up drunk, flopping down beside her and then playing with her hair.

"Stop that," she whispered to him.

"Stop? Why, I can't touch you in public, dear wife?" he howled at her.

"Shh," she said, patting him on his knee. "Don't talk so loud."

Austin pushed his chair away and left the room. Eve's heart sank, but she soon felt a bit thankful, in a strange way, as shortly after Austin's exit, Clement leaned forward and vomited all over the brand new dress Inez had made for her.

"Clement, for heavens sake!" Eve yelped, jumping out of her chair.

"Oopsssh, I'm sooorrry, wifey," he slurred. But the shame of her husband's behavior did not compare with the relief she felt that Austin had not seen the humiliation.

TWENTY

Less than half an hour after Mrs. Harris' departure, the stillness of Orchid Crescent erupted in a cacophony of wailing sirens. Two police cars swerved up onto the pavement outside the house directly opposite Eve's. She stood like a ghost peering from behind the living room curtains, watching the activities at Number 9 with intense interest.

Eve jumped backwards with fright when she saw a police officer coming up the path to her front door, as fast as he could walk. He kept his finger on the doorbell far longer than was necessary. Eve waited awhile before responding, straightening her cardigan and skirt as she approached the door.

"Good afternoon, ma'am. Sorry to disturb you." The officer tilted his cap.

"How can I help you, Officer?"

"Have you seen this little girl?" He shoved an eight-by-eight photo of a child with shoulder-length red curly hair and brown freckles at the shaken lady of the house. The girl was dressed in a navy-blue school uniform.

"Little Sarah Cohen is missing. She lives at Number 9." He pointed across the street where his car had jumped the curb. The Cohen's front door was wide open. Eve stared at the school photo for a second.

"No, Officer. I haven't seen her for a few days. I don't get out much."

"Sorry to be a bother, ma'am."

"No bother at all. Sorry I couldn't be of more help. How awful for her parents. I hope you find her soon."

Eve closed the door behind her and made her way to the kitchen, wracking her brain: *When, exactly, was the last time I saw that little girl? Two days ago, I think, playing hopscotch in front of her house, her red hair bobbing up and down as she jumped from one square to another.* Eve sauntered into her kitchen to start the evening meal, but thoughts of Sarah still plagued her.

If only she'd been more attentive that morning, she thought, maybe she would have noticed a stranger hiding in the bushes watching her every move. She might have seen a van parked at the bottom of the street and some weirdo trying to offer her a lift to school, luring her with sweets or even money, God knows… If only she'd paid more attention to all those details that morning. Anything that would give the police a clue to help bring that little girl back safe and sound to her parents, she could have helped avoid the terrible pain they would feel if the police did not find her.

But she'd seen nothing, not even a happy little girl waving goodbye to her mummy, and clutching her leather satchel across her chest as she ran off to catch her school bus. Eve felt a lump in the pit of her stomach, the same lump that stayed there during the days her family was missing after the train crash. She tried to push Kendal out of her mind, but every calamity brought her saddest emotions back to the fore.

She opened a cabinet door and studied the rows of spices. Almost out of curry powder. Eve picked up the phone and called Clement.

An unfamiliar female voice answered, "Jackson & Associates."

"Oh hello," Eve said quite startled by the new voice.

"Who am I speaking with?"

"This is Miss Watkins," the chirpy voice replied. "How may I assist you?"

"I am Mrs. Jackson. Can you put my husband on the line, please?"

"He can't come to the phone right now. He's busy."

"Please ask him to call me when he is free." Eve settled the receiver on the stand, staring at it with scorn.

Who was Miss Watkins? How come Clement hadn't mentioned her to me? He had a new employee. How long had she been working there? Eve tried to concentrate on her cooking, but her thoughts kept slipping back to the chirpy voice. 'He can't come to the phone right now. He's busy.'

Who was she to tell me I can't speak to my husband? Her chopping accelerated with a vengeance until the knife slashed her index finger.

"Owww…!" she cried as she sucked on the finger. Eve grabbed paper towels from the nearby wall and sopped up the blood. Inner chaos was made worse by the trill of the phone.

"Hello, sweetheart." It was Blue. "You needed something?"

"Yes. I've just started cooking dinner."

"I'll be home a little late. Don't bother to cook for me."

"But I've already started," Eve protested.

"Okay. I'll be home soon, but I really can't stop long. Did you need something?"

"Well, I'll soon run out of curry powder—but more importantly, I wanted to tell you little Sarah is missing!"

"Who is Sarah?"

"The little red-headed school girl across the street from us. At number 9."

"Oh, that is Sarah," he paused. "I think I saw her today over by the Common."

"Over by which Common?"

"Clapham Common, darling. Maybe I should drive over there and see if she is still there."

"That's so far for a little girl to just wander off—shall I tell the police?"

"No. Let me just go back there and look first."

★★★

Eve could still hear Miss Watkins' voice circling inside her head.

"He can't come to the phone right now. He's busy."

"I've got to stop this broken record right now," Eve said aloud as she abruptly stopped cooking and ran toward the telephone. She pressed her index finger into the dial and began circling. "Seven, four, five… two, nine, nine, seven…" Inez' number was always on the tip of her tongue. For the first time, she spoke each digit as she dialed.

"Hello—Inez?"

"What's the matter dear? You sound a little upset."

"I'm wondering if you can clear up something that's bothering me," Eve said, already thinking she had been too impetuous.

"I was just thinking, do you know the new assistant working with Clement ?"

"Oh yes, Enid Watkins. Yes you know her family, too. They just send for her. Her mother asked me to find her a likkle work so I told her to call Clement… Eve, is she messing up his work? What did she do?"

Inez was beginning to get frantic.

"Oh no. She hasn't done anything wrong. I was just curious to know who she was, because Clement hadn't said a word to me about someone new working with him."

"Eve, you cannot be suspicious about every move your husband makes. You'll drive yourself crazy."

"Sorry I asked."

"I'm not scolding you my dear, but relax a little. Your husband is not all bad. And if it makes you feel any better, I hear the little miss likes women."

"Oh," Eve said nonchalantly, hiding her relief. "Okay Inez, thanks. Let me get back to my cooking. See you tomorrow. Bye."

Eve returned to the kitchen and put all her effort back into her cooking. She dipped the spoon into the pot and stirred briskly, then blew on it to taste the results. She closed her eyes, no longer embarrassed about calling Inez. *Mmmm... This curry sauce was almost as good as her mother's cooking,* she thought.

★★★

Within an hour, Clement was home with Sarah. He had her neatly wrapped in a blue blanket with diamond shapes on the edges. He handed the trophy to the Cohens, who had been inconsolable all day.

"She had fallen and sprained her ankle and couldn't move," he announced to her parents.

"Oh, thank you so much, Mr. Jackson. Come in. Come in."

"Oh thank you, thank you," cried Mrs. Cohen "How can we repay you for this?"

"You would do the same for me if I had kids, wouldn't you?"

From that moment on, they were the celebrated couple of Orchid Crescent, and they—actually, mostly Clement—became the Cohens' best friend. News spread quickly around the entire area that "Clement had found Sarah."

"Let me arrange an interview with the *South London Press* and the *Gazette* – I'm going to them right now." He skipped out of the room while Sarah clung to her mother.

Glowing headlines did not take long to appear.

LOCAL HERO OF ORCHID CRESCENT FINDS MISSING CHILD.

The front page headlines hung over the photo of Clement's big broad face.

Clement and Evelyn Jackson were invited to tea, the 25th wedding anniversary, to Mr. Cohen's promotion at the bank, Sarah's birthday party, and Jonathan's bar mitzvah. Any invitation to celebrate and they were invited. One minute, they were invisible and the next, they had risen to prominence.

"Oh, it's wonderful what your husband did," said Mrs. Goldberg, peering over the garden fence. "You must be so proud of him."

The whispers and rumors died down, and with it, the silence of Orchid Crescent died forever. Icy grins melted into warm smiles, and there were greetings on everyone's lips. Clement was complimented on his looks, his dress, and his manner.

Eve should have been happy that Sarah had been found and that she was safe. She should have been happy that she and Blue were now noticed and welcomed into the community of Orchid Crescent. She had waited so long to be embraced by the neighbors, to have tea with them, to talk about each other's families and to exchange recipes and favorite-television-programs talk over the garden wall. She wanted to tell them about her Jamaica, her real home, the land she loved and had left behind, the family she once had that was now just an aching memory. Now that the time she had longed for had finally come, it was shrouded with suspicion.

She was haunted by thouhgts of what Clement could have been doing by the Common in the middle of the day. *Who was the voice on the end of the phone at his office? Why had he not told Eve about his new employee? How had her husband known where to find Sarah? What if Clement himself had had something to do with the little girl being snatched?*

TWENTY-ONE

Flashing lights, fire engines and a mass of confusion greeted Austin as he turned the corner of the street. He walked faster, his tired legs leaden, his heart pounding. "Oh my God, please let Aunt Pearl and Uncle Dudley be safe." He pushed his way through curious onlookers and petrified neighbors who had spilled out into the streets like hot but curious lava.

Aunt Pearl was perched on a wall huddled under a coarse Army blanket.

"Aunt Pearl," Austin shouted as he raced toward her.

"Are you okay?"

"Yes, yes my dear." She clung to Austin for dear life. Her teeth chattered and her small body trembled against his.

"Thank God you're okay," he sighed with relief.

The firemen extinguished the last offending flames from the ground-floor rooms. The water from the hose hissed violently against the yellow flames, remaining insistent until the fire dissipated into plumes of black smoke.

"What happened?"

"Little Margaret's dress catch a fire on the paraffin heater. Poor Mrs. Duncan. Her girl burn up bad. Then the next thing we know the whole house gone up in flames. Every one of Vincent's books burnt to a cinder."

"You know how many times I tell that silly woman not to leave that little girl alone with that paraffin heater on. But no, she doesn't listen to me. If Vincent never call me, I woulda get trapped upstairs."

"Everyone move back please—move back!" The firemen roared, ushering the curious crowd backwards, creating a guard rail by locking arms. Mr. Carr emerged, bobbing on his wooden leg through the confusion and congestion toward Aunt Pearl.

"Who is responsible for this mess?" he yelled, as he threw his hands in the air.

"Don't you want to know if anyone is hurt?" said the fireman.

"You are responsible for this, gas stoves on the landing, paraffin heaters everywhere. It's no wonder the place didn't go up in smoke before now. These people have been living in a death trap, thanks to you, Mr. Money Bags! People like you should be hung, drawn and quartered!!" The fireman spat at him. He poked his gloved finger into the middle of Mr. Carr's chest as he heaved with anger.

"This is the third fire this week caused by these wretched paraffin heaters. There should be some kind of law against you landlords." He rattled on, his voice rising like the whirl of smoke above us.

"I hope you people have somewhere to go, because you can't go back in there."

"Not even to collect my things?" Aunt Pearl said.

"Everything is burnt to a crisp on the ground floor and we will have to check the rest of the house for safety. Which rooms are yours?"

"The ones at the top," she said, pointing.

"I think we caught the flames before they reached up there, but you still can't go in there right now.

"Do you have somewhere else you can stay?"

"I suppose I can go to my niece's house in Dulwich."

"Okay. Please make the necessary arrangements."

"Give us a few days and then if it is safe you can collect whatever is left of your things."

"Come on, Austin, call Eve."

"Call Eve and tell her what, Aunt Pearl?"

"Tell her that we'll have to stay with her for a few nights."

"I'm not going to Eve's house to stay. No way."

"Oh, Austin, why do you always have to be so difficult? I am too tired tonight to argue with you. How long are you going to keep up this nonsense? I'll call her myself." She stomped off, the blanket slipping from around her shoulders and dragging on the pavement. Austin searched his mind for a solution.

"Aunt Pearl, wait for me," he called after her. "I'll find somewhere else to stay. I'll stay with Inez or at a friend's house, but I can't and won't live under Clement Jackson's roof. I can't give him the pleasure."

"This would be a good time to settle your differences with them. Since your sister has been married, you haven't visited her once. Your father would roll over in his grave if he knew this was how you were treating her."

"That is exactly why I can't go there. I have not been there at all. I have my pride too, Aunt Pearl. I would rather be homeless."

"Swallow your pride, Austin."

Austin removed his coat and placed it around Aunt Pearl's shoulders. "Don't worry about me, I'll be okay. I didn't come to England to cause you any pain or trouble. I will help you when we can get back in the house to move." she said, softening her tone.

"What about the partner money?"

"Look." She pulled out a big brown bulging envelope. Her face lit up.

"When Vincent called me, I was counting the money. I just pushed the envelope in my pocket and ran out of the house. All I really want in the flat now is Grace's photos. Everything else I can live without. Even me china cabinet." She nudged him, grinning like a Cheshire cat.

"I'll call Dudley at work. We will have to take Vincent with us too," Aunt Pearl said, nodding at him.

"I am sorry about your papers, Austin."

"Not to worry, Mr. Vincent. All my learning should already be in my head anyway."

"Come on, Vincent. We're going to Eve's."

The three of them cut through cold night air to the corner phone box to call Eve. Austin put them into a taxi. He, in turn, deposited himself and his pride in the safe love of Inez.

***

Two weeks later, Austin kept his promise and followed Aunt Pearl back to their former home. The apartment house was now just a scarred hulk and a pile of debris. Aunt Pearl mopped the sweat from her brow. The pair pushed their way through the charred rubble. When evening arrived, they had not found Grace's photo.

"That's all I want out of this mess. Where is it? Where?!" Aunt Pearl said, her frustration palpable. They struggled through the debris, cursing the weakness of the street light.

"Aunt Pearl, we'll have to come back another day when the light is good."

"Where can it be?" she murmured. "It has to be here somewhere."

Both their knees were covered in grime, eyes sore and burning from the soot and stifling air, but they continued to scan through the rubble. Aunt Pearl thrust her hands, now stiff and painful, back into the cold ashes.

"Please God, let it be here," she prayed.

Seeing a sudden glint in a pile of broken glass fragments, she pulled out the cherished image and kissed it. It was blackened, but only by ash and smoke. She could easily make it good as new. "There you are," she said.

Austin brushed the soot from his trouser leg and wiped the black grime from his hands onto his handkerchief. Wrapping his arms around his Aunt Pearl's shoulder, Austin whispered, "It's finished. Let's go home."

★★★

It wasn't always love that propelled Austin regarding Inez. When he abruptly decided to move in with Inez, it was pride. He would not and could not humble himself enough to live under Clement Jackson's roof. *I can't accept charity from dat boasy bwoy they call my brother-in-law,* he said to himself, thinking he would rather die first. If Inez would not have him, he'd join the ranks of the homeless under Waterloo Bridge rather than live in the same house with Eve's husband.

Inez had been waiting for him and only she knew that one day he'd come to her. She asked no questions about how long he might stay, for she had no rules about housekeeping. She welcomed him with an open heart and mind. It was strange how things turned out; in his foolish arrogance, he resisted the idea at first, not wanting her to "get any ideas in her head about marriage." As far as Austin was concerned, he was going back to Jamaica, so marriage wasn't on the table. *Wives cost too much money anyway and staying with Inez for a while is my cheapest option,* he selfishly told himself.

Inez, Austin admitted, was all any man could desire of a woman. She was a beautiful, sensuous, caring and ambitious woman. His heart, however, was as cold as concrete since the death of his family. He felt that life had dealt him an unfair hand and he could not shake his anger at being robbed of his loved ones. While Aunt Pearl pushed and pulled him in different directions and Uncle Dudley coaxed and coerced him into his social activities, Inez simply allowed Austin to indulge in his pain, anger, and self-pity. When he chose to be still and quiet, she said nothing. When he ranted and raved about how much he hated England, she held her own counsel.

"I'm not staying in this bloody cold country much longer. As soon as I finish my studies, I am getting the hell home. Home is where I belong." he yelled. Inez allowed him to dream his foolish dreams, too. She never voiced that she would not go home with him or whether or not she wanted to marry him. She never scolded him in his self-pity, nor did she ask questions about his parents or try to get him to talk about Kendal the way Uncle Dudley did.

So many times, Austin wanted to just pour out his heart to her. He wanted her to know how much he missed her parents, how he felt that life was so unjust, letting so many who deserved to die live, but could not spare his family. He just could not say those words out loud. Instead, everything remained locked inside. Her presence was the only thing that consistently soothed him.

There were days when he thought he'd go clear out of his mind. There were nights when Austin could only think of Sarge, nights when he imagined he could will his father to surface from the wreckage and come home. His father was so fearless. He had survived a war; if anyone should have survived that train crash, he should have been the one. Although Austin was forever grateful for Donovan's return, Sarge should have returned too.

When Austin was a boy, Sarge took him everywhere. He believed that Austin spent too much time around the womenfolk. "You'll be a sissy," his father mocked, and kept his son hungry for hours or left him sitting in the police station while he took care of other business.

He'd wake the boy up in the middle of the night and walk him through pitch-black country roads.

"You're going to be a man one day," he'd say, "and if anything happens to me, you have to know how to take care of your mother and your sisters. How are you going to take care of anyone if you're afraid?"

"He's too young, he's just a baby," Mother would quarrel with Father.

"Ruth, you're raising the boy too tender. He's going to be a man one day."

Now the boy was a man. He was not as fearless as Sarge wanted him to be, but neither was he as tender as Sarge feared. Despite being honest about his shortcomings, Austin considered himself a 'good man.' He was so accustomed to living with his two sisters that all Sarge had taught him did not help him now. Being so close to his sisters prepared him for his existence with Inez and Marge. *How could I marry a woman like Inez when I have nothing to give her? No money, no love, no heart, nothing to make her feel secure…*

***

After the fire, the three of them, Marge, Inez and Austin lived together in a tiny one-bedroom flat. There wasn't enough room to swing a cat, but they managed. Marge and Inez shared the bed and Austin took the lumpy settee in the living room-cum-dining-room-cum sewing room.

Sometimes Marge slept at her boyfriend's house. He was a young man from Barbados and there was nothing about him that found Inez' approval. Austin thought he was an alright chap, but Inez didn't think him worthy of her cousin. They had some privacy when Marge stayed with him, but in the small cramped space, they generally lived like one. There were no quarrels about money, housework or cooking. And almost no sex.

Lovemaking was rare in the new domestic arrangement, but intense when it found freedom. Inez loved to straddle Austin like an experienced rider. He, at first, wasn't very comfortable about a woman taking the lead. But her sexual dominance gradually aroused him even more, and he allowed her to take control. Although he did not ever consider her a promiscuous woman, Austin often wondered where she acquired those particular skills. He wasn't ready to hear the truth, on account of how blunt Inez could be at times.

Austin was plagued with thoughts that she and Clement might have been lovers, but he knew better than to ask, because he could not ever settle with that knowledge, if it were true. So he reconciled himself to the indulgence of enjoying every moment with her, nestling between her voluptuous thighs and dreaming that he had died and gone to heaven.

There was no more sneaking around the back of the house, no more zinc fences and worn linoleum floors, his pants flagging around his ankles, his bottom bare to the world. There were no more days of creaking bedsprings or muffled moans. They were free to express this love in whatever natural way they felt.

Inez would lay him down on soothing rose- or lavender-scented sheets and rub him down with oils that hypnotized him. She caressed Austin's slender frame from head to toe with her soft hands and sucked on his navel, which sent his strong heart stampeding. When he was sick with a cold, which was fairly often, she rubbed his chest with her concoctions of vapor rub and almond oil. She even brewed dried mint leaves she had found in a tea shop on the cobblestone streets of Covent Garden.

The touch of her lips was like that of no other woman he had known. Austin would wake up in the middle of the night hot with sweat from his nightmares of Kendal. If she was working at her sewing machine, she would stop as soon as she heard him stir, come over to the bed, lay down beside him, rub his head, massage his temples, and caress and soothe him back to sleep. No matter how early he tried to wake the next morning to do something nice for her—like make her a cup of tea or prepare some toast—she was always up and dressed before he was.

Like an Obeah woman, Inez erased all the memories of his worst hurt, and although no one could replace his mother's love, being in Inez' arms was sheer ecstasy. The longer Austin stayed with her, he knew in his heart that as much as he wanted to go back to Jamaica, he could not leave her behind. How could he not marry a woman like her? But he just couldn't. He wanted to go home. *I must go home. I need to do the things that I set out to do,* he kept telling himself.

***

Many nights, he watched Inez hunched over the sewing machine with the dim light of a desk lamp, listening to the rustling of wheels and the humming of the pedal, intently making colored fabrics into amazing creations. Just the simple color of a piece of thread excited her. Nothing was too difficult or too much to ask of her. What he loved most about Inez was her passion for her life and her craft.

Inez came from the country, without certain privileges, but she knew more than he did about British politics and social issues. Since she had arrived in England, she taught herself etiquette, and improved her reading, discovering all kinds of books from Shakespeare to C.L.R. James. She listened to the World Services when she sewed, and studied the news so she could hold a conversation with just about anyone on just about anything.

She was friendly around Austin's family, could break into patois if she wanted to, but at any given opportunity she had in which to socialize with the English nurses or hospital officials, she'd drop everything to be with them. She observed their mannerisms, which helped her to iron out any of the lingering cultural wrinkles from her below-poverty upbringing. She listened carefully to the way they spoke and worked incessantly to change her Jamaican lilt into a more controlled British tone. She sometimes even corrected him.

Bloody cheek, Austin often thought to himself, because he had come from 'privilege and class' and didn't need the likes of her to tell him how and what to say. But he suffered his irritations in silence, because he knew her corrections came with no malice. She was a chameleon who could slip in and out of the various dialects, from cockney to standard English to patois with ease, although she limited her patois to a bare minimum. Often when he closed his eyes, he couldn't think of her as Jamaican.

Inez had as many books as she had yards of fabric. Austin's worries about not wanting to marry her soon began to disappear, because as much as she loved him, nothing or no one was going to get in the path of her success. It even dawned on him that Inez didn't care one iota whether he proposed to her or not; she was so driven by her own ambitions.

Having sung her praises—mostly to himself—there were two things about her that drove Austin crazy. *I sound like an ungrateful bastard, I know, but they bother me no end.* First, Inez never cooked. All his life, he had been surrounded by women who cooked and pampered him. Miss Ruby, his mother, Aunt Pearl, his sisters, all fussing, cooking and caring for him. Austin had no idea how to cook and it never occurred to him that he could or should learn.

His palate soon adjusted to the various foods being prepared and cooked outside. They went to the chippy and often ate steak and kidney pies, Cornish pastries and sausage rolls from the local bakery. All the home-cooked meals were now being served up at Eve's house, but as long as the family was living with Eve, those scrumptious curry dinners prepared by Aunt Pearl became a thing of the past. He was simply not going to Eve's house, not even for a plate of rice and peas and curry chicken, which he missed—oh, how he missed that cooking.

The second thing that bothered him was Inez' tight friendship with Clement Jackson. There was nothing that Austin could do about that either. Inez and Eve were close and so he relied totally on Inez for information about his sister. Austin never probed her, but on occasion she'd spoon-feed him like a baby with tidbits of the happenings in his sister's household. He was sure Inez was prone to omit any part of Eve's life with Clement that she knew would tick him off. As loyal as she was to Austin, she never spoke an ill word about Blue in his presence.

God, how he missed his sister.

"Don't whisper a word of evil," his mother always told him. "Think evil thoughts, then evil things happen. Do bad, and bad follows you. Do good and good walks behind you."

Her soft voice rested in his memory. But every time Austin thought of Clement Jackson or heard his name, the blood in his body simmered, ready to bubble over.

TWENTY-TWO

Austin's darling Inez was always immaculately dressed. Not a day went by when she wasn't wearing something outstanding and unique. She never left home without her face made up, her lips painted with ruby-red lipstick and every strand of her short hair intact. She was not the definition of Jamaican beauty as he had been conditioned to believe a woman should be, but she was the most stunning woman he had ever laid eyes on.

He often saw English women with hair rollers hiding under a scarf or slippers they had dragged onto their feet when they popped out to the corner shop, but not his Inez. When she stepped out of the house, she was dressed for the world to see her and to see her appearance as her trademark. In fact, when Austin thought back, he had no recollection of ever seeing her in an old ragged dress or nighties.

She left the house one particular evening in the middle of winter in a two-piece orange brocade suit. She had just finished it over the weekend. The jacket had raglan sleeves, was cut short and sat on the round of her bottom. The skirt stopped just below her knees. Her long knee-high leather boots gave her legs no chance to be exposed to the winter air.

She had sewn false flaps on the front to look like real pockets, although if she had not pointed it out to him, he would not have been any the wiser. She hated fooling around with pockets on a garment that was not making her any money, so all the shortcuts went into her clothes. Just as she lavished Austin with love and affection, she indulged her customers with tiny tucks, hand-sewn sequins, beads, and lace. Nothing was too much for her creations. When she was overloaded, she commissioned Eve's help. Rain or shine, Inez was the perfect student. She never missed class no matter how tired she was. Austin studied until she returned home, and they ate whatever dinner she brought home.

One particular night, she burst through the doors like a gust of wind.

"Wake up," she said as she prodded her lover in the chest. He opened his eyes to see the clock glaring *10.30 p.m.* He had dozed off over his books. "Guess what?" she said. "My teacher invited a special guest to our class tonight. I've been given a great assignment. I can finally leave my lousy job. My days are numbered there."

"What happened?" said Marge, rising from under the candlewick bedspread, where she had dozed off on the settee. "Did we win the pools yet?"

"No, no, not yet, but I am going to work for the Queen."

"Which Queen? What are you talking about? Have you been drinking?" Marge said.

"Shut up and listen. I am going to work at Buckingham Palace under the supervision of Norman Hartnel," said Inez.

"Who's Norman Hartnel?" Austin asked excitedly.

"Her designer," she paused, prodding Marge. "Are you hearing me? He has chosen me to be one of the collaborators for the Queen's spring wardrobe. There are several state dinners and foreign diplomats who will be coming, and I've been commissioned to design one of her new dresses."

Nothing Inez said made any sense to them yet, but they both sat bolt upright and paid attention. *Inez was going to do what? Work for the Queen?!*

"How much will you get paid? And when do you start?"

"All the details will be sent to me through Mr. Hartnel's secretary. They will send a car to collect me and take me to the Palace on the nights I will be working there."

"You are going to Buckingham Palace? Lawd have mercy, wait till I tell the people at work," Austin said.

"In the meantime, I have to come up with a dozen evening dresses. I'll have to cancel all my other assignments and find someone to make the dress for Cherry's wedding." She paced the floor, mumbling to herself.

"You can't do that," piped in Marge.

"Don't start losing your mind. You will get a bad reputation all through South London if you suddenly abandon your local customers."

"But this is for the Queen of England, don't you get it? Her Majesty Queen Elizabeth the II."

"Yes, and when the queen is still in Buckingham Palace not thinking about you, it's your community that you'll have to face," Marge said, sounding just like so many people's mother. "You have to come back to Miss

Charmaine and make christening gowns and other dresses for her sisters."

"Think, girl, think," Marge shook her shoulders.

"Find a way to work it out, but don't cancel her."

"You're right, you're right," Inez conceded. You are always my con-science." She kissed her cousin on the forehead.

"Tomorrow I'm going to call in sick. I have so much to do to be ready for my meeting with Mr. Hartnel." Inez kissed Austin and rushed down the stairs.

"Where are you going this time of night?" he yelled from the top of the flight.

"To call Eve. I'll need her help." Before Austin could catch her to hand her a coat, she had reached the door, flown the lock and dashed outside into the night.

★★★

There were eight meetings in a quaint tea shop in St. James' Park before Inez finally set her foot inside the Palace walls for the first of several trips to work inside England's most fabulous house. On one of those great occasions, Austin decided to go along with Inez. *Why not? When would I ever have the chance to see inside Buckingham Palace? If they turn me back, at least I tried.*

Austin had taken the afternoon off from work, lying to his supervisor that his aunt was sick so that he could be home on time and not fight the evening rush hour or make Inez late. The gleaming black Bentley arrived promptly at the Palace, stopping at the Service Area to the the south of the building at 6.30 p.m. They were received by uniformed guards at the Royal Mews, some of whom were familiar with Inez's cheerful face.

"Good evening, Miss Wright... And who do we have 'ere then?"

"My husband," she lied. "He's just come along to keep me company," Inez said with quick assurance.

"Sign here, sir," the guard said, raising an eyebrow at Austin.

The Palace at this end was much less grand than the Eastern entrance with its main facade and ceremonial gallery. Still, it exceeded Austin's capac-ity to imagine it before he saw it.

At the end of a long corridor, they took a left turn, passing several por-traits of one King George, a King Edward and some others, and then a right turn into a small anteroom that fronted the Ballroom. Before she settled down to work, Inez made sure Austin was shown how to find the toilets.

Soon, Austin got to meet the famous Norman Hartnel. He was a tall, slender man who wore a beige herringbone wool suit and two-tone brogues that you could see the world in. He sported a large gold ring with an emerald on his little finger. His upright posture made one immediately want to straighten up one's own back. His hair was parted on the left side of his face and some premature grey was evident at his temples. Brylcream, or something like it, held down any stubborn strands. He pronounced every word with precision, as if he had a plum in the middle of his mouth. He was more than likely 'the other way', as they would say. You know, 'queer,' but it didn't bother Austin. In his way of thinking, his Inez would be safe with Hartnel.

"Mr. Wright, such a pleasure to meet you."

Austin shook his hand without correcting the name.

"Likewise."

Austin forced a smile to go with the handshake, then sat quietly in the corner of the room. The dim light forced his eyes to narrow as he read the small print of a newspaper, while Inez and the others worked furiously on an emerald-green organza skirt. Inez held tiny pins in the corner of her mouth. Not once did she speak to him, but she looked over and gave him that magical smile without losing a single pin from her pursed lips.

The team of designers had tape measures around their necks, plus chalk, scissors and various other tools. They worked without a word spoken amongst them. A penciled sketch design, attached to an easel served as the Bible for the team.

A large door creaked slightly as it opened, and two officious women walked in. Behind them stood the Queen. The actual Queen. Two ladies in waiting followed about a yard or more behind her.

Austin's newspaper fell to the floor and his heart skipped some beats. He wanted the wallpaper to devour him so Inez wouldn't get into any trouble for having him there, but it was too late. He had stood as still as a statue but the paper fell off his knees to the floor, exposing him with its gentle flutter.

Her green eyes met his and Austin bowed his head.

"Who is this, Mr. Hartnel?" her Majesty said, looking directly at Austin.

"Mrs. Wright's husband, Mum. We got clearance from the guards."

She nodded in a small movement of her head and reached out her hand for Austin to take. It was as soft as any hand he had ever felt, and she smiled at him with that reassuring way only the high-born take for granted.

The Queen was much smaller than he had imagined her. It was hard to believe that the entire British Empire rested on the shoulders of someone so young and petite. Her face had a pallidness to it, but she was an exceptionally attractive woman. Her thick brown hair, swept off her face in tiny waves across her head, shone with health beneath the dim light. Austin had never seen her without something on her head. No crown, no hat, not even a scarf. She turned toward Inez and reached out the same hand in welcome.

Inez, in return, curtseyed as she had been shown when she was a schoolchild, lowering both her knees and bowing her head (she had been advised by Mr. Hartnel that the depth of the curtsy was very important).

"I'm hoping you will add a little bit of Caribbean flair to my evening gown collection," the Queen chuckled.

"Mr. Hartnel informs me that you are from the Caribbean colonies." The word 'colony' stuck in Austin's throat like a fishbone. He tried to swallow without showing it.

"My favorite, of course, is Jamaica. My father, King George, took me there when I was a girl and I returned not long after. I had the most delightful time there. How long have you been here?"

"Ten years, Ma'am. I came on the *Empire Windrush*," Inez replied, her voice croaking as she answered.

"You must be frightfully homesick…?"

"Yes Ma'am, but I do like it here," she responded quickly.

"Well, we have to make sure we compensate you enough so you can take a nice trip home—but after my dresses are finished, of course," she chortled. Inez nodded and made sure her laugh did not exceed the Queen's.

They stood the whole time while the Queen kept her hands in front of her, as if she were lost without a handbag or a scepter to hold onto. Austin stood with his hands behind his back and tried not to shake or rock, but he was so nervous he found it extremely difficult.

"Well, it was so nice to meet you, Inez." Queen Elizabeth II, ruler of the United Kingdom, Canada, Australia, New Zealand, South Africa, Pakistan and Ceylon left the room. Everyone stood at attention. Nobody was at ease until it was certain she was out of the reception hall. Then a collective sigh filled the air.

***

At the end of her tenure at the Palace, Inez was paid a thousand pounds, given a sealed letter of recommendation and a set of official photographs of the Queen wearing her new dresses at state events. Inez' name was never published in the papers in connection with the pieces. Mr. Hartnel took all the credit; that was the protocol of the Palace. Inez didn't seem to care at all; she had money in the bank, a round trip ticket with British Overseas Airways Corporation to go home and visit her family and a letter of reference from the Palace.

"This is enough to get me started with my own company. Inez Designs. Can you see it?" A smile ran across her face.
Inez returned to the hospital to collect the belongings she kept in her locker.

"What are you doing, Inez?" the matron asked.

"I'm resigning as of today," she said, as she handed in her letter. "I just came to collect my things, if you don't mind."

"But you cannot just leave like that, Inez. You have to give proper notice and all the paperwork takes time—and where will you go?"

The Matron stuttered over her words. "You cannot just throw away a good job like that. You'll never get a reference if you do it this way."

"Where I'm going Matron, I don't need a reference." She flashed her cheekiest gap-toothed smile while she stuffed her belongings into a carrier bag.

"What's going on?" came the voices around the exit Inez was preparing.

"Inez is leaving." By now all the orderlies had gathered around them.

"Good on you, girl," shouted one of the nurses.

"Good luck, my love," were the echoes she heard as she walked with an inner warmth she had not felt since she had arrived in London. All the hospital staff cheered and clapped as she exited the doors.

"Don't forget us when you're rich and famous!"

***

Inez moved into a bigger flat and for the first time in years, she lived in a house with an inside toilet and bathroom. There was now a room where she could sew and a parlor in which to entertain customers. Visitors came to the house, saw the two photos of the Queen perched on the top of the coffee table and wondered why Inez was so patriotic. It was not until they looked closely at the photos that they saw her name written in the Queen's own hand.

Thank you, Inez, for making me look so beautiful.
Elizabeth R.

That was impressive, and those who had judged her unfairly now revered her.

The royal car that arrived for Inez had caused a lot of gossip in the neighborhood and soon Inez was sewing for everyone. The summer months were her busiest time as her clientele grew. Her clients needed summer dresses for leisure at Bournemouth, Brighton and Butlins summer camps.

Inez was now soaring and Austin was genuinely happy for her. He knew that any hope of her returning to Jamaica with him was now lost forever. Do I love Jamaica more than I do Inez? Could I really live without her and start a life again with someone else? There was a lot to think about.

Soon after the glorious Buckingham Palace adventure, Austin found a crumpled air mail letter amongst some magazines. He unfolded it, assuming it was from Esther, but when he looked closer at the handwriting it was clearly not his sister's. He read it anyway.

Dear Inez,
Hope fine. Thanks for the postal order you send me and the nice photograph of the Queen. Is you really make that dress in the picture? When you have time to do all that when you working at the hospital? Don't form the fool and lose you good nurse job. We glad to see you whenever you can come home. Ever boddy dying to see you. We are all doing fine and your brothers send them love.
Your loving father.

Austin folded the thin blue airmail letter and smiled. One of these days I'll take Inez back to Happy Grove and introduce myself to her father as her husband.

He placed the letter exactly where he'd found it, between the two old copies of *Life* magazine being put out with other paper for garbage collection. That was when he saw it. There, in the same spot was another air letter, addressed to someplace in Jamaica, but crumpled before anything was written inside, except for the words "Dear Pappa" in his girlfriend's distinctive handwriting. It struck him then, once and for all, that Inez was never going to Jamaica. Why should she go back to her nothingness? He doubted if he could coax her to live where he had lived in Kingston. That was not enough to satisfy her yearning, the things she dreamed of. If he were to keep Inez, he would have to change his ideas about England.

TWENTY-THREE

As selfish as it sounds, Eve was more than a little glad for the fire. It bought her family back to her. Where else could they go? She had seen so little of Aunt Pearl and Uncle Dudley since she got married. They came to her reluctantly, but thank God they came. Finally, the bedrooms on the top floor were filled. One was also ready and waiting for Austin. She hoped and prayed that the day would come when he would sleep there.

The Scott family refugees had been the luckiest of all the Mitcham Street tenants. Miss Clarke lost everything, including little Margaret, who did not survive her burns. Mr. Vincent attended to her until the ambulance came. She struggled for life for four days and four nights and on the fifth day surrendered her soul. Miss Clarke, devastated by the loss of her only child, took a train to Liverpool to her cousin's house and was never heard from again. Even Margaret's death did not stir Eve enough to feel any remorse for having her family back.

Aunt Pearl was able to rescue her beloved photo gallery and the china cabinet, with everything intact at that.

"Some hot soapy water will get the soot off everything," Mrs. Harris advised.

"We will have them looking spic and span, good as new in no time," she said with her usual optimistic sing-song voice.

"Thank you, Jesus," Uncle Dudley rejoiced.

"Me radiogram and all me records survived too." Uncle Dudley bent down and kissed a jazz LP from his beloved record collection.

The cellar was packed to the brim with the rescued books, clothes, and furniture. Eve's home now bounced with the energy that she knew in Jamaica. *God has delivered them to me. He has answered my prayers and as long as I can keep them there with me, I will*, she thought.

"Don't worry. We won't be staying long." Uncle Dudley assured.

"You can stay as long as you want, Uncle Dudley."

"No, you're are newlyweds. You don't need all of us hitching up under you," he persisted. "It's just not right."

"Come Monday morning, we will start looking for somewhere to live."

"You can stay here as long as you want. There is plenty of room for all of us to be comfortable," boasted Clement who had popped in on one of his usual cameo appearances at home.

"Any room upstairs is yours. There is even room for Austin if he changes his mind.

"Everything happens for a reason. Now is the time to bridge the gap between us and really be a family again," Aunt Pearl said, nodding as she spoke.

"Make yourselves comfortable. I'm off to a meeting." Clement kissed Eve on the cheek and closed the front door behind him.

One month raced into six more and no matter how hard they searched for a place, from East London to South London, Pearl and Dudley found nothing. They even looked as far as Notting Hill Gate. All the signs for rooms to rent had the same message in their windows.

NO DOGS
NO IRISH
NO COLOREDS

"Every room and flat I have looked at seems to be worse than the one before," Aunt Pearl complained as she rubbed her aching feet. "I looked at a place yesterday; the wallpaper was peeling from the wall. Not even a decent piece of carpet on the floor, and then when the landlady opened the kitchen door, mice scurried to their homes in the wainscot."

"'Never mind them,' she had the nerve to say to me."

"Never mind dem, nuh? I wouldn't put a dawg to live in a place like that , much less me family. I run out of that place so quick, I never even say goodbye. Maybe we should try to buy a place. Dudley try and get some extra work and I will do a double shift at the hospital."

"You don't have to do that Aunt Pearl," Eve pleaded. "There's enough space for all of us here."

"Darling Eve, we can't be dependent on you and Clement. It is not a good way to start a marriage, with all your people in your house one time."

"That's how we lived in Jamaica, Aunt Pearl. Look how long Aunt Martha and her family lived with us, and then there was the time Uncle Cork and Aunt Daphne stayed when they first moved to town and even you and Uncle Dudley lived with us for a while before you came here."

"Chile, that was a different time. How we lived in Jamaica can't work the same way here."

"Why not? We can try. We can start a new Jamaica in London."

"No, me sweetheart. Eve, you are still a girl and so naive you already got three people too many in your house. We will work harder and save everything so we can get somewhere quick."

Eve listened to Aunt Pearl's moans and groans about her aunt's search, but secretly longed and prayed that their attempts would continue to be futile so that they would have to stay with her. With them there, the emptiness of the house disappeared, gradually beginning to look, smell, feel and vibrate like a real home. Eve didn't want to lose that just after she had found it.

Clement was gone all day and most evenings. The family filled the void of Eve's long and lonely days. They cheered up her dampened spirits and distracted her from the despair and disillusionment of her marriage. Clement put up a good show in front of them and for a while no one suspected anything—or so she thought.

It didn't take Uncle Dudley long to adjust and, sooner than Eve was prepared for, the domino games began on the posh dining table. Uncle Dudley's friends were now traipsing through the house the way they had at Mitcham Street.

How grown men could talk so much foolishness over a box of small white tiles was beyond Eve. But she relished the sounds of clattering and slamming and the boisterous chatter. Her home was alive again and she wanted it to stay that way forever.

Aunt Pearl was now revered throughout the community. She had restored the missing partner money. Wagging tongues and false statements swept through the community. Some said, "Miss Pearl run into the burning house and grab our money. She brave, you see."

No matter how everyone tried to dispel these stories, they grew and grew and Aunt Pearl became a larger-than-life figure among her crowd.

Everyone wanted to save their money with her. The partner scheme grew to such a level that even Clement got involved in banking the money.

"It's not wise to have so much money in the house, Aunt Pearl," Clement warned her. "I'll take it to the bank on Mondays."

Mr. Vincent soon joined the family, too. He had no relatives in London to stay with and his exams were approaching. Leaving London was not an option. He had lost everything, every book, file, scrap of paper, his passport, clothing, even the photo of his beloved family. Everything burnt to a cinder. But he never uttered a word about his loss. He stayed quietly in his room quietly, went to work, gradually bought many books again and continued his studying as if nothing had happened. To him, Mitcham Street never existed, just like the memories of his homeland, while Eve clung to every memory of home.

He spoke less and less and for hours stayed locked away in his room. Out of respect for Eve he never smoked inside the house. Most nights he joined Aunt Pearl at the bottom of the garden by the apple tree. Hunched at the shoulders, and with collars upturned, they puffed on their cigarettes in the freezing cold.

"I've found a small room in Brick Lane," Mr. Vincent announced out of the blue one night.

"Brick Lane! You can't go there," Eve insisted.

"I can't stay here any longer. You have been so good to me but I must not outstay my welcome. In my country, this is unacceptable behavior for a man of my stature."

"We don't want you to go. You are part of our family, Mr. Vincent. Aunt Pearl and Uncle Dudley are saving to buy a house. Why don't you just wait until they move and you can move with them? We won't let you go to another one of those awful tenement homes. Brick Lane is the worst area in London for us. It is not safe there at nights with those Teddy Boys roaming the streets, beating up any black man they can get their hands on," Austin pleaded.

"But it is near the hospital, and easy to get to work."

"No," everyone said in unison.

Vincent clutched his Woolworth carrier bag tightly. He stood tall with nothing but his pride and the clothes on his back. His eyes were sad but too proud to shed a tear.

"I am unaccustomed to this manner of kindness, but I thank you for it. All I have lost is not important. It is what is on the inside—in my head and my heart—that matters more. From my heart I thank you for your generosity. I will repay you one day. I promise. I can still take my exams without my books." He paused.

"I need to talk to Austin, to encourage him not to give up," said Mr. Vincent.

"Don't worry about Austin. He's in good hands with Inez," Aunt Pearl said with a smile.

"Good night and thanks again from the bottom of my heart." He bowed his head and left the room.

Vincent climbed the stairs to his room, slowly and precisely. In the middle of the night, Eve could hear him pacing the floor reciting his knowledge for his exams, praying, humming. Then one night it came. His tears from years of pain and disappointment flooded his empty nights. Eve knew those tears, because she had cried them all before he came. She had mourned the loss of her family, and cried for the injustices God had chosen for her. She also cried over her love for Clement, too proud to say to Austin, "You were right." Mr. Vincent cried for all of us.

Of all the people in the household, it was Mr. Vincent who Eve watched over the most. Old enough to be her father, he was like her child. Aunt Pearl had her cigarettes and Uncle Dudley was her rock. Austin was his own master and Austin had Inez, but Mr. Vincent was as vulnerable as a newborn.

Eve never let on—especially not to Mr. Vincent—that she heard him cry at nights. She respected and loved him too much to embarrass him. He had a vision as clear and as strong as Austin's, and a passion as deep as Esther's. And how could she not love a man who was so committed to his dream, when he had sacrificed his family, dedicated his soul to become a doctor to return to his homeland to heal his people? How could one not love him?

★★★

The arrival of Madge's daughter was cause for the family's biggest celebration ever, even bigger than when Inez worked with the Queen, or when Aunt Pearl was promoted to matron, which Claudia Jones splashed across the front page of the West Indian Gazette. Madeline's party was more elaborate than Aunt Pearl's and Uncle Dudley's housewarming. Cakes were baked and decorated weeks before her arrival. Colored balloons floated in the corners of her room; the house was buzzing with excitement. All of Inez' customers wanted to be a part of the welcoming party, bringing plates of food and toys for the newcomer.

Aunt Pearl unlocked her china cabinet for the third time and every single item in it was used. An army of friends and family trudged up to the West End to Bourne & Hollingsworth and bought out the entire toy department.

Aunt Pearl, Madge, Inez and Eve stood on the cold platform eagerly awaiting little Madeline. "There she is—there she is!" Madge waved frantically in the air. For the first time, we saw the gleam in Madge's dark eyes. Her smile shone from inside her heart, up into her eyes and across her cheeks. While she glowed with joy, not one ounce of excitement surfaced on Madeline's little face when the clan greeted her at Victoria Station. Her face was more precious than any photo Eve had seen of her. She had the biggest dark-brown eyes and deep-set dimples.

"Hello, my darling, my precious little girl. I'm your mummy," Marge said, bending down and kissing her on her cheek, lifting her and squeezing her too hard.

"No, you're not," the little voice replied. She spoke with a lisp, which just made Eve's heart melt when the child opened her mouth.

"My mummy is in England," she replied in a cooing voice.

"But you are in England now, and I am your mummy."

Four years with her grandmother and a barrelful of clothes had not been sufficient for Madeline to know her mother's face, her smell and the ring of her voice. Madge took an entire two weeks off work to reacquaint herself with her daughter, playing with her and her dolls, reading *Alice in Wonderland* and *Dick Whittington* to her until she knew all the stories by heart. They saw all the London sights, and splurged on tickets to the London Palladium, Madame Tussaud's and the London Zoo.

Eve wondered how any father could walk away from such a beautiful child. Madeline was the quietest child she had ever met. She sat for hours without a sound, playing with her dolls and her plastic tea sets. It did not take long before Madeline was acquainted with all of Inez's customers. Aunt Pearl, Eve, and many of Inez's customers showered the child with blue-eyed blond-haired dolls of all descriptions and sizes.

"What a darling little girl you have," they cooed around her.

"Can we have her as a flower girl in my wedding?" one of Inez' customers asked.

"Of course, of course, as long as she doesn't cry."

"She won't cry, Madge. She's a big girl." The customer pinched Madeline's cheek.

Before long, Madeline became the co-star and the official flower girl at every wedding. She became as important as the bride and groom themselves, and no wedding was complete without her. Madeline was well-behaved and took beautiful photos, and no matter what color dress was chosen for her, her blue black skin glistened against the vibrant colors.

She took everyone's breath away, throwing rose petals or confetti from her basket and smiling at the congregation as she made her way down the aisle, the hem of her dress swishing and swaying as she walked. Growing up in Jamaica with her grandmother had seasoned her to be in the presence of adult company. She was neither shy nor precocious.

Then one day, out of the blue, Madeline took Madge's hand and squeezed it.

"You can be my mummy if you want to. You're a nice lady. I don't think my mummy is coming for me again anyway."

"I'd be happy to be your mummy." Madge lifted Madeline up in the air and swung her tiny body around her as she spun and laughed with her daughter.

Marge's days were complete and happy. Had she not been so quick to marry Clement before he changed his mind, Eve would have waited for Madeline to have been her flower girl. How she envied Madge. What a joy motherhood must be. Eve waited patiently for that day to be hers while she over-indulged Madeline as if she were her own.

TWENTY-FOUR

Long before little Sarah Cohen went missing, long before Eve saw the strand of honey-blond hair staring right back at her on the nape of Clement's thick neck, she suspected her husband's infidelities. They had been married less than six months. She moved closer to him, pulling the thin strand of hair from his body. He rolled over on his back like a whale, having gained some weight in the short time they had been married. He said it was "well-fed contentment," but later Eve realized he was eating two dinners. In time, Clement staggered home from his pub tours drunk almost every night, except for the nights he chose to sleep somewhere else.

When she first suspected his infidelities, her first reaction was a resolution to make him a dead man. *How should I kill him? Should I smother him with a pillow while he sleeps? Should I sneak up from behind when he's in a drunken stupor, or should I stab him with the sharpest kitchen knife?* she would ask herself. *Should I pour hot water over him? Or should I just cut off his joystick? Yes, that was the offending part of his body.* He was dipping it in so many honey pots that Eve had caught several infections from him. Every doctor's visit became a humiliation. She thought her suffering gave her the right to retaliate.

Watching him sleep, she remembered that it took a lot to stir him. She could crush his skull like a pumpkin. She wanted to hurt him as much as he had hurt her. She had loved this man with all her heart and argued with her brother and with her Uncle over him. She had been wrong, yet she was not ready to concede that to the family. She would be patient about that, as well as his punishment. But she wanted more proof to confirm her suspicions; she just had to be patient.

My mother once told her, "What happens in the dark my love, will surface in the light."

She had waited this long; another few days, months, a year would make no difference. Time was on her side.

What brought Eve back to reality was the thought of spending the rest of her life behind bars, in Holloway Prison or someplace worse. If she thought she could get away with murdering her husband, he would have already been dead for the pain and suffering he had caused her. But she couldn't go to prison and shame her family; neither as a Catholic woman, could she leave her marriage and shame herself.

When those thoughts swam around in her head, she turned to her Savior. Eve opened her Bible and comforted herself with prayers. She still had not found her rosary beads, after looking high and low for them. So she prayed from memory and intuition.

Hail Mary, full of Grace,
the Lord is with Thee,
Blessed art thou among women,
and blessed is the fruit of Thy womb...

"My little wife is always praying," Blue mocked her. "My little Catholic wife, say a prayer for me nuh?" he would chuckle. He had no idea that her prayers were keeping her sane and him alive.

Holy Mary, Mother of God,
pray for us sinners,
now and at the hour of our death,
Amen.

He awoke rubbing the sleep from his eyes, smiling and licking his lips, as if he had just experienced another sexual encounter.

"Marnin', me love," he grinned up at her.

She turned her face to avoid his kiss. Those luscious lips she once craved, that had sent her heart aflutter, now repulsed her. Eve jerked backwards to avoid the morning breath that was now tinged with stale alcohol and cigarettes. When they were first married, he must have thought that his early-morning ritual of clearing the phlegm from his throat by hawking and spitting was like music to her ears. It had always made her sick to her stomach.

"Morning, darling," he sang out. Eve feigned a smile, moving quickly off the bed to protect her only shred of evidence. She wasn't quite sure what she was going to do with it. She just hurried down the hallway to her sun-lit kitchen for solitude.

★★★

The long-awaited truth surfaced like unwanted dust on a polished table. It came on a day when Eve was ill-prepared, a day when it wasn't raining and the sky was bright from the noon-day sun. English sun was never hot like Jamaican sun, just tepid. The days were never warm enough to go about sleeveless and carefree, where you could throw a blanket on the grass, have a picnic, and pretend you were on a beach. But it was a day when Mrs. Harris, the district nurse, was not there to share her wisdom and comfort.

Clement had surely lived up to every antic her brother Austin, Aunt Pearl and Uncle Dudley had expected of him. Inez watched him like a hawk and it was dear Inez to whom Eve turned in her hour of need. Eve had no proof of infidelity by Clement, nothing but a bellyful of doubt. Doubt can't hang a man, but it can surely kill the love inside, and fill you up with contempt for a person once loved and adored. Eve's doubt consumed her. Now there was no room to breathe, to trust, and to believe in the man she loved, a man for whom she had been willing to forsake her family.

The phone rang, disturbing her muddled thoughts.

"Hello, Inez," Eve said in her best nice-lady voice.

"You want to come for a drive with me, Eve? My client never showed up for her fitting."

Her soft voice fluttered through the phone line.

"I'm going to check on her. Should I swing by and pick you up?"

"Okay. Mrs. Harris isn't coming today. I'd love the drive; it's such a nice day outside." With just a cardigan thrown around her shoulders, Eve was like a five year-old, ready and waiting at the door when Inez arrived.

"It's so unlike her not to show up. She is maid of honor at Cherry's wedding in two weeks."

They approached the street on Rosewood Park and found a small detached house with manicured lawns and neatly pruned rose bushes. They parked and walked toward the house. Inez gave a gentle tap on the polished brass doorknob. A small woman with rosy cheeks, dressed in a paisley pinafore, opened the door. Her sleeves were rolled up above her elbows as if the pair had disturbed her day's washing. Her ice-blue eyes greeted them with a challenging stare. Her shoulders slouched forward, her streaked blond hair straggling around her pudding face. The woman's breasts had a middle-aged sag and her stomach curved generously and unevenly below the waist-band of her skirt.

"Yes, can I help you?" She asked, wiping her soapy hands on the end of her apron.

"Does Charmaine Carter live here?" Inez asked, straightening out the crumbled paper in her hand.

"Oh yes, me dear."

She moved to one side of the door to let them in.

"Are you the nurse?"

"Yes, I am." Inez lied.

"She's quite poorly, the poor love. She's been like that a few days now. Groaning and crying like a baby. She is in the room on the right at the top of the stairs."

Eve bounced in behind Inez, acknowledging the landlady with a nod and a nervous smile. They gingerly climbed the carpeted stairs.

"I'm right here if you need me," she said, craning her neck from where they left her below.

They disappeared onto the landing. Inez knocked on the door and without waiting for a response pushed it open.

"Charmaine—it's me, Inez. Good God, where is the light in here? Why're you lying in the dark like this?"

Eve's eyes slowly adjusted to the darkness. A mild kind of rotten-egg, musty odor engulfed her nostrils. She fanned her nose, ready to retreat.

Inez fumbled toward the edge of the bed and plunked herself down onto the unmade bed. "What's wrong, my darling? You didn't come for your fitting yesterday and you didn't call. Have you got the flu?"

Eve was still stuck at the door, frozen by the appearance of the room.

It was furnished exactly the same as Eve's bedroom, with dark oak fur-niture and soft thick carpet. Seeing the candlewick bedspread with pink soft rose petals made her stomach churn. Identical ornaments and paintings hung on the wall. The same velvet drapes and the same heart-shaped picture frame held the same face of her husband. Draped on the bed head were Eve's mother's crimson rosary beads. The musty smell that greeted her now faded.

Now the room reeked of something more familiar. Clement. His style, his smell, his taste.

"Shall I open the curtains?" Eve's voice trembled. She didn't wait for an answer, and moved toward the window and pulled the thick velvet drapes open. As the light entered the room, there in front of her was the dirty truth: the broken wall, the ditch, the grassy Common, where Clement had told her he had found Sarah. So this is where the wretch was the day Sarah was missing. This is how he knew where to find her. Her knees buckled.

Under the same blue blanket with diamond-patterned satin edges—the one that he had used to wrap Sarah—Eve saw a small frame curled up in a ball.

"Miss Inez, I've messed up everything this time."

"Tell me what's wrong, darling."

"I'm being punished," Charmaine sobbed. Inez carefully moved the blanket away.

"Lawd me Jesus, look here, you need to go the hospital, girl, or you will bleed to death if you stay here."

"I can't go, Miss Inez. I have been to a doctor. It was a doctor he sent me to, to get rid of it. Some African called Okapi or Agabi or something like that. But I did not want no African touching me. So I paid another doctor to take care of it."

Eve felt the sweat breaking out on her forehead. She froze when she heard, "He said I could not keep the baby because he was married, Miss Inez. All this time I didn't know he was married." Her words were muffled by her cries and as she lifted her hands in a silent prayer. Eve could now see the gold crucifix that she had bought for Clement to mark their first Christmas together. It hung from her pale thin neck.

She raised her head for one moment toward the light, and Eve could see her face clearly now. Even with her matted and unkempt hair, she was an attractive girl. Her face was angelic and childlike, her blue eyes red and swollen with tears. Her thin, delicate lips trembled. She could not have been a day over seventeen.

Charmaine stared at Eve, looking for sympathy but Eve had none. Her anger was not with Charmaine, certainly not, but the proof she had been awaiting for so long, was now staring right at her. As pathetic as it seemed, her husband was an adulterer. She could not listen anymore to what

Charmaine had to say. Eve already knew the story. Her pain was Eve's.

Eve fumbled at the doorknob and ran down the stairs as fast as her legs could carry her, almost knocking the landlady out of the way.

"Is everything alright up there? I can't afford no scandal 'ere you know," said the lady who was left downstairs.

"Call an ambulance. Please." Eve choked on the words.

She pushed the front door open, gasping for breath. She flung open the car door and threw herself into the passenger seat, wheezing. She just sat there, crying soundlessly for a while. But when her tears stopped, she stole a glance at the upstairs window where the light had revealed the truth. Behind those windows, behind those curtains that were the same as hers, a baby had been conceived, a baby that she had prayed and begged for, and Charmaine had discarded it like a bag of stale chips.

"Bastard!" Inez railed for the whole building to hear. "Just say the word, Eve, and I will kill him for you with my bare hands. I won't even wait to tell Austin. I'm so sorry, Eve. I'd never have brought you here if I had known. I wonder how many other Charmaines are scattered across London?" She shook her head in pain and disgust.

When she had finally collected her thoughts, Eve said, "Please don't tell my brother, Inez." That was all that seemed to matter.

"Promise me, Inez. Promise me."

"I promise," Inez assured her.

"Here." Inez said as she pulled Eve's arm toward her and put something in her hand. "I think these belong to you. You said you couldn't find them." It was the rosary. "Nobody should have your mother's rosary but you, Eve." Eve held Inez close to her as the tears rolled down her face.

"Thank you, Inez." Eve sobbed. A silence hung thickly between them until the car pulled up outside Eve's house.

"Do you want me to come in and stay with you for a while?"

"No, I'll be alright," Eve lied.

"Did you know, Inez?"

"Darling Eve, I wouldn't be that cruel to you. I love your brother, but I'm a woman too. I wouldn't want this to happen to my worst enemy."

Eve closed the door behind her, pressed her back against the other side and slid down to the floor. She cried all evening and all night. *This was the man I loved. This was the man I had forsaken my family for. Why God? Why did you send me a man to hurt and humiliate me?* But God was silent. God did not reply, and all that was left in the stillness of the room was the painful truth.

★★★

The early drizzle of the afternoon continued steadily until late evening. The constant rain turned into a heavy downpour beating hard on the windowpane. Outside, the thunder sounded farther away but the rain beat furiously against the glass, insistent as hell.

It rained for five consecutive days without letting up for a second. Clement did not come home. There was no word, not a phone call. A mosquito net of silence surrounded Eve. Her sobs almost suffocated her. She lay on the floor and cried until she was too exhausted to continue and she became quiet. The pain was so overwhelming, her breathing became difficult and a sharp electric sensation ran through her chest.

"Fucking bastard," she cursed into the air, beating her fists against the floor.

If anyone had been present, they wouldn't have believed that such foul language could come from the mouth of a good Catholic woman like Evelyn Scott.

"Fucking bastard. I hate you!" she shouted louder.

Her mind was a mass of confused, painful, even embarrassing thoughts. What was she going to do now? Every day she had waited for the truth to surface. Now her tomorrow wasn't tomorrow any more, it was today. Today was here, and although she had waited so long for this day, she was still completely floored by the news, unable to tell the family. Eve had begged Inez not to tell Austin, but who knows what words are whispered between lovers at night?

Eve's eyes had grown accustomed to the dark, and the curtains were not quite closed. She strained to stay awake by focusing on the diagonal lines the streetlight made on the hardwood floor, but eventually her thoughts drowned in sleep.

On the seventh day, Clement surfaced.

"Eve, I'm so sorry. I had to go to Scotland on business. It was very sudden and I had to just drop everything and go…"

"Blah, blah, blah," Eve said, covering her ears with her small hands. "I don't want to hear your cock-and-bull story."

"Chuh Eve man, don't g'wan so. It's not like you."

"Tell me about Charmaine. Start there!" she yelled at him.

"That likkle piece of trash. She been here causing you trouble?"

"No, she has not been here. How could she come here when you sent her to some back street butcher?"

"Me sah?! Me never send har nowhere. What a lying likkle wretch."

"So you admit that you know her then?"

"It's not what you think Eve; chuh, man." He stopped and searched his mind for explanations. "I was helping out me cousin Jocelyn. Is Jocelyn's girl and I send her to Agabi. She tek it up pon herself fe go somewhere else."

"A young girl lying in bed, bleeding to death is nothing to you? Then why isn't Jocelyn's face in the photo by her bed?"

"Backside!!," he murmured. "Look, Eve, baby, you are going to make yourself sick again."

"Get away from me." She pushed him backwards. "How could you take my dead mother's rosary and give it to another woman? How could you do that?!"

"I can explain…"

"Clement Jackson, you are a dirty dawg!" she yelled at him.

"Don't say that, Eve; give me a chance. I can explain."

"The crucifix I gave you is hanging around her neck."

By now her fists were pounding in his chest. She didn't realize he had got so close.

"So you want to fight me now—You don't want to hear my side?"

"No, absolutely not. I can't listen to your lies anymore. I once trusted you, lived off your every word. My brother was right about you all along."

"No, baby, you can't listen to your brother. Him never like me from time. Him never think me was good enough fi 'im likkle sister."

Eve crawled into bed, breathless. With no warning, a sharp pain shot through her. That was all she remembered.

TWENTY-FIVE

That Monday morning, anger was welling up inside Austin as he inched his way along the crowded Kennington station platform, conscious only of his lack of everything. He was penniless in a country where he really did not belong. The British Government lied when they said they welcomed Jamaicans. *We aren't welcome here at all. We are needed to clean up after them, but we are not welcome to dream our dreams or achieve them here.*

And Austin Scott's dreams were fading fast. He had not been accepted in any of the major cricket clubs, nor had he saved as much money as he had planned. He didn't have the money for his family's memorial, not even return fare home to his beloved Jamaica. He still had one more year of studies to go. Clement Jackson, on the other hand, had everything. Money, reputation and Austin's beloved sister. He missed his sister, but he could not back down now. Not now. She had married his worst enemy, and so he washed his hands clean of her. His parents would roll over in their graves if they could see Eve now.

How gratifying it must have been, to be Clement Jackson and to be so revered. He had the latest motorcar, a big fancy house in a posh part of South London, and a wife who would tolerate anything. Adoring friends hung off his every word, everyone falling over themselves at his every beck and call, just because he had a bit of money and a business.

Austin once had a life that most young men dreamed of. Back home, he didn't have a care in the world. From sun-up to sundown, he played cricket. His meals were made on demand and everyone worshiped the ground he walked on, including his sisters. He cursed God every day for changing that and taking it away from him.

Like Aunt Pearl, he just existed. She was apparently smoking herself to death. An inferno of anger raged inside Austin. He wanted to shift his anger to a positive place, but every time he tried, something else happened. Truth be told, he had nobody to blame but himself. For every five shillings he earned, he gambled three at the bookies, convinced that he'd strike it rich. But every time he got lucky, instead of being grateful, like a fool he'd squander every last penny of it again. He combed his brain for various ways to make quick cash, but nothing legal ever came to mind.

He could easily fiddle the books at work, but they expected him to do something stupid anyway, so he decided to prove them wrong. Uncle Dudley was his saving grace; after all, he had got Austin the job in the first place. What shame he would have brought on his family, he thought, if he were caught stealing. The risk wasn't worth it, but he needed money fast.

What restored his pride was the West Indies cricket team's tour of England. Austin tagged along with Uncle Dudley and his boisterous friends everywhere there was a match from Henley to Lords, from Egbaston to Old Trafford and every other ground. *Boy, oh boy, our men in white were my heroes and did us proud. Their dark skins glistened against their whites as they strutted out onto the green to play and perform sheer magic. We had perfected the game of our colonial masters and made our opponents seethe with envy. It sweet me so till, to turn up at work on a Monday morning and poke fun at my colleagues.*

"Cricket, lovely cricket," Austin would sing and burn their ears.

★★★

Austin stood on the escalator, staring at the back of the bowed heads in front of him. Every Monday was very much like the last, but before he walked through the doors of his department, his gut told him that something was wrong. He could feel it, just like when Eve had taken a turn, or on the night of the train crash. He recognized those despondent faces, had lived around them for years.

"Good morning all," he chirped. But by the look on everyone's face, it was not.

"Is someone going to tell me what the bloody hell is going on then?"

"It's…Mr. Stewart," stuttered a voice from behind Austin.

"What's happened to him?"

"He died of a heart attack over the weekend. You're in charge until Head Office decides what to do."

"Me, in charge?!"

"Yes sir. That's what the notice says right here from Baker Street. Look." The clerk pushed the typed letter under his nose. His boss, Mr. Stewart, had been a considerate man. His consideration, however, had been for the other accountants in the department and not for him.

"Austin, you got to understand my position," he would say, straightening his tie as he spoke. "There would be such an uproar. I can't afford to ruffle everybody's feathers, son. Be patient. A promotion comes at the right time for all of us."

As he seethed, Austin had watched others less competent than himself get promoted to senior positions and then Mr. Stewart had the nerve to ask him to train them. His counterparts watched him like a hawk, looking for ways to trip him up, but he knew his job like the back of his black hand. Now Stewart was dead and by default, Austin became Head of the Accounting Department.

He even got a mention and a photo in the South London press. The caption, in bold print, read:

AUSTIN SCOTT, THE FIRST BLACK MAN TO BE HEAD OF DEPARTMENT OF THE SOUTH LONDON DIVISION OF THE LONDON TRANSPORT

There was no mention, thank goodness, that Austin had not yet completed his degree. They moved him to an office with a window and a substantial pay increase, although it probably did not match his predecessor's. His promotion came as a bigger surprise to him than to everyone else. Although Mr. Stewart had always said promoting him would be a problem, no one seemed to give a toss.

His new sense of authority filled the void that had sat inside him for years. He was doing exactly the same job, training new arrivals, budgeting and planning but now he was getting the recognition that came with it. His future was suddenly clear. This was a cause for celebration.

***

The West Indian League was having its annual dance, an appropriate time for Austin Scott to announce his good fortune. Because of his accounting skills, he had been roped into being a more active member of the League's financial committee and secretly enjoyed the role of Treasurer. The handling of such responsibilities propelled him to work hard and he wanted everyone he knew to become a member.

"Come on, Aunt Pearl and Uncle Dudley. Life cannot just be about work," he encouraged them.

"Come to the League's annual dance and celebrate my promotion. Come on, you two."

"Alright then, son." Uncle Dudley replied.

The sale of succulent, spicy curry goat and rice, piled mountain high on paper plates, the abundance of rum punch, Babycham, Cherry B and Guinness Stout made the West Indian League's dance a great success. The church hall was packed with bodies bouncing and gyrating to the blaring blue beat rhythms from the popular South London sound system, 'Count Suckle.' Some couples were waltzing, some bending their knees and twisting their feet to Chubby Checker; other couples kicked their heels in the air and fox-trotted around the hall like their bodies were on wire springs. Others just bobbed their heads, swinging their arms back and forth to the 'ska beat.' Nobody was seated.

Inez stayed at home. She was already chalking out and cutting new fabrics and designs for the next event. By now every woman they knew, both Jamaican and English, wanted one of Inez's new creations. Austin looked forward to having a few dances with some of her clients. He could manage the flirting with ease. After all, wasn't it his duty to compliment them on how wonderful they looked? What he had not anticipated was a run-in with his notorious brother-in-law, Blue.

It was bad enough that he consistently left his sister at home, humiliating her by flirting with everything that moved in a skirt. Austin tried to ignore Blue as he staggered in his direction.

"My dear brother, have a drink on me."

The words belted from his mouth, loud and uncouth from twenty feet away.

"Let's celebrate your good fortune this week, nuh man." He staggered closer. Austin could feel his blood boiling. The muscles around his neck were tight and his fists clenched. He gritted his teeth and took a few firm steps backwards to avoid his rum breath as he spluttered all over Austin.

"Come on, man. Have a drink with me, nuh? For old time sake?"

Austin tried to contain himself, but his patience was being stretched. He snapped. The next thing he knew, Austin had pushed Blue much harder than he intended. Oh Shit!

"Is what, church boy—you think you better than me? Is me the head of your family now." He pounded his fists on his chest.

"Is me a save your family bwoy!" he spat, spraying liquor and saliva. "You is nothing but a hypocrite. You think you better than me because you educated, and you go church."

He wiped his mouth on the back of his hand.

"But is me ah save your raas hide inna dis ya town now. The whole of you is de damn same. That's why you family dead off inna Kendal."

The words lit a special fire within Austin, just as Blue rushed toward him, catching him off guard. He saw the fist coming and tried to dodge it, but Blue still caught Austin above the left eye, knocking him backwards against a table and sending chairs flying. The room tilted for a second. Austin gasped and caught his breath just as he saw Blue closing in on him again.

Clement tried to hit him again, but this time Austin was ready. Steadying himself he threw a open palm forward and shot him a box—*buff!!!* Then his fist connected with the edge of Blue's left jaw. *Now I feel kinda like Joe Lewis, to rahtid! Buff!* Austin dodged the punch, then threw a fist that caught Blue clean on the chin. The uppercut sent the man reeling backwards so fast that he lost his balance and fell. *Budoff!!* His large frame staggered back. The rum glass fell to the floor, shattering into tiny pieces. Blue's body followed in a kind of slow motion, crashing onto the hardwood floor.

There was a deafening silence in the hall, as all three hundred eyes stared at him.

"Come on, man. Tek it easy, nuh?" Uncle Dudley and Mr. Vincent ran over, pulling Austin aside. He cupped his bruised knuckles as he watched the blood trickle from the corner of Blue's mouth. His fist hurt like hell, but he felt a sense of relief as he stepped over his adversary's limp body.

"You will never be my brother," he said, looking down at the man who now tried to rise.

"You are not worthy of my sister, or any decent woman for that matter. You are nothing but a hurry-come-up, country-ass fool!"

The needle slid across the vinyl 45 record and the music stopped.

Mouths fell wide open and all eyes were centered on Austin, but nobody could stop his verbal assault. What he had felt about Clement Jackson for years was now unleashed.

"You can't manipulate me the way you do everyone else, just because you have a little bit of money. You are a disgrace to your family and our community!"

Onlookers stood in astonishment. One was heard to whisper, "But stop, is Austin a g'wan so? I don't know this side of him at all...!"

"Still rivers run deep fi true," he heard another say.

Austin knocked back a swig of rum, straightened his tie, grabbed his hat off the floor, dusted it off and plunked it back on his head. The carefree dancers parted, and then stood still like a *tableau vivant*. He stomped past them and made his exit without a word. The winter air felt good on his face as he stepped outside into the car park. Austin's fist throbbed but that was all that hurt. The burden of quiet anger, self-pity and guilt that had weighed him down for so many years was now lifted. *I suddenly feel free to rahtid!!*

Austin started up his faithful Zephyr and drove straight home to his beloved Inez. *How could I have been so bloody stupid, not speaking to my sister all this time because of this fool?* He shook his head. *Ughh—to allow an ediat like him to come between the two of us. Aunt Pearl told me a thousand times how foolish I was, Esther had written me countless letters from Jamaica, with the same gentle persuasion in each one. Uncle Dudley quarreled with me over dominoes, during cricket matches, over glasses of Guinness... but it wasn't until I busted up Clement Jackson that I realize I've been a damn jackass all this time.*

Austin pulled up outside the house and approached the door with renewed determination. In the morning, he would make amends with Aunt Pearl and Eve, the two women he loved so dearly. He would beg Eve's forgiveness, apologize for hitting her husband and for being so bull-headed and stupid. Yes, that was what he would do.

Eve had been so loyal to him and this was how he had repaid her? His sister had had two miscarriages and not a word of sympathy or comfort had come from Austin. No prayers or reassurances that all was going to be well. That was his job now that their father was dead. He'd failed her. If she had not been sick, that day in September in 1957, he would have been buried alive in the train wreck at Kendal. He owed her his life. Tomorrow, he would tell her how he had missed her and how much he loved her. Over the years, he had dug a ditch self-pity for himself. It was so deep he could not crawl out.

As he slipped under the blanket, into bed beside his beloved Inez, she stirred and gave a gentle sigh. "You're home." He ran his hand over her hair and kissed the nape of her long neck.

"Yes I'm home, darling."

Austin cuddled up beside her body like a child, filling the gaps of her curves. He drifted off to sleep with the comforting realization that he could now make so many things better.

★★★

It seemed as if Austin had only slept for a minute when he felt an urgent prodding in the ribs.

"Austin, wake up! There's been an accident. We have to go to Eve."

"Accident?!" He was awake instantly, as if he had always been ready for such a moment. He felt a wave of panic washing over him.

"What kind of accident? What happened to my sister?"

"She's okay." Inez reassured him.

"It's Clement." She paused. "He's dead."

"Kiss me neck! Him dead…? Is me kill him? What happen to him?!"

"Sod's law. The one time he wasn't drunk, he was hit by a speeding car that ran through a red light. He died on the spot," Inez reported in a robotic tone.

"Mi rahtid!!! I must go to Eve." Austin bolted out of bed, dragged on his trousers and dashed down the stairs two at a time. He hunched over the steering wheel while the Zephyr pissed and panted. He forced it into unfamiliar speeds, and somehow managed to get to Orchid Crescent. Austin ran up the unfamiliar path, where he was greeted by Uncle Dudley.

"She's through there, son." He pointed at the living room door.

Eve was sitting by the fireplace, her face drawn, her eyes red-rimmed and swollen. He ran toward her with his arms wide open. Her small body felt like a block of ice.

"My darling sister, I am so sorry. So sorry. I have treated you so shabbily. Please forgive me."

His words were muffled by her wailing sobs. She buried her head in his chest and cried uncontrollably, but all he could think about was his own guilt and wretchedness for all those years of stupidity.

★★★

The telegram read:

DEAREST ESTHER: CLEMENT IS DEAD. THE FUNERAL IS ON NOVEMBER 14. PLEASE TRY AND COME. YOUR SISTER NEEDS YOUR SUPPORT, SO DO I. IF YOU CAN'T COME I UNDERSTAND BUT TRY YOUR BEST. I CAN ARRANGE YOUR FLIGHT FROM HERE AND FOR YOU TO TRAVEL WITH CLEMENT'S BROTHERS. YOUR LOVING BROTHER, AUSTIN

TWENTY-SIX

Funerals bring out the best or the worst in things. On the good side of that equation, Clement's funeral brought Esther and his son back to Austin. He was up at the crack of dawn, pacing up and down the entire airport in anticipation of their arrival from Jamaica, his face pressing against the glass window searching for the aircraft that would reunite them. He was two hours early.

There she stood, dressed in her stiff straw hat and white cotton gloves, as if she was going to church. Her dark nutmeg skin glistened in contrast against her pastel cotton floral dress. Esther had not gained one ounce of fat, nor a wrinkle in her face. She had lost her teenage chubbiness and her face was more narrow. Now, she looked like their mother.

Austin's feet felt light and his pace quickened; his heart tightened in his chest until he could hardly breathe. His son and Esther were now running to him at the same pace. The little boy with the elfin ears got to him first, flailing and shouting. Austin held out his arms and imagined hearing the word "Daddy."

"Come to Daddy, little man," he said as he picked up Austin Junior under the arms and held him high above his head. His heart sang with joy when the child said the word: "Daddy." My son is the dead stamp of me, just as Esther had described him in all her letters. He squeezed Esther as tight as one arm could reach around her thin waist. They hustled from the airport and made their way home to prepare for the home-going of Clement "Blue" Jackson.

***

Austin really had no desire to go to Clement's funeral, much less be a pall bearer for a man he had loathed all his life. He had his Royal Air Force clan, his clients, and his cricket and domino club members to do him the honors. Eve had insisted, however, and with great reluctance, he dutifully put on his black suit, tie and black shoes. Esther, Junior, Inez and Austin drove over to Eve's house.

Out of respect for his sister, he took his position beside the other men. Clement's cousin Jocelyn, three of his brothers who had flown from Jamaica, and two army officers from his old unit carried the coffin. It was irrelevant that Austin detested funerals. In this case, he felt no grief for the corpse in it.

The church was bursting at the seams with all kinds of people. Ex-servicemen were bedecked with medals from the wars they helped to win, for a country that granted them no respect. They came in droves from Birmingham to Brixton, and from Cambridge to Clapham. Friends from all walks of life filled the church. Respectable people like Claudia Jones from the *West Indian Gazette*. Businessmen like Mr. Dyke, Mr. Dryden, Mr. Goode, Mr. George Crossdale and members of the West Indian League and the Caribbean Ex-servicemen's Association attended. The Cohens and other neighbors from Orchid Crescent, and even Mr. Coburn, the milkman, showed up. Every living soul from the surrounding pubs, the bookies and their customers flocked to the funeral. The world arrived to pay their last respects to the great Clement "Blue" Jackson.

Everyone filed passed him as if he was some kind of important statesman who had saved the world or something. Clement lay like an angel surrounded by all the white ruched satin. Clement's brother wanted him to be buried in his RAF uniform, but Eve had chosen his favorite brown tweed suit instead. It was the suit he had worn when she had met him; she liked the irony of it. His linen handkerchief, signature gold watch and cuff links adorned his stiff body. Austin sat in a semi-daze as he listened to Father Stephen droning on about him as if he had been some kind of saint. What Austin felt was inconsequential, because as much as he hated the man, he was highly admired by so many.

There were mountains of blue flowers everywhere in lush bouquets, an enormous wreath from the West Indian League, even small delicate handmade bunches of bluebells, irises and lilies of the valley decorated the pulpit and the area around the casket, looking as elaborate as his life had been.

Austin kept his eyes focused on the brand tag that had been forgotten on the jacket sleeve of the gentleman in front of him. *Did this occasion really warrant a new suit?* he asked himself.

It was so easy to recognize his lovers. Yes, Lawd, every woman he ever kissed or lay down with was there. The women showed no compunction about bawling openly and loudly in their hankies throughout the service. Without shame or apology.

One woman was dressed to the nines in a black dress that was too short and too tight to be respectable. She bent over and kissed his mouth, and lay a single long-stemmed red rose on his chest. Her breasts threatened to ooze out of her dress; a gold crucifix lay tightly in her cleavage. Austin sat on his pew, rigid and helpless. Even in death, Blue still disrespected his sister. The congregation gasped at the sight of the woman, bending low to plant her last kiss. Someone whispered, "Is who she think she favor?"

Austin turned to look at Eve and wondered what was going through her mind. She sat there calm and controlled as everyone filed by to pay their respects. But he could not see her face; she held her head low and kept the veil of her hat close to her face. Beside her, stiff as a flagpole, Esther held her hand. His two sisters reminded him of coconut trees, bending with the winds of time, or the harshnesses of life, no matter what came their way. He loved and admired their courage and strength. It seemed as if their past quarrels were meaningless now. It occurred to him then that they were gathered for the first time to honor a loved one—albeit very flawed and undeserving. There had been no funeral for their own family because there had been no bodies recovered at the train wreck. Not one single body to lay to rest in a manner that was deserving of them. But here we were on ceremony for "Blue."

Austin bowed his head and whispered his mother's name. "Ruth Miriam Scott, may you rest in peace. Neville Archibald Scott, may you rest in peace, Uncle Cork and Aunt Martha, may you both rest in peace," and so he continued in a shallow whisper, creating his own private ceremony for those he truly loved and had lost four years before. He did not shed one tear for Eve's loss but cried in his heart. He cried for his own. The tears he had not shed for his family in all that time, he now let flow. He cried for the funeral that they never had, for faces to which they never said goodbye, for a future so promising snatched away from them. For the months he had been stupid with malice for his sister. For the years his life had changed without preparation or warning. As much as he hated Clement, he had bought them all together for the first time since they had left Jamaica. He had gotten Esther out of the house and on a plane to England. As much as it would have given him an opportunity to return home to just lie under a shady tree, to see Donovan again, he had abandoned that opportunity.

"It's right that you should bury your husband here, Eve," Austin whispered. "I don't think Blue cared whether he ever saw Jamaica again. He didn't love the island the way we did. So why waste good money flying him home? It would be such an unnecessary expense. Plus we would be denying the community of his homecoming. This is his home, Eve," he reassured her.

She nodded her agreement. For the first time in years, Eve and Austin did not argue. She had waffled over his resting place, but Austin made it feel like the right choice.

After the casket was lowered, Eve stepped forward, throwing a bouquet of bluebells and irises on his coffin, whispering her final farewell.

He stepped closely behind Eve to steady her, but his legs were the ones that buckled. Austin held onto the shovel to steady himself, pushing his foot hard on the spade and digging deep into the dirt. He scooped up the earth and threw it into the grave. The particles clattered loudly against the buffed wood.

What the hell are the gravediggers for? Austin asked himself.

His eyes became a watery haze and he blinked several times to fight back new tears. As dirt rained onto the coffin, his feelings for Blue dissipated from nonchalance and anger to sympathy.

The whistling wind whipped through women's hemlines, blowing their hats. The weeping of the mistresses and wellwishers continued around the graveside even longer than it had inside the church. Amens and yesses traveled on the murmurs of the crowd. They closed ranks, forming a tight circle. As everyone bowed his or her head, the mourners seemed as if they would sing every hymn they knew:

For every mountain you brought me over,
For every trail you brought me through
For this I give you praise ....

And then:

Then sings my soul
My savior God to thee

How great thou art
How great thou art

    And then

Rock of Ages cleft for me...

    It went like that until the grave was full and the ground was even. People walked back and forth against the wind, bringing all the flowers out of the church and placing them on top of the mound. The Scotts lay Blue to rest at Grove Park Cemetery on a blistering November afternoon, almost precisely four years from the day they first arrived in London.

TWENTY-SEVEN

It seemed like an eternity before Blue's family and friends finally left Eve's house. It was Austin, Aunt Pearl and Uncle Dudley who ushered the droves of people in and out of the house. There were people hanging off the banisters, up the stairs, in the hallway, piled up in the kitchen. Esther and Austin went to Eve's room where they lay curled up on the bed together, just as they did back home. There was no Miss Ruby to bring them piping hot mugs of cocoa tea, but Mrs. Harris was very helpful.

Every time she entered the room she smiled. "Esther, you are the spitting image of your sister," she said in that angelic way of hers. She shook her head and left the room. "My, my, you both could pass for twins."

Every morning when Eve awoke and rushed to the bathroom, she threw up everything she'd eaten the evening before. Nausea and dizziness became her new companions, but there was no pain. This feeling was new to her.

"I think I'm getting sick again, Esther. Every morning I feel so bad."

"It's probably just stress. With all that you have been through these last couple of months," Esther told her.

"I'm fine the rest of the day, but it's just the mornings that I have this terrible feeling and no pain like before."

"When Mrs. Harris comes again I must ask her what she thinks is wrong. Anyway, enough about my aches and pains. Esther, you really should do some sightseeing while you're here. You've just been cooped up in the house since you got here."

"I'm not really interested in seeing anything, plus it's too cold to go anywhere," she said, leaning against the radiator and rubbing her hands.

"But there are so many wonderful sights to see throughout London. Uncle Dudley is an excellent tour guide."

"I'm sure he is, but I don't want to go out in the cold."

"So I hear you don't want to go sightseeing, Esther," said Uncle Dudley, walking into the room without knocking. "You can say what you want to your sister, but I'm not taking no for an answer. You can't come this far and not at least see the Palace. I gave Eve her first tour around London and you must get the same."

With Esther still resistant, they piled into Uncle Dudley's car and took the route he had dutifully taken Eve and Austin when they had first arrived. Now Eve was the official tour guide"

"This is the House of Commons where the government meets to make decisions about their country and ours too. And the big clock beside it is Big Ben. We are actually on Westminster Bridge and the River Thames is below. I think they say twenty-six bridges span the river." Esther stared expressionlessly at Big Ben.

"Do you want to get out and walk around?"

"Oh no, it's far too cold to do that. I'll just look at everything from the car."

"Okay, then let's go on to the Palace." They drove down the Mall. "Here on your left is 10 Downing Street where Prime Minister Harold McMillan lives."

"Hmm," Esther said nonchalantly. "What is that line for?" She pointed at a long queue that had formed further out along the Mall.

"Oh, everyone is waiting to see the Changing of the Guards."

"Where is the Palace?"

"Just a second. As we turn around the corner we'll be able to see it."

As they drove closer to the Palace, Esther perked up in her seat. "What room were Austin and Inez in when they met the Queen?" she asked.

"I don't know from the outside, but I'm sure Inez can tell you when we get back home," Eve said.

"Do you want to do some shopping in Harrod's or Bourne & Hollingsworth?"

"Bourne & Hollingsworth. That sounds like it costs money..."

"Their prices are reasonable. It's Harrod's that has the shocking prices."

"No, I'm not really interested in shopping, let's go home. It's so cold."

"How do you all live in this cold, Eve? It's a wonder you all don't turn into ice."

"You get used to it after a while," Eve tried to convince her with little success.

"You really think I could get used to this cold?"

Back at the house, no matter how high Eve turned up the thermostat, no matter how many flannel nighties and layers of cardigans she wore, Esther's teeth chattered and her body shook against the cold.

Mrs. Harris brought an extra hot water bottle for her; they all covered her with extra blankets and she even slept with socks on, but nothing kept her warm. Eve's sister was one of the first women to fly to England—and probably the only Jamaican woman to fly back so quickly. Whereas most people were trying to make a life in England, Esther wanted no part of it. As much as she loved them and missed them, Jamaica was in her heart.

Finally, all the mourning activity stopped. No more plates of food arrived at their doorstep, no more well-wishers, or folk who knew Clement (or who were just curious about his infamy) came filing through the house.

When Esther left, Eve cried more at the airport than she had at the funeral. When she returned from the airport, she sat in the still of the room, staring into space. She did not feel as wretched as everyone had thought. Rather, a sense of relief had overtaken her. She would never have left her marriage, but with all that Clement had done to her, Eve wasn't sure how long she could have endured. His unexpected death, just like that of her parents, caused her to wonder if she could ever love anyone again.

Eve began to hum the song that Miss Ruby always sang to her.

One day at a time, Sweet Jesus...

"Cheer up, luvvy," said Mrs. Harris, interrupting her thoughts.

"You can't sit around the house moping all day. Pardon me for saying so, but good riddance to bad rubbish. That's what I always say. That husband of yours was no bloody good for you in the first place."

"Oh, Mrs. Harris, please hold your tongue."

"Hold my tongue, young miss? What do you think I've been doing all these years I have been coming here? You are better off without him. You mark my word, young miss." She wagged her finger in her face. Eve always liked Mrs. Harris' blunt honesty, but this version had come sooner than she expected.

"You deserve so much better, so much more. Trust me, as God is my witness, you will get better. You know, I have never been one not to call a spade a spade, but Mr. Jackson was bad blood from the beginning."

Without taking a breath, Mrs. Harris continued. "I don't want to speak ill of the dead, but he got his comeuppance good and proper. You'll get what's coming to you on this earth, my angel. You mark my words."

"But how can I get what's coming to me Mrs. Harris. I've been feeling so sick these past few days. Not the kind of sick that makes my heart ache or my breathing shallow but just this awful feeling which only seems to come in the morning.

"In the morning? She smiled.

"What is it? Is something else wrong with me?"

"Nothing is wrong with you me dear." She paused. "You're having a baby, that's all."

"A baby? I'm having a baby?!"

"Yes, luvvy, that dreadful feeling you are having is 'morning sickness.' It will soon go away. She patted Eve on the shoulder and waddled off into the kitchen with her medicine tray and used syringes. With a smile from ear to ear Mrs. Harris said, "Eve is having a baby…"

***

As the days drifted into each other, Eve welcomed the solitude. For the first time in her entire life, she was living alone. Esther had tried to persuade her to return to Jamaica with her. How Eve loved her; she missed Jamaica but wasn't ready to leave England just yet.

In the next few days, everyone came with advice, with food, with sympathy, with their concerns, with instructions. Eve had been lonely in the house with Blue. Without him, she now had peace. Her pride was restored, her mind no longer muddled.

"What are you going to do with such a big house? How are you going to manage with no steady income to pay the bills?" She was bombarded with questions.

For once, Austin was silent. He was comforting, held her hand, but gave no advice, no comments on the situation at hand. Eve had her brother back—but a new brother, one who loved her as much as her beloved Sarge.

"Whatever you decide to do I will support you, Eve, and I know Inez will too."

Having been sheltered all her life, Eve didn't know how she was going to manage. She had never paid a bill in her life and didn't even know where the gas meters were in her own house. All she knew for certain was that she was not leaving Orchid Crescent.

"God will find a way," she said aloud.

"You should sell it and get something smaller," Aunt Pearl chipped in.

"Maybe Austin and Inez can move in with you."

"God will find a way."

"Yes, but he don't write checks," said Uncle Dudley.

"But whatever you decide to do, we are behind you, me love." Aunt Pearl said.

The sound of the doorbell saved Eve from the family interrogation. She moved quickly toward the front door, where she greeted the postman. He had a registered letter in his hand.

"For Mrs. Evelyn Scott Jackson. Could you sign here, please?" The man pushed the pen and the clipboard in front of him. Eve signed and took the package.

"Thank you," she said without raising her head. She closed the door behind her, still fixated on the envelope marked "Lloyds of London".

She opened the envelope, took the letter out and read it.

Dear Mrs. Jackson:

I am deeply sorry to hear of your loss. We had been instructed by the late Mr. Clement Jackson, before his passing, that in case of any illness or accident that we notify you of his financial commitments. Enclosed is a copy of Mr. Jackson's insurance policy and a copy of his will.

Please do not hesitate to contact us if you require any further assistance. Our company sends its deepest sympathy to you at this time.

Yours sincerely
Alan Bosworthy
Partner

Eve knew absolutely nothing of Clement's financial affairs. He had always dismissed the idea that she should know. He would always say, "I'm going to take care of you, Eve, so don't worry." But she did anyway, because he gambled, he drank, and he squandered his money on women and all kinds of foolishness. "Everything I have is yours," he would tell her.

Her entire life had been at the mercy of men; Sarge, Austin and then, that of Clement. During the time she was married, any little money that she could get her hands on, she had saved some of it. She spent less on groceries when she sent someone to the store, never giving Clement back any change. Anything she needed, she told him it cost more. He never checked, and why should he? He was married to an imbecile, or so he thought.

Eve felt the rush of adrenaline as she read the contents of the letter. Clement's life insurance policy was to be paid to her in full. This meant that the house was paid for and she would receive a sum of ten thousand pounds. The will also stated that she would inherit everything and that two thousand pounds was specifically dedicated to building a memorial for the Scott family. The check was not made payable to Eve. It was made out to 'Austin Scott.'

The vanilla-embossed letter fell from her hands and floated to the floor. A powerful sense of relief brought her to her knees. She raised her head to the ceiling and, closing her eyes, she whispered the prayer that had given her all the strength to bear all the pain she had endured over the years.

The Lord is my Shepherd
I shall not want
He maketh me to lie down in green pastures
He restoreth my soul
He leadeth me in the paths of righteousness for his name's sake
Yea though I walk through the valley of the shadow of death
I will fear no evil
For thou art with me
Thy rod and thy staff they comfort me
Thou prepareth a table before me in the presence of mine enemies
Thou anointest my head with oil
My cup runneth over
Surely goodness and mercy
Shall follow me all the days of my life
And I will dwell in the house of the Lord
Forever.
Amen

TWENTY-EIGHT

Gone are the days when I sat around the house staring into the emptiness, wishing and willing my family to come home. Miss Ruby, Donovan, and a school full of potential pianists became my family now. They are my hope and my happiness. I often find myself singing Billie Holiday songs at the top of my lungs, just the way Mummy did. When I catch myself singing I let out a slight chuckle. I am truly my mother's child and she is right there on my shoulder, watching over me as she had always done.

At the end of the day I sit on the verandah, watching the sky change from powder blue to purple to ink-black. Beyond the gate is a world to which I do not belong. At least, not now. The sign "Piano Lessons Here" rests cockeyed against the wooden post, the layers of dry paint peeling away. The upper hinges of the gate are now broken and held together by a piece of rope. I listen to the harmony of nature, the thud of a mango as it hits the ground, the gentle serenades of the crickets humming in the last warmth of the evening as they lull me to sleep. I am at peace now because every corner of my home echoes with the spirits of my family.

Not even my terrible sin of killing Marse Joe haunts me anymore. All I hear is my mother's soft footsteps on the wooden floor and her voice as she sang to her students or to Eve.

"Try it again in C minor this time." This is what I hear now: Sarge's voice floating by me as he orders someone to do something for him; Aunty Daphne rushing into the kitchen, saying "Ruth, have you got a cup of sugar?"; Uncle Cork shouting, "Where's that boy Donovan?" All the memories of my life with them are right here in this house, and I feel safe and secure. I somehow know that I will never feel desperate or helpless again.

I have a memorial to plan, but there's no rush. I'll wait for Eve's baby to arrive and I'll make sure every related Scott in the world can attend. I no longer fear the world beyond the gate, but I live for the cool evenings at home. Some nights, a cool breeze caresses the nape of my neck or sweeps past my face. On those nights, I can sense the family around me and I'm fully connected with all of them. Their spirits filter through the wooden shutters, beneath my bed, above the roof, within the cracks of the walls. I walk and breathe their spirits every step of the way. They are all here with me and nothing can take me away from my home. Nothing.

EPILOGUE

On July 30 1938, 32 people were killed and over 70 were injured in a rail accident. Traveling from Kingston to Montego Bay, the train's engine jumped the rails at Balaclava and embedded itself firmly into the mountainside. The coaches followed, piling themselves on top of each other in layers of chaos and death. At the time, it was one of the world's worst-ever rail disasters. Yet Balaclava remains a quaint Jamaican country district, and nobody connects it with disaster. Not the way Kendal is remembered.

Rail service in Jamaica began as one of those great examples of colonial need being met by British engineering ingenuity. As part of the first railway built anywhere outside England, the Jamaican trains were a source of pride for locals and colonists alike. That first link created between Kingston and Spanish Town in 1845 must have seemed a genuine marvel, as evidenced by the many local songs that have romanticized trains in the ensuing 150 years.

St. Anne's Roman Catholic Church still stands on the corner of 5 1/4 Percy Street. The red stone building is beautifully maintained on the jagged edge of a sometimes forgotten community. Inside, toward the back of the church and mounted on the wall, are two marble plaques in memory of the lives lost at Kendal. The day I visited the church, children were rehearsing Christmas carols. An elder of the church who knew my grandparents showed me where my entire family sat each Sunday. Reverend Father Eberle, who led that congregation in 1957, survived the train crash and died in Kingston in 1965. Father Mallet, the other priest who rode the train that day, left the church, married and moved to America. One Catholic youngster who witnessed the horror, Richard Mock-Yen (now Monsignor) became a priest a few years later.

My character, Miss Ruby, came from my own imagination and with no knowledge that someone like that had existed in my family. The real Miss Ruby is Miss Ruby Grey, a woman I met in Ocho Rios. She was proud to tell me she had lived in my grandfather's house while her mother worked as a housekeeper there. After her mother's passing, she continued to live with my grandparents and they raised her as their own. The only reason she was not on the train the day of the crash was that she had misbehaved the day before and was being punished. She told me that she felt she had been orphaned twice.

There are blueprints for a Kendal Cenotaph that was planned for erection in Spanish Town, (the island's original capital) in a new cemetery to be called La Caridad. To date, no further work has been done to get this project off the ground.

During my numerous research and interview sessions, more than 300 elaborate ghost stories were told to me over and over. These stories still circulate today. Some tales are similar with moderate variations, and others inspired parts of the story—hence the reason to create Lucy.

In its years of operation, the Jamaican railway provided a means of transportation for people of many races and classes. It afforded more people the chance to engage in islandwide travel. The fares were relatively low, allowing a large segment of the population to move about by rail.

In 2007, the Jamaican Government was still conducting discussions with a team from the Rail India Technical and Economic Services (RITES) regarding the resumption of the national rail services. The first phase, commuter services between Kingston and Spanish Town and then from Kingston to Linstead, was expected to have been up and running by January 2001. There has been no new launch date put in its stead.

Initial investments required for the first phase were set at approximately US$8 million. The Government was said to be considering an initial 40 per cent shareholding to be used for improving infrastructure, loading stock and the purchase of new trains.

Today, the Jamaican Railway Corporation (JRC) appears to be defunct and is closed to the passenger public, having ceased operations in 1992. The railway system's only customer is the Bauxite Company, which runs eight trains daily. These trains travel from Williamsfield Station, also known as Kirkvine, through the Porus and May Pen stations without stopping, then coming to a halt at Bodles Junction Station at the Port Esquivel site in Old Harbour, then through Spanish Town and on to the Bog Walk/Linstead station. They bypass Kendal without so much as a pause or a whistle. The final stop is Ewarton Plant, now known as WINDALCO (West Indies Alumina Company). In 1957, at the time of the Kendal Crash, the Bauxite company was known as Alumina Jamaica. It was largely responsible for digging the rescue road to the site.

Kendal's train station is now derelict, with only platform steps, an overgrown railway track and rusty carriages left behind to show the life of a thriving train service that once existed. Although I read that a plaque had been placed at the crash site, I never found any marker that acknowledged the loss of so many lives—despite several searches.

The JRC's Kingston Terminal, hanging on in hope the way Esther did, has very few employees. An empty train sits in the station. There is nobody on the platform. Fifty years after Kendal, the waiting room stands frozen in time, looking almost like it did on the day my family and so many others went there for the last time.

An official inquiry was supervised by the British shortly after the tragedy. A scathing report detailing negligence and mismanagement was released in 1958. Although there had been talk of compensation for the passengers, only some survivors or the victims' families were ever paid anything by the Railway Company. The surviving Easts received eight pounds Sterling.

★★★

Of the fourteen East Family members lost, none of their remains or personal effects was ever identified or returned to Kingston.

ABOUT THE AUTHOR

DANNY DACOSTA

For more than two years, she transferred her life back to Jamaica to reconnect physically and spiritually with her ancestral roots as she researched the 1957 Kendal Crash, which is still the worst disaster in the island's living memory. *Reaper of Souls* claims power over what had eluded her for so long – the truth about Kendal and a sense of closure in the face of so much tragedy for one family.

Beverley East is a Washington, DC graphologist and the bestselling author of *Finding Mr. Write: A New Slant on Selecting the Perfect Mate.* She divides much of her work and family time between Kingston and London. Her website is www.writeanalysis.com.

Cover Design by MG Design LLC.
Cover Illustration by Warren Field

MORE PRAISE FOR
reaper of souls

66 Beverley East has put her heart and soul into this gripping family saga that shuttles between the past and present with the locomotive power of a speeding train. With terminal points in England and Jamaica, *Reaper of Souls* is a tumultuous journey teeming with characters who will live with you in memory for a very long time."
—Colin Channer, author of *Waiting In Vain, Passing Through,* and *The Girl With the Golden Shoes*

66 Like many other history-making events in the life of Jamaicans, the story of the Kendal Crash was only whispered like some mysterious duppy (ghost) story until Bev East courageously used her family's tragic experience as grist for this touching and riveting story..."
—Barbara Ellington, *The Daily Gleaner*

Made in the USA
Charleston, SC
14 March 2014